THE HONOUR OF ROME

By Simon Scarrow

The *Eagles of the Empire* Series

The Britannia Campaign

Under the Eagle (AD 42–43, Britannia)
The Eagle's Conquest (AD 43, Britannia)
When the Eagle Hunts (AD 44, Britannia)
The Eagle and the Wolves (AD 44, Britannia)
The Eagle's Prey (AD 44, Britannia)

Rome and the Eastern Provinces

The Eagle's Prophecy (AD 45, Rome)
The Eagle in the Sand (AD 46, Judaea)
Centurion (AD 46, Syria)

The Mediterranean

The Gladiator (AD 48–49, Crete)
The Legion (AD 49, Egypt)
Praetorian (AD 51, Rome)

The Return to Britannia

The Blood Crows (AD 51, Britannia)
Brothers in Blood (AD 51, Britannia)
Britannia (AD 52, Britannia)

Hispania

Invictus (AD 54, Hispania)

The Return to Rome

Day of the Caesars (AD 54, Rome)

The Eastern Campaign

The Blood of Rome (AD 55, Armenia)
Traitors of Rome (AD 56, Syria)
The Emperor's Exile (AD 57, Sardinia)

Britannia: Troubled Province

The Honour of Rome (AD 59, Britannia)

The *Wellington and Napoleon* Quartet

Young Bloods
The Generals
Fire and Sword
The Fields of Death

Sword and Scimitar
(Great Siege of Malta)

Hearts of Stone (Second World War)

Blackout

The *Gladiator* Series

Gladiator: Fight for Freedom
Gladiator: Street Fighter
Gladiator: Son of Spartacus
Gladiator: Vengeance

Writing with T. J. Andrews

Arena (AD 41, Rome)
Invader (AD 44, Britannia)
Pirata (AD 25, Adriatic)

Writing with Lee Francis

Playing With Death

SIMON SCARROW

EAGLES • OF • THE • EMPIRE

THE HONOUR OF ROME

HEADLINE

First published in Great Britain in 2021
by HEADLINE PUBLISHING GROUP

1

Cataloguing in Publication Data is available from the British Library

ISBN 978 1 4722 5849 6 (Hardback)
ISBN 978 1 4722 5848 9 (Trade paperback)

Artwork by Tim Peters

Typeset in Bembo by Avon DataSet Ltd, Arden Court, Alcester, Warwickshire

Printed and bound in Great Britain by Clays Ltd, Elcograf S.p.A.

Headline's policy is to use papers that are natural, renewable and recyclable
products and made from wood grown in well-managed forests and other
controlled sources. The logging and manufacturing processes are expected
to conform to the environmental regulations of the country of origin.

HEADLINE PUBLISHING GROUP
An Hachette UK Company
Carmelite House
50 Victoria Embankment
London EC4Y 0DZ

www.headline.co.uk
www.hachette.co.uk

To Jonathan Mills, who taught me history and inspired a love for the subject ever since.

SOUTH-EAST BRITANNIA AD 59

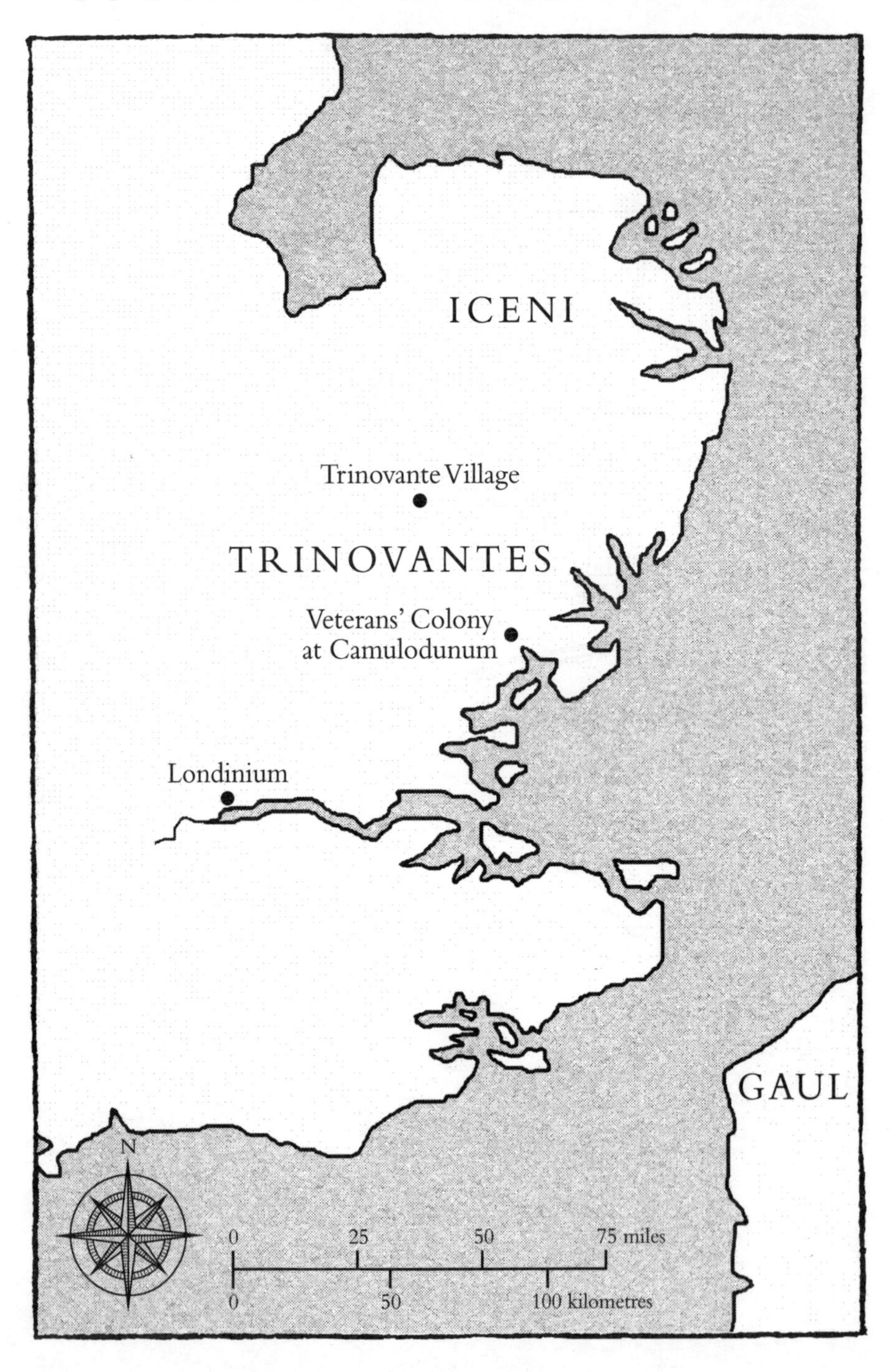

LONDINIUM AD 59

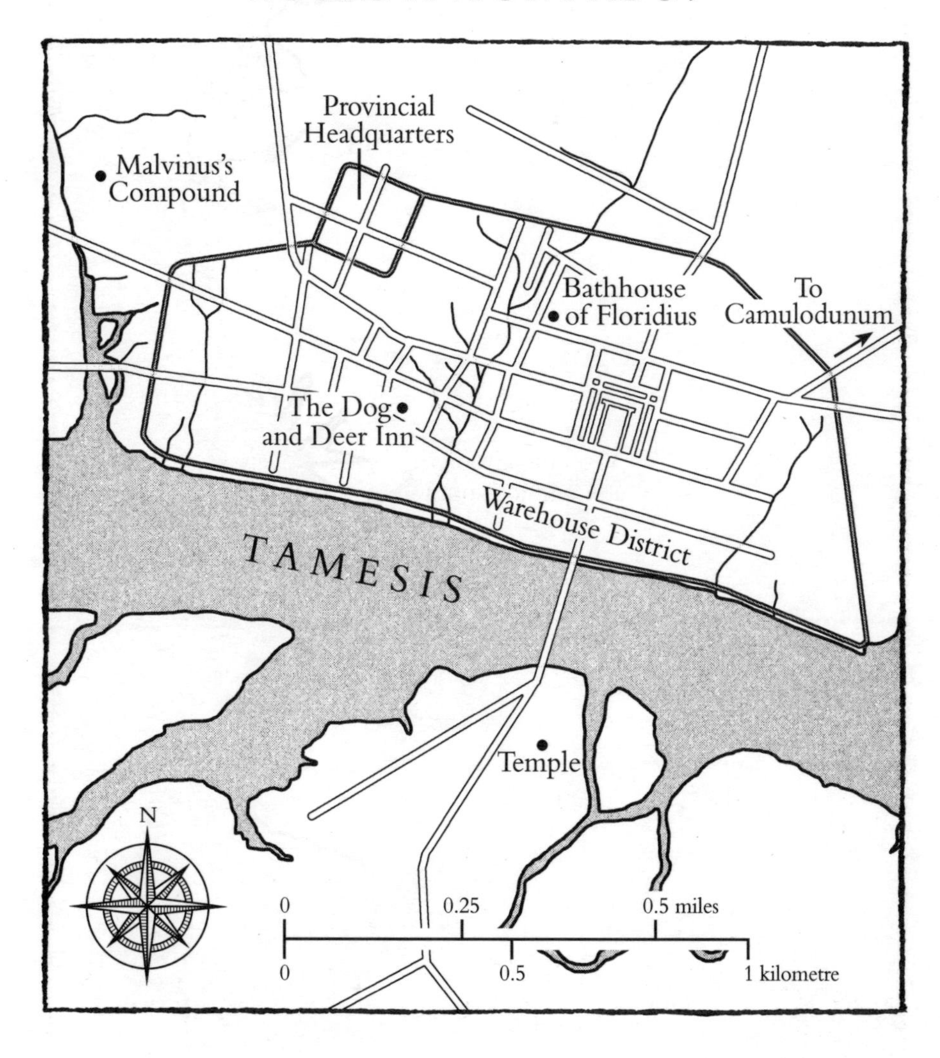
Provincial Headquarters
Malvinus's Compound
Bathhouse of Floridius
To Camulodunum
The Dog and Deer Inn
Warehouse District
TAMESIS
Temple
N
0
0.25
0.5 miles
0
0.5
1 kilometre

CHAIN OF COMMAND, BRITANNIA AD 59

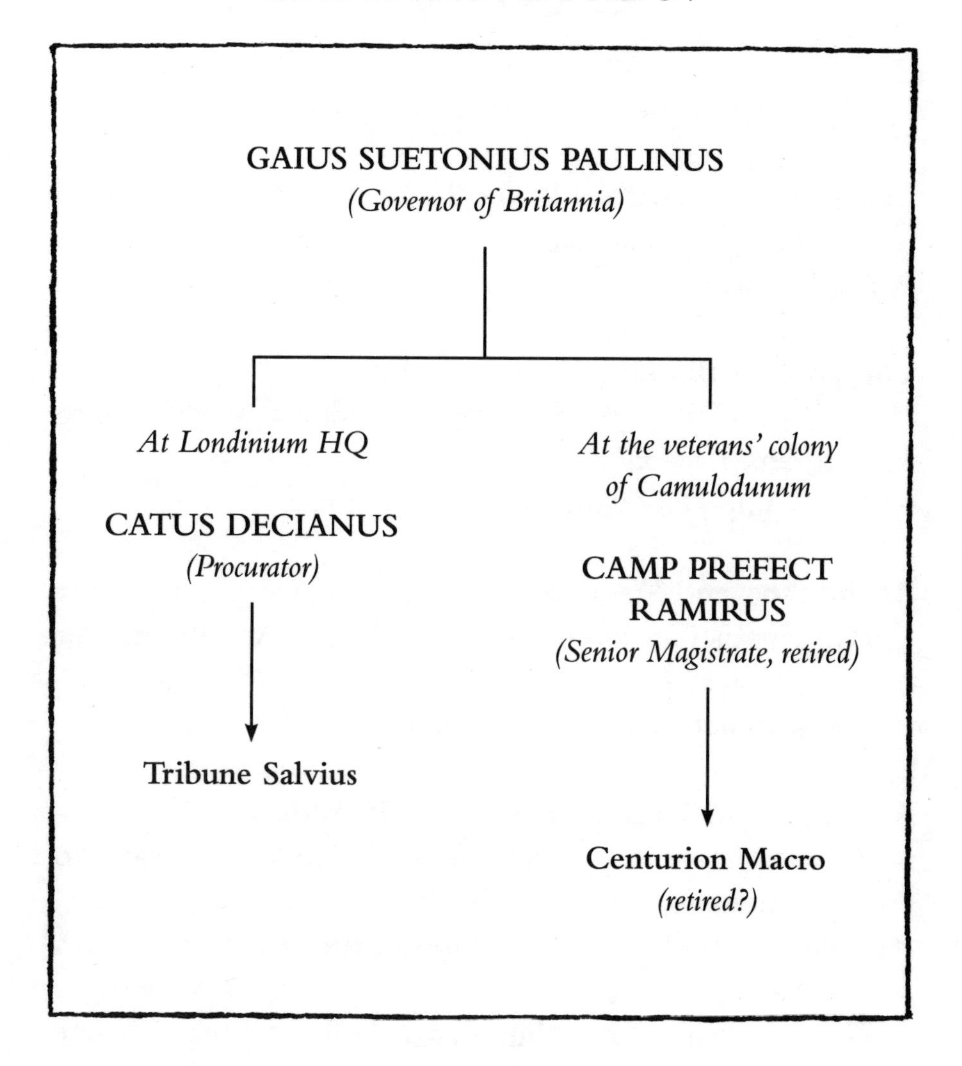

Cast List

Centurion Macro: a hero of Rome, looking forward to a peaceful retirement in Britannia, or so he thinks . . .

Petronella: wife of Macro, looking forward to the same

The crew of the *Dolphin* cargo ship

Androcus, Hydrax, Barco, Lemulus: an edgy crew sailing into troubled waters . . .

Parvus: ship's boy with the heart of a lion

At the Dog and Deer inn

Portia: mother and business partner of Macro. An entrepreneur in tooth and claw . . .

Denubius: her handyman, and more

At the provincial headquarters at Londinium

Tribune Salvius: a young aristocrat looking forward to returning to Rome

Procurator Decianus: a flawed bureaucrat sent to Britannia as a punishment

Governor Paulinus: an ambitious man looking to make a name for himself by completing the pacification of Britannia

The Gangs of London

Malvinus: leader of the 'Scorpions' and a man who makes offers it is dangerous to refuse

Pansa: his second in command

Cinna: leader of the 'Blades' with ambitions to make his gang the most powerful in town

Naso: a 'Blade' with a nasty streak running right through him

At the Veterans' Colony of Camulodunum

Ramirus: retired Camp Prefect, looking forward to drinking his retirement away in peace

Cordua: wife of Ramirus

Tibullus: officer in charge of an isolated outpost not far from Camulodunum

Laenas, *Herennius*, *Ancus*, *Vibenius*: retired veterans, willing to enter battle one last time

Cardominus: a native guide who does not get on with the natives

Mabodugnus: an elderly chief of the Trinovantes

Iceni Royalty

Prasutagus: King of the Iceni, but sadly stricken with terminal illness

Boudica: wife of Prasutagus, a fierce defender of her tribe's interests

Visitors from Rome

Prefect Cato: best friend of Centurion Macro. An accomplished soldier without permission to be in Britannia

Claudia Acte: lover of Cato and former mistress of Emperor Nero, who thinks she died in exile

Lucius: son of Cato by his dead wife

Cassius: a ferocious-looking mongrel with a ferocious appetite

And also

Caius Torbulo: a cargo gangmaster with a quick eye for business

Camillus: an innkeeper on the road between Londinium and Camulodunum

Gracchus: the owner of a tannery in Londinium who is being skinned by the gangs

CHAPTER ONE

The Tamesis river, Britannia, January AD *59*

'There's a boat approaching,' Centurion Macro said, and pointed down the river. The grey-streaked curls above his brow stirred in the cold breeze as he squinted over the water. The others on the deck of the *Dolphin* turned to see a small, low craft being propelled by four men at the oars, while another three sat in the stern and one more stood in the bows, holding a rope to steady himself. It had rounded a bend in the Tamesis no more than a quarter of a mile away and was approaching fast. Macro swiftly calculated that it would soon overtake the sluggish merchant vessel carrying his wife and himself upriver to Londinium. Although the men wore no armour and Macro could see no spears or other weapons, something about their demeanour caused a wary tingle at the back of his neck.

'Are we in any danger?'

He turned to his wife, Petronella, a heavily built woman with an oval face fringed with dark hair, who was only a little shorter than Macro. They had been together for a few years now and she knew that, though Macro had left the army, his senses were well honed to detect any potential threat.

'I doubt it, but better to be safe than sorry, eh?'

He left Petronella to watch the approaching boat and

addressed the captain of the merchant vessel in a casual tone. 'A word with you, Androcus.'

The captain caught the warning look in Macro's eye and followed him aft to where the baggage lay, covered by a goatskin. Macro folded the covering back and undid the latch of the chest holding his kit. Reaching inside, he rummaged for his sword belt then quickly buckled it on, adjusting it so that the handle of the sword settled into its usual place against his hip. He handed a spare sword belt to Androcus. 'Put it on.'

The captain hesitated and glanced towards the oncoming boat. 'They look harmless enough. Are weapons really necessary?'

'Let's hope not. But in my experience it's better to have them at the ready and not need them than not have them ready and need them.'

Androcus took a moment to digest the comment before he took the belt and hurriedly fastened it around his slim hips. 'Now what?'

'Let's see what they do.'

A dull sun shone through the grey overcast, bleakly illuminating the river and the drab landscape on either bank. The sound of the oars splashing into the water carried over the surface to those aboard the merchant ship. The boat held its course and passed within thirty feet of the larger vessel, and Macro saw the man in the bows scanning the deck, his gaze quickly passing over what cargo was visible before settling on Macro and Androcus. Like the others, he wore a cloak, and his hair was tied back with a leather thong.

Macro cleared his throat and spat over the side as he raised his hand in greeting, making sure that his cape opened enough for those on the boat to see the handle of his sword protruding from the scabbard. 'Hello, friends. It's a cold afternoon to be out on the river, eh?'

The man in the bow nodded and grinned as he muttered an order in the native dialect to his companions. The men at the oars rested and their craft began to slow at once. 'Aye, cold enough.' He switched to a heavily accented Latin. 'You bound for the town?'

'We are,' Androcus replied. 'And you?'

The man gestured upriver. 'A fishing village a couple of miles that way. Looking forward to our supper. May the river god keep you safe.'

He tapped a finger to his forehead in farewell and then spoke in dialect again to the men at the oars. They took up the strain and the low craft lurched forward and continued upriver, water swirling in its wake.

Androcus let out a relieved sigh. 'Seems there was no cause for concern after all.'

Macro watched the boat surge away as it made for the next bend in the river. Mist was spilling out from the reeds along the bank, and the boat disappeared from view even before it reached the bend. 'I'm not so sure. What reason do you imagine they have to be out on the river on a cold winter afternoon?'

'How should I know? Some might ask the same question of a captain crossing from Gaul at this time of year.'

Macro reflected a moment. 'That village he mentioned. Do you know of it?'

Androcus shook his head. 'There are several along the river, but none as close as he says.'

'Are you certain?'

The captain looked offended. 'I've been plying my trade between Londinium and Gesoriacum for the last five years now. I know the Tamesis like the back of my hand. I'm telling you, Centurion, the nearest village is at least ten miles away. That said, there might be some settlement at the end of any of the creeks that feed into the river. But none that I'm aware of.' He turned to look in the direction the boat had taken. 'You may be right. I don't like the look of those men.'

'You don't say.' Macro sniffed. 'I think we may be in trouble. I don't think it's safe for us to stop for the night.'

'Sail at night?' Androcus shook his head. 'No chance of that.'

'You said you know the river.'

'By daylight, yes.'

'It's still the same river at night,' Macro countered. 'I have every confidence you'll be able to guide the ship a safe distance from those men. What's the worst thing that can happen? If we run aground, it just means we'll have to wait until the tide rises and floats us off.'

'If we sail into a mudbank at any speed, the impact could take the mast down.'

'Then take it slowly. Even if you lose the mast, it's better than losing your ship, your cargo, your crew, your passengers and your life to a gang of river pirates.'

The captain rubbed his jaw. 'When you put it like that . . .'

'That's exactly how I am putting it. We keep going.'

Macro turned away and made his way back along the deck towards his wife. He offered her a reassuring smile. 'We're not stopping along the riverbank tonight.'

'Why? Because of those men?' Petronella responded shrewdly.

He nodded. 'Just to be on the safe side.'

'Are they dangerous?'

'It's best we don't wait around to find out.' He paused to think briefly and called out to Androcus. 'Have you and your lads got any weapons?'

'Some axes, knives and the belaying pins.'

'What about armour?'

'We're sailors, Centurion, not soldiers. Why would we have armour?'

'Fair point,' Macro conceded. 'Just make sure your men are armed, and keep your eyes skinned when we get moving again. If we are attacked, it will be a fight to the death. Pirates won't want to leave any witnesses alive. No quarter will be given. Understand?' He looked round the crew to make sure they grasped the seriousness of their plight.

'What about me?' asked Petronella.

Macro regarded her thoughtfully She might be a woman, but since they had met, he had seen her deck more than a few men with her solid punch. She was as fierce and formidable in a fight as many men he had known. He kissed her on the cheek. 'Just try not to kill too many of our lads in the darkness, eh?'

As the winter sun declined towards the horizon, the crew and passengers kept watch for any signs of danger from the reed-lined banks on either side.

'We gave up a comfortable life in Rome for this?' Petronella gestured at the bare landscape. The Tamesis, being a tidal river, exposed broad expanses of mudbanks as the tide ebbed. Beyond the reeds at the water's edge, low mounds were dotted with clumps of brambles and trees stripped of their leaves.

She shook her head and shrank into the fur collar of her cloak as Macro shrugged. He had been discharged from the army nearly two years earlier. They had set off for Britannia soon after but had been delayed in Massillia for several months when Petronella had fallen ill. Once she had recovered Macro had been keen to complete the journey as swiftly as possible, even if that meant crossing the sea in the depths of winter. In addition to the generous bounty he had received from the imperial treasury in thanks for his many years of honourable service, he had also been granted a parcel of land at the military colony of Camulodunum. More than enough to set him up comfortably for retirement, he reflected with a smile.

'Oh, it's not so bad here,' he replied.

'No?' She glanced at him and raised an eyebrow. 'Why would Rome want to turn this . . . bog into a province?'

Macro laughed, his lined face creasing up and emphasising the handful of scars etched across the skin. He wrapped an arm round her shoulders and drew her close. 'You're not seeing it at its best. When summer comes, it's quite different. There's rich farmland, forests teeming with game. The trade routes with the rest of the Empire are opening up to all manner of creature comforts.' He paused to nod towards the rows of wine jars tightly packed into the grass matting in the hold. 'Give it a few years and Britannia will be no different to any other province. You'll see. Ain't that right, Androcus?'

The captain was standing on the small raised deck at the bows, scanning the river ahead. He turned and nodded. 'Aye. There's more ships crossing between here and Gaul every month. You should see Londinium now, miss. It's grown from a trading post into a huge town in the space of a few years. Bit rough and ready at the moment, but it'll be a fine place once things settle down.'

'Hmph,' Petronella muttered, and returned her gaze to the dismal sprawl of mud and mist stretching out on either side.

Macro frowned and slowly sucked in a breath, sensitive to the likelihood that anything he might say would not improve matters. That was how it was with women, he thought to himself. If you could not read their minds and say what they wanted to hear, it was best to say nothing. However, silence ran the risk of provoking the accusation that men were unfeeling, insensitive brutes incapable of being supportive of their wives. Accustomed as he was to the battlefield, it perplexed Macro that there was no winning strategy in such matters. Women had their men completely outflanked, and all that remained was to retreat into the corner and face the end with defiant stoicism.

The captain glanced up at the band of cloud moving in from the east. 'Let's hope that's not snow.'

Macro followed the direction of his gaze and nodded. It would be dark in an hour or so, and he did not relish the prospect of spending another freezing night aboard the ship.

'So what's waiting for you in Londinium?' asked Androcus. 'A posting to one of the legions, is it?'

Macro shook his head. 'I'm done with soldiering. Me and the wife are here to make some money and live out a comfortable retirement. I own a half-share in an inn. My mother's been running it for the past few years.'

'Oh? I might have heard of it.'

'The Dog and Deer is the name of the place. In a good position, not far from the river. Doing a brisk trade, according to her letters.'

'The Dog and Deer . . . No, can't say I know it. But then I don't spend much time in Londinium. Just long enough to unload my cargo and take on the next load before sailing back to Gaul. I take my drink at a place on the quayside.'

'If you want to give my place a try, I'll stand you the first drink,' Macro offered companionably.

'Thank you, sir.' Androcus smiled. 'I may well take you up on that.'

A movement amongst the reeds of the nearest bank drew both men's attention. A moment later, a startled heron struggled into the air and flew off across the water. The pair exchanged a relieved smile and returned to their vigil.

★ ★ ★

The temperature dropped sharply the moment dusk gave way to night. Androcus, anxious about running aground in the darkness, ordered his crew to take in two reefs to slow the ship down. The *Dolphin* glided upriver in the middle of the broad expanse of the Tamesis. Their progress seemed unbearably slow to Macro, and he cursed Androcus for being too timid to risk continuing under full sail. However, it was the other man's ship and Macro knew better than to try to tell the captain how to do his job. Besides, he needed to keep alert for any sign of danger. If it came to a fight, he would be the only one aboard trained to deal with it; he had little confidence in the crew being able to defeat a gang of river pirates who were accustomed to killing and looting.

Petronella was standing beside him, hefting a belaying pin to test its weight. Macro put his arms around her and held her close for a moment before speaking softly into her ear. 'If anything happens and it goes badly for us, get away however you can. Even if that means jumping over the side and swimming for it. When you get ashore, make for my mother's place. She'll take care of you.'

They fell silent and, like the captain and his crew, kept watching for any sign of the boat that had passed them less than two hours earlier.

'Look there,' Macro said, and pointed to the south bank. In the gloom he could barely see the two figures that had emerged from the stunted undergrowth and climbed a small mound overlooking the river. They paused to look towards the *Dolphin* before breaking into a trot down towards the bushes at the foot of the mound and disappearing from view.

'What are they up to?' asked Androcus.

'Tracking us, I imagine. If there's any way you could make

this tub go faster, it would be a good idea to see to it now.'

The captain raised his hand briefly before he responded. 'There's virtually no breeze. It's the tide that's doing most of the work. And that'll help those pirates if they attack, since they have the lighter craft.'

The fear in his voice was palpable, and Macro turned and grasped him by the shoulders as he spoke in a fierce undertone. 'Listen, if it comes to a fight, your crew will be looking to their captain. You set the example on the ship. So take a deep breath and get a hold on yourself, Androcus.' He eased his grip and patted the man on the arm. 'Besides, you've got me, and I've been in more battles than most. I'm more than a match for any bog-hopping barge bandits. Hold your nerve and we'll come through this and reach Londinium safely. Is that clear?'

'Y-yes.' The captain cleared his throat. 'I'll do my duty.'

'Good for you.' Macro chuckled reassuringly. 'For now, just get us upriver fast as you can.'

Androcus approached his crew, who were lining the side facing the south bank, scanning for any further sign of the pirates, and quietly ordered them to shake out one of the reefs. A moment later there was a rustle of leather and a faint *phwap* as the breeze filled the sail and the water gurgled along the waterline. Scanning the banks on either side, Macro could see that they were making some progress now. Overhead, heavy clouds rolled in from the east, beneath them a greater darkness indicating rain, or snow. If fortune was on their side, the weather would make it harder for the pirates to find them in the darkness. On the other hand, Macro reflected, the same weather might conceal the approach of an enemy vessel until the very last moment. With that in mind, he decided that it would be best to talk to the crew while there was still time to think clearly.

'Lads,' he spoke just loud enough for the crew to hear him clearly, 'a word with you. Those pirates will be thinking that the *Dolphin* is just another cargo ship, with a crew they can easily overwhelm. They'll be depending on our fear to weaken any resistance we offer. That'll be their best weapon against us. So we have to show them we're not afraid. If they come for us, I want to hear you give them as bloodthirsty a greeting as possible. And we don't wait for them to get on board before we fight 'em. Find something to throw at the bastards as soon as they draw close. And if they attempt to get aboard, we meet them at the ship's rail and knock them on the head before they can get a foot over the side. If you have the urge to run from the fight, just remember, there's no place to hide. So we drive 'em off or go down fighting, eh?'

He paused and looked over the dark figures standing before him. The ship's boy remained at the steering paddle. Macro recalled what he had learned about the crew during the short voyage from Gaul. Besides the captain, there was his first mate, Hydrax, a burly, good-humoured man who seemed a competent sailor. He had stuffed an axe in his broad leather belt. Beside him stood the other two sailors, Barco and Lemulus, both of whom had been friendly in their dealings with the two passengers. Barco had armed himself with a stout boathook while his companion carried a belaying pin. The captain had Macro's spare sword and stood with his hand resting on the pommel. It was then that Macro realised he had not learned the name of the ship's boy. The lad, no more than twelve or thirteen, had not spoken a word the entire time and had been addressed by his crewmates simply as 'boy' whenever they had spoken to him.

'Lad,' Macro called over to him. 'What weapon have you got?'

The shadow at the stern reached his spare hand to his side. There was a dull rasp and he raised his arm, revealing the just discernible shape of a dagger blade.

'Good,' Macro responded. 'Then we all know what we must do.'

'What about your wife?' asked Androcus.

'I'll feed them their own balls,' Petronella purred menacingly, and Macro was pleased to hear the men laugh in response. They were as ready for a fight as any bunch of civilians could be, he decided.

Something brushed his forehead, and he glanced up to see fine shapes swirling down from the darkness. Snow, then, not rain. The first small specks soon gave way to large, feather-like flakes that settled on the deck and the cloaks of those watching for danger. In moments the dark timbers of the upper works of the *Dolphin* were covered in a thin layer of snow. Macro had to shield his eyes as he squinted across the water, blinking as the blizzard blew at an angle into his face.

'Can you see anything?' asked Petronella.

'Not much, but then neither can they.'

The falling snow had a deadening effect on the sounds around the ship. On all sides the twisting specks blotted out even the vaguest hint of the banks beyond the dark flow of the river, so that the vessel felt cut off from the world, with no sense of direction.

'We'll have to lower the sail,' said Androcus. 'We're steering blind and I can't see anything more than fifty feet away. If we run aground now, we'll lose the mast, if not the whole ship and her cargo if the hull is breached.'

'Hold your course,' Macro replied firmly. 'A little longer. Just until the blizzard abates.'

'Who says it will? It's too dangerous.'

The captain turned to his crew and was about to shout an order when the snowstorm passed beyond them. On either side they could see the banks of the Tamesis again. More by luck than any nautical expertise, the *Dolphin* seemed to be almost exactly in the middle of the river; there was no danger of her running aground as Androcus had feared. Ahead of them the dark band of the blizzard receded swiftly.

Then, emerging from the snow, moving at an angle across their course, came the dark outline of the pirates' boat. Its crew worked the oars hard as they were urged on by their leader to close in on their prey.

CHAPTER TWO

'Here they come!' Macro called out, and the crew of the cargo ship turned to look in the direction he was pointing. It was already clear that there was no chance of escape. The boat would cut directly across their bows.

Lowering his arm, Macro looked round at the others, their faces clearly visible thanks to the faint loom of snow that covered the deck and picked out the rigging in fine white lines against the night sky. It was pleasing to see that Androcus and his men no longer looked so terrified. Their expressions were grim and they appeared to be resigned to fighting a battle they could not avoid. Petronella's expression, by contrast, was deadly. Her head was slightly lowered and her dark eyes glowered as she clenched her teeth.

'That's my lady.' Macro smiled. 'Give those bastards a thrashing they'll never forget.'

She sniffed with derision. 'They're not going to live long enough to forget when we're through with them.'

Macro nodded and turned back to watch the approaching pirates. Their boat had drawn ahead slightly, but they made no attempt to change course towards the cargo ship.

'The odds are almost even.' He spoke calmly to reassure the sailors. 'And they'll have to climb the side to get at us. We have the advantage. All we have to do is hold our nerve and stop them getting aboard. Once we kill or wound some of 'em, they'll lose heart and scarper. Are you with me, lads?'

Androcus and his crew nodded uncertainly.

Macro thrust his sword into the air. 'Then let's give them something to be afraid of.'

He let his jaw drop, sucked in a deep breath, then roared, 'For the *Dolphin*!'

Far from working the crew up, he saw them flinch slightly, and he clenched his spare fist and gestured to them. 'Come on, let's hear it from you! *Dolphin*! *Dolphin*!'

The others joined in, hesitantly at first, but then, as their resolve hardened, louder and louder, brandishing their weapons at the pirates. The men in the boat turned to look across the water until their leader bellowed to the men at the oars and they continued to propel the craft forward, ahead of the cargo ship.

Macro edged towards the bows to keep the boat in sight. 'They'll be turning towards us any moment.'

As he watched, the boat pulled directly ahead of the cargo ship and slowed to match its pace.

'What are they waiting for?' asked Androcus.

Macro strained his eyes ahead for a moment before he replied. 'I don't know. Unless . . .'

He climbed onto the small platform in the angle of the bows and grasped the shroud as he glanced round, straining his ears for any sounds other than the soft creak of the rigging and the muffled swish of the boat's oars from ahead. Then he heard a cry from the darkness to his left, and turned towards the south bank as a voice on the pirates' boat called out in response. He felt a chill grip the pit of his stomach. The pirates' plan was obvious. The first boat would wait until the new arrival was in position, and then they would attack the cargo ship from both sides. Macro had been counting on being at the head of the fight, but now he would have to divide his tiny force and place Androcus in command of half of it. He was not convinced the ship's captain had the heart for such a fight.

'Listen here, Androcus,' he began calmly. 'I want you to take two of your men and defend the port side. Hydrax can fight alongside me and my wife.'

'What about the boy?'

Macro glanced at the slight figure holding the tiller of the steering paddle. 'Tell him to stay where he is and keep the vessel on course. He won't be much good in a fight. Not enough to make a difference. But lend him a knife in any case. He may need it.'

'If you say so,' Androcus replied grudgingly.

Macro caught his arm. 'Remember, this is a fight to the death. We drive them off or they will kill us all. There is no other outcome. They won't spare any witnesses to their piracy.'

The captain nodded. Macro released his grip and the man made his way aft.

'Do you think we can rely on him?' Petronella asked quietly.

'What choice do we have?' Macro forced a smile. 'Are you ready?'

'Hmph.'

The two parties moved to either side of the ship and made ready as they watched the second boat surge across the current. There was a brief shouted exchange before both smaller craft turned towards the *Dolphin* and raced downstream, closing quickly as they made for each beam of the cargo ship. Macro drew his sword and tested his grip in the icy air to make sure that his fingers were supple and could be relied on to grasp the handle tightly.

As the first boat closed in, he saw a figure rise up between the rowers and take aim with a bow. An instant later, an arrow hissed close overhead and Hydrax flinched and ducked. There was just time for the pirates to attempt a second shot; this time the iron head of the arrow buried itself in the timbers beneath Macro with a sharp splintering crack. Then the boat glanced off the bows and swept down the side. The dark shape of a boarding hook arced over the rail, struck the deck and was instantly hauled tight so that the points lodged in the wooden frame and secured the boat to the ship.

Macro raised his sword and hacked at the thin rope stretched over the rail, but it slipped towards him at the last moment and the blade bit into the wood. He tore it free as the first of the pirates was hoisted by two of his comrades, sailing up and over the side to land on the deck. He was lithe and nimble and did not stumble as he readied a short axe in one hand and a dagger in the other. There was a thud from the other side of the vessel as the second boat came alongside, and the pirates gave a lusty cheer, but there was no chance for Macro to turn and look before he rushed the first enemy to board the *Dolphin*. The pirate crouched as he swung his axe back, but Macro powered forward before the man could strike, easily parrying the dagger, then slamming shoulder first into the pirate's chin and sending the lighter man flying backwards to crash onto the deck. Macro was standing over him before the man could snatch a breath, and he drove his short sword down into his opponent's throat and twisted it left and right before tearing the point free and backing off to face the next pirate.

A second man vaulted over the rail between Macro and Petronella, while a third clambered up just beyond Hydrax. Macro twisted round, but before he could move, fingers closed round his ankle. The pirate he had knocked down was scrabbling on the deck, gurgling horribly as blood pulsed from his wound, splattering black across the snow-covered planks. He had dropped his axe, but his dagger was still in his other hand, and now he slashed at Macro's calf. The point went high, tearing through the hem of Macro's breeches and scoring a shallow wound. Macro swung his other boot into the man's head, kicking hard. It took two blows before the wounded pirate released his grip and freed Macro to help Petronella. She was locked in a tight embrace with a shorter man, and snarled as she flailed at the back of his head with her belaying pin. As Macro watched, she butted her head against her foe's nose, and then bit into his cheek. The pirate let out a shocked cry of pain and made to punch her with the fist grasping his axe.

'Not my bloody wife you don't!' Macro bellowed. He grabbed the man's wrist and twisted it viciously so the axe head slapped into the pirate's back, driving the air from his lungs in a loud gasp. Then he drove his sword at an angle up into the pirate's side before thrusting him against the rail, where Petronella gave him a violent thrust so that he toppled with a splash into the river.

There was no time to share a brief moment of triumph. Macro saw that Hydrax had been driven to his knees by a blow from a studded club. At the same time, the pirate sensed the danger from behind him and glanced over his shoulder just as Macro brushed past Petronella and charged towards him. Spinning round, the pirate swung his club, knocking aside the sword that Macro had raised to parry the blow. It was snatched from his numbed fingers and clattered onto the deck several feet away. The pirate's lips parted in a triumphant snarl, and he shaped to strike again, but his expression twisted in agony as Hydrax's belaying pin smashed into the side of his knee with a bone-shattering crack. As he began to topple to one side, Macro sprang at him and swung a powerful hook into his jaw. The pirate's head snapped back before he collapsed in a heap on top of Hydrax.

'Macro! Help!'

Macro looked round to see another attacker wrenching Petronella's hair from behind and dragging her towards him. She tried to pull free but could not break his grip. Macro snatched up the studded club and stepped round her, swinging a quick blow at the man's elbow. It was enough to make him release her. At once she turned on him and clamped her hands round his throat, shrieking with rage. The pirate clawed at her hands as he struggled to retain his balance. She thrust him against the rail, then snatched her right hand back, balled it into a fist and punched him on the nose. At the same time, she released his throat and pushed him hard on the collarbone so that he tumbled over the side into the pirates' boat, where he lay groaning.

The three pirates still waiting to board looked up warily, weighing up their chances. Seeing their hesitation, Macro dropped the club and swept up the axe of the first boarder he had felled, then swung the blade down on the grappling line stretched tightly across the ship's rail. It parted on the third blow, and the boat lurched away and fell astern of the *Dolphin*.

Breathing hard, he turned to look across the deck to where Androcus and one of his men were struggling against the attackers from the second boat. The other man lay still on the deck. The captain had his back to the mast as he fended off two pirates armed with swords. As Macro started to cross the deck to come to their aid, he saw one of the attackers feint. Androcus half turned to defend himself, and at once the other assailant darted forward and drove his sword into the captain's side. He doubled over and dropped to his knees, his own sword falling to the snow-covered deck as the pirates closed in to finish him off.

Macro raised the axe and hurled it at the nearest of the pirates. The edge struck him between the shoulder blades. Even though some of the impact was absorbed by his cloak, the blow winded him and he let out a deep groan as he staggered forward into the path of his companion. Macro stooped to pick up the captain's sword, then gave the pirate a vicious shove in the small of his back to make sure he collided with the other boarder. Following up, he hacked at the pirate's exposed head, and the skull gave way with a soft, wet crack. The man's arms spasmed and he trembled violently as he sank to his knees. Macro pushed him aside and confronted the second pirate, who backed off a pace as he watched the centurion warily.

'What's the matter?' Macro growled. 'Not fond of an even fight, are we?'

Suddenly the night lit up as if a bolt of lightning had struck the vessel, and a haze of brilliant white seemed to fill his eyes. He heard Petronella shout his name before something slammed into his body and laid him out. As the light faded, he felt the cold of the snow against the side of his face and found that he could not breathe. He saw dark figures at an angle, and then another, smaller figure leaped into his blurred field of vision. There was a clatter of metal, some grunts, and then a body fell across Macro's legs. He felt hot breath on his arm, ragged as the man struggled to breathe for several heartbeats, then twitched and lay still.

'Macro . . .'

His head was turned and cradled and he saw Petronella looming over him, just visible against the cold stars that glinted from a sky now clear of clouds. It was painful to breathe and all he could manage was a hoarse whisper. 'Finish them . . .'

Behind her he could make out two figures: a man on the deck, arms raised to protect his head, and the smaller figure wielding an axe as he hacked at his opponent's body. Still supporting Macro's head with one hand, Petronella looked round, club raised, ready to strike, and then set it down beside him. 'It's over. They've given up.'

He felt dazed, and struggled to make sense of the situation around him. Nausea gripped him and he fought down the urge to vomit.

'Let me help you up,' said Petronella. She dragged the body off Macro's feet, then gripped her husband under the arms, swearing under her breath as she heaved him onto his feet and held him steady. Macro grasped the ship's rail and looked out over the water to see the two boats making for the south bank, the surviving pirates working the oars. Then he turned to survey the deck.

Hydrax was sitting on the edge of the helmsman's platform nursing his head. Barco lay still, his skull cloven almost in two by an axe blow. Lemulus was standing over the body of the pirate he had killed. Androcus was leaning with his back to the mast, a hand clasped over the wound in his side, his chest heaving. The boy was squatting against the ship's rail, rocking slowly to and fro as he held his right hand over a cut in the other arm. There were five pirates on the deck, two of them still moving weakly as they groaned. The others lay still. It was then that Macro recalled the slight figure that had flown at the pirate who had been about to finish him off. He cleared his throat and leaned over to pat the boy on the shoulder.

'Thank you, my young friend. I owe you.'

The boy looked up, smiling shyly, before he grimaced and glanced down at his arm.

'Here. Let me have a look,' said Macro. He eased the boy's

hand away, and at once blood pulsed down his arm and dripped onto the scuffed snow on the deck. The wound was about six inches long, but seemed shallow. Macro eased the boy's hand back into position. 'Hold it there. Bet that wound stings like a bastard, eh? But it'll heal. Trust me.'

Petronella had taken a cloak from one of the pirate's bodies and was using a dagger to tear it into strips for makeshift dressings. She applied one to the boy's arm before moving on to Androcus.

'Better let me have a look at that. Take the belt off and raise your tunic.'

When he hesitated, she clicked her tongue. 'Save your modesty for someone else, Captain. I've seen it all.'

Androcus did as he was told, and Petronella leaned closer to examine the wound. The point of the pirate's sword had gone through the flesh just below the ribcage and pierced the skin at the back.

'Nasty,' she muttered.

'Am I going to die?'

'We all die one day. But I don't think this is the day for you. Not unless the wound goes bad. Let me get a dressing on it to stop the bleeding. When we reach Londinium, you can have one of the garrison's medical orderlies treat it properly. For now, brace yourself.'

She folded a wad of wool into a tight bundle and pressed it against the entry wound. The captain gritted his teeth and hissed.

'Hold that in place,' she ordered, then cut a wide strip from the cloak and tied it over the wadding. When she had done, the captain let his tunic drop and Petronella moved on to see to Hydrax.

'Quite a woman you have there, Centurion,' Androcus said

admiringly. 'Fights like a demon and knows her way around wounds. Any more like her at home?'

'No chance. She's one in a million, and she's all mine.' Macro grinned briefly, then indicated the ship's boy. 'What's the lad's name?'

'He doesn't have a name. I found him starving on the wharf in Gesoriacum and took him in. He wouldn't speak at first, then I discovered why. Someone had cut out his tongue. If you lift the hair from his ear, you'll see it has been clipped. He was a slave. Might have been a runaway, or might have been abandoned by his master. He can't say which, of course. Once I'd fed him up, he was capable of light duties about the ship and taking a turn at the helm when the ship's in calm waters. He's not much good for anything else.'

'Well, he saved my life.'

'So I saw. I'd never have guessed he had it in him,' Androcus mused. 'Brave lad.'

A shift in the direction of the breeze caused the sail to billow, and Androcus took a couple of steps towards the helmsman's position before drawing up sharply with a groan and clasping a hand to his wound.

'Sit down,' Macro ordered, then turned to the ship's mate. 'Hydrax, take command. Get us under way again, before those pirates recover their nerve enough to try another attack.'

Hydrax turned towards his captain, who growled an affirmation before slumping down on the deck and bowing his head as he fought off another wave of pain. His subordinate turned to the ship's boy. 'Lad, are you up to taking the helm?'

The boy glanced up and nodded, then climbed to his feet and made his way aft, nursing his injured arm across his chest. He took the tiller with his other hand and stood ready. Lemulus was still stupefied by the recent violence and had to be shaken roughly by Hydrax before his wits returned and he grasped the sheets that controlled the angle of the sail.

'Anything I can do?' asked Macro.

'Best that you and your missus stay out of the way. This is no time to be teaching landsmen how to do a sailor's work.' Hydrax paused and lowered his head apologetically. 'What I mean to say is, you've done enough already, sir. We'd be goners if it weren't for you.'

'Fair enough.' Macro gave a good-natured laugh.

He shepherded Petronella aft and let her dress the wound on his leg. When she was done, she stood and regarded him in the dim starlight.

'What about your head?'

'Just took a slight knock, that's all.'

'Looked like more than a slight knock to me. Let me see.'

Before he could respond, she reached up and tenderly felt her way over his scalp, stopping as she came across a patch of matted hair and felt blood ooze between her fingers.

Macro winced. 'Go easy. You're supposed to be treating a wound, not tenderising a joint of ham.'

'Poor baby,' she responded mockingly. She cut another strip of cloth to wrap around his head. 'There you go. That'll help stop the bleeding at least. I'll have a proper look at it when there's enough light.'

She peered round into the darkness, squinting to make out what she could of the riverbank before she spoke softly. 'Do you think they'll be back?'

'I doubt it. We gave them more of a fight than I imagine they're used to. Most likely they'll retreat to lick their wounds and grieve for their dead before picking easier prey in future. Speaking of the dead . . .'

Macro recovered his sword and cut the throats of the two

wounded pirates, then tipped their bodies over the side along with those who were already dead. They splashed into the water and caused a brief commotion on the surface of the river before they fell astern and disappeared from view. Rubbing his hands together to try to restore some warmth to his numb fingers, he kept a steady watch over the water around the ship as the *Dolphin* glided up the Tamesis towards Londinium.

An hour or so later, another band of clouds swept in from the east and a fresh fall of snow soon covered the streaks of blood and other signs of the desperate struggle. Mercifully, Barco's body, with its mangled head, now lay under a pristine shroud of snow.

As the first glimmer of dawn seeped over the winter landscape, there was enough light to navigate more easily. There was no sign of the pirates, and already a handful of other trading craft were visible heading in both directions along the river.

'So much for a peaceful retirement,' Macro muttered to himself.

CHAPTER THREE

Londinium was the kind of frontier town a person could smell before ever they saw it. An acrid stench of sewage, smoke from fires and the indefinable assortment of tanneries, rotting vegetation and the sharp tang of animals and the people who kept them. The odour wafted downriver as if it was borne along with the flow of the Tamesis, and the river's naturally muddy colour thankfully served to hide the brown streaks emerging from the drains and culverts that carried the town's waste down to the water's edge.

Androcus pointed out the greasy haze pierced by columns of smoke that stretched across an expanse of the horizon, befouling the crisp blue sky beyond. It contrasted unpleasantly with the gleaming white blanket of snow that covered the landscape either side of the dark waters of the Tamesis. The captain of the *Dolphin* had relieved the boy at the tiller, and the latter was now curled up under some spare cloaks, fast asleep. 'Two more bends to round and we're there. And I've never been more keen to see port at the end of a voyage,' Androcus added with feeling.

Petronella had examined everyone's wounds as soon as there was enough light to see clearly. Fresh dressings and bandages had been neatly applied. Hydrax was sitting cross-legged on the deck as he sewed up the cloth that covered Barco's corpse. He had used the sailor's two cloaks for the job, and he pulled the sturdy twine threaded through the sailmaker's bone needle tightly with each stitch so that the wool hugged the contours of the corpse. Lemulus had already collected the dead man's meagre belongings in a basket to hand to his family when the ship returned to Gesoriacum.

'What'll you do with the body?' asked Macro.

'There's a low ridge outside Londinium where they cremate the dead. We'll take the ashes back with us when we sail for Gaul. First, though, I'll need two new deckhands. One to replace him, and one to help me out until I recover.'

'What about the boy?' asked Petronella. 'He'll need time for his wound to heal as well. He can't do much with one arm for the present.'

Androcus nodded and thought for a moment before he sniffed. 'It might be time to cut him loose. I can't afford to feed him if he can't work.'

'I think you *can* afford it,' Macro said quietly. 'Given what we paid for the voyage, on top of what you'll earn from the cargo.'

'All right then, I can afford it, but I ain't going to keep him if I can't get a decent day's work out of him. I'm a businessman, not a worthy cause, Centurion.' The captain's lips lifted in a cynical smile. 'If you're so concerned about him, you can have him.'

Macro was not the kind of man who liked to play games, and he decided at once to call the other man's bluff. 'Fine, we'll take him.'

Petronella arched an eyebrow. 'Will we?'

Macro shot her a quick warning glance while the captain struggled briefly to get over his surprise at the centurion's reaction. Then he swallowed and drew himself up, grimacing as his attempt to adopt an assertive posture caused pain from the wound to shoot up his side. He sucked in a quick breath and gritted his teeth. 'Of course, when I say "take him", I mean that he is yours for a price. After all, he's young, with plenty of good years ahead of him. Feed him up and exercise him regularly and he'll turn out fit and strong. A good investment, I'd say.'

'But just now you were all for cutting him loose.'

'A figure of speech.' Androcus forced a smile. 'Come now, Centurion, you didn't really think I'd just dump the lad. Why, in some ways he's become part of the family.'

Petronella sniffed. 'Not any family I'd want to be a part of, I'm thinking.'

'I agree,' Macro said firmly. 'I think we'd be doing the captain a favour taking the lad off his hands.'

'Now see here,' Androcus protested. 'He's the ship's boy and that means I've got the right to decide what happens to him, as I do for any of my crew.'

'How much?' Macro interrupted him.

The captain's eyes narrowed shrewdly. His passenger had an honourable discharge, which meant he had plenty of seed money to fund his retirement. 'Given the boy's potential, I'd say he'd fetch a good price in the market. So two hundred denarii would be the going rate.'

'Bollocks to that. If he ain't got a tongue, he's only ever going to be good for manual labour. I'll take him off your hands for fifty.'

'Fifty!' Androcus clapped a hand to his chest theatrically. 'That's—'

'That's all you're going to get from me. Final offer.'

'Fifty?' Androcus chewed his lip. 'From the imperial mint,

mind. Not them debased coins doing the rounds in Gaul.'

'Imperial mint,' Macro confirmed. 'Do we have a deal?'

The captain affected a moment's reluctance before he spat into his palm and held his hand out. 'Fair enough. But I'm robbing myself, so I am.'

Macro took the coins from the locked chest in his baggage and handed them over. Androcus counted them carefully before tipping them into the leather purse hanging from a thong around his neck. 'He's yours. And good riddance.'

Macro felt a moment's doubt at the swift transaction. There was no record of ownership, nothing to guarantee the legal transfer of the boy from one master to another. He wondered if it was even a legally binding transaction. A few feet away, the lad lay curled up on his side, his head resting on his hands, breathing easily as he slept, unaware that his life had taken a new direction. Macro wondered how he would take the news.

As Androcus turned his attention back to steering the ship, the centurion stared down at the boy, hands on hips. Petronella stood beside him and put her arm around his back.

'Well, that was unexpected. Centurion Macro, I swear that as long as I live you will never stop surprising me.' She shifted round and stood in front of him, giving him a quick hug and a kiss on his bristly cheek. 'Why did you do it?'

'Fucked if I know.'

'Really? I think it might have something to do with the lad saving your life last night.'

Macro shrugged. 'Maybe. Maybe I'm just a soft touch. Either way, the kid is going to be another mouth to feed. Once his arm is better, I'm sure we can put him to work at my mother's inn.'

'I suppose.' Petronella looked at the boy with a sympathetic expression. She eased herself down beside him and stroked his dark curls gently. The boy gave a moan, shifted slightly and then let out a contented sigh. She smiled affectionately.

'Now don't you get too attached to him.' Macro wagged a finger. 'I bought him as an investment. We'll do as Androcus says. Feed him up and work him hard, and he'll do well for us when the time comes to sell him on.'

Petronella gave her husband the kind of knowing look that discomforted him. He prided himself on being hard and unsentimental. Yet those who knew him best were wise to his warm heart, and it infuriated him to be so transparent. But then, he was a soldier. Not a politician, or worse, a lawyer. He had no time for artifice, and his natural blunt honesty made any lasting attempt at deceit doomed to failure.

'Hmph . . .' He made his way forward, and as the ship rounded the last bend before Londinium, he fixed his gaze on the sprawling port that gradually revealed itself. Just beyond the last navigable stretch of the river, a long trestle bridge had been built across it from a spit of land on the south bank. Beyond that point, only far smaller boats could trade upriver. Scores of ships, large and small, were moored alongside a timber wharf, while others rode at anchor waiting for a berth. Androcus's ship would have to take her turn. Beyond the wide strip of the wharf lay the warehouses where imported goods would be landed and assessed for tax. Fortunes were to be made supplying the appetites of the wealthier native tribes, who had developed an insatiable taste for wine and other luxuries produced by the more established provinces of the Empire. There, too, would be stored the slaves, dogs, hides, silver and gold trinkets, grain, and ingots from the newly established mines destined for export.

The roofs of the warehouses and the buildings beyond were covered in a thick mantle of snow, and it was hard to discern any regular street pattern in the dwellings, workshops and businesses clustered along the river. On higher ground to the north was a larger structure that appeared to be a modest basilica, and further off on another rise stood the walls of a fort, beyond which rose a tall building that might once have been the garrison commander's house. If it was the building Macro remembered, it had been extensively expanded in recent years. Londinium had changed completely from the far smaller settlement he had last seen nearly seven years earlier. He doubted he would even be able to find his way to the inn run by his mother.

As the *Dolphin* rode the last of the tidal current, Androcus steered towards a timbered hard at the end of the wharf. He called out to Macro, 'Centurion, I'll moor there and you can unload your baggage before I drop anchor out in the river.'

Macro stared at the point the captain had indicated. The timbers were stained green and streaked with mud and other filth. 'I'd rather we landed on the wharf.'

'Then you'll have to wait until there's a spare berth.'

'How long is that going to take?'

Androcus shrugged. 'Hard to say. Hours . . . days, maybe. Your choice.'

Macro exchanged a quick glance with his wife, and Petronella nodded without much enthusiasm. 'We'll use the hard.'

The captain ordered Lemulus to make ready to lower the sail as the ship approached the bank. At the last moment, he turned neatly upriver and bellowed the order to let the sheets fly, and the *Dolphin* bumped softly against the end of the hard close to one of the piles driven into the riverbed. Lowering the spar and sail across the deck, Lemulus took the mooring cable from the bows and dropped over the side, splashing into the ankle-deep water at the end of the hard. Slipping a loop over the pile, he threw the line back up to his captain, who fastened it securely to a cleat.

'Give me a hand with the gangplank,' he instructed Macro.

They slid it over the side and down onto the timbers. One of the gangmasters on the wharf was already picking his way across the churned snow and ice covering the slippery timbers, and he cupped a hand to his mouth.

'Do you need porters?'

When Macro nodded, he turned and bellowed towards a group of men leaning against the side of the nearest warehouse, sheltering from the cold breeze. Several of them pulled away from their companions and hurried to join the gangmaster as he approached the ship and smiled a greeting.

'Caius Torbulo at your service.'

He paced nimbly up the gangplank and hopped down onto the deck. Macro looked the man over warily. Torbulo had a swarthy complexion, and his tunic, cloak and boots looked hard-worn, but he appeared trustworthy enough. Macro jerked his thumb at the baggage on deck. 'We've got four chests, some kitbags and bales of cloth.'

Torbulo glanced past him. 'I've got eight men. Should be enough for one trip. Where are you headed, sir? If this is your first time in Londinium and you're looking for accommodation, I know some comfortable places at decent rates.'

'It's not my first time here, and we've a place to stay. An inn called the Dog and Deer. Do you know it?'

'Know it?' Torbulo chuckled. 'Who doesn't? One of the few places where the wine isn't watered and the whores don't pick your purse behind your back when you're on the job.'

Macro felt a tinge of pride at the words of recommendation. Clearly his mother had made something of a success of the business they both owned.

'I should warn you about the woman who runs the place, though. Portia's as tough as old boots, and you don't want to get on her wrong side, I can tell you.'

'I can imagine,' Macro interrupted quickly, not wanting the man to run on with his description of his mother's attributes in front of Petronella before she had a chance to make up her own mind. 'Let's get on with this. My wife and I want to be warming our arses in front of a decent fire as soon as possible.'

As they waited for the porters to reach the ship, Torbulo sized his customers up. 'I dare say you're a soldier, sir. You have the look of one.'

'Used to be.' Macro drew himself up. 'Centurion Marcus Lucius Macro, late of the Praetorian Guard.'

Torbulo's brows rose appreciatively, then his eyes narrowed and Macro felt a stab of irritation at having made the casual boast. No doubt the gangmaster was already deciding how much he might increase his fee for his distinguished customer.

'From the bandage on your head, it looks like you've not long since left the line of battle, sir.' Torbulo glanced round and saw the dressings on the others, then noticed for the first time the body sewn into a woollen shroud on the far side of the deck. 'Jupiter's cock, what happened?'

'We were jumped by pirates last night.'

'Pirates?' He clicked his tongue. 'Those bastards are becoming more of a problem all the time. It's a wonder the governor doesn't do something about it. Well, if not him, then that new procurator of his. Bloody waste of space. He's been in office over a month and he's done fuck all so far. Pardon my language, ma'am.' He bowed his head apologetically towards Petronella.

'Oh, don't mind me. I've heard worse.' She rolled her eyes.

Torbulo glanced round again and noted the blood still staining the snow. 'Must have been a tough fight.'

'It was.' Macro nodded. 'But they came off far worse than we did. I dare say that gang will be licking their wounds for at least a month before they work up enough courage to try again. Anyway, enough banter. Get our baggage unloaded and then take us to the Dog and Deer.'

'Wait,' Petronella interrupted. 'We need to agree the price first.'

'What?' Macro frowned. 'Well, all right then. What's the charge?'

'A sestertius for each chest and bag is the going rate.'

He shook his head. 'Try again. I'm not some wet-behind-the-ears son of the aristocracy on a grand tour of the provinces.'

Torbulo nodded towards the wharf. 'I don't see any other gangmasters rushing down to offer their services. Fact is, the port is busy enough to keep us fully occupied, even in winter. If you think the price is too high, you're welcome to carry your own baggage, sir.'

Petronella's eyes narrowed and she drew a deep breath. Macro knew the signs well enough to know that he must act before she dismissed the gangmaster and sent him scurrying off under a storm of the most unladylike abuse.

'Very well, a sestertius for each item, but mind your men don't drop anything. I'll hold you responsible for any breakages or spoils. That clear?'

'Yes, sir.' Torbulo smiled cheerfully. 'You can trust my lads.'

As he turned to bellow the orders to the men waiting at the bottom of the gangplank, Petronella steered her husband towards the mast and poked him in the chest. 'Why did you agree? He's conning us. That's twice the going rate back in Rome and you know it.'

'We're not in Rome. It's the way things are on the frontier. Prices are higher. Besides, my head's killing me and I'm cold and tired. We've been on the road for several months, one way and another, and I just want the journey to be over.' Macro sighed. 'So we'll pay what he's asking and just get it over and done with.'

She chewed her lip for a moment, and he feared she was going to protest, but then she nodded. 'Let's go and find your mother.'

'First things first. We need to wake the boy.'

Macro crouched down beside the sleeping youth, who was snoring lightly, and gave him a gentle shake. 'Come on, lad. Wakey-wakey.'

The boy's eyes flickered open and he sat up with a nervous start, looking round anxiously at the strange men clambering up the gangplank.

'Easy there, this lot ain't pirates. At least not in the same way as the others we saw off last night.'

The comment was loud enough for Torbulo to hear, and he glanced round and affected a hurt expression.

Macro lifted the boy up onto his feet and rested a hand on his shoulder. 'You're coming with me and Petronella. The captain's agreed to let us look after you while you recover from your wound.'

The lad glanced towards Androcus, who gave a dismissive shrug and then turned away to order Lemulus to stow the sail. The boy looked surprised at his sudden change in fortune, then bowed his head in acquiescence.

'Where's the boy's kit?' Macro asked the captain.

'Kit?' Androcus sniffed. 'He's wearing it. That's all there is.'

Petronella plucked a spare cloak from one of the chests before the porters carried it ashore and wrapped it round the boy's thin shoulders. 'There you are, my lamb. That'll keep you warm.'

'That's one of my cloaks,' Macro protested. 'You can't just hand it over to the lad like that.'

'It *was* yours.' She smiled sweetly. 'Things are different on the frontier, eh?'

They bade Androcus and what was left of his crew a curt farewell and carefully descended the gangplank onto the timbers below, where Torbulo and his porters were waiting.

'Watch your step,' the gangmaster advised. 'It's slippery going until we reach the wharf.'

Fifteen years before, Londinium had been no more than a small trading post next to a ford. A place where the more daring of the merchants from Gaul had come to do business with tribesmen curious to sample wares from across the Roman Empire. After the invasion, on the heels of the legions that fought their way inland, came a veritable flood of merchants and slave-traders keen to establish a foothold in the new province and make their fortunes before a second wave of traders arrived to compete for the spoils.

Beyond the long line of timber warehouses roofed with shingle lay a warren of smaller buildings, a mixture of native wattle-and-daub shelters covered in thatch, and larger, more angular buildings constructed from timber. Despite the bitter cold, the narrow thoroughfares were crowded, and the streets were covered with a thick slush of melted snow, mud and sewage. Macro and Petronella marched behind the gangmaster and his porters in order to keep an eye on their possessions. There were bound to be some petty thieves on the lookout for easy pickings; the kind of sharp operators who could cut a small opening in a bag or bale of cloth and snatch the contents before the victim was ever aware that something was amiss. Besides, Macro did not wholly trust Torbulo and his men, who could just as easily help themselves the moment their customers' attention was distracted.

Petronella shepherded the boy along to make sure he was not lost in the crowd. The seething mass of people and animals and the cacophony of shouts, the bellowing of animals and the cries of hawkers made him nervous enough to stay between her and Macro.

Macro was relieved when they emerged onto a much wider street that ran parallel to the river. A wooden drain, four feet across and two deep, ran down the middle, leaving enough room on either side for heavy wagons to pass. Shops and workshops lined the route, and the sour tang that hung in the freezing air was pierced here and there by the smell of baking, roasting meat, and the very occasional scents of spices and perfumes brought to the town from the farthest corners of the Empire. There were the odours of animals as well, the heavy stench emanating from the thick hides of oxen, mules and dogs, who added their steamy breath to the puffs and plumes of the people making their way through the brown slush.

'You wouldn't recognise this street,' Torbulo mused. 'This and the other main street fifty paces further in were laid down in Governor Paulinus's time. One of the few things he achieved before he died. That was less than two years ago. It's quite an impressive sight, no?'

'Impressive?' Petronella wrinkled her nose in distaste. 'Not quite the word I was thinking of.'

'Ignore her,' Macro chuckled. 'This is her first visit to the northern frontier. She's not used to the cold. You'll get used to it, my love. It's not as if it'll be like this for ever. Once winter's over, you'll see the province at its best.'

'It would be hard for that not to be an improvement on the present,' she responded.

Macro refused to let her mood sour his own. In truth, he had come to like the climate of the island during the years he had campaigned in Britannia. While it was true that the cold and damp endured for months longer than he would have preferred, he savoured the sharpness of the winter air and the pared-back starkness of the landscape. Each season had a peculiar beauty of its own, and the temperate weather made marching far less onerous than in the scorching heat of the eastern provinces he had served in. He briefly recalled the searing deserts of Aegyptus and Syria and shuddered at the memory of unquenchable thirst aggravated by swirling dust and buzzing insects that contrived to explore every inch of a man's exposed face and skin. True, the fleshpots, food and wine of the East were unsurpassed, but there was more excitement and opportunity to be had in a province still in the making, like Britannia.

He turned back to Torbulo. 'It's been several years since I was last here. What's been happening outside Londinium?'

The gangmaster sucked his cheeks with a loud click as he collected his thoughts. 'The lowlands are peaceful enough. Most of the tribes have been content to adapt to the new management. The only one that's caused us any trouble has been the Iceni. They gave us a bit of a scare ten years back, but Governor Scapula put them in their place in short order. Since then, they've kept to themselves for the most part and not welcomed any traders on their lands. They handed in some of their weapons and armour after the uprising, but the rumour is that they hid most of their kit away. Which tends to make the powers-that-be a bit nervous. That's why a veterans' colony was established at Camulodunum, close enough to the Iceni to make them think twice about any mischief.'

'I've been given a parcel of land at the colony,' said Macro. 'If the growth in Londinium is anything to go by, Camulodunum should be thriving. Being the capital of the province and all.'

Torbulo laughed. 'No chance, sir! The colony's remained a bit of a backwater, despite Rome's ambitions for the place. They've got a theatre, forum, senate house and a bloody great temple under construction, but the real action has shifted here.' His voice took on a proud tone. 'This is where most of the trade passes through. The most recent governors have made Londinium their headquarters. They've already started work on a palace on the hill where the fort is. A few years from now, there will be no doubt about where the real capital of the province is. Whatever the veterans at Camulodunum may have to say about it.' He glanced anxiously at Macro. 'Not that I have anything against veterans, sir. Bloody heroes, every man of them. And I'm sure Camulodunum will be a fine place in its own right.'

'Save the flattery, man. I've already decided you won't be getting a tip. How far to the Dog and Deer now?'

'Right at the next junction and then down to the corner of the next wide thoroughfare. It's a good spot to catch passing trade, and there are plenty of soldiers and officials from the governor's headquarters who step in for a drink. You'll find it lively enough.'

'Sounds good to me.'

The porter at the head of the small party led the way across a board crossing over the drain and turned into the alley Torbulo had mentioned. There were fewer people using this route, and the buildings on either side were poorer-looking than those on the main thoroughfare. Macro felt his optimism slip a little. Then, at the end of the alley, he saw a two-storey timber-framed building looming above the surrounding dwellings.

A painted board hung from an iron bracket. It was decorated with a well-executed painting of a dog chasing a deer through a winter landscape. It was possible the hound was hunting the larger animal, but to Macro it looked more like they were playing together. To one side of the building was a wall some ten feet high with a gateway leading into a yard behind the inn. He indicated the opening. 'In there will do.'

The porters led the way into a large open space surrounded by storerooms, a stable and a couple of pens where chickens pecked amid the frozen mud, while three pigs huddled together beneath the rickety remains of a thatched shelter. As the porters set down the baggage and chests, a heavily built man emerged from one of the storerooms and hurried towards them, wiping his bloodied hands on a leather apron and nodding a familiar greeting to Torbulo. He appeared to be a few years older than Macro, and his grey hair was close-cropped above a pair of bloodshot brown eyes that seemed to bulge from their sockets. He looked dubiously at Macro's bandaged head, and the sling that Petronella had tied for the boy, and Macro realised that he might easily be taken for a brawling ruffian rather than a highly decorated, and wealthy, retired officer of the Empire's elite Praetorian Guard.

'May I help you, sir?'

'Indeed you may. Would you tell the owner of this establishment that her son and his wife have arrived?'

CHAPTER FOUR

The man let out a low whistle, and then smiled. 'Can't wait to see the look on Portia's face when she sees you. This way, please.'

'Just a moment.' Macro took out his purse and paid Torbulo, then looked round and pointed to one of the storerooms, which looked to be empty. 'Have your men put the baggage in there.'

Once they had done as he had instructed and left the courtyard, Macro retrieved the small pay chest containing his savings, closed the door and secured the catch, then set the boy in front of it.

'You're on guard here, understand?'

'He's a kid,' Petronella protested gently. 'A kid with an injured arm. What kind of a guard does that make him?'

'Might as well start earning his keep.' Macro drew his dagger and handed it to the child, who regarded the weapon with wide eyes. 'Now, boy, if there's any trouble, you stick it to them and come running to find me. Think I can trust you to do that?'

The boy grunted and nodded, his eyes gleaming with excitement as he brandished the dagger.

'Easy, lad!' Macro ruffled the boy's unruly hair. 'Can't be

having you knifing your centurion by accident. Keep the blade tucked into your belt until it's needed.'

The boy sighed with disappointment as he carefully slipped the blade into the belt around his tunic so that the handle protruded above and the gleaming point beneath. Then he struck a pose in front of the storeroom, jaw jutting, shoulders back, one foot slightly advanced.

'Just as long as he doesn't trip over and impale himself,' Petronella cautioned.

'He'll be fine.' Macro turned to the man, who stood waiting by the rear door leading into the Dog and Deer, and swallowed nervously. It had been several years since he had last seen his mother, and over two years since he had received a terse report from her informing him that the business was running well and it was time he took on half the burden. 'Let's go in. I can't wait to introduce you.' He smiled widely at Petronella. 'You'll get on famously. Once you see that she has a heart of gold.'

The man slipped the latch and pushed the door inwards, stepping over the lip of the wooden frame. Macro took his wife's hand as he followed. The door opened onto a short passage, twenty feet in length. To the left were three storerooms containing wine jars on shelves, while cheeses, sacks of grain and cuts of meat hung in string bags suspended from iron hooks in the beams in order to keep them out of the reach of rats and mice. To the right was a kitchen with a cooking fire in the middle, above which were iron griddles and a roasting spit. The ashes were grey and no kindling had yet been placed for the day's cooking. A sullen-looking woman in her early twenties with heavily powdered cheeks glanced up from the tub where she was scrubbing clothes as they passed by, then went back to her work.

The corridor gave out onto a counter and a large space beyond filled with trestle tables and benches. Straw was strewn beneath them, covering most of the stone floor except for around the fireplace. At the far end was a studded door with two shuttered windows on either side, slightly ajar to admit some light through the iron security grilles. A fire blazed near the right-hand window and warmed the thin figure hunched over some waxed tablets at one of the benches. She looked up at the sound of footsteps, the brass stylus in her hand poised above the long list of figures she had been working on.

'What is it?' she demanded curtly. 'I thought I told you not to interrupt me when I'm doing the accounts.'

'Begging your pardon, Mistress Portia, but you have visitors.'

'Not visitors,' Macro corrected him. 'Family.'

Her brow creased as she squinted towards the shadows at the rear of the inn, and then her jaw sagged and she dropped the stylus. 'Oh . . .' she gasped.

Macro grinned as he paced towards her, arms outstretched. 'Is that the best you can manage, Mother? After all these years?'

Portia stood up, hands on hips. 'You might have warned me. It would have been better if you had told me you were coming.'

Macro stopped in his tracks. 'I—'

'And look at the state of you,' she clucked. 'Have you been fighting again? I'd have thought you'd be too old for that by now. Have the army finally had enough of you then? And who is this with you? Some tart you picked up in Rome?'

'Heart of gold, eh?' Petronella muttered, just loud enough for Macro to hear. 'You'd better set her right about me, straight away.'

'Of course,' Macro responded quickly. He raised a hand to interrupt his mother, but she continued in a hectoring tone.

'I've heard nothing from you for over two years, and now you think you can just pitch up here expecting a warm welcome. Well, I'll tell you . . .'

'Mother, please, let me just—'

'. . . a dutiful son would have made sure—'

'Quiet!' Macro bellowed, his voice filling the large room so that the man who had shown them in flinched. 'I did write to you, Mother. I wrote to say I would be getting my discharge and coming to join you with my wife.'

Her eyes widened. 'Wife?'

Macro put his arm behind Petronella's waist and gave her a gentle push. His mother cocked her head slightly and moved aside to let more of the light from the window fall on the pair of them. Her steely gaze fixed on the other woman and her lips pinched together.

'This is Petronella. We were married two years ago, in Tarsus.'

'I see. Well, I can't say I am impressed, my girl. You bring my boy in here looking like he's been in a street brawl. You should have stopped him. Did you put that dressing on? He looks like an unholy mess.'

Petronella opened her mouth to answer back, but Macro jumped in before she could speak. 'Mother, it wasn't like that. We were attacked by pirates on the river.'

'Pirates?' Portia sniffed. 'A likely story.'

'It's the truth.' He sighed. 'I had hoped for a warmer welcome.'

There was a brief moment of stillness, the only sounds coming from the street outside. Then Portia suddenly lurched forward, threw her skinny arms around him and buried her face against his shoulder. 'My boy . . . my Macro. At last. Thank the gods!'

He was taken by surprise, and his arms hung limply for a beat before he reached round her and held her close. There was something in her tone, some hint of desperation that concerned him. 'I'm here now, Mother. For good. And so is Petronella.'

Portia stiffened and released her grip on him, then stepped back, cuffing away some tears with her hands as she looked at Petronella.

'I trust you have been a good wife to my son.'

'She is as fine a wife as a man could have,' said Macro. 'You'll see that for yourself the moment you two get to know each other.'

'She doesn't have much to say for herself, does she?'

'I might have,' Petronella smiled sweetly, 'provided I can get a word in edgeways.'

Portia bristled with umbrage for a moment, and Macro feared she might unleash an outburst of rage. Instead she suddenly threw her head back and cackled. 'She has some spirit then! Good, she'll need it to cope with the both of us.'

She gestured to the bench on the other side of the table she had been working at. 'Sit down there.'

Turning to the man who had shown the new arrivals in, she adopted a more imperious manner. 'Denubius, bring us some wine. Get the fire lit in the kitchen and heat up some of the stew, then bring us some cold chops and bread.'

'Yes, mistress. Which wine would you like?'

'Use one of the jars from Gaul. Water it down well, though. And bring some more wood for the brazier.'

He nodded and hurried out of the room.

Macro eased the bench out and waved Petronella in first so that she could be closest to the warmth of the logs burning in the brazier. The smoke curling from the flames was acrid enough to overcome the pervasive odour of the filth in the street outside and the tang of sweat and spilled wine and ale inside the room. There was an aroma of boiled vegetables and roast meat as well, and he felt his stomach grumble as his appetite got the better of him.

Once all three were settled, Portia hugged her arms around her skinny frame. 'I suppose the obvious question is how did you two come to be married? I'll be honest, I didn't think Macro was the marrying type. Where are you from, girl? Tarsus?'

Petronella shook her head, trying hard not to react to being referred to as a girl. 'I met your son while I was serving my old master.'

'That was Cato, Mother. My commanding officer. You remember him?'

Portia gave him a frosty stare. 'I am old, not stupid. Of course I remember Cato. How is the dear boy? Still alive, I hope.'

'Very much so. At least he was when I last saw him, before we left Rome.'

'So he didn't leave you the girl in his will, then?'

'Obviously not,' Petronella responded tartly. 'Master Cato set me free so that I could marry your son.'

'Set you free?' Portia arched an eyebrow before she addressed Macro. 'You fell for a common slave, then?'

Macro took his wife's hand and squeezed it with as much desperation as affection as he tried to head off any expression of outraged indignation. 'There is nothing common about Petronella, Mother. I knew it almost as soon as I first saw her. She's honest, strong and smart, and I love her.'

'You love her. Since when was love a good reason to marry anyone? Did her master give her a decent dowry when he set her free to marry you?'

'Cato was generous.'

'Glad to hear it. So, apart from the qualities you mention, what use will she be to our business here?'

'I can answer perfectly well for myself,' Petronella cut in. 'I can read and write and deal with numbers. I may have been a slave once, but I was born a free person, and now that I am free once again, I'll not be beholden to anyone I don't choose to be. And that includes you, Portia. I'll speak my mind as I see fit to anyone. Even my husband's mother.'

The blood had drained from Macro's face, and now he forced a smile as he tried to ease the increasingly strained atmosphere between the two women. 'She also has a fine right hook to deal with any troublemakers who might kick off in this place. She's kind of a cross between a barmaid and a doorman. Very useful indeed.'

Petronella shot him a hostile glance. 'Well, thank you indeed for such kind words.'

Portia scrutinised her daughter-in-law for a moment and then gave a resigned shrug. 'I suppose you'll have to do. Time will tell. I'll be watching closely to see how you cope. Settle in and play your part in the business and I think we may get on well.'

They were interrupted by Denubius, who returned balancing a tray laden with a platter of cold meat and two small loaves in one hand, while in the other he held a jar with four small cups hanging from the rim. He set them on the table and then made to sit down next to Portia.

'You've work to do,' she said sharply. 'Make sure the bedcovers are washed and then get the whores to clean out their cells.'

'But I thought I might introduce myself to your family, mistress.'

'Later. Be off with you.'

Denubius turned away with a pained expression, shoulders stooped. Portia saw the look of pity on her son's face.

'Oh, don't you worry about him. He's used to the sharp edge of my tongue. He'll be fine once his mind turns back to his chores.'

Macro gave their surroundings a closer inspection. 'You've got girls working here?'

'Not in here.' Portia gestured towards a curtained doorway to the side of the room. 'The brothel is in there. It's a nice earner given all the soldiers and sailors who pass through Londinium. I bought the next-door building a few years back and knocked through. There's another entrance onto the main street that customers can use if they don't want to drink first. But most come in here to have a few jars before they go on to the girls.'

'How many women do you have?' asked Petronella.

'Twelve. I own six of them. The others rent their cells and pay me a cut for each client they service.'

'Twelve?' Macro let out an appreciative whistle. 'You've obviously done well for yourself, Mother. A brothel as well as the inn. Now that I'm here, I can help expand the business even further.'

'Just make sure you keep your hands off the women,' Petronella warned him. 'Or you may well be on the receiving end of that right hook you admire so much.'

'Oh, I don't think I need much help in expanding the business,' Portia said. 'I've managed without you for seven years. Besides the inn, the rooms I let to travellers and the brothel, there's a bakery and a butcher's shop, and I have plans for a wine-importing business as well. It's not common knowledge yet, but I've just bought a warehouse close to the wharf. Once I get regular shipments from Gaul, it means I can cut out the middle men and supply the inn for far less cost, and make money from selling to other inns in the town.' She sat back with a satisfied smile. 'I've made a tidy return on our initial investment. Of course, I've been doing all the hard work while you've been swanning around the Empire with the army. Still, I dare say you've saved a decent sum for your retirement. With your money, there's plenty more we can do. Although I've been getting by fine without you, the extra money would be useful to expand the business.'

'I'd be happy to put some silver into the business, Mother. But I have also been given land at Camulodunum. So we'll be spending time there getting a farm up and running, as well as working here.'

'Perhaps that's something Petronella could take on while you help me. She has the right build for agriculture, and the clean country air will do her a power of good, I'm sure.'

'It's my land and I'll see to it personally. With Petronella's help.'

'As you wish. You never listened to my advice when you were young. Some things don't change.'

'Perhaps I never had the chance to listen to your advice, because you ran off with that marine and abandoned me and my father.'

Portia stiffened and folded her arms. 'Your father was a waster.'

'At least he wasn't a traitor, like that bastard you hooked up with. Just as well he came to a sticky end.'

The tense silence returned to the room as old wounds were plucked open and the vintage poison of unforgotten and unforgiven sins bled afresh. At length Macro folded his hands together and cracked his knuckles. 'Let's try and put that behind us, Mother. For both our sakes. We're in business together now, and we're the only family we have. So let's make the most of it, eh?'

'Fair enough.' She scratched her chin. It was a gesture that Petronella had seen Macro perform in almost exactly the same way. She contained a smile.

'Londinium is growing larger all the time,' Portia continued. 'I've made a small fortune so far, but there's still plenty to be made by those who got a foothold early on.' Her expression creased into a frown. 'Of course, places like this attract scum as well . . . those who feed off the hard work of others.'

'Who are you talking about?'

'Who do you think? The same street people who prey on shops and merchants in Rome.'

'The gangs?'

'Who else? I suppose it was only a matter of time before they saw the rich pickings to be had in the new province. They arrived three years back and have been leeching off honest traders ever since. The guilds have asked the governors to do something about it but they're too interested in fighting the tribesmen and winning glory to bother with such matters. So we're stuck with the gangs. They take a cut of my profits. It hurts, but I can still get by and get on.'

Macro's expression had darkened. 'Now that I'm here, I'll put an end to that bollocks.'

'You'll do no such thing.' Portia wagged a finger at him. 'I don't want you causing any trouble that hurts my interests. You've just arrived here, and you need to watch and listen until you learn the lie of the land rather than kicking off without any idea of what you are getting yourself into, and dragging me along with you.'

'Mother, I've been a soldier for most of my life, and I've

been a good one. I've faced the toughest barbarian warriors on this island and beaten them. Same goes for pirates in the Adriatic and the Parthians of the eastern frontier. So I think I can handle a few street thugs. Point me in the right direction and I'll soon deal with them.'

Portia shook her head sadly. 'You're no longer a soldier. Your hair is going grey and what sense you may have had has been knocked out of that thick skull of yours by spending too long in the army. The men I'm talking about don't come screaming at you from the front. They give you no warning, and you can't pick them out in a crowd. The first thing you'll know about it is when they stab you in the back, or close in around you in a dark alley when you're alone. They don't fight like soldiers, my son.'

'They sound like cowards.' Macro snorted with derision.

'I don't think they are too concerned what men like you think of them. And if you get all high and mighty about it, then you can be sure they'll make an example of you to show the people of this town what happens to anyone who challenges them.'

'Let 'em try.'

Portia rolled her eyes and turned to Petronella. 'Does he listen to you?'

'He's been known to. Not often, but it happens.'

'Then talk some sense into him before he causes any trouble.'

Petronella thought for a moment before addressing Macro. 'We're new here. You're no longer a soldier and you promised me that we'd have a quiet life. You promised. I think you'd be wise to listen to your mother.'

Portia gave a thin smile of satisfaction. 'There. Maybe your woman's brighter than I thought. If she gets the point, then surely you can.'

Petronella ground her teeth. 'I'm not certain how much more of this I can take,' she muttered. 'But listen to her, Macro. She might be right. Let's not cause problems for ourselves the moment we arrive, hmm?'

Macro sighed deeply. 'I'm outnumbered. Not that that has ever been a problem before. But now I'm outnumbered and outflanked. What can I say? I surrender.'

Petronella stared at him briefly and shook her head. 'If I hadn't heard it with my own ears, I'd never believe it. Somehow I don't see you surrendering to anyone. Not even your wife, or your ferocious mother.'

'Ferocious? Me?' Portia scowled, then caught the humorous glint in the other woman's eyes and suddenly cackled with laughter as she reached out a gnarled hand and pinched Petronella's wrist. Coming from another person it might have been a purely affectionate gesture, but there was an extra pressure from her fingernails that Petronella had to force herself not to react to.

'This girl's a treasure. Make sure you look after her, Macro. If you're lucky, she'll turn out to be as astute as your mother.'

'May the gods have mercy on me,' Macro responded wearily. 'Now that I've promised I'll behave, can we please get started on the food and wine and stop all the needling? When I said I wanted a peaceful retirement, I didn't mean getting it in the ear from the two of you. I'd sooner march myself down to the recruiting depot and sign on as a fucking recruit all over again.'

'Language!' Portia reached over and clipped his ear. 'Watch your tongue, lad. There are ladies present.'

Macro straightened up and made an elaborate show of scanning the room. 'Where?'

Petronella barked with laughter and kissed him impulsively on the cheek. 'You dog, you.'

He put his arm round her and squeezed her close before he spoke to his mother again. 'There's one other thing. We've picked up a young lad. He's outside in the yard. He'll be staying with us for a while, I imagine. We'll need a place for him too.'

Portia threw her hands up in despair. 'There I was thinking I'd invite my son into the business, and he turns up with a small horde of gatecrashing freeloaders into the bargain. What's a poor woman to do? You two can have a room. The boy sleeps in the kitchen, unless you want him to share the room with you.'

'Ah, no,' Macro responded. 'A man and his wife need a little privacy. The kitchen will be fine.'

'So much for gratitude,' said Petronella, rising from the bench. 'I'll go and fetch him.'

'Why not?' said Portia. 'Might as well have a free-for-all banquet for every waif and stray my son cares to take under his wing.'

Once Petronella had left the room, Macro leaned forward and fixed his mother with an intense stare. 'Well, what do you think of her? Try to bite back on your bitter nature and be honest with me.'

'Honestly?' Portia picked up a chop daintily between the tips of her finger and thumb. 'I think she's far too good for you.'

CHAPTER FIVE

Early the next morning, Macro put on his best tunic and buckled on his sword belt. Petronella had cleaned the wound to his head and applied a small dressing before she handed him his cloak. Once he had put it on, she stood back to look him over, then stepped forward to adjust the cloak marginally.

'There you go. As presentable as you can be.'

The boy had been sitting watching them as he hungrily consumed the porridge Petronella had made for the three of them. He smiled as he caught Macro's eye.

'What are you smirking at?' Macro growled. 'I imagine you think Petronella wears the breeches, eh?'

The boy grinned. 'Hngggg.'

Macro regarded him with a frown for a moment. 'We're going to have to find a name for you, lad. "Boy" isn't good enough. What do you think, my love?'

Petronella shrugged. 'One name's as good as another.' She turned to regard the youngster. 'Poor little thing,' she mused.

'Parvus it is then,' Macro decided. 'Hey, lad, your name is Parvus from now on. If you're not happy with it, just say so.'

The boy struggled to swallow his mouthful of porridge, then gave his response. 'Hmmghnh!'

'I'll take that garbled nonsense as a yes.'

Petronella put her hands on her hips and gave her husband a scornful look. 'You have a cruel sense of humour sometimes, my love.' She stood over the boy and patted his cheek. 'Poor lad. If I could get my hands on the swine who cut your tongue out . . .'

Macro ruffled Parvus's hair. 'I won't be long. Just need to report into the garrison commander. Then we'll have a look over the town and get our bearings. Maybe buy you some furs to keep you warm, and something to replace those rags Parvus owns.'

Petronella nodded, and Macro picked up his centurion's vine cane and turned to step through the door of the inn and out into the street.

The sun had not yet risen above the roofs of the surrounding buildings, and the light had a blue hue in the muddy street. There were not many people or carts abroad at this hour. Macro strode around the corner onto the second of the town's main thoroughfares. He had got directions to the administrative quarter of Londinium from Denubius as the latter had appeared from the direction of Portia's room just before dawn. There had been an awkward pause before Macro cleared his throat and made his request. The other man had provided the details before making the excuse that he needed to split logs for the kitchen and the braziers and dashing off.

Macro's brow creased as he made his way along the street. If his mother had taken Denubius as a lover, why hadn't she mentioned it the previous day? Maybe she was embarrassed by her hypocrisy. Having berated her son for marrying a former slave, it seemed likely that she was sleeping with the paid help. Macro was not sure how he felt about that. Not until he got to know the man better. He had planned to take care of his mother in her old age once he and Petronella reached Londinium, but it seemed she was quite resilient and successful and in little need of help. Still, there was the matter of the gangs she had mentioned. If they were giving her trouble, Macro was not the man to stand by and let it happen, despite her admonition to leave well alone.

Some two hundred paces along the street, he spotted the blacksmith's on the corner of a junction that Denubius had described to him, and turned north towards the partially walled area where the original fort had been constructed to cover the Tamesis ford in the early days of the invasion. As he drew closer to the gatehouse, he saw that the gates had been removed and there was no sign of anyone on watch in the tower. He followed a man leading a string of mules inside and saw that much of the open space beyond was filled with market stalls, many of which were being opened up in preparation for the day's business. People were setting out their wares and produce, while others were rubbing their hands or stamping their feet to warm them.

Although the purely military purpose of the fort had long since been made redundant by the pacification of the island's lowland tribes, most of the buildings remained and now served as the seat of government for the town and the wider province. The headquarters block had been surrounded by a new wall to fill fully a quarter of the space that had been contained within the original rampart. The remaining barracks within the enclosed area were still being used for soldiers in transit as well as the small garrison that policed the town. The new wall had been hurriedly constructed, however, and parts of the rampart were crumbling, leaving piles of debris. Beyond these, sections of the ditch had been filled in with rubbish. It was clear to Macro that the original defences offered little protection if an enemy was to descend on Londinium. But then it seemed there was little danger of such an attack now that Caratacus – the most formidable warlord of the Britons – had been captured. The last of the warriors he had once led had been driven into the mountains far to the west and north of the province. It should only take a few more years before every tribe of the island was tamed and Britannia would enjoy peace and prosperity like any other province of the Empire.

A pair of auxiliaries were standing sentry at the arched entrance to the headquarters courtyard, and one of them raised a hand to halt Macro as he approached.

'What's your business, friend?'

Macro lifted his vine cane in an informal salute. 'Centurion Lucius Cornelius Macro come to register for the provincial reserve.'

The auxiliary stiffened and saluted. 'Yes, sir.'

'Where can I find the commander of the Londinium garrison?'

'Main block, sir. Ground floor. Ask for Tribune Salvius.'

'Tribune Salvius. Thanks.' Macro returned the salute and the sentries stepped aside to let him pass.

Inside the wall, there were more sentries at the entrance to the main building, and previous falls of snow had been cleared from the flagstones and banked up around the perimeter. A squad of auxiliaries were working under the watchful eye of an optio as they swept the most recent snowfall away.

'No slacking there, Lucanus!' the optio bellowed, striding over to an auxiliary who had paused to rest. 'This is the army, not a fucking holiday spa. Shift yourself, my lad!'

It had been a few months since Macro had last set foot inside a fortification, and the familiar surroundings brought on a pang of regret that he had been discharged and was now no longer a part of this way of life. All that remained for him was to help his mother run her businesses and spend as much time as possible with Petronella. There was the additional burden of Parvus to be considered, of course, but he was sure he could find ways for the boy to earn his keep. He had noted his wife's growing affection for the mute lad, and was under no illusion about her intention to take him under her wing and treat him as if he was family. While Petronella had been a slave, she had been responsible for raising Prefect Cato's child, Lucius, and when the time had come for Macro and Cato to part company, she had grieved over being parted from the boy. If Macro was any judge of her personality and needs, it was a sestertius to an aurus that she was looking to make Parvus the replacement for Lucius.

Still, his connection with his army days was not completely severed. Like every other veteran, he would be considered a reserve for as long as he was capable of fighting, and would be called on in an emergency. Moreover, there would be many more like him who had been granted land at the veterans' colony at Camulodunum. Old soldiers who would be happy to swap tall stories over a drink, or several drinks if Macro had his way. As the saying went, you can take a soldier out of the army, but you can't take the army out of a soldier.

Having been passed into headquarters, Macro stopped a clerk for directions and was pointed towards an office at the end of the main hall. The door was open, and he saw a slender young man with prematurely thinning hair hunched over a table as he worked on a wax tablet. There was a long table at the side of the room where three clerks were equally busy, working by the light entering a window high up on one wall. Because of the overcast weather outside, the room was dim and felt chilly as Macro rapped on the frame and entered.

'Tribune Salvius?'

'A moment!' The man marked a spot on the tablet with one

finger and then glanced up. His face was thin, his complexion sallow and his expression tired. Macro could well imagine that the young officer was looking forward to completing his compulsory military service as swiftly as possible before returning to Rome to continue to the next step of the political ladder. Although Britannia was a place where reputations could be made, it was equally true that there were far more clement places around the Empire that served the same purpose for the likes of the junior tribune.

'What do you want?' Salvius demanded.

Macro advanced towards him, stopped a pace from the far side of the desk and stood to attention. 'Centurion Lucius Cornelius Macro, sir. Honourably discharged from the Praetorian Guard. Just arrived from Rome to take up my grant of land at Camulodunum. I'm here to register for the reserves.' He fished into his sidebag and took out the bronze plates that were issued to Praetorian veterans listing their service record, decorations and details of the bonus and land grants awarded to them by the emperor on their discharge. He handed them to the tribune and Salvius read them over carefully before returning them with a more respectful demeanour.

'You've had quite a career, Macro. I'm pleased that a man of your quality will be playing a leading role at the colony. Camulodunum could use a senior officer to lick them into shape. They're way behind schedule on building works. Just as well that the place has fallen out of the running to become the provincial capital.'

'Ah, well, I intend to spend most of my time here, sir. I have business interests to attend to in Londinium. Though I will need to establish a farm at the colony.'

'Oh . . . that's a pity. Still, I'm glad you're here. We need every good man we can get at the moment. Officers with your experience are thin on the ground, given the casualties we suffered in the most recent campaigns.'

This was the first report of the situation in Britannia from a military figure that Macro had heard since leaving Rome. The popular view was that the province was on the verge of finally achieving a hard-won peace.

'I had the impression that we had the upper hand here, sir.'

'We have done ever since we set foot on this island. And yet there's always a handful of tribes that cause us difficulties. The Silures, Ordovices and their Druid friends are still holding out in the mountains. And then there's the ongoing tension with the Brigantes in the north and the Trinovates and the Iceni not far from Camulodunum.'

Macro raised an eyebrow. 'What kind of tension, sir?'

Salvius gestured to the bronze diploma in Macro's hand. 'You've served here before, so you'll know about the trouble we have had keeping Cartimandua of the Brigantes on the throne and making sure her tribe stay loyal to Rome. But the more worrying reports are coming from the other two tribes. The Trinovantes are screaming blue murder over the liberties taken by some of the veterans at the colony. Of course, it's not going to get them anywhere. Woe to the vanquished and all that. But you don't want to push people too far . . . As for the Iceni?' He shrugged. 'Who knows what they are really up to? Since the last uprising, we've established a line of outposts around their territory, and they do their best to keep Romans and traders out. We have a treaty with them that says we are allies, but how long they'll respect that is anyone's guess.

'Now that Governor Paulinus is mobilising an army to finish off the mountain tribes and the Druids, he's having to scrape together every soldier he can find to fill out its ranks. Even though there are four legions stationed in Britannia, three of them are under-strength, and the Second is acting as a training depot for the new recruits arriving from Gaul. That's why Paulinus has had to ask for veterans at Camulodunum to rejoin the legions. There are over two thousand of them there, and more than five hundred have answered the call. You can be sure that will not go unnoticed by the troublemakers amongst the natives in the region. Which is why I hoped you would be settling there. Men like you will be needed if there's any trouble. You've picked an interesting time to return to Britannia, Centurion Macro.'

Macro smiled wryly. 'Interesting times seem to have followed me everywhere since I first joined the army, sir. But my soldiering days are over. If the natives know what's good for them, they'll keep their noses clean and behave. They've had enough experience of being on the receiving end of our swords to grasp what happens to those who choose to defy Rome. Once the governor has cleared up the last of those still holding out in the mountains, Britannia will settle down, you mark my words.'

The tribune briefly considered Macro's remarks and puffed his cheeks. 'I admire your sanguine point of view, Centurion. I hope you are right. The last thing the Empire needs right now is any further trouble in Britannia. We've been fighting here for fifteen years now. The cost in men's lives and silver has been bleeding us white. There are some who say we'd be better off if we abandoned the province. Others think we should never have invaded in the first place.'

Macro could not help smiling to himself when green young officers like the tribune talked as if they had been involved in the fighting. The man in front of him had been a toddler fifteen years ago. What did he know of the desperate battles Macro and Cato had endured in the early days of the invasion and the years of conflict that followed? But then there were plenty of people back in Rome who boasted of Rome's achievements and dared her enemies to defy her while never exposing themselves to anything more dangerous than food poisoning or a brief encounter with a footpad in a dark street. The bellicose courage of the mob and the boastful rhetoric of politicians were far more easily come by for them than victory in the field for those who actually had to fight and die for it. For Macro, and soldiers like him, the measure of a man was judged by his deeds, not his words. So his mild amusement over the tribune's easily won military insight was tempered by a shadow of contempt all the same.

'You know what they say in the army, sir. There's no gain without pain. Rome has earned this province the hard way. She'll not let Britannia slip through her fingers.'

'I suppose you're right.' Salvius reached to one side and sorted through a pile of wax slates before he found the one he was looking for and made some quick notes. 'I'll have you added to the reserve list. Aside from the colony at Camulodunum, where can you be found if we need you?'

'I'm billeted . . .' Macro caught himself and smiled at the slip of his tongue. 'I'm living at the Dog and Deer inn. Do you know it?'

The tribune chuckled. 'Who doesn't? The best wine and whores in Londinium. And the woman who owns the place makes sure fights are kept to a minimum, which keeps the provosts happy. She's a tough old bird is Portia. Have you met her yet?'

'She's my mother.'

Salvius did a swift double-take as he recalled his most recent comment, and then looked relieved that he had not said anything that might be taken as offensive. A slightly embarrassed expression flitted across his face as he continued quickly. 'Well, that would explain where you get your martial qualities from, Centurion. That's a family to be reckoned with.'

'Yes, it is, sir. And you haven't met my wife yet.'

'An equally bold woman, then?'

'I'd put good money on her against almost any barbarian I've ever met in battle. She can strike a man down with one blow of her tongue, and finish the job with her fists.'

Salvius hesitated before he responded. 'I'm not quite sure whether to congratulate you on finding such a formidable partner to match the qualities of your mother, or whether to offer you my deepest sympathy at the prospect of living between two such women.'

'You understand my position perfectly, sir.'

The tribune made a note of Macro's lodgings and then pushed the slate aside. 'Welcome to Londinium, Centurion. I wish you a long and peaceful retirement, given the circumstances.'

'No doubt I'll be seeing you at the inn sometime, sir.'

'You can count on it.'

As he made his way back to the Dog and Deer, Macro reflected on Salvius's assessment of the situation in Britannia. While it was true that it was taking far longer to crush the resistance to Roman rule than had been anticipated, the very fact that the fighting had been so tough made Macro fiercely determined that the job had to be seen through to the end. Anything less would be a humiliation, as well as robbing the sacrifice of so many of its meaning. It was deeply concerning to hear, once again, the gossip that powerful men in Rome were considering abandoning Britannia and withdrawing the garrison to Gaul. Should that happen, what would become of all those who had followed in the footsteps of the invading army? If they chose to stay, who would protect them against the wrath of the tribes Rome had subdued? Tens of thousands of merchants, traders and settlers, including Macro and his mother, would have to give up their investments in the new province and return to Rome in penury. It was a disturbing prospect indeed, and it dampened his earlier good mood.

As he approached the inn, it began to snow again, large flakes swirling round and down as they were borne on a rising breeze. Within moments the muddy, rutted surface of the street was covered in a thin sheet of white, and Macro hastened his pace. He ducked inside the door and closed it quickly before turning in the direction of the counter.

A handful of early customers, burly-looking men, were sitting around the brazier while Parvus struggled in with a basket of split logs. Macro tousled his hair as he passed by and made for Petronella, who was setting up cups on a shelf behind the counter.

'All done with the formalities, my love,' he announced cheerfully. 'My retirement begins.'

As soon as he saw the strained expression on her face, Macro felt his guts twist with anxiety. 'What's happened?'

'Those men came in not long ago. Their leader asked to speak with your mother.' Petronella nodded to the corridor leading towards the yard at the rear of the inn. 'She told me she would deal with him and to stay in here. Macro, I don't like the look of them.'

He took a deep breath. 'All right. I'll see to it.'

CHAPTER SIX

The room his mother used as a storeroom and office was narrow, with a high barred window overlooking the yard. Shelves ran along one wall, stacked with jars of wine and the more valuable commodities she traded in as part of her burgeoning range of business interests. On the floor beneath the shelves there was a strongbox squeezed in between two blocks of stone and secured to each of them by heavy iron chains. On the opposite wall was a long, narrow table on which were stacked neat piles of wax tablets and an iron stand from which hung four oil lamps.

Portia was sitting alongside a thin man wearing a green tunic with a geometric pattern woven into the cuffs and collar. His knee-high boots were of the same colour but soiled with mud. An emerald-green cloak lay folded on the table next to him. As Macro entered the room, he turned to reveal a broad, pleasant face with a ready smile beneath dark hair carefully arranged into tight curls that gleamed with oil, as did his neatly trimmed beard. His age was hard to determine. Anything between late twenties and forty, Macro estimated, as the man addressed him.

'And who might you be, friend?' His tone was cordial, but there was a cold glint in his eyes as they sized Macro up.

'This is my son,' Portia said hurriedly. 'Come from Rome to help me run the business.'

'Son?' The man's eyebrows rose. 'You never mentioned a son before, my dear Portia. I have to admit that after doing business with you for over two years now, I had assumed we knew each other well. It seems you have been keeping secrets from me.'

'It's no secret,' she protested mildly. 'You never asked me about my family.'

'That's true.' He nodded. 'I'm just disappointed that you did not see fit to tell me, given our close working relationship. But look, I'm being rude.' He stood up and offered Macro his hand. 'My name is Pansa. I came here from Rome some years back to seek my fortune. There's nothing like a freshly minted province for an enterprising man to make his mark on the world. I imagine that's why you have come such a long way to join your mother. And your name would be?'

'Lucius Cornelius Macro.' Macro gave the extended hand a cursory shake, noting the firmness of the other man's grip and the tattoo of a scorpion on his forearm.

'Macro?' Pansa's lips lifted in a slight smile at the humorously inappropriate cognomen. 'It's a pleasure to make the acquaintance of another man from the capital. Although I can't place your accent. Which part of Rome are you from?'

There was a hint of wariness in the way the question was asked, and Macro wondered if Pansa's reasons for leaving Rome were as innocent as they sounded.

'My last billet was at the Praetorian barracks.'

'A soldier?'

'A centurion.' He stood stiffly, shoulders back.

'But retired now, I'd say, from the look of you.'

'That's right.'

'You must be very proud of him, my dear Portia.'

She made no reply, and Macro could see from the way she clasped her hands together tightly and sat rigidly that she was acutely uncomfortable.

'Well, I mustn't tarry here when I am sure you two still have so much to catch up on.' Pansa turned back to Portia and nodded to the mug on the table. 'Thanks for the wine. It's been good to clear the air. I'll let Malvinus know that normal business relations will be resumed. He'll be pleased to hear that. As you know, he doesn't like any . . .' he paused, as if searching for inspiration, and then clicked his fingers, 'unpleasantness! That's the word. So let's not burden him with such things again.'

He picked up his cloak, flicked out the folds and swung it over his shoulders before he glanced up at the window. 'Must be about my business before the snow delays me. It's a pleasure to meet you, Centurion Macro. Former centurion, I should say.'

Macro stood his ground and the other man was obliged to step round him. As they stood close together, Pansa looked down at him and spoke softly. 'Just remember that your fighting days are over once and for all and I'm sure we'll get along famously.' Then he strode out of the room and turned towards the bar, barking an order to the men sitting by the brazier.

Macro stepped out into the corridor and watched as Pansa led his companions out into the street and the door closed behind them. Then he returned to his mother. He was shocked to see her trembling as she poured herself another cup of wine from the small jar on the table and knocked it back.

'What was that all about?' he asked.

She swallowed and set the cup down sharply. 'You don't want to know. Rather, I don't want you to get to know him. Stay away from Pansa and let me deal with him.'

'What business do you have with him, Mother?'

'Whatever it is, it is not *your* business, my boy.'

'It's *our* business now that I am here.'

Macro was about to close the door behind him when there was the sound of footsteps in the corridor and Denubius appeared, breathing hard, his cloak speckled by snowflakes. He nodded a greeting to Macro before turning to Portia anxiously.

'I saw Pansa leaving as I came back from the market. Is it settled?'

'Leave us alone,' Portia snapped. 'Go and rouse the whores. There'll be customers looking for warmed wine, a roaring fire and a woman in this weather. Go!'

Denubius hesitated, then his shoulders slumped as he turned and trod heavily back along the corridor. Macro closed the door and sat on the stool that Pansa had occupied. He folded his arms and stared levelly at his mother. 'I think you'd better tell me exactly what's going on.'

Portia winced. 'Keep your voice down. If someone's listening . . .'

Macro saw the terror in her expression. 'By the gods, who is he that you should be so afraid of him?'

'Pansa has had men killed for cursing his shadow. I'm warning you, be careful what you say about him. There's no telling who is listening. And show him respect when you next meet him, for all our sakes. D'you hear me?'

'I'll respect any man who earns it.'

'You fool, you're no longer in the army. You don't lightly make enemies in a place like Londinium. Certainly not enemies like Pansa and his master.'

'Who is his master?'

'Malvinus is his name. He runs the biggest gang in the town, the 'Scorpions'. There's another, almost as powerful, run by Cinna. They call themselves 'Cinna's blades'. The handful of other gangs are small affairs and they pay tribute to these two. If they don't, their leaders are killed and their men have the choice of serving either Malvinus or Cinna. Or being killed themselves.'

'I can imagine how effective that incentive is. But what was Pansa doing here? What were you talking about before I turned up?'

Portia worked her hands together anxiously. 'Can't you guess? Surely not every grain of sense was knocked out of you in the army? Malvinus is running a protection racket. Every business in Londinium has to pay him a cut. If someone refuses, he cuts a finger off their child or wife. Once he has taken all the fingers, the head follows, then the whole family. Pansa was sent to arrange my next payment. He's demanding six hundred sestertii within the next three days. Only I haven't got it. I've invested in stock, wine from Gaul, that was supposed to have arrived nearly a month ago, and the warehouse. With the winter storms it was a bit of a risk, but if the wine had arrived I'd have been able to charge premium prices for it. More than enough to pay off Malvinus. But now . . .' She shook her head and closed her eyes. 'I don't know what I'm going to do. I have to pay him or . . .' She made a cutting motion with one hand across the other.

Macro leaned forward. 'That isn't going to happen, Mother. I won't let it. If Pansa and his thugs try anything, I'll deal with them.'

She shook her head. 'You'd only get yourself killed. And your wife along with me as well. We have to find the money. I can sell what stock I have, but it won't be enough. I could get rid of one of my business interests, but it might be difficult to find a buyer in time.' Her brow creased in concentration. 'I could—'

'I can pay it,' Macro interrupted. 'I have more than enough money. Anyway, you said you could make use of a further investment from me.'

'No. This is my problem. I'll handle it.'

'Since I own half the business, it's my problem too.'

'But you need that money to set yourself up in Camulodunum.'

Macro shrugged. 'I can take it back when your wine shipment arrives. For now, let me sort the payment out. All right?' He stroked the wrinkled flesh on the back of her hand with his thumb. 'Let me deal with it.'

She stared at him intently, then seemed to shrink into herself as she let out a sigh. 'Thank you. Once the wine comes in, I'll be fine. I'll have enough to pay off Malvinus and make a decent profit besides. I'll be fine,' she repeated, to reassure herself as much as Macro.

Macro cleared his throat. 'Perhaps if I have a word with Malvinus, I can cut a better deal for us.'

'No!' She clamped her hand over his. 'Stay away from that bastard! You hear me?'

'Mother. Sometimes a man-to-man conversation gets results. Besides, it's not as if I'm just some civvy who doesn't know how to handle himself in a fight. Malvinus would be wise not to cause me any trouble.'

'Bollocks. What is wrong with you? Do you think he's gouging me for money just because I'm a woman? Doesn't matter if you're male or female, old or young, weak or strong, Malvinus and his type will always take their cut. So don't even think of trying to change things. All that's likely to achieve is him making an example of you to discourage any other fools from challenging his authority. Promise me you'll do nothing to make things worse for us. Promise me!'

Macro hesitated before replying. He was shocked by the vehemence of her tone, and the abject surrender to Malvinus that betokened. There was a surge of anger in his veins that she should be forced into such a state of mind. And there was disgust too, for the kind of coward who would happily bully an old woman into paying up. If there was one quality a long career in the army had imbued him with, it was contempt for bullies. But his mother was sitting before him, anxiously trying to read his expression. She needed to be reassured, even if he had to be a little dishonest with her.

'Very well, Mother, I promise I will do my best not to make things worse for us.'

'You're not serious?' Petronella shook her head as her husband outlined his intentions. 'If this man is half as dangerous as Portia says, that is twice the reason not to even think about confronting him.'

Macro, whose grasp of numbers was never as good as he might wish, spent a moment getting his mind around her comment before he scratched his cheek, fingernails rasping over the thick stubble. 'Well, we can't afford to let some petty criminal bleed our business white like some fucking horsefly. We came here to make a fortune and then retire and live an easy life. I have no intention of the three of us working our fingers to the bone while that louse Malvinus grows fat off our labours.'

'I thought he was a horsefly.'

'Either way, he's a parasite and needs to be dealt with.'

'You think you can just walk up to his kind and announce that you've had a think about the situation and decided not to do business with him?' She shook her head. 'Oh, my dearest Macro. You have the heart of a lion but the brain of an ox.'

'Look, I'll just have a word with him. Man to man. There may be a way out of having to pay him in future. Or not paying him so much, at any rate. It's worth trying. If he's a reasonable man and I approach him reasonably, I'm sure something good can come out of it.'

'I can't say the idea of you being reasonable comes easily to mind.'

'Thanks, wife.'

She took his face between her hands and stared intently at him. 'For the love of the gods, Macro, please reconsider. You have enough money from your savings to pay him off and still have plenty to invest in the business and a farm at the colony. I'm sure if we work hard, we can earn enough to make Malvinus's cut easy to swallow.'

'You don't see it, do you? If we pay what he asks for now, we've set a floor for future payments. If the business struggles, how willing do you think he will be to take less? And if it does well, he'll only demand more and more from us. I'm not prepared to appease him. You give cunts like that an inch, they'll always want more. I have to draw a line under this matter. Surely you can see that?'

'All I can see is that you're putting yourself and the rest of us in danger.'

Macro took her hands and lowered them, then leaned forward to kiss her on the forehead. 'Trust me. I've survived bigger dangers, haven't I?'

There was no denying that, and she let out an exasperated sigh. 'Just be careful, and be calm when you speak to him.'

'I'll do my best.' Macro smiled encouragingly. 'Come now, we've only just arrived in Londinium and you're all doom and gloom. This is supposed to be the start of a new life for us both. Look, once we've sorted out our belongings, we'll go to Camulodunum and pick a spot for a villa on my land. Chances are we'll be spending most of our time there once the place is built and we have a small farming estate up and running. When my mother goes into the shadows, we can sell the businesses and cut any ties we have with Malvinus. How does that sound?'

'It sounds good,' she conceded. 'But we have to stay alive long enough to reach that point. How do you intend to find Malvinus in any case?'

'Easy. Where does any man of business spend much of his time in a Roman town? I'll go to the best bathhouse in Londinium and ask about. Someone will point me in the right direction.'

'Just swear to me that you will be careful.'

Macro had already made an equivocal promise to his mother and had his answer ready at once. 'I'll do my best to be careful, I swear.'

CHAPTER SEVEN

The bathhouse of Floridius was not the largest in Londinium, but it was almost certainly one of the most upmarket. It was one of the small number of brick buildings in the town. A wall surrounded the modest complex of storehouses, furnace rooms and slave quarters, as well as the far larger structures containing the hot, warm and cold rooms, pool, steam room, massage room and exercise courtyard. A large man with the physique of a wrestler stood at the gateway in the wall to make sure that no one but customers and tradesmen entered. A wise precaution; many of the public bathhouses in Rome were frequented by pilferers, pimps and sundry perverts. Clearly Floridius had decided that his establishment was going to cater to a better class of client.

Although Macro had not been told where to find the man he was looking for, it seemed only logical to begin his enquiries at the best bathhouse on offer. It was where Londinium's lawyers, senior civil officials, army officers and wealthy merchants came to relax, catch up on gossip and carry out business. He presented his ring to prove his equestrian status, and the guard at the gate ushered him through. A flight of steps led up to a simple portico sheltering a studded door, which was opened for Macro by a slave standing behind a small viewing grille. Inside, the temperature was comfortably warm, although there was no sign of a brazier or fireplace, and Macro raised an eyebrow appreciatively as he realised that the hypocaust system extended even to the lobby. That was a refinement he had never seen before.

Across the small lobby was a counter with a large rack of pigeonholes behind it. A clerk wearing a neat tunic bowed his head to Macro. 'How may I help you, master? The standard entrance fee? Or will you require any extra services?'

'Depends what's on offer and how much you charge.'

'The fee is five sestertii. That gets you access to the hot and steam rooms, the pool and the courtyard. A massage costs the same again. As does the oil and scrape and the barber.'

Five sestertii was a steep price. Steep enough to immediately put Macro off any of the other services on offer. 'Just the entrance fee.'

He took the coins from his heavy purse and paid them over to the clerk, who smoothly swept them into the slot on top of a money chest and then rang a small brass bell. At the sound of the shrill tinkle, another slave hurried out through a narrow door behind the counter. The clerk gestured to the pigeonholes, many of which contained cloaks and sidebags. 'You are welcome to leave your valuables here, master.'

Macro stared at him shrewdly. 'Will they be safe?'

The clerk looked disdainful. 'This is the bathhouse of Floridius, master. There are no petty thieves here. Your possessions will be quite safe, I can assure you.'

Macro was beginning to perspire under his heavy tunic and cloak, and he took off the latter and handed it over to the clerk, who folded it and turned to place it in a pigeonhole.

'The second one,' he instructed. It was easy to recall, being the number of the first legion he had served in.

'As you wish, master. What about your sidebag? Shall I take care of that too?'

'No need,' Macro replied quickly as he placed his purse in the bag and flipped the cover over it. 'I prefer to keep it with me.'

'As you wish, but it will be perfectly safe here.'

'I am sure, but I'll hang on to it all the same.'

The clerk clicked his tongue and then turned to the slave. 'Show this gentleman to the changing room.'

The slave bowed to Macro and indicated the corridor leading off the lobby. On one side were a number of alcoves containing shelves of oil jars, sponges and strigils and piles of neatly folded cloths. The other side had two closed doors. A third stood open, and the slave showed Macro inside. A room thirty feet by ten or so was lined with tall hanging spaces and pegs. Macro moved to the nearest one that was free, removed his boots and began to undress. The slave darted off to a cupboard at the end of the room and came back with a large linen sheet, which he held up until Macro was naked, and then quickly wrapped it around him. As Macro bent to pick up his clothes, the slave coughed.

'I will take care of those, master.'

'Oh? Very well.' Macro slipped the strap of his purse over his head so that the heavy leather pouch hung against his chest. 'There.'

'The facilities are through the arch at the end of the room, master.'

Macro nodded and made to turn away, then hesitated. 'Perhaps you can help me. I've only just arrived in Londinium on business, and I've been told that the man I need to see is someone called Malvinus. Is he a client of this bathhouse?'

'Indeed, master.'

'Is he here today?'

'Not yet, master. He usually arrives around the third hour.'

'Do you know where I might find him when he does arrive?'

The slave shook his head. 'I only work in the changing room, master.'

'Fair enough,' Macro responded. 'Look here, if he does turn up, I'd like you to find me and let me know. There's a sestertius in it for you. But I'd be grateful if you didn't let him know I asked for him. Clear?'

The slave nodded enthusiastically and Macro tossed him a coin from his purse and dismissed him with a curt nod. Then, adjusting the sheet, he made his way through the arch into a large chamber some sixty feet long and twenty wide under a barrel-vaulted ceiling. Massage tables were arranged along one side while benches stretched along the opposite wall. The temperature was noticeably warmer here, and he gave an appreciative grunt at the quality of the engineering. At this hour, no one was having a massage. That would come after the early-morning clients had worked their way through the hot room and cold plunge bath. Several men were already sitting in a group on the benches, chattering loudly, their voices echoing off the walls, which were decorated with geometric patterns in a dull red, interspersed with paintings depicting serene pastoral vistas at odds with the harsh winter landscape outside. On closer inspection, the renderings were crude compared to those of even a modest bathhouse back in Rome. But they served as a reminder of home to those merchants from Italia who had come to Britannia in search of a fortune.

Macro crossed over to the men and nodded a greeting as some of them turned towards him. 'Morning, all. I'm new in town. Mind if I join you?'

A fat man with heavy jowls, and rolls of flesh below his

chest, waved him on with a flabby arm. 'Not at all, my dear fellow. Come, sit you down.'

As Macro had expected, they were eager enough to welcome him. Partly because of any news of the wider Empire he might offer, but mostly because he might be a source of business or at least a useful connection to cultivate. The fat man made brief introductions as Macro settled on a bench at the fringe of the group, reeling off the names of his companions before looking meaningfully at the newcomer.

'Lucius Cornelius Macro, Praetorian centurion, retired.'

'Retired? To Londinium?' The man arched an eyebrow. 'Hardly the place for someone of your rank to retire, my friend. Would have thought you'd be more comfortable in some Campanian town.'

'I have family here.' Macro clicked his tongue. 'So here I stay.'

'It's your funeral, Centurion. If the cold and damp doesn't get you, those native bastards surely will.'

'I had been under the impression they were under our thumb. You're not the first to tell me there may be trouble. What's the problem?'

'Nothing that couldn't be handled until that new procurator, Decianus, pitched up. Word is he has been sent to Britannia to bleed the tribes dry. The emperor wants his taxes and there are powerful men in Rome who are calling in loans made to many of the tribal rulers. It'll do our cause no end of damage, I can tell you.'

Some of the others grumbled their agreement.

'How so?' Macro asked. 'Things seem settled enough in Londinium. Barring a handful of pirates making a nuisance of themselves along the Tamesis.'

'It's stirring things up amongst the tribes. Why, one of my

men was given a hiding the last time he took a wagon of goods up beyond Camulodunum. Same settlement he'd traded with for the last two years. Only this time the stock was looted, and he was beaten up and just managed to escape with his life. Of course I went straight to the governor's headquarters to complain and demand the natives be punished and forced to pay compensation. I was told there were no spare men for the job, thanks to Paulinus making his preparations to finish off the mountain tribes and their Druids. What kind of message does that send out, eh? Once word gets out that you can steal a merchant's property and thrash his servants, there'll be no end of those bog-dwelling barbarians preying on honest Roman merchants.'

There was another chorus of angry muttering before the fat man continued. 'We pay our taxes. We're entitled to protection. Why aren't there any soldiers marching out to teach those Trinovantian bastards and their Iceni cronies a lesson?'

Macro raised his hands. 'I can't answer that. Not my job any more, friend. Best take it out on the governor.'

'That's just it, he's seldom in Londinium these days.'

'Then what about the procurator? He's next in the chain of command.'

'Gah, he doesn't give a shit about honest merchants like us. All he's interested in is the tax take.'

Macro sighed regretfully. 'I wish I could help you. Like I said, my soldiering days are over. I'm a civvy now, in the same boat as you.'

'A pity,' the other man said.

Macro cleared his throat. 'I wonder if you could help me out with something?'

'We'll try. Always happy to help out one of the Empire's finest. What do you need? Good building land? Slaves to work it? Builders? A loan? If so, you're speaking to the right men.'

'I'm after information about someone.'

'Oh?'

'Fellow's name is Malvinus. I'm told he comes here regularly.'

At once, the amiable ambience withered. Anxious glances were exchanged, and the fat man gathered up the folds of his sheet and threw a length over his shoulder before he stood up.

'You'll have to ask someone else, Centurion. I'm afraid I don't know anything about Malvinus that would be of any use to you. I, uh, look forward to seeing you again some day. Have to run now. Business to attend to.' He bowed his head and waddled off towards the door leading to the hot room, and one by one the other men made their excuses and followed him.

Macro watched them with a faint smile. 'Well, well,' he muttered. 'Seems like Malvinus has quite the reputation.'

He eased himself back against the wall and settled comfortably. When Malvinus turned up, he would inevitably pass through the warm room, so Macro decided to enjoy the soothing heat while he waited. He closed his eyes and indulged himself by imagining the layout of the villa he intended to build outside Camulodunum. There would be a small courtyard to the front where guests would pause to admire the fine lines of the building. Then there would be the hall, giving out onto the inner courtyard with a small pond in the middle. The dining and sleeping chambers would be arranged around the colonnade that bordered the courtyard. There would be a kitchen at the rear of the villa, and he decided that it would be a fine idea to have a room on the other side to share the cooking fire, so that he and Petronella could warm themselves during the province's bitter winters. Having laid out the interior of the villa, he turned his mind to the crops they would grow, and as he did so, he fell into a pleasant slumber.

Which made it all the more annoying when he felt himself being rudely awakened by someone shaking his shoulder.

'Hey, wake up!'

Macro had long since mastered the soldier's art of falling asleep and waking swiftly and fully, and he sat up, eyes snapping open. The man who had woken him drew back and retreated half a step. He was a few inches taller than Macro, some ten years younger and solidly built. His jaw was firm, and along with his broad brow it gave his face an almost square shape. Dark eyes, widely spaced, stared at Macro as he adjusted his linen sheet.

'You were snoring. Loudly.' He spoke in a level tone that betrayed neither anger nor humour. 'I like to relax when I come to the bathhouse. I can't do that if people snore.'

Macro stretched his shoulders. 'Apologies. I was waiting for someone. But the warmth . . .' He paused and shrugged. 'You know how it is.'

The other man did not respond immediately, but looked round the room warily before returning his gaze to Macro. 'Who are you waiting for?'

'A fellow by the name of Malvinus. Do you know him?'

As soon as he asked the question, Macro guessed the man's identity. The faint flicker of caginess in his expression as he retreated a step confirmed his suspicions.

'What is your business with Malvinus?' the man demanded.

Macro stood up in order to make his acquaintance on more equal terms. 'You're Malvinus, I take it. Leader of the Scorpions.'

'Maybe. Who are you?'

'Centurion Macro.'

'And what would an army officer want with me, exactly?'

'I'm no longer a serving officer,' Macro explained. 'Retired. As for my business, well, it's a shared business really. I own a half-share of the Dog and Deer inn, along with some other concerns.'

'I know it well. But the place is owned by Portia.'

'She's my mother. I fronted her some money several years ago to get the place up and running until I took my discharge and came to join her.'

'I see. How is that connected with wanting to see me?' There was no change in Malvinus's tone. None at all. Just a flat voice and a cold, dead look in his dark eyes as he watched Macro closely.

'It seems you have been forcing my mother into a protection racket. She says your man Pansa has demanded six hundred sestertii from her.'

'That's right.' Malvinus nodded slowly. 'What of it?'

Macro cleared his throat. 'I've come to renegotiate the deal on her behalf. She can't afford to pay six hundred. Nor should she have to.'

'Renegotiate?' The corners of Malvinus's mouth lifted for a moment in a smile. 'I don't renegotiate deals, Centurion Macro. I don't even negotiate them in the first place. I set a price for my services and my customers pay it. That way, everyone knows precisely how things stand.'

'As far as I understand it, you don't offer any services. You tell people to pay up or else.'

'That is the service I offer. To everyone I approach. No exceptions.'

'My mother is an exception,' Macro said firmly. 'And so am I. That's what I came here to tell you.'

Malvinus tilted his head slightly to one side, as if contemplating Macro's statement carefully. 'And now you've told me.

But that changes nothing. Your mother must pay what she owes me. She should be grateful I have not asked for more. I would, were it not that I have a degree of admiration for the wizened old stick.'

Macro eased his hands behind his back and clenched his fists as he tried not to let the backhanded compliment to his mother rile him.

'Go back to her, Centurion. Tell Portia to pay her dues before I raise the amount or she loses a finger. How is that for renegotiating?'

Macro clenched his jaw as he struggled to control his rising temper. 'It's not acceptable.'

For a moment the two men stared at each other without blinking, and then Malvinus barked out a laugh, his square face crinkling with amusement. 'Ah, but I do like you army veterans. You make a refreshing change from the usual whining merchants and traders I have to deal with. You soldiers are all stiff-backed and unyielding. But you will yield. You may rule the roost in army camps and on campaign, but here in Londinium, I am in charge. Since you're new here, I'll be happy to explain things to you. I wonder what you have heard so far?'

'I've heard about what happens to those who don't pay up.'

'That's good. I don't want you to be in any doubt that what you have heard is true.'

'What if they can't pay?'

'That's their problem.'

'What if they make it your problem?'

Malvinus stroked his chin slowly. 'Are you threatening me, Centurion? I've had men gutted and flayed alive for defying me, let alone threatening me. Be thankful that we are talking man to man. If you had said that in front of a wider audience, I'd have had you struck down on the spot. You are new here and have no idea who you are dealing with, so I'll let your foolish comment pass on this occasion. But if you ever repeat it, to my face or in the hearing of any man who answers to me, then you, your mother and any of your family I can track will be killed. Do we understand one another?'

Despite the warmth in the room, Macro felt a cold tingle inch its way up the back of his neck. He had no doubt that this man meant what he said, but there was another aspect to this that Malvinus might not appreciate.

'What do you think will happen to you if you have me killed? Do you think the governor will sit idly by when he hears that a gangster has murdered one of the emperor's Praetorian officers? If Nero was to find out then it would go very badly for the governor.'

'The emperor would have to hear the news first. And Londinium is far from Rome.'

'Not far enough, unfortunately for you. Once Nero knows what you have done, he'll send word to the governor to have you arrested and executed.' Macro paused briefly to let his words sink in. 'So spare me your threats.'

Malvinus sniffed. 'Maybe I can't have you killed. But I can destroy you just as surely. I can have your businesses burned to the ground. I can simply give the word that no one in Londinium is to do business with you and your mother. Or I could have poison added to your wine so that you are held accountable for your customers' sickness or deaths. You are a soldier. You know how it is. You can only guard yourself from one direction at a time, and I can strike from any direction, at any time.'

'You can try,' Macro countered stubbornly, even as he accepted that he was in a more vulnerable situation than he had first supposed.

Malvinus shook his head in pity. 'I would hate to have to

cause you harm, given the sacrifices you have made for the Empire. The same sacrifices that have won us this province and provided me with the opportunity to grow rich. There is nothing to stop you and your mother making your fortunes, even after paying what is due to me. We can all come out of this better off, Centurion. That's how you should think of it. Play along, like everyone else in Londinium, and we all profit. If you refuse, you may cause me a little inconvenience, but that is all, while you and yours will be crushed. I am sure you can see that makes no sense. Besides, I could always use a man like you at my side. Someone with a talent for violence. I would make it worth your while.'

Macro sneered. 'Work for you? Sweet fucking mother of Jupiter. I'd sooner stick my balls in a meat grinder.'

Malvinus smiled wryly. 'I think I may have found your weak spot, so to speak.'

Macro felt his temper rising and bunched his shoulders as his fists clenched. It took great effort to force himself to stay calm as he responded through gritted teeth. 'I am not your man. Nor will I ever be.'

'You say that now. I can understand that you need time to consider my offer. In the meantime, be sure to pay me what I am owed.'

Reaching for the cord around his neck, Macro slipped it over his head and tossed the purse to Malvinus, who caught it deftly.

'There's your money,' he growled. 'That's what my mother told me she would pay. But now that I am here, that's the last of it.'

'If you agree to work for me, then it will be. Otherwise . . .' Malvinus hefted the heavy bag of gold coins, 'I'll be expecting the same again in three months' time. If you choose to defy me, you know what to expect.' His expression darkened. 'And if you do defy me, I swear by all that I hold holy that you will regret this moment for what little will be left of your life. I suggest you go back to your inn and consider my offer. I'll give you ten days to let me know your answer.' He took a few steps towards the entrance to the hot room, then paused to look back over his shoulder. 'Think it over carefully, Centurion. One other thing. I don't take kindly to talking business at the bathhouse. So stay out of my way. If you see me in here again, walk away. While you still can.'

CHAPTER EIGHT

Macro was in a sombre mood as he strode through the gateway into the governor's headquarters once again. The snow had stopped falling shortly before, and the clouds were breaking up to reveal the sun for the first time in days. A fresh blanket of white had covered the muddy slush in the streets and the soot-stained roofs; Londinium was clad in a dazzling shroud that strained the eyes. For a less distracted soul the scene might have been a cause for delight, but Macro trudged through it heedlessly, his thick eyebrows knitted above his dark eyes. He tucked his vine cane under his arm and rubbed his hands together briskly to try to warm them. Now that any hope of cutting a deal with Malvinus had been dashed, he and his mother would either have to bow down to the gangster's will or face the consequences.

When he had returned from the bathhouse, he had taken Petronella into the yard at the inn to relate what had happened out of earshot of his mother.

'Do you think his threats are serious?' asked Petronella. 'I've never heard of any of the gangs in Rome being so ruthless.'

'Maybe not, but we aren't in Rome. This is a frontier town, and different rules apply.'

'What rules? If Malvinus can get away with this, what is the point of there being any laws? And if there is no law, there is no civilisation and then what separates us from the barbarians?'

'Oh, Jupiter's arsehole!' Macro groaned. 'You're starting to sound like Cato. Be careful what you say next. I'll not have you compare Rome with a bunch of gangsters.'

'I was wondering about that.' Petronella thought a moment. 'After all, isn't that what you once told me about the deals we cut with client rulers? Do what we say and pay up, or else. Doesn't sound much better than a protection racket run by the likes of Malvinus.'

'Maybe,' Macro conceded reluctantly. 'But where does that get us? Me, you and my mother? And Parvus, for that matter, now that he has joined our happy little brood. He might have been better off taking his chances on the streets.'

'I doubt it. He'll do fine now that we're looking out for him.'

'But who is looking out for us? That's the problem.' Macro took her hand, and felt how cold her skin was. He threw his cloak round them both and held her close to warm her. 'Much as I hate to say it, I think Malvinus has me backed into a corner. We've only just arrived in Londinium and we don't know who we can trust or call on for help.'

'Portia must know someone.'

'No. We'll keep her out of it.'

Petronella leaned back and looked into his eyes. 'You didn't tell her you were going to speak to Malvinus.'

'No. She told me not to. You've seen what she's like. Doesn't take much imagination to realise how she'd react.'

Petronella could not help smiling. 'By the gods, I've finally discovered the one thing that frightens the great Centurion Macro. If only your pals in the Praetorian Guard could see you now, they'd piss themselves laughing.'

'Stop making fun of me,' he responded angrily.

She relented at once and reached up to clasp his face. 'It's all right, my dear husband. You are right to be afraid of Malvinus and you cannot hope to take him on alone. You need help.'

'Where am I going to get that?'

'Why not report this to the governor? Surely he won't tolerate a Praetorian centurion being treated this way.'

'The governor's not in Londinium. He's away making preparations for a campaign.'

'Then who has he left in charge? There must be someone.'

Macro nodded. 'The procurator is next in line of command. I suppose I could try to speak to him.'

'Then do it. Tell him what's going on and that he has to take action against Malvinus and the other gang leaders.'

'Easier said than done,' Macro muttered to himself now as he kicked the snow from his boots and entered the administration hall. Since leaving Petronella at the inn, he had had time to reflect on what good putting the matter in front of the procurator would do. While Malvinus operated outside the law, an imperial official was obliged to play by the rules, and that handed the advantage to the enemy. Macro smiled at the term. It seemed there was no peace for him in this world, even in retirement. Well, if the situation demanded that he wage war on Malvinus, then he was as likely to make a good job of it as the next man.

He caught the eye of the same clerk he had spoken to the previous day and beckoned to him.

'How can I help you this time, sir?' the man said tersely. 'I'm afraid the tribune is not around today.'

'It's not him I want to see. It's the procurator. Decianus. Is he here?'

'Yes, sir. I can take you to his offices.'

'Thank you.' Macro drew the man towards the side of

the hall, away from the other clerks and any officials passing through. 'How long have you been serving at headquarters?'

'Four years, sir. Why?'

'You've been here long enough to know what kind of man the province needs. What do you make of Decianus? Is he up to the job?'

'He's only been in post a short time, sir. It's hardly fair for me to say.'

'But you do have a view of him, I'm sure.'

The clerk glanced round to make sure they would not be overheard, then lowered his voice. 'Since you ask, I'd say our new procurator has been given a very narrow remit by his superiors in Rome.'

Macro frowned. 'What do you mean?'

'He's spent most of his time pulling together the financial records. What every tribe has been paying in taxes, right down to each settlement. He's also been going through the outstanding loans made by the emperor and others to the local rulers. Looks to me like someone has ordered him to settle all the province's debts as soon as possible.' He gave Macro a meaningful look.

Macro shrugged in response. 'So?'

The clerk just managed to suppress a sigh. 'What does that suggest to you, sir?'

'Look, I don't fucking know, all right. Just spell it out.'

'I can't be certain, but it looks to me like someone settling accounts before selling up. Now, I have work to do, sir. You'll find Decianus on the second floor, on the side overlooking the courtyard.'

'You said you'd take me to his offices.'

'That was before you started asking me questions, sir. I have work to do for the tribune. Duty calls.'

Before Macro could respond, the clerk had dipped his head

in a swift bow and turned to hurry away. For a moment Macro glared after him and considered bawling at him to halt and turn about. But he was no longer a serving officer, and the man might not respond to the command. That would be a humiliation too far for Macro. So he turned to the stairs and began to climb to the floor above.

Decianus's office was a large room with four desks on each side, two clerks sitting at each. At the end of the room was a dais with a larger table and a cushioned seat beyond from where its occupant could keep an eye on his minions. The chair was empty, but a slender man wearing a thick woollen tunic was standing by a brazier at the window, gazing out over the courtyard, and Macro guessed this was the man he was looking for.

As he approached, he saw that the procurator was bald, save for a fringe of dark hair that stretched from one temple to the other. Decianus glanced round as he became aware of Macro's approach to reveal two large eyes, wide apart, that were dark and manic-looking.

'Yes?'

Macro nodded a greeting. 'Good day to you, sir. My name's Lucius Cornelius Macro. I need a word with you.'

'Oh?' A slight frown formed on the man's brow.

'Assuming you are Catus Decianus, that is.'

'Yes. Make an appointment with my secretary. I'm a busy man. I can't just stop work for anyone who happens to be passing.'

Macro nodded to the window. 'Nice view. I imagine it can be distracting for those who have the time to be distracted.'

The frown deepened for a moment, but the pointed comment had struck home.

'Oh, very well. What is it?'

Macro briefly related his circumstances and the meeting with Malvinus. 'So as you can see, it's a nasty situation for us. Not to mention all those others who are victims of the gangs of Londinium. It ain't good for trade and it can't be good for tax revenue,' he added, hoping that might help to pique the procurator's professional interest. 'If the governor doesn't stamp down on this kind of thing, it will only get worse.'

'Then you should be addressing this matter to the governor, not me.'

'The governor's not here, sir. And with the preparations for the coming campaign taking up his time, I imagine he won't be back in Londinium for a while. You are next in the chain of command, so it's your responsibility now.'

Decianus sighed. 'It's not as if I am not already burdened by demands on my time, Centurion Macro. In any case, what would you have me do?'

'Send some men out, gather evidence and then prosecute Malvinus. Confiscate his property and banish him and his gang from the province, and let the businesses of Londinium get on with their job of bringing commerce and the benefits of civilisation to Britannia.'

'What is the nature of your business, Centurion?'

'My mother and I own an inn with a brothel attached, sir. There are a few other businesses we have interests in.'

'Intoxicating drink and prostitutes, eh?' Decianus sniffed. 'Would you mind telling me how those constitute the benefits of civilisation?'

Macro pressed his lips together in umbrage before he responded. 'We pay taxes like any other business, sir. The same taxes that pay for the roads and garrisons that help keep peace in the province. That's how.'

'Fair enough,' Decianus conceded. 'I'll look into the matter when I find the time. If these gangs are hitting our tax take, then there'll be cause to investigate and put a stop to it. The gods know, this barbaric island is already causing enough of a drain on the imperial purse. It was a fool's errand invading Britannia in the first place.'

Macro's irritation with the man was shading over into a darker sentiment, and he had to force himself not to react angrily. He took a calming breath before he spoke.

'I imagine there are many soldiers, retired and still serving, who might not take kindly to hearing that, sir.'

'So I should think. No man likes to be taken advantage of.' Decianus gestured towards the door. 'Leave this with me, Macro. You may go.'

It was a curt dismissal, but Macro had had enough of the procurator's haughty attitude and was happy to quit headquarters and return to the inn. On the walk back, the clear blue skies and bright sunshine on clean snow did much to raise his spirits, and he was happily whistling an old marching song when he turned into the yard. If the procurator was as good as his word, there was a fair chance that the threat of Malvinus would be dealt with.

The frightened cries of a woman cut through his thoughts and the tune died on Macro's lips. As a fresh shriek sounded, he broke into a run, crashing through the rear door and running down the corridor that led into the bar. The door to the street was open, and light flooded into the room, revealing a frozen tableau of violence. He took it all in in a heartbeat. Parvus shivering in the corner, hugging his knees as blood trickled from his nose. Petronella shielding Macro's mother from a cloaked man who stood in front of them brandishing a dagger. One of the whores lay on the ground between upturned tables and benches, her face battered and bleeding; another thug stood over her, fists bunched. A third man stood at the opening to the brothel, holding the other women at bay with a studded club. The injured woman was sobbing as she curled up into a ball, her movement breaking the spell.

'What in Hades is this?' Macro growled as he tightened his fist around his vine cane and stepped round the counter. 'Who the fuck are you?'

The man who had been beating the woman straightened up, chest heaving.

'If you're the new man here, we've been sent to give you a message from Cinna.'

'Cinna?' Macro took a step closer. 'What message?'

'Cinna says he is taking over this street. You'll pay him and not Malvinus from now on. If not . . .' The man gestured to the woman at his feet.

'I see.' Macro adjusted his balance so that the weight rested evenly on the balls of his feet, and tensed his muscles. 'I imagine Cinna wants a reply.'

The thug smiled, revealing stained and uneven teeth. 'There's no need for a reply. You'll do what he says.'

'All the same, it's only polite to offer one.' Macro bared his teeth in a grin.

The other man frowned. 'Polite?'

Macro hurled himself forward, punching the gnarled end of his cane into the man's stomach, throwing his weight into the blow. The thug doubled over with a gasp, and Macro smashed his knee into the man's face, feeling the nose crunch. He finished the job with a savage slash of the cane on the back of the skull, and the thug dropped to the ground beside the woman, who rolled away with a screech.

The man brandishing the knife in front of Petronella had turned round as his friend collapsed and now let out a roar as he charged at Macro, dagger held out, ready to thrust. Macro had already recovered his balance and stood poised, feet apart and braced. He parried the blow with a sharp rap from his cane, then stepped lightly to the side as the impetus of his charge carried the man a step beyond and Macro delivered a powerful kick to his knee. The man let out a cry of pain as his leg gave out, and he slumped against a bench.

'Look out!' Petronella cried, and Macro saw a blur of movement as the third of Cinna's men rushed him, club raised to strike. If they had been in the open, the fight would have gone against Macro at that moment. The blow would have landed, and even if he had tried to raise an arm to protect himself, the limb would have been shattered. As it was, the nailed head of the club struck the beam that crossed the room, supporting the floor above. There was a loud splintering crack, and the impact caused the man to draw up sharply. He jerked the nailed head free of the beam and made to swing it in an arc, but the mistake had given Macro just enough time to react, and he snatched up a stool with his left hand to act as a makeshift buckler.

'You stupid cunt,' the man snarled. 'When Cinna hears about this, he'll cut your balls off and make you watch as he kills your women before he gouges your eyes out.'

'He can try,' Macro replied quietly. 'But if he's sensible, he'll keep his distance when he gets my reply to his message, eh?'

The comment served its purpose, provoking the man into another attack. This time he made a jab at Macro's face, which the centurion blocked with the stool. Then he whipped the club round in a horizontal arc, aiming for the side of Macro's head. Macro ducked, throwing his shield arm up and trusting it to deflect the blow while he struck with his cane, thrusting it at the man's groin. He followed up with another thrust that caught the man under the chin, snapping his jaw shut and his head back. The thug staggered to the side, one hand clutching his balls, the other releasing his grip on the club so that it dropped to the floor. It was then that Macro felt the agony in his left hand where the club had glanced off his knuckles, grazing the skin. He let the stool go and tucked his hand under the opposite arm, clenching his jaw.

There was a chorus of angry shouts and cries as the prostitutes poured through the opening from the brothel and set upon the man who had been beating the woman. They tore at his exposed skin and pounded and kicked him. His victim rose into a crouch with a pained expression, then snatched up the discarded dagger and made to strike at her abuser.

'Stop!' Macro roared, sweeping the women back with his vine cane. 'Get back!'

'Leave him to us,' the injured woman snarled.

Macro raised his cane. 'I'm warning you. Back. Right now.'

The women edged back, angry expressions etched on their powdered faces. Once he was sure they posed no danger to the men on the ground, Macro turned to Petronella.

'What the bloody hell has been going on?'

'They came in here shortly after you left. Two of them ordered a drink and sat down while their mate looked round the place and then went with one of the women. A bit later I heard a ruckus and went to see what was happening. He'd had his way and refused to pay her. I told him he'd better hand the money over, and he slapped me. Parvus went for him and got thrown back against the wall. The other men joined in. They told us they were from Cinna's gang. That's when your mother—'

Portia pushed Petronella aside. 'That's when I told them we were under Malvinus's protection and they'd better get out.

They laughed at me. Said they didn't give a shit about Malvinus and that we needed a lesson.'

Macro saw that she was trembling, and gave a nod to his wife. Petronella put her arm around the old lady's shoulders and steered her towards the brazier, sitting her on the nearest bench. Meanwhile Macro leaned his cane up against the wall and rubbed his hands together gingerly before searching the three men. Two were groaning; one was out cold. He took their purses and the silver torcs they wore around their necks, and tossed the purses to the women crowding the doorway leading to the brothel. 'That's for your pains, ladies. We look after our own here.'

As they eagerly divided the coins, Macro pocketed two of the torcs and examined the last one closely. He squinted as he held it up to the light and could just make out the wording etched into the metal. *Cinna's Blades*.

Tossing the torc onto the nearest table, he gave one of the moaning men a light kick in the ribs. 'Cinna's Blades. That's your gang name, I take it.'

The man groaned and nodded.

'All right. You and your mate, get up and pick him up. Then get the fuck out of my inn. You can tell Cinna that the next time he sends men here, I'll let our women kill what's left when I've done with them.'

Macro stood, fists on hips, while the thugs scooped up the inert figure of their comrade and staggered out into the street. He waited a beat before following up and closing the door, slipping the locking bar into its iron brackets. Then he crossed over to Parvus and helped him to his feet. 'My thanks for defending Petronella. You've earned your keep.'

The boy grinned and grunted happily, wiping away the blood on his face with the back of his hand.

As Macro sat down opposite Petronella and his mother, the latter looked up anxiously. 'What's to become of us now? We're caught between Malvinus and Cinna. If one doesn't finish us off, the other surely will. Ruined . . . we're ruined.'

'Not yet,' Macro replied firmly. 'Not by a long way, Mother. You'll see.'

Brave words, he thought to himself. But against the two gang leaders and their thugs, bravery would not be enough. That much he was certain of.

CHAPTER NINE

For the rest of the day, Macro remained in the bar, keeping a watch over the customers who came in, studying them closely for any signs of trouble. In addition to his vine cane, he had positioned his sword on the shelf beneath the counter, both within easy reach.

The inn had only been closed for as long as it took to clear up the broken jars and cups and to carry a bench and stool to the yard to be repaired at a later time. The doors were reopened in time for the midday trade, which was always brisk, Portia informed him, thanks to the inn being situated between the wharf and Londinium's largest market. A steady flow of merchants, stevedores and officials from the governor's headquarters stepped in off the street and warmed themselves by one of the braziers before coming to the bar to order drink and food. Portia offered stew at two different rates, with grilled meat, freshly baked bread and cheese for an extra price. The cheapest option was a thin gruel that reminded Macro of the plain fare consumed by legionaries on the march. The pricier stew contained a mixture of root vegetables and chunks of meat that were not wholly gristle.

While Macro served at the bar, his mother supervised Petronella and Parvus as they worked in the kitchen, perspiring freely in the confined heat and smoke of the small room. Petronella cooked the meat on the iron grill, and Parvus fed fresh logs onto the glowing embers of the cooking fire and scuttled to and from the storeroom with slabs of pork and mutton.

Once the customers had finished their meals and downed the last of their wine, a handful made their way through to the brothel to sate a different appetite. Macro nodded approvingly at the coins that clinked into the strongbox. 'This place is something of a gold mine, Mother,' he said as Portia sat down on a stool beside him to rest for a moment.

'Thanks to years of hard work, not to mention knowing how to apply that work to best effect.' She tapped the side of her head and allowed herself a thin smile. 'Lucky for you that your business partner made the most of your investment. Proud of your mother, eh?'

Macro kissed the wiry hair on top of her head. 'If only the Empire was in the hands of a businesswoman like you, instead of those conniving cunts in the Senate and that clown in the palace. That would be something.'

'Yes, it would.' Her smile faded. 'It would be even better if I wasn't being squeezed by the likes of Malvinus. And now there's Cinna added to the mix to make things even more difficult.'

'We'll deal with them both if it comes to that,' Macro responded firmly. 'I didn't spend the best days of my life fighting for Rome and hoarding the loot I've shed blood for just to see it pissed away into the coffers of some low-life parasites like those two. I've dealt with far harder men during my time in the army.'

'Like I told you before, you're not in the army now.'

Macro glanced round to make sure that Petronella was still in the kitchen and out of earshot. 'More's the pity. Much as I thought I was looking forward to being demobbed, I have to say I'm missing my old life.'

'You couldn't carry on with it for ever, my boy.'

'Maybe not, but I could have served for several more years yet.'

'You may think that, but you grow older than you imagine you feel and one day your body will betray you badly. If you keep up your soldierly bravado, it'll happen soon enough. You'll see.'

Macro raised an eyebrow sardonically. 'My, but you are a little sunbeam today, aren't you?'

'Call me what you like, but I'm the one who's been living in Londinium all these years and has had to deal with Malvinus and his kind. It would be sensible of you to learn from my experience. Ah, what's the point? When did a parent's hard-won wisdom ever influence anyone? You should think about how your young wife will cope if anything happens to you. If you have any regard for her, let alone love her, you'll stop playing the fool and tread carefully.'

Macro instinctively bridled at the insult. If it had come from anyone other than his mother – or Cato or any other superior officer – he'd have decked them then and there. Instead he kept his mouth shut, and gave a nod to welcome a fresh customer at the bar. The man slapped a sestertius on the counter.

'What will that get me, friend?'

Macro deftly swept the silver coin into the strongbox as he replied. 'A bowl of our finest stew, a jug of wine and, if you have another sestertius, the pick of our girls.'

The man chuckled. 'Just the meal. I don't have to pay for my women.'

Macro called out over his shoulder to pass the order on to Petronella and then scrutinised the customer. He looked to be a few years younger than Macro, although his face was heavily creased and his hair was mainly grey, with a few dark streaks remaining. He had heavy shoulders, but there was no hint of a stoop in his posture. He wore a blood-red tunic and cloak. Macro instantly recognised his soldierly bearing.

'You still serving, brother?'

'Sadly not. I parted ways with the Ninth Legion many years ago. Just made centurion when I was discharged.'

'Oh?' Macro prompted.

'Took a spear in the leg.' He patted his thigh. 'Never fully recovered, so the army kicked me out.'

'That's tough,' Macro responded with sympathy. He'd seen many good men crippled in the line of duty long before they had served their time. If the man before him really had attained the rank of centurion, he must have been one of the best. It was a damned shame that he had not enjoyed the rank as Macro had for so many years. He lifted the lid of the strongbox, took out the silver coin and handed it back.

'It's on the house, brother.'

The other man looked surprised. 'There's no need for that. I can afford to pay my way.'

'Keep it. A favour from one old soldier to another.'

The man gave him a quick searching look. 'Thought as much. Which unit?'

'Take your pick.' Macro grinned. 'Spent most of my time with the Second Legion, but I also served with auxiliary cohorts before I ended up in the Praetorians. A centurion, like yourself.'

There was no doubt about the admiration in the other man's expression as he held out his hand and they clasped arms.

'Well met, brother. The name's Decius Ulpius.'

'Lucius Cornelius, though most know me by my cognomen, Macro.'

'Macro it is then. It's a pleasure to make your acquaintance, brother. I take it you're new here. I've not see you in the Dog and Deer before.'

'Recently arrived from Rome. I own a half-share of the inn.'

'I see.'

Macro noticed two more men at the bar waiting to be served. 'Find yourself a table and I'll have the food and wine sent over. If you're a regular, we can share a jug sometime.'

'I'd like that.' Ulpius nodded and held up the coin. 'And thanks.'

He turned and picked his way over to a table where he could sit with his back to the wall, and Macro felt a twinge of pity as he noticed his limp. Then one of the men waiting further along the bar rapped a coin on the wooden surface to draw his attention.

'No need for that, friend. What do you want?'

The afternoon passed swiftly, thanks to the constant coming and going of customers. Outside, the winter sun inscribed its shallow arc across a clear sky and edged towards the roofline of the buildings lining the street. Gradually the customers in the bar thinned out as they returned to work or ambled home, sated by the comestibles and services on offer at the Dog and Deer. A less honest proprietor than Portia would have used the wine as a means to fleece the unwary, but as she explained to Macro, establishing a good reputation ultimately generated more profit than gouging clients. Graft not grift was her credo, and it had served her well. It was quite a change from most of the establishments Macro had visited during his army days, and he was surprised that so few innkeepers had failed to take the longer, and more profitable, view. The proof of it lay in the coins heaped within the strongbox.

Ulpius had long since finished his stew and wine but was still seated close to the warm glow of the brazier, seemingly dozing off his meal with a contented smile. Every so often Macro noticed him looking around at the other customers. He sensed that Ulpius was a kindred spirit, thanks to his military background. Such a man might well be a useful ally to have at his side given the situation. He poured himself a cup of wine and made his way across the bar.

'Mind if I join you?'

'Not at all.' Ulpius smiled. 'In fact I was hoping you would.'

'Oh?' Macro arched an eyebrow as he pulled up a stool and sat opposite.

'I was wondering if we might be able to do a deal, what with you being a fellow centurion back in the day.'

'Actually, I was thinking the same thing.' Macro cradled his cup in his hands.

'I doubt it. You haven't heard what I'm offering yet. What's on your mind, Macro?'

Macro took a sip before he replied. 'I may be in a tight spot in the days to come. I could use a man who knows his way around a fight. Someone with a handy blade and an eye for the ground. Someone who can back me up if there's trouble.'

'I see.' Ulpius scratched his jaw, letting his thumb linger on a scar that ran across his chin. 'What kind of trouble?'

'Drunks and petty thieves mostly.' Macro hesitated. 'And maybe heavies from some of the local gangs.'

'Sounds like dangerous work.'

'Not for a one-time centurion. Despite your leg, you look like the kind of man who can handle himself.'

Ulpius laughed. 'Oh, I'm pretty sure I can handle myself, not to mention the kind of men you are talking about.'

'Good. Then are you interested in the job? I can make it worth your while.'

'I doubt it. I'll have to decline your offer, brother.'

Macro sighed. 'That's a pity.'

'Do you want to hear about my proposal?'

Macro had no need of any other work. The inn was taking up all his time at the moment. Besides, he still had to claim the land that had been awarded him at Camulodunum. There would be boundaries to establish and plans made for the building of the villa he had dreamed of sharing with Petronella. Still, he would be interested in hearing the other man out. He drained his cup and gestured at the bar around them. 'I'm kept busy, as you will have seen since you came in. All the same, what did you have in mind?'

Ulpius folded his hands together and cracked his knuckles. 'I too need some muscle. A man like you who is accustomed to giving and taking orders would be perfect for the role.'

'What role, brother?'

'Taking charge of my men. Keeping them fit and training them to fight. They need to be ready to act when the time comes.'

'What time would that be?' The first inkling of doubt crept in, making Macro anxious.

'The time when I take control of the other gangs of Londinium and destroy those who stand in my way.' Ulpius paused. 'I must apologise, I have not been wholly honest with you. I wanted to observe you before I made my offer. That's why I came here to size you up, as well as consume your excellent stew and passable wine.'

Macro's eyes narrowed. 'Who are you?'

'My name, my full name, is Decius Ulpius Cinna.'

Macro's fist closed around the cup in his hand as he tensed

in immediate readiness for action. He scrutinised Cinna closely, looking for the first telltale sign that he was about to strike. Instead, the other man smiled knowingly.

'You are not in any danger, Centurion Macro. Not today, at least. Nor am I at risk from you. If you were to try and harm me, I have but to raise my voice and my men waiting outside will come charging through that door in a heartbeat. If you were to kill me, they have orders to kill you and every member of this household. Your awareness of that guarantees that you will not raise a finger to me. So, now that you know who I am, let's continue our conversation. I wish we could talk with the same warmth as before, but I dare say that won't be possible.'

'You think?' Macro growled.

Cinna affected an offended expression. 'Come now, we were both soldiers. We understand one another and what we have been through better than most men. For many soldiers, their comrades are closer than any family. We have ties that bind us. So hear me out and think through the opportunity I have come to offer you.' He waited a moment to allow Macro's edginess to abate slightly, then continued. 'You took down three of my men this morning. Admittedly they weren't the best, but they were competent enough and they outnumbered you.'

'You need to hire yourself better men if you are going to send them against me.'

'Don't flatter yourself too much, Macro. If I send more men, they will be better prepared. Next time, you will lose.'

Macro gave a scornful sniff. 'We'll see.'

'Pray that we don't have to, brother.'

'Don't call me that.'

Cinna looked bemused. 'Come, I want to help you. Like I said, I need someone to train and lead my men. You would be the best man for the job. The way you dealt with the lads this morning proves it. They need kicking into shape. They need discipline and training so that I can take on any rivals. Particularly Malvinus. I'd make it worth your while. There's so much wealth flowing through Londinium these days, it can make rich men of us both provided we act swiftly and take control of the streets.' He gave Macro a calculating look. 'I appreciate it isn't proper soldiering, but it's as close as you are going to get now you are a discharged veteran. Tell me, honestly, that you don't miss the old days. I don't think the soldier in you is happy at the idea of living out his days pouring wine, wiping down the counter and turfing out the odd drunk. Am I wrong?'

Macro felt the truth of his words, and Cinna's offer was fleetingly tempting. But there was a vast difference between training soldiers to fight for the glory of the Empire and helping gangsters to bully honest businesses and extort protection money. Then there was the question of how Cinna might react to Macro's rejection of his offer. It was unlikely that he would tolerate the humiliation that had been dealt to his reputation this morning. He would almost certainly make an example of Macro to show what happened to those who defied him. Macro thought quickly and chose his words, and the tone in which he spoke them, very carefully.

'I'll admit, the idea is appealing, but as you say, I am a soldier through and through. I don't know much about your line of work.'

'You wouldn't have to. Indeed, I would not want you to. It's better that you stick to what you know best and keep your nose out of anything else. After all,' Cinna smiled, 'I wouldn't want you learning enough to challenge me for control of the gang, would I?'

Macro heard Petronella's voice and turned slightly as she

emerged from the corridor leading to the kitchen. Seeing that Macro was in conversation, she raised an eyebrow enquiringly. He shook his head and gave the slightest of gestures to warn her to stay back. It was not lost on Cinna, who glanced in her direction.

'A fine-looking woman. Yours? Or one of the whores?'

'My wife. And she's no man's property.'

'Feisty, eh? Just the kind of woman a soldier needs.'

'Well, she's all I need, at any rate.' Macro set his cup down and folded his arms. 'Tell me something. How did a soldier, a centurion at that, come to be a gang leader in this town? It doesn't feel like an honourable way out for the kind of centurions I knew in the army. What happened to you?'

'If it's my life story you're after, I haven't the time, or inclination, to relate it to you, brother. Let's just say that I left the army under a cloud.'

'There's no shame in a medical discharge. Unless there's more to it than you told me.'

Cinna thought a moment and then nodded. 'Very well. Since we're old comrades, I'll tell you. I got the wound like I said. Only it happened because some fine young tribune was out to win himself a reputation. The tribune was in command of a fort in Silurian territory at the time. I was his senior centurion. One day a native scout told us that an enemy warband was camping in a valley not five miles from the fort. He said he knew of a path through the hills that would allow us to fall on them by surprise. I was suspicious from the start. You know how untrustworthy the barbarians on this island can be. But the tribune would have none of it. He ordered me and two centuries of my boys to follow him, and we set off into the hills.

'A few miles from the fort, the scout led us into a ravine and then told us to wait while he went ahead. I ordered the column to turn back to the fort. The tribune blew his top and demanded we stay where we were. I told him we shouldn't disagree in front of the men. So we walked a short distance into some trees to continue the conversation. He said he'd put an end to my career for confronting him. He'd have me broken back to the ranks if I didn't order the men to follow him against the enemy.' Cinna paused and scratched his cheek. 'You've met his kind. Glory-seeking thrusters who don't give a shit about the men they put at risk. Good men. Fine soldiers. I knew that if we carried on into the ravine we would be ambushed. So I punched the bastard. Knocked him cold and went back to the men. That's when the Silurians hit us and I got my wound. We managed to fight our way out, but lost half the column by the time we reached the fort.'

'What happened to the tribune?'

'What do you think? A patrol found his body several days later. Naturally there was an investigation by the legion's commander, but he never got the truth. But someone must have said something, because they gave me nothing when I was discharged. No bounty, no land. Nothing. I came to Londinium looking for a ship to take me to Gaul, only I fell in with a gang. And that's how a good centurion became a low-life gang leader, brother. Breaks your fucking heart, doesn't it?' He gave a sardonic laugh. 'That's why I say fuck the glory of the Empire. It's every man for himself in this life.'

'That's tough,' Macro agreed. 'But what you're doing now is not worthy of any man who once bore the rank of centurion. Frightening civvies and scaring old women like my mother ain't the same thing as taking on an enemy warrior.'

'No, it isn't. It's a lot less dangerous and a damned sight more profitable, and if it offended my pride then I got over that a long time ago. As you will.'

'You seem pretty sure that I'll throw my lot in with you and your gang.'

'Of course I am. What choice do you have, brother? I can't be letting people know that you got away with thrashing three of my men. It won't sit comfortably on my conscience to have a fine soldier done away with, but I'll get over it. Come now, Macro. Do the right thing by your wife and mother, and that scrap of a boy you've picked up. Think about their safety. I'll let you have a few days to get over your pride and come round to seeing what you must do. You can find me at the Painted Celt. It's my place at the end of the wharf.'

He stood up and stretched his shoulders. 'Just don't leave it too long. I'm not a patient man, Macro. Good day.'

CHAPTER TEN

The mood around the bar was sombre that night. After Cinna had left, Macro had closed the doors and sent the prostitutes away. There had been some complaints about losing trade, but a payout from the strongbox had been sufficient to put a smile on their faces. Once the women had gone, Macro spoke briefly to the rest of the household.

As night fell over Londinium, Petronella served up the remains of the food that had been prepared that day as Macro, Portia, Parvus and Denubius sat around the table closest to the brazier that had been kept alight to provide light and warmth. Once the stew had been ladled out, Petronella took her place next to her husband.

'What's the plan then, my boy?' Portia asked as she mopped up the dregs of her stew with a hunk of bread. 'We can't afford to pay off both gangs. You can't risk refusing to serve either Malvinus or Cinna, and you certainly can't accept both offers.'

It was a succinct appraisal of the situation, and Macro stared back at his mother with a glum expression before he shook his head. 'I don't have a plan. Not yet. If only Cato was here. He'd think of something. He always does.'

'Well, he ain't here,' Portia snapped, and jabbed a thin finger at her son. 'It's down to you to sort it out. Things were bad enough before you arrived. Now you've made them much worse. I'd have been better off if you'd stayed in Rome. I wish you had.'

Petronella scowled. 'That's no way to speak to Macro. If it weren't for him putting up half the money in the first place, you wouldn't even have this business.'

Portia did not respond to her directly but continued addressing Macro. 'I don't need backchat from some gold-digging freeloader. You tell her to remember her place.'

'You bitter old crone!' Petronella snarled. 'How dare you?'

Denubius stared down at his bowl, fearful of getting drawn into the confrontation, while Parvus looked on with an amused expression.

Macro slapped his hand down on the table, making the bowls and cups shudder. 'Jupiter's balls! Will you two give it a rest? There's no point wishing for things we can't change, Mother. We're here, and we're in the shit and we need to dig our way out. We haven't got much time to spare. Strikes me that I'm the one Malvinus and Cinna want to get their hands on first. I can buy us a little time by getting away from Londinium for a while.'

Petronella looked surprised. 'Running away? That doesn't sound like you.'

He bristled irritably. 'I ain't running away. Sometimes you have to retreat and regroup before heading back into battle. Malvinus and Cinna will have to wait until I get back.'

'Back from where?' Portia demanded.

'Camulodunum. I need to sort my land claim out. The sooner the better, before all the choice plots are taken. I'll take Petronella with me. You managed well enough with

Denubius before I turned up. Parvus can help out while we're gone.'

The boy's expression turned to one of alarm, and he stared pleadingly at Macro and then Petronella.

'You'll be fine, lad. Just do as you're told.' Macro turned his gaze back to Portia, who sniffed with derision.

'What good will it do us if you bugger off to the colony for a while? We'll still be facing the same problem when you get back.'

'Maybe. Maybe not. Depends on how things go in Camulodunum. There's hundreds of veterans there. Good men who aren't under the influence of the gangs. If I can get some of them to back me up, we might be able to deal with Malvinus and Cinna. Or at least discourage them from giving us any further trouble.'

'And why would any veterans want to help you?'

'For the reason I'd do the same in their place. If someone threatens a comrade, others will come to his aid. Besides, I dare say there'll be a few who fancy a bit of action to relieve them from the usual routine of retirement.'

'Is that how you see it?' asked Petronella. 'Settling down with me ain't good enough for you?'

'I didn't say that, did I? I was talking about the other veterans.'

'Oh yes, sure you were.'

Macro saw another trap opening up and quickly moved on. 'It'll cost us, but no more than we're already paying out to the gangs. Once I've sorted out my affairs at the colony, I'll come back with enough muscle to make sure we're safe.'

'And how long do you think they'll be prepared to stay? We won't be able to pay them indefinitely. Besides, they'll need to get back to their own farms and businesses at the colony. And once they're gone, we'll be vulnerable again.'

'Only if the gangs are still here.'

'What? Are you suggesting that you and whatever men are fool enough to follow you are going to take them on?'

'If they force the issue, yes.'

Portia rolled her eyes. 'Sweet Jupiter, you'd turn the streets of Londinium into a battlefield and get us all killed. It's like death follows at your heels like a hungry dog. Everywhere you go you leave a trail of bodies in your wake.'

'Only those who cross my path.'

She touched a hand to her chest. 'And what happens to those of us who stay here while you lie low? Who is going to protect us until you return?'

'You have Denubius. You seem to think you managed well enough before I arrived. If he's not up to it, hire some extra muscle to protect the inn. The gangmaster who brought our baggage from the ship might be keen for some extra work for him and his lads.'

'Not when he realises who he's up against.'

It was a fair point, Macro mused. He thought for a moment. 'If it looks like there'll be trouble, close the place up and join us in Camulodunum until we're ready to come back.'

Portia rubbed her forehead. 'I don't like this. There's no plan here to deal with the situation. You're just winging it and hoping for the best. I thought soldiers were supposed to be good at plans.'

'Soldiers fight. Commanders plan. Not that they often get the plans right . . . We're in a fight, Mother. When it comes down to it, it'll be decided by the bastard with the quickest blade and the guts to get stuck in.'

'Listen to yourself. Get stuck in? What kind of fool thinks that's a solution?'

Petronella nudged him. 'She's right. We need to think this through carefully and come up with something that avoids fighting. We're supposed to be running a business here, not a war. We have to think of a way to cut a deal with the gangs. A deal we can afford.'

The bitterly cold spell had passed and milder weather settled in as Macro and Petronella made their way along the military road leading from Londinium to the colony at Camulodunum, some sixty-five miles away. A short section of it had been paved, and the two-wheeled covered cart provided by Portia rattled, jolted and slid over the cobbled surface. Macro was pleased that they had left the dirt and stench of the town behind them, and his gaze happily feasted on the stark winter landscape either side of the road. It felt good to be out in the open countryside. Petronella was not so sanguine; every so often she glanced back to make sure that they had not been followed from the town. There were a few others on the road, traders and drovers making their way between the two settlements, and some exchanged greetings; others, natives mostly, fixed them with a wary or hostile look as the cart passed by. A rider in the livery of the imperial courier service cantered by, exchanging a brief wave with Macro.

After ten miles they came to the end of the paved stretch and encountered the work gangs toiling away as they extended the road. Most of the men were slaves, dressed in rags and chained together at the ankles as they were urged on by overseers shouting orders and threatening punishment for those who slacked in their efforts. Macro noted that many of the men bore the swirling tattoos favoured by the warriors of the island's tribes. He felt a surge of sympathy for these emaciated figures who had once been haughty opponents, and who were now defeated and enslaved and fated to spend the rest of their lives in servitude. Barbarians, yes. But brave all the same, and worthy of a better end than this.

'Poor creatures,' Petronella muttered.

'Fortunes of war,' Macro responded gruffly. 'If they had been victorious, they would have treated their Roman prisoners the same way, or worse.'

She turned her gaze towards him. 'Worse?'

'Some of the tribes, especially those under the thumb of the Druids, sacrifice their prisoners to their gods.'

He felt her shudder even through the folds of the cloaks they were wearing.

'We found the bodies of some of our captured men with their hearts cut out; others were disembowelled, impaled or decapitated – the Celts love to take heads as trophies. Some were burned alive.'

Petronella's face twisted into an expression of disgust. 'Barbarians.'

'Indeed.' Macro nodded. 'Still, given the benefits of our civilisation, there are some who believe that inside every barbarian there is a Roman trying to get out. Unfortunately, no one's explained that to the tribes that are still holding out in the mountains to the west. It'll be a while yet before Britannia is completely pacified. If ever.'

'I thought you said we'd be safe here.'

'And we will be, my love. The fighting is far away and there'll be no trouble in the lands around Londinium and Camulodunum. Mark my words,' he concluded reassuringly.

'I'm sure you're right.'

They passed the last group of slaves, who were cutting turf away and levelling the bed of the new road, pounding it with large wooden piles to compact the soil ready for the first layer of gravel that would serve as the foundation. A short distance beyond, the diverted track turned back onto the military road. From there on, the route comprised little more than cleared ground with corduroys of logs covered by soil carrying the road across stretches of wetlands. The snow was steadily melting in the glare of the sun, and the path of the road was easy to follow as it stretched across the landscape: a straight brown line of churned slush that made no concession to the geography it negotiated. Since the shortest route between two points was always a straight line, that was how the Roman engineers went about it. Such an approach was a source of pride to Macro, yet one more demonstration of the uncompromising superiority of Roman civilisation. Any barbarian who encountered such a road for the first time could not help but be in awe of the engineering prowess of their enemy.

Along the route there were many small settlements, farmsteads and the occasional villa, and here and there the small mounds marking the last traces of the military outposts that were no longer needed to protect the road and those passing along it. They stopped at the end of each day in one of the inns that served travellers. These were small and spartan compared to the Dog and Deer and the other inns of Londinium. All the same, they provided decent if simple fare, a warm hearth and a comfortable bedroll for the night. There were only a few other customers at this time of year, and the innkeepers were grateful for the business.

The night before they expected to reach the colony, they were the only travellers, and after they had eaten and settled down in front of the fire, the innkeeper stepped out of the kitchen holding up a wine jar.

'Do you mind if I join you for a drink, Centurion?' He had already introduced himself as Camillus, a demobbed optio from the Twentieth Legion.

'If it's on the house, it'd be our pleasure!' Macro grinned. He had already shared a jar with Petronella as they ate, but he was not going to turn down a free drink.

Camillus pulled up a stool opposite the bench where his guests sat and placed the jar on the woven reed matting between them before he built up the fire.

'You'll be joining the colony, I take it.'

Macro scratched his neck. 'I'll see how it goes. From what I've heard, the best place to make money is Londinium. But the wife and I are keen to get a farm up and running at Camulodunum all the same. I imagine we'll be passing here regularly.'

'Suits me. I can use the business.' Camillus clicked his tongue. 'I'd hoped this place would make me more money, being close to what was supposed to be the province's capital. But trade's been falling off every year since I set up. Partly down to merchants moving to Londinium, but also because there's less and less appetite to trade with the local tribes.'

'Why's that?' asked Petronella.

'Mostly because they're not a friendly bunch. Surly buggers are scaring off the merchants. They haven't got much to trade and there are some who are downright hostile and refuse to let any outsiders into their settlements. The Iceni are the worst of them all and make no bones about sending any Roman traders packing. You can imagine how much the merchants have been bending the ears of the decurions at Camulodunum and demanding that they teach the Iceni to mind their manners.'

Macro reached for the jar and filled all three cups. 'Good luck with that. The Iceni were prickly bastards from the moment we landed in Britannia. As stiff-necked as any barbarians I have ever fought.'

'Just as well their fighting days are over then,' said Camillus as he raised his cup to make a toast. 'Roman peace. Here to stay.'

Macro nodded in agreement and both men took a healthy swig, but Petronella looked down into her cup and swirled it thoughtfully.

'Is there a problem with my wine, lady?'

She glanced up and forced a quick smile, then took a sip to reassure their host. 'It's fine.'

Macro chuckled. 'She's new to Britannia. Not used to the cold, nor being so close to real barbarians. Puts the wind up her a bit.'

Petronella scowled at him before turning back to address Camillus, mimicking Macro's manner. 'Come to Britannia, love. Perfectly safe, and within a few years you won't be able to tell it apart from Campania . . . What a load of bollocks that's turning out to be.'

Camillus laughed. 'Didn't your mother ever warn you to never believe a word a soldier tells you?'

'Anyway,' Macro interrupted hurriedly, 'we're here now and we're going to make the most of it. Come what may.'

'Oh yes, and we've made such a fine start of settling down peacefully, haven't we? You can't go anywhere without stirring up trouble.'

Camillus raised an eyebrow. 'Trouble?'

'A little misunderstanding with some of the locals in Londinium,' Macro responded.

'Ha!' Petronella laughed mirthlessly. 'We'll see about that. There'd better not be anything like it at Camulodunum. I've had enough of gangsters.'

'There's none of that at the colony, lady,' Camillus reassured her. 'The veterans wouldn't stand for it. Anyone who tries to start up any of that nonsense gets flung out and sent on their way with a quick prod of a sword point. The biggest dangers there are old soldiers in their cups, and you look like you know how to handle their kind.'

'And how . . .' Macro added under his breath, then drained his cup and reached for the jar again.

They talked and swapped soldiers' tales long into the night. After a while, Petronella excused herself and dragged a bedroll near to the fire before covering herself with a cloak and a thick blanket and curling up to sleep. After a while she began to snore faintly, and Macro leaned closer to the innkeeper and spoke quietly.

'That business about the local tribes – anything I should be worried about?'

'No more so than any other frontier province. Although . . .'

'What?'

'I had a wine merchant in here a month ago. He'd tried his hand at trading with the Iceni. You know how the tribesmen like our wine, so he thought he had a good chance of succeeding where others had failed. He sold some jars in the first two villages he came to, but after that they went cold on him. Refused to buy a thing. He tried to reason with them, but they got angry and chased him away. He says he saw someone watching him from the edge of the village as he drove his wagon away. A Druid, he reckons.'

'And how would he know? I don't recall seeing any wine merchants in the ranks when we took on those Druid bastards during the early years of the invasion. We put paid to them back then, and the governor is about to deal with what's left of them. I very much doubt your merchant would know a Druid if he saw one.'

'I hope you're right, Centurion.'

The next day they set off as soon as there was enough light

to see the road ahead, determined to make sure they reached their destination well before dusk. The temperature had dropped below freezing again, and the slush of previous days crunched and crackled beneath the iron rims of the cart's wheels as it shuddered and slid across the bleak landscape. The mule plodded ahead dutifully in its harness, steamy breath pluming from its nostrils. Macro was leaning forward on the driving bench, occasionally flicking the willow switch against the mule's rump when the beast slowed its pace. Beside him, Petronella sat brooding. There was something in her expression that warned Macro off trying to make conversation. So he started humming an old marching song to himself.

At length Petronella cleared her throat. 'I think we made a mistake coming here.'

'The colony's a safer bet than Londinium at the moment.'

'That's not what I meant and you know it. I don't think we should have come to Britannia. It's not safe here. We're in danger.'

'I can handle a few jumped-up street thugs and I can protect you.'

'If you seriously believe that, you're a fool. And you are no man's fool, my love. So stop trying to pull the wool over my eyes. I deserve better than that. Those men back in Londinium will not let you show them up. Even the fact that you are a highly decorated veteran, and one of those chosen to serve in the Praetorian Guard, won't save you if Malvinus's mob, or any of the others, decide to do you in. We should have stayed in Rome, or bought a small farm somewhere nearby.'

'But I had sunk a small fortune into the businesses here,' Macro protested. 'What happens to them when my mother is no longer able to run them? They'll go to rack and ruin without us around.'

'Then sell up and let's return to Rome. Your mother can come with us.'

'Why? We're making good money and we can make more as Londinium grows. We'd be fools to turn down such an opportunity. Anyway, just how big a farm do you think we could afford back in Italia?'

'I'd sooner be alive and living more modestly, than a dead fool.'

'Pah!' Macro growled in frustration.

'It's not just the gangs in Londinium,' Petronella continued. 'I don't like the way the natives are looking at us. I get the feeling they'd stab us in the back at the first opportunity. You heard what that innkeeper said about the tribes near the colony. They don't want to be part of Rome.'

'They don't have a choice about that any more, do they? We're here and we're staying. Rome ain't going to give way to a bunch of leery barbarians. They'll get used to the situation in time and accept our ways.'

'And if they don't? What then?'

Macro sniffed. 'Then they'll have to be taught a lesson they won't easily forget.'

Petronella shook her head wearily. 'What if they decide to teach Rome a lesson?'

'Let 'em try. That's all I am going to say about that.'

Macro did not like the direction the conversation was taking. There was an unsettling ring of truth to her words, and it challenged his view of the world. He gave the mule a sharp whack with the switch. 'Get a move on, you bloody idle brute! At this rate, we'll never get to the colony.'

CHAPTER ELEVEN

The light was starting to fade as the cart trundled onto the low rise that overlooked the veterans' colony of Camulodunum. Macro was immediately struck by the difference in scale between the province's notional capital and the thriving town of Londinium. It was fifteen years since he had last seen Camulodunum, shortly after the great battle fought in the presence of Emperor Claudius. The enemy's capital had been taken and Caratacus had fled west with what remained of his army.

Back then the settlement had been a sprawl of round huts centred on the hall of the Catuvellaunian king. The only other notable structures had been a handful of small warehouses beside the river, where traders from across the sea had been dealing with the natives for many years before the first soldier landed on these shores. Since then a legionary camp had been built beside the native settlement before much of it was levelled to prepare the ground for the colony. A few of the larger military buildings remained, but the rest had given way to civilian structures. The square outlines and shingled and tiled roofs of the Roman houses and shops contrasted sharply with the tribal huts nearby. Down at the river, a handful of small cargo ships were moored alongside a short wharf, and there were a few more warehouses present than when Macro had last been there. Rising above the colony was the timber scaffolding and the timber limbs of cranes around a number of construction sites, the largest of which was the temple dedicated to Claudius. It wasn't going to be finished for many years, Macro mused, as he noted that work had only progressed as far as the pediment and the precinct wall that ran around the temple complex. At this rate the grandest Roman edifice on the island would be completed long after the colony had become no more than a provincial backwater.

'Is that it?' Petronella demanded. 'That's Camulodunum?'

'Even Rome wasn't built in a day, my love.'

'Maybe not, but that can't be more than a quarter of the size of Londinium.'

If that, Macro thought. He shared her sense of disappointment even if he would not admit it to his wife. She was being critical enough already without him providing any further encouragement.

He took tighter hold of the reins as they followed the road down the slope towards the gate leading into the colony. The gate dated from the time of the camp and had two narrow arches. There was a short stretch of wall on either side, no longer than twenty feet, Macro estimated, and the ditch that had once surrounded the camp had long since been filled in and built over in places. Snow covered the only other traces, so that the overall impression was of a fortress barely begun and then abandoned. Even though it would have been possible for anyone approaching the settlement to simply walk around the ends of the wall either side of the gate, there was still a red-cloaked sentry keeping watch from the top of the gatehouse, and two more standing in the shelter of the open gateways. Old habits died hard, Macro reflected approvingly. The veterans who made up most of the colony clung to the rituals of their military days.

Macro gently pulled on the reins as they approached the gate, and one of the men on watch approached. His face was heavily lined, and grey stubble covered his chin. Between the folds of his cloak Macro saw the dull gleam of scale armour and the hilt of a short sword.

'What's your business on this cold day, my friend?' the sentry called out as he paced towards the side of the cart.

'Business with the colony. Where can I find the magistrate?'

'Business, eh?' The sentry looked Petronella over.

'She's spoken for,' said Macro.

'Too bloody right I am!' Petronella snapped. 'I'm his wife.'

'And who is "he"?' the sentry grinned.

'Praetorian Centurion Lucius Cornelius Macro.'

The sentry took a step back and saluted. 'Apologies, sir. My lady.'

'Bit late for that,' said Macro. 'Just tell me where I can find the magistrate.'

'The headquarters block, sir. That's where the colony senate meets.'

'They're in session?'

'In a manner of speaking, sir.'

Macro nodded his thanks and flicked the reins, and the cart rumbled through the gate. On the far side he could see that the street grid had been clearly set out with surveyors' poles, but barely half the area within the lines of the old military camp had been built on. They were almost all single-storey buildings, a mixture of homes, shops and other businesses lining a large open space that seemed to be designated as the colony's forum.

'I've seen villages in Apulia that look more developed than this,' Petronella commented.

Macro followed the main route that cut across the colony and made for the large building at the heart of the settlement, close to the temple building site. Woodsmoke rose from most of the buildings and an acrid tang hung in the cold air. Another veteran was on guard outside the entrance to the headquarters building, and the sound of cheering and shouting came from within.

Macro slipped the switch into its holder and slipped down from the driver's bench. His buttocks ached, and he rubbed them as he stretched his back and shoulders.

'Going to help me down?'

He turned to his wife with a guilty expression and supported her arm as she stepped down beside him. Taking the reins, he hitched them over a post to one side of the entrance, which was framed by a pair of plain limestone columns supporting a simple entablature.

'Stay with the cart,' he instructed Petronella. 'I shouldn't be long. I'll find us a billet and we can deal with all the admin tomorrow.'

'Stay with the cart?' Petronella frowned. 'It's freezing out here.'

'Then move about. It might keep you warm until I get back.' Macro turned to the sentry, who had been watching the brief exchange with a faint look of amusement. 'Centurion Macro. I have business with the magistrate.'

The sentry bowed his head in an informal salute and waved Macro inside. He did not like leaving Petronella out in the cold, but women were not permitted to enter the senate of any Roman city, town or colony.

A small vestibule lined with pegs for cloaks and kit led through to the main hall of the headquarters block, where officers and men had once assembled under the shelter of the tiled roof that towered above. Now the space was given over to a semicircle of benches at one end where the colony's ruling council met and debated. The benches were deserted. At the other end, gathered around a large iron brazier and seated at tables and benches, was a small crowd of men wearing a mixture of faded military tunics and others of various hues. Wine jugs and cups covered the tables, along with the remains of a meal. Several slaves, locals by the cut of their clothing and the tattoos visible on their exposed skin, were clearing the tables and piling fresh logs by the brazier. The old soldiers were belting out a chorus of a song unfamiliar to Macro as he strode towards them, flicking the folds of his cloak back over his shoulders.

'Who's this?' one of them called out. Those around him stopped singing and looked at Macro with vague expressions of curiosity. The rest continued their cacophonic effort with no regard for the new arrival.

Macro stopped by the man who had first spotted him and bent down to speak in order to be heard above the din that echoed back off the sides of the hall. 'Which one is the magistrate?'

'Ramirus? He's the tall one there. To the right of the brazier.'

Macro's gaze followed the direction indicated. He saw a giant of a man in a military tunic with a medal harness strapped over his torso. Ramirus had a broad face, a heavy jaw and dark curly hair. He raised a wine jar and grinned as he addressed the gathering.

'Watch this, lads!'

He braced his feet apart and arched his back as he raised the jar to his lips and began to drink, his throat pulsing at each gulp. Around him the others cheered and stamped their feet, their cries rising to a crescendo until Ramirus lowered the jug with a flourish and upended it to allow the last few drops to spatter onto the flagstones. Then he opened his arms and thrust his chest out in triumph as the other men roared his name.

Macro waited a moment on the fringe, and when the cheers subsided, he made his way over to the colony's senior official. As soon as Ramirus saw him approach, he raised a finger.

'Who's this fellow, then?'

This time everyone turned to look, and the conversation died away as they regarded Macro curiously.

'What's your name and your business here, fellow?' Ramirus demanded. 'Don't you know you are interrupting a meeting of the colony's council?'

There were a few laughs at the remark, and Macro made himself smile as he responded. 'So I heard. Sounds like my kind of politics.'

Some of the men raised their cups to him and grinned.

'The name's Lucius Cornelius Macro, former centurion in the Praetorian Guard.' He stepped up to Ramirus and held out his hand. After the briefest of hesitations, the other veteran clasped his forearm.

'Welcome, brother. You're a long way from Rome.'

'Best place to be a long way from. That's why I've chosen to have my land grant here in Britannia.'

'Here? At Camulodunum?'

'Why not? Can you think of a better place for an old soldier than amongst former comrades at a military colony? Better than eking out my days with fat merchants and playboys in some seaside town in Campania.'

'If you say so. At least the locals there aren't looking to stick a knife in your back the moment you drop your guard. Give this place a couple of years and you'd sell your mother for a billet in Herculaneum.'

'Don't tempt me.' Macro sighed. 'Anyway, here we are.'

'We?'

'My wife's waiting outside.'

'I'd better not keep you then, brother. What can I do for you?'

'I need to mark out the land I've been granted and register it with the colony. That can wait until the morning. Meanwhile, I need a place to stay until we can get something built.'

Ramirus rubbed the back of his neck. 'There are a few rooms at the rear of the yard that have been put aside for official visitors. You can have one of them for now if you like.'

'That'll do.' Macro nodded his thanks, then gestured to the other veterans, who had returned to their drinking and banter. 'I'll let you get back to your meeting. Seems like there's quite a few items still on the agenda. How often do you meet?'

'Almost every day. We're busy men – drinking is a serious business. I'll add you to the council once you're settled. We can always use another wise head to help run the show.'

'I'm always up for a bit of liquid politics.'

They shared a laugh and Ramirus clapped him on the shoulder before Macro turned away and made his way back outside to the cart. Petronella was squatting on the driver's bench. She had pulled a fleece over her cloak and sat there hunched and shivering, looking up when she saw him emerge.

'Well?'

Macro offered a big smile. 'I think we'll do fine here. Just fine.'

The next morning, Macro woke to find that a bright beam of sunlight had fallen across his face. He squinted, groaned and then sat up, shielding his eyes against the glare of the open window not far from the door. A faint sizzling sounded from the corner of the room, and he turned to see Petronella stirring the contents of a cooking pot suspended from an iron tripod over the flames of a brazier. The aroma of cooked meat immediately sharpened his appetite, and he threw back the blankets and fleece under which he and his wife had slept the previous night. The floor was cold and he slipped his feet into his boots before he went to her.

She glanced up and smiled. 'Sausage. I went out first thing and bought some in the market. He was just opening up, so I got the pick of what was on offer.'

Macro lowered his head to sniff, and blinked as a tendril of smoke stung his eyes.

Petronella stirred the chunks of sausage around in the pan as she continued. 'Are we going to be staying in this place long?'

'As long as it takes for us to build a house of our own. There's no chance of that happening before we return to Londinium, but at least we can get the work started and pay someone to complete the job before we come back here. I can get the farm under way at the same time.'

'Good.' She smiled happily. The prospect of settling down with Macro in a villa at the heart of a small farming estate had been her long-cherished ambition ever since they had married and contemplated Macro's retirement.

He read her expression and chuckled as he slipped his arm around her hip. 'We'll have all we spoke of some day very soon. I'll hang up my sword and we'll enjoy the peace and quiet.'

It was what he knew she wanted him to say, and if that meant putting aside any comment about his fondness for his army days, he was content to do so for the sake of the woman he loved.

'I wouldn't be too sure about that,' she responded, her smile fading.

'Why's that, my dear?'

'Just something the butcher told me. Seems there's been some trouble with the local tribe. The Trinovantes. One of their settlements refused to pay their taxes and roughed up the collector and his escort before sending them packing.'

'That sort of thing happens from time to time in frontier provinces. The natives just need a firm reminder to put 'em back in their place.'

'And whose job would that be?'

Macro could see where this was headed, and shifted warily. 'Camulodunum's a veterans' colony. Those who are still fit enough are obliged to answer the call if there's a need for armed men. That will include me.'

'I thought so.' She stopped stirring and ladled the chunks of sausage into two mess tins, sharing the fat out equally before tearing a small loaf in half and handing Macro his piece. There was no other furniture in the small room, and they sat on the bed as they ate in silence. Macro could tell that she resented the prospect of him taking up arms again. For his part, he hoped he would be called on. It would be an opportunity to acquaint himself with some of the other veterans, and get to know the landscape that surrounded the colony.

After they had eaten, Macro put on his best tunic, cloak and boots and went to the administration office at the rear of the main building. In the days when the headquarters complex had been at the heart of the legionary fortress, the clerks in the office would have been busy with the myriad duties of record keeping, writing orders, issuing requests for supplies and replacement equipment and maintaining strength returns. Now, the lesser needs of running a civilian settlement with a population of barely half the complement of a legion meant that only four clerks occupied the office, sitting at tables at one end of the room. Macro handed over the wax slates stating his land entitlement at the colony and the clerk fetched a large roll of vellum from the shelving that ran along one wall. As he unrolled it on one of the empty tables, Macro saw that there was a grid diagram of the colony with many names and details already filled in. The clerk leaned over and tapped a finger to indicate an area not far from the modest-sized market.

'That's the zone reserved for centurions, sir. On slightly higher ground, so the drainage is good. There are still five plots available; you can take your pick.'

Macro stared at the map for a moment. 'I'll take the one closest to headquarters, there.'

The clerk nodded and made a note of the location on Macro's wax slates, then handed them back to him. 'I'll get that added to the registry and put a board up on the site, sir.'

Macro smiled. Petronella would be delighted to have a well-positioned townhouse. He glanced back at the clerk. 'What about the farmland?'

'Not so straightforward, sir. Camulodunum's surrounded by the richest lands of the Trinovantes, and there are also small estates owned by the Catuvellauni nobles who settled here before the invasion. They haven't taken at all kindly to having the veterans' land grants carved out of the area.'

'I can imagine.'

'There's been no overt resistance to the veterans' allocations. They know the score. When Caratacus was defeated, the property of the Catuvellauni became spoils of war. Nothing was done about that at first, thanks to the continued fighting in the west, but once the colony was established, Rome started appropriating the land for veterans.'

'Quite. Still, that's how it goes. They'll get used to the new arrangement. They haven't much choice.' Macro put his hands on his hips and stretched his shoulder joints. 'So which parcel of land can I claim? I want good land, mind you.'

'Of course, sir.' The clerk ran his finger down a list of plots, most of which had names already appended to them. He paused at the details of one of the vacant listings. 'I think this one will suit you, sir. Five miles to the east of the colony. It borders the river. There's woodland, and it includes four Trinovante homesteads. Very productive, according to the record. Their rents should be a nice little earner. The surveyors have already staked out the boundary, so it'll be easy to find.'

Macro, who knew little about farming, was relieved at the prospect of leaving that to the natives on his land. 'Very well, I'll take it.'

'Yes, sir. I'll have it entered in the colony registry, along with the plot in the town. Will there be anything else?'

'Not at the moment. That'll do.'

The clerk rolled up the vellum and returned it to the shelf. Macro turned to leave the office, his heart warmed now that the document granting him land had been translated into tangible assets that he could develop and enjoy with his wife. This morning, life was good, he reflected as he made his way across the main hall towards the entrance. He was now a landowner, a happily married man, and his stomach was filled with a fine breakfast.

Voices from the far end of the hall interrupted his happy musings. He glanced towards them and saw Ramirus in earnest conversation with a slight figure in a mud-stained cloak. Four armed men waited a short distance away. Close by stood a native, his face tattooed above the patterned weave of his cloak. At the sound of boots crossing the flagstones, Ramirus looked in Macro's direction.

'Centurion! A word, if you please.'

Macro changed direction, and as he approached, the man Ramirus had been talking to turned round. It was the procurator, Catus Decianus.

'We've got a problem, brother,' Ramirus announced. 'Decianus needs our help.'

'Oh?' Macro turned to the procurator, who looked tired and anxious.

'There's been an attack on one of the tax collectors and his escort near the colony.'

'Yes, I heard. So?'

'The collector and one of his men died from their wounds. A courier reached Londinium with the news two days ago. The governor has sent me to deal with it. I need to raise an armed force to teach the natives a lesson. You and Ramirus are the senior men of the reserve at the colony. Find me fifty more good men. Then we'll hunt down those responsible and make them pay with their lives.'

CHAPTER TWELVE

'You said your fighting days were over!' Petronella stabbed a finger at him. 'You promised me!'

Macro held up his hands. 'There's nothing I can do about it. I'm on the reserves for five years after being discharged, as long as I am fit enough. It's the same for every soldier, my love.'

'Don't you "my love" me!' she snapped back. 'We were supposed to be living out the rest of our days in peace. That was the deal when I agreed to come to Britannia with you. Instead we've battled river pirates, taken on two crime gangs, and now you want to go and stick it to some barbarians.'

'In fairness, the pirates and the gangs were not my fault. I didn't pick a fight with them.'

'That's a matter of opinion.'

'And the attack on the tax collector ain't on me either.'

'You could choose not to be involved. The procurator is only asking for fifty men. You don't have to be one of them.'

'He asked for me directly. I could hardly refuse. What would you have me say? I'm sorry, lads, but the wife won't let me join you? I'd never be able to look anyone in the eye again.' Macro took her hands in a warm grip. 'You understand.'

She gritted her teeth and hissed, 'I understand. You'd better go then. Before I do something you'll regret.'

He released her and turned to the small pile of baggage in the corner of the room. He took out his sword, canteen and a spare tunic and cloak, which he rolled up and tied with two short lengths of rope. His armour and shield were with the rest of his belongings in Londinium; he'd have to find some spare kit from whatever was available in the colony's quartermaster's store. Tucking the roll under his arm, he turned towards Petronella, but she was sitting on the bed with her back to him.

'I'll be back as soon as I can. Safe and sound.'

She sniffed with derision but said nothing in return.

'Goodbye then,' Macro growled, and left the room.

He had barely gone three paces before the door was wrenched open and Petronella surged towards him and threw her arms round his shoulders, holding him tight. He could feel her hot breath on his neck as she whispered urgently, 'Come back to me, Macro. Don't leave me alone in this world. I couldn't bear to live without you.'

'I'll come back. I swear it.'

She pulled away, stared into his eyes one last time, then returned to the room and closed the door behind her. Macro smiled and shook his head. 'As long as I live, that woman's going to be full of surprises . . .'

The small band of veterans summoned by Ramirus were waiting in the walled courtyard along with Decianus's four-man escort. A native had been paid to guide the column to the settlement. It was an hour or so before noon, and a biting wind had risen and now nipped at what little flesh the men exposed. Some hugged themselves, while others stamped their booted feet or blew hard into clasped hands before rubbing them together vigorously. They had an assortment of weapons and armour that they had retained from their time in the army, and even though their kit had seen better days, the equipment was well cared for and gleamed dully. Beside them on the ground were their marching yokes, with sleeping roll, mess tins, spare clothes and rations bundled up in a second cloak. A string of six mules were hitched to a post in the corner of the courtyard. They were laden with marching rations and worn tents that had been found in the quartermaster's storeroom.

Macro had equipped himself with a scale-armour cuirass, a battered shield – the best that remained in the storeroom – and a legionary helmet. There were no officer's crests available to attach, and he recalled the day, long before, when he had joined the Second Legion and been handed his ranker's equipment. He would have liked to have his medal harness and vine cane with him to signify his rank, but both were at the Dog and Deer. Looking round at the other men, he saw that the youngest of them was in his forties, and most had lined and scarred faces with grey-streaked beards or bristles on their ruddy cheeks. An aged group of men they might be, but they were veterans all and would give a good account of themselves in any fight. Not that Macro was expecting any serious action. The purpose of the brief expedition was to intimidate the rebellious tribespeople and arrest those responsible for the attack on the tax collector and his escort. They would be condemned to death, or sold into slavery, according to what the procurator decided was a suitable punishment. The tax due would be collected, in addition to a punitive fine, and the column would return to Camulodunum leaving the tribespeople to rue the day they decided to defy the power of Rome. That was how it was likely to go, Macro reflected. But you could never tell. Some barbarians buckled at a display of strength, while others met the challenge head on. If the latter happened, greater bloodshed would be unavoidable.

He caught sight of Ramirus and Decianus emerging from headquarters and quickly cleared his throat. 'Officer commanding present! Detachment, form up!'

At once the veterans formed two ranks, with the auxiliaries to the left. Macro took his place at the right flank and raised his head as he called the others to attention. Ramirus's last position in the army had been as the senior centurion of his legion, and so he outranked Macro. He was an imposing figure in his red military cloak, helmet with transverse crest of dark crimson, and medalled harness across his mail vest. By contrast, Decianus, wrapped in a blue cloak and with wool breeches tucked into knee-high leather boots, looked like the cosseted political official he was. He hung back as Ramirus addressed his men.

'Brothers, by now you will all know the reason we have been called out.' He half turned to indicate Decianus. 'This is the provincial procurator, Catus Decianus, sent from Londinium to oversee the matter. But make no mistake, I will be in charge. Our newly arrived comrade Centurion Macro will be second in command. It'll take us no more than two days to see it through and get back to our families.'

His words were greeted by groans and some muttering, and Ramirus raised his vine cane and called for silence.

'I know you'd rather be sat in front of your hearths, but we're veterans, and when we're called on to do our duty, we must serve the emperor once again. Besides, I've persuaded the procurator here to pay a bonus of ten sestertii for all who take part.'

The mood of the men changed instantly from mild disgruntlement to amused pleasure at the prospect of being paid for their efforts. Enough to keep them in wine for several days on their return to the colony.

'Centurion Macro!'

'Yes, sir?'

'Prepare to march.'

Macro turned to the veterans and felt the excitement stirring in his heart as he drew a deep breath. 'Detachment . . . packs up! Form column!'

The men picked up their yokes, shifted them onto their shoulders and slung the shield straps onto the crossbar, then shuffled into formation, four abreast. Age and loss of habit meant they took longer than they would have done in their prime, and Macro was tutting under his breath until they were in position. Then he turned to Ramirus, Decianus and the four men of the procurator's escort, who had mounted and were waiting a short distance away. Their native guide stood close by, ready to accompany them on foot.

'Column ready, sir!'

Ramirus turned towards the archway leading out of the courtyard and swept his arm forward as he urged his horse into a walk. A moment later, Decianus flicked his reins, trotted round Ramirus, his escort following, and took his station at the head of the column. Macro gave a wry smile. The procurator seemed to believe he was in charge, whatever Ramirus might have said. Well, that was something the two of them would have to sort out between them. Macro was more than content with his own role, even though he had no horse to ride and was once more a foot-slogger. Given the small size of the column, it reminded him of his days as an optio many years before. He did not resent the effective demotion; it was good to feel like a soldier once more, with no burden of command on his shoulders.

'Detachment . . . advance!'

With Macro at the head of the detachment, calling the time every so often, they tramped out of the courtyard and along the main street of the colony, past clusters of completed buildings and the frames of those still under construction. Small groups of women, some with children huddling at their sides, had come to bid farewell to their men marching off once again in the service of Rome. Macro looked for Petronella, but she did not seem to be present. Ahead lay the gate, still looking as futile as ever with the lack of walls on either side. As the riders passed through the arches, Macro saw a lone figure off to one side, standing by a pile of construction timber. It was a woman, swathed in a cloak, her hood pulled up. Closer to, he could see it was his wife. He smiled and gave her a wave. She half raised a hand in response, holding it still for a moment before it dropped.

Then Macro was passing through the arch and she disappeared from sight. Once he was on the road beyond, he looked back over his shoulder, past the bundle on his yoke, but she had already blended in amongst the other women turning away to return to their homes. He felt a sudden pang for her, a need to enfold her in his arms before he marched away. But it was too late for that.

For five miles the veterans trudged along behind the men on horseback before turning off the road to Londinium and onto a rough track. The route wound its way through the rolling landscape that had once been the kingdom of Trinovantes, before they were overwhelmed by the Catuvellauni and conquered by Rome in turn. At first there were many native farmsteads and a handful of small Roman villas and farm buildings where the forests had been cleared away. As the day wore on, these became more sparse, and the dark lattices of the bare limbs of trees and patches of evergreens closed in on the narrow, rutted track.

Dusk was settling over the weary veterans as they came in sight of one of the outposts that Governor Ostorius Scapula had ordered to be built in order to keep watch on the tribes that had threatened to rise up several years earlier. Only a small garrison remained; a section of auxiliaries. Just enough to mount a constant watch over the surrounding land and light a signal beacon if there was any sign of trouble.

The outpost consisted of a fortified tower surrounded by a palisade atop an earth rampart and a ditch outside. It was positioned on high ground, and the gentle slopes around had been cleared of any trees or undergrowth that might conceal an enemy stealing towards the defences. At the veterans' approach, a challenge was shouted by a figure in the tower, and Ramirus called back, stating their identity. A moment later, the gates opened and the soldier in command of the outpost crossed the narrow causeway over the ditch and gave a smile as he saluted.

'Been a while since we've seen you up this way, sir.'

'Not much game to be had this time of year,' Ramirus answered. 'How are things, Tibullus?'

'Apart from being bored fucking rigid, fine, sir.'

The riders dismounted and led their horses as they followed Tibullus into the outpost. When the last of the veterans had passed through the gate, one of the auxiliaries closed it behind them and placed the sturdy timber locking bar back into the iron brackets that secured it.

The interior of the outpost comprised a space fifty feet square, with timber store sheds on one side and living quarters on the other. There were no stables, merely a small pen that stood empty. Macro mused that the outpost might once have held as many as twenty men. It would be a tight squeeze for the garrison and the veterans that night, but at least they would not be camping in the open, with the discomfort and risk that entailed.

'Detachment! Fall out!'

The men set their yokes down with a chorus of groans and stretched their stiff muscles as they looked round them. Macro put his yoke down beside the entrance to the modest barracks and strode over to join the other officers and the auxiliary.

Ramirus had already introduced the procurator, and now gestured at Macro as he approached. 'And this is Macro, formerly a centurion of the Praetorian Guard.'

Macro exchanged a salute with Tibullus and the latter clicked his tongue. 'I imagine this is a far cry from the comforts you are used to, sir.'

'Do I look like some pansy, bed-wetting son of a senator to you, lad?'

'Er, no, sir.'

'Good. I served my time in the legions.' Close to, Macro could see that the auxiliary was in his early twenties, with a sparse scattering of bristles on his jowls that was unlikely to ever grow into a beard. 'I was fighting my way through the bogs of this benighted island while you were still sucking at your mother's tit.'

Ramirus laughed. 'Ah, go easy on the boy, Macro. Tibullus is a good sort and one of the best hunters you'll find in the army. He can track down and pike a boar or shoot a deer before either knows he's near them. Ain't that right, lad?'

The auxiliary smiled at the praise and Ramirus punched him lightly on the shoulder before his expression became more formal. 'We can talk about hunting another time. Meanwhile, see to our horses. Have them fed, watered and tethered for the night.'

'Yes, sir.'

As the auxiliary saluted and hurried away, Ramirus turned to Macro. 'Get the men settled into the barracks and join us in the room under the tower.' He gestured towards their guide. 'He can join them.'

'Yes, sir.'

The interior of the barracks was lined with bunks, two racks high. The first veterans through the door hurriedly claimed the empty bunks while the rest found spots on the floor. The structure, like most buildings in the region, was timber-framed and daubed with a mixture of mud and straw, and had a roof made up of wooden shingles covered with thatch from the reeds that lined the local waterways and marshlands. It kept out the wind, rain and snow even if it smelled and felt damp. There was one brazier at the end of the room, and Macro ordered two of the men to carefully manoeuvre it to a more central position and then build it up to warm the new arrivals.

Having assigned the watch rota for the night, he left the men to eat and rest and picked up his yoke before making his way to the foot of the tower. The six horses were champing contentedly into their feedbags as he passed by. A narrow door led into the small room there, while a ladder climbed the side of the tower to the platform where one of the auxiliaries stood watch.

A cheery blaze from another brazier illuminated the interior, and Macro saw that Ramirus and Decianus had claimed the two bunks there, while Tibullus was spreading his bedroll out on the ground to one side. Macro closed the door and set his pack down before he sighed wearily. 'Rank hath its privileges, eh?'

'Too fucking right it does,' Ramirus answered. 'I didn't work my way up to camp prefect just so that I could sleep like a squaddie.'

Decianus shook his head. 'If this is the best there is, then where's the privilege?'

Ramirus rolled his eyes. 'It seems the procurator thinks he's a cut above the likes of us veterans, eh, Macro?'

'Being in the field is something of a social leveller. He'll get used to it.' Macro undid his bundle and took out his thin bedroll. He laid it out opposite Tibullus and slumped down, resting his back against the wall.

Decianus sighed. 'Gentlemen, I am in the room, you know. Believe it or not, I did my time as a junior tribune in my youth.'

'Oh?' Ramirus propped himself up on an elbow and stared at the procurator as the latter rummaged in his saddlebag and drew out some flatbread and a wedge of cheese. 'Which legion did you serve with?'

'The Fifteenth Primigeneia on the Rhenus frontier.'

'See any action?'

'Not much,' Decianus admitted. 'A few punitive expeditions along the river when the barbarians on the far bank mounted a raid. Only ever amounted to a skirmish.'

Macro grunted. 'That's more action than most junior tribunes ever get to see.'

'Maybe.' Decianus tore off a strip of flatbread and chewed. 'At any rate, it convinced me that soldiering was not for me.'

'And yet here you are.'

'On sufferance. The governor ordered me to deal with this matter in person. Said that since I was new to the province, I should get some dirt between my toes.'

Macro's heart warmed to the governor. It seemed Paulinus was the kind of leader who didn't pamper his subordinates, no matter what rank they held. That or he just didn't like Decianus. Certainly the procurator's sour and superior demeanour was unlikely to win him many friends. It occurred to him that there were a couple of matters he could bring up now that he and the procurator were confined to the tower room for the night.

'That native guide you've hired, can we trust him?'

'Cardominus? I think so. He's from the Cassivellauni. There's no love lost between them and the Trinovantes. They'd been at each other's throats for generations before the Cassivellauni finally got the upper hand. He knows these lands well. His father was one of the nobles who continued the fight here when Caratacus fled to the mountains to stir up the Silures and Ordovices into continuing to resist Rome.'

'Did your man fight on with his father?'

'Hardly.' Decianus smiled. 'It was Cardominus who sold his father out. He led us to their camp in the forest.'

Macro sniffed. 'Doesn't sound like the kind of man I'd trust.'

'Maybe not, but I'm told he's loyal to Rome.'

'Loyal to Roman silver, you mean.'

'If that's what it takes. It's the same with most men, in my experience.'

'Not me.' Macro patted his left breast. 'I'm loyal to Rome, right to the core. There are some things you can't buy with silver.'

'Maybe you just haven't been offered enough yet. Every man has his price. That certainly goes for me, and I dare say it's true for Tibullus and Ramirus too.'

Macro gave Ramirus an appealing look. 'Tell him it ain't true.'

Ramirus grinned wolfishly. 'I'm as loyal as the next man. As long as the next man isn't Cardominus. Don't you worry, Macro. I'm keeping an eye on him. At the first sign of treachery to his paymaster, I'll ram my sword down his throat.'

'I doubt he'll give us any problems,' Decianus said confidently.

Macro saw his chance to move the conversation on to the

other matter that was preoccupying him. He cleared his throat. 'Strikes me you're going to have your hands full dealing with the problems this province will throw up during your posting here.'

Decianus chewed hurriedly and swallowed. 'What do you mean?'

'Once we've taught our recalcitrant tribal taxpayers a lesson, you'll need to sort out a few problems in Londinium.'

'Problems?'

'Come now, you remember? I told you about the gang problem when we met at the governor's headquarters at the end of last month.'

'I remember. I had hoped you wouldn't bring it up. Not right now, at least, when we're tired and need some sleep.'

'What better time?' Macro grinned. 'You can hardly fob me off here and now. It's something you and the governor need to deal with. If Britannia is going to pay its way, you can't afford to let criminals like Malvinus bleed honest businesses dry. If they don't make a healthy profit, then where are the province's taxes going to come from? You need to sort the gangs out before they ruin us all.'

Decianus shrugged. 'I doubt I'll be in Londinium long enough for it to be my problem.'

As soon as he had made the remark, the procurator froze for an instant then quickly glanced round the other men in the room. Tibullus was busy pulling a pair of cloaks over himself and Ramirus was fishing about in his haversack for something to eat. Only Macro was looking at him, and for a moment the two men stared at each other before Decianus affected a yawn and blinked.

'It's been a long day. We'd better get some sleep. We'll reach the village tomorrow. We'll need to be alert.' Without waiting for a response, he swung his feet up onto the bunk, pulled up his covers and turned to face the wall.

Macro regarded him for a moment, wondering about his comment. Why would a newly arrived official of his rank be recalled from Britannia so soon after his arrival? It made no sense, unless perhaps Decianus had some patron with influence at the palace who might swing him a more significant and lucrative appointment in another province. Macro frowned as he contemplated that possibility. Britannia was the place where reputations were being made. If anything, men like Decianus would be pushing for an appointment here. So why did he seem certain that his posting would not be for any significant length? And if that turned out to be the case, what was the real reason for his appointment? Assuming it wasn't intended as a punishment of some kind.

Macro's eyelids felt heavy and he welcomed the prospect of sleep. Unlacing his boots, he put them within easy reach in case he was roused in an emergency during the night. Then, covering himself as best he could with his cloak, he lay on his back and stared up at the angled wooden planks of the ceiling. The smoke from the brazier curled up to the small opening above the centre of the room and disappeared into the darkness. Outside, the wind was building up and moaned softly over the outpost as flecks of snow drifted through the opening.

He puffed his cheeks. If there was a night of heavy snow, it would hamper their progress the next day. The quick resolution of the situation and a speedy return to the colony might not be possible. That would be a pity, thought Macro; he was missing the presence of Petronella at his side. It was the first night they had been apart since the campaign he had fought in the previous winter. If it took longer to deal with the troublesome natives than planned, she would be sure to worry. Worse still, she would be certain to take it out on him when he returned, whether it was his fault or not. Even so, he smiled at the prospect. That fierceness of hers was one of the reasons he loved her as much as he did. He closed his eyes as he continued to think about his wife, and very soon he was snoring in a deep rhythm.

Ramirus looked towards the source of the din. He had been eating a strip of cured meat, and he threw the final bit of gristle at Macro. His aim was true and it bounced off the centurion's shoulder. Macro snorted and turned his back. 'Fuck off.'

CHAPTER THIRTEEN

Morning revealed that another six inches of snow had fallen, and thanks to the wind that had blown through the night, drifts had formed in and around the outpost. The weather had moderated with the coming of the dawn, but the mood on top of the outpost's tower was sombre as the three men regarded the view. Ramirus's cheery demeanour gave way to frustration as he looked out over the freshly blanketed landscape beneath a sky streaked with clouds. Where the sun pierced through, the snow gleamed serenely.

'That's going to make progress difficult. I can't see any sign of the route we were following yesterday.' He glanced at Decianus. 'Are you sure your man can still find his way to the village?'

'That's what he says. He won't get paid until we've carried out the mission.'

Macro listened in silence as he regarded the way ahead of the column. There was scant sign of life amid the heavily forested landscape. He could only see three thin trails of smoke and one darker smudge far off that might mark the presence of a settlement.

'That might take rather longer than we first thought,' said Ramirus. 'We'd better get moving before there's any more snow. Centurion, get the men ready to march.'

* * *

Once the snow had been cleared from the gate to allow it to open, the column left the outpost, picking a path over the snow as they followed the native scout north, in the direction of the distant smoke Macro had seen from the tower. The fresh snow sank beneath the men's boots with a soft crunch, while the horses' hooves constantly flicked up white spray, so that Macro held up the column to allow the mounted men to pull a short distance ahead. Their pace was markedly slower than the previous day, and more tiring, and the older and less fit amongst the veterans were breathing heavily as the morning wore on.

Even though the Trinovantes had been humbled by two conquests, there was a palpable tension hanging over the column as they passed through the winter wilderness. There was very little sign of movement, save for some birds and a small herd of deer that ran along the edge of a forest as soon as they caught sight of the men and then turned into the trees and disappeared from view. Nor was there much sound, due to the deadening effect of the snow. What at first had seemed starkly beautiful to Macro soon became oppressive. The only thing that relieved his mood was the thought that it would be almost impossible to mount any kind of surprise attack in such terrain. Any movement by the enemy would be easily detected, and the snow would hamper the speed at which an attack could be attempted. Yet he could not help feeling a growing sense of wariness the further they marched away from the outpost and the nearer they drew to their destination.

Decianus was all for driving the men on, but Ramirus, conscious of the condition of the veterans, rested them every two hours. So it was not until late in the afternoon that the column approached the village. The clouds had thickened steadily since noon, and now the sun was no more than a dull metallic disc low above the western horizon. They approached a wooded ridge beyond which the smoke resolved into discrete columns curling up until they dissipated. Cardominus indicated a gap between the trees on the crest and spoke in broken Latin.

'There's the village. Should I scout ahead?'

Decianus took his meaning and shook his head. 'There's no need. We've wasted enough time. Let's just get this done and get out of here.'

'Get out of here?' Macro scoffed. 'There's no chance of us returning to the outpost before dark. We're going to have to spend the night in the village, unless you are going to make the men sleep in the open.'

He had spoken loudly enough to be overheard by the other veterans, and they glared at Decianus as he turned and gauged their mood.

'We'll shelter in the village tonight,' he announced. 'After we have resolved our purpose here. Ramirus, get your men moving again.'

Cardominus had watched the exchange closely, and now he caught Macro's gaze and shook his head, frowning. Macro rolled his eyes in acknowledgement. He would have preferred to have scouted ahead to spy the lie of the land before they made their presence known to the natives, even though there was scant risk of danger. It always paid to be cautious when they were some distance from safety.

The column moved off again, climbing the gentle gradient. Now Macro could discern the track they were following from the low curve of the banks either side. As he reached the crest, he looked down on the native settlement half a mile or so ahead. Perhaps as many as fifty round huts were clustered together in a rough circle. Most were of a modest size and had pens and smaller huts close by. Swine, goats and a few cattle stood in the pens. Piles of logs were stacked close to the low entrances of the huts, and smoke issued from the holes at the top of the thatched roofs. There were many people moving amongst the huts and across the surrounding open ground, which had been cleared for several hundred paces to make way for crops and pasture. A party of hunters, armed with sturdy spears and accompanied by large shaggy dogs, were picking their way across the snow from the direction of a sprawling forest. In the centre of the settlement was a much larger hut, surrounded by a compound defined by a palisade. There was a long, low building to one side that Macro took to be stables, judging from the steaming dark mound at one end.

It did not take long for the Romans to be spotted. Figures stopped in their tracks and faces turned towards the ridge. Some people pointed. Others ran, women scooping up infants and driving children into the huts. A number of men – no more than twenty, Macro estimated – hastily assembled in an open area in front of the compound; some were armed with hunting spears while others carried axes and clubs. There was no sign of any armour or swords; those had been forbidden to the natives by Governor Scapula to ensure there was little chance of his rear being endangered when he led his forces west into the mountains to hunt down Caratacus. Yet Macro was not naive enough to believe that a good quantity of armour and weapons of war had not been hidden by the warriors of the region.

As the slope gave way to even ground, Macro lost sight of the natives behind the outermost huts. At once he felt his heartbeat quicken. To lose sight of the enemy was to lose the initiative. Then he smiled grimly. These villagers were not the enemy. They were a subject people who needed to be reminded of the authority of Rome. An example needed to be set, and there should be no need for fighting. Yet his senses, finely honed to detect threats, told him there was danger ahead. Glancing over his shoulder, he could see that the veterans behind him shared his anxiety and needed reassuring.

'Easy now, lads,' he called out in an even tone. 'Keep your eyes open, but don't reach for your weapons unless the order is given. We didn't come here for trouble.'

Cardominus dropped back behind the mounted men and fell into step alongside Macro as the column closed up on the edge of the settlement. The centurion shot him a look of contempt. 'Not friends of yours, I take it.'

The guide spat to one side. 'The Trinovantes have had nothing but hate for the Catuvellauni since we conquered them.'

As the column entered the settlement, the round huts crowded them on either side. Despite the fresh fall of snow, there were some well-worn tracks winding between the native dwellings, and the air was thick with the acrid scent of woodsmoke and the sour tang of animals. Macro was aware of faces peering out at them from around the edges of the thick hides covering the entrances to the huts. More of the villagers watched from behind the huts, but there was no attempt to speak out in greeting or insult for fear of attracting the attention of the Roman soldiers.

A hundred paces into the settlement, they came to the open ground in front of the compound. Beyond the palisade rose the roof of the chief's hut. The group of men they had seen earlier were gathered in front of the gate. A tall figure in a patterned cloak stood in the middle of the front rank, holding a sturdy boar spear. He raised a hand as Decianus and Ramirus walked their horses steadily towards him and shouted defiantly in the native tongue.

'Detachment, halt!' ordered Ramirus.

Macro relayed the instruction in the loud, clear voice he had used on the parade ground, and the veterans stopped, more or less in time.

'Detachment, close up!'

They moved closer together, right hands resting on the pommels of their short swords as their eyes swept the surrounding huts, searching for any sign of an ambush.

Decianus drew himself up in his saddle and placed his spare hand on his hip in an imperious manner as he addressed the men before him.

'I am Catus Decianus, sent here by Paulinus, governor of the province of Britannia. I have orders to collect the taxes due by this settlement, and to arrest those responsible for the recent assault on an imperial tax collector and his escort. You will surrender the perpetrators to me immediately!'

There was no reaction to his declaration in word or deed; the natives merely stared at him in open hostility. Decianus waited a moment before he spoke again. 'Is there anyone here who speaks Latin?'

There was no response, so the procurator twisted in his saddle and gestured towards the guide. 'Cardominus! Step forward and translate what I told them.'

The Catuvellaunian reluctantly took his place to the side and slightly behind Decianus. At the sight of him, the native with the spear snorted in disgust and made a comment that caused his followers to laugh.

'Tell them!' Decianus ordered. 'Speak up, man!'

Cardominus winced, drew a breath and called out to the tribesmen, gesturing to the procurator before sweeping a finger across the ranks of the Trinovantes.

The procurator did not wait for a response before he

continued. 'Tell them that any refusal to obey my instructions will be met with force.'

As Cardominus translated, Decianus turned to Macro. 'We'll advance into that compound and take control of it. I don't want any clashes with those men. If they don't budge, push them firmly but gently. No weapons are to be drawn.'

Macro nodded, then cleared his throat. 'Detachment, prepare to advance!'

The moment the guide stopped speaking, Decianus waved his men forward and the horses walked on, making directly for the leader of the men barring their path.

'Advance at half-pace!'

The veterans marched forward in the shuffling slow step they used in battle to keep their formation. For a beat the natives did not move; then, when Decianus's horse was almost upon them, they stepped aside, just enough to allow the riders and the veterans on foot to pass by. As Macro came level with the tribesmen, he was acutely aware of the hostile expressions on either side, along with the muttered insults, but there was no attempt to resist as the Romans passed through and entered the compound. The tribesmen followed them inside and took up a new position either side of the entrance to the chief's hut. The man who seemed to be their leader ducked inside; a moment later, he re-emerged supporting a thin, frail old man with a white beard, who raised an arm and pointed a trembling, gnarled finger at Decianus as he spoke in an indignant tone.

'He demands to know why we are trespassing on the lands of his tribe,' Cardominus translated.

'His tribe?' Decianus repeated. 'He is the chief here, then? What is his name?'

'Mabodugnus, sir.'

'Very well. Then you tell Mabodugnus that I speak for the

governor of the province. These lands are the property of Rome, and thereby subject to the taxes that Rome levies on those it rules. The Trinovantes and their Catuvellauni overlords did not ally themselves with Rome when they had the chance, and chose instead to become our enemies. You lost your lands the moment Rome defeated Caratacus outside Camulodunum. So spare me any accusations of trespassing. Furthermore, you not only refused to pay the taxes due to the provincial treasury, you attacked imperial officials going about their lawful duties, two of whom subsequently died. I am here to collect the taxes that are due, together with punitive damages, and to arrest those responsible for the deaths and injuries inflicted on citizens of Rome. Tell him, Cardominus.'

Macro shook his head subtly. He doubted whether the tax collector and his henchmen were Roman citizens. Most likely the collector was one of the many Greek tax farmers involved in the lucrative contracts handed out by provincial headquarters. His men would be locally hired thugs tasked with coercing the more reluctant taxpayers.

By the time Cardominus had finished, the old chief was quivering with rage. He clenched his spare hand into a fist and brandished it as he shouted back in a reedy harangue.

'Centurion Macro!' Decianus called out over the chief's cries.

'Sir!'

'Arrest this man and disarm the others. All of them are to be held in the stable block over there while we resolve matters in the village.'

'Yes, sir.' Macro turned to the veterans. 'Down packs, draw swords!'

There was a series of soft thuds as the old soldiers dropped their yokes to either side, and then hard rasps as their blades came out. At once the tribesmen raised their motley collection of weapons. Cardominus hurriedly addressed them and pointed emphatically to the ground as the veterans fanned out either side of Macro. There was an instant of acute tension, and Macro was keenly aware that a bloody, one-sided conflict was only a heartbeat away. He took a calming breath, then slowly sheathed his sword and stepped towards the man still supporting the chief. Reaching out his right hand, he indicated the spear in the man's grip.

'I'll have that, if you don't mind,' he said gently. 'Come on, lad. Let's not start any trouble.'

The younger man glared back, his lips pressed together in a thin line beneath his drooping moustache. At his side, the chief's eyes widened in alarm as he surveyed the confrontation between the two sides. Then he coughed and called out to his followers, repeating his words more urgently to the man standing defiantly before Macro. There was a long-drawn-out hiss as the man breathed out, and then his shoulders slumped slightly. He pushed the shaft of his spear towards Macro and released his grip.

'There's a good boy.' Macro gave a slight nod as he caught the spear.

On either side other men dropped their weapons at their feet, and Macro indicated the stables. 'Over there, then. Let's be having you.'

The chief turned and shrugged off the hold of his companion as he led the way across the compound, followed by the tribesmen, while the veterans covered each flank. The stable was some fifty feet long and divided into eight stalls, with stores at the far end. There was a warm animal odour inside. Once the last of the natives had entered, Macro closed the doors and fastened the latch. He posted two men at each end of the stables and two more to patrol the sides before he returned to the rest of the detachment, who were being given their orders by Ramirus.

'I want four sections of eight men to scour the village. Search every hut. Confiscate any weapons you find and take any gold or silver, including jewellery.' He paused to lend his next words some added weight. 'Don't abuse their women. I'll personally cut the balls off any man here who mishandles them. I know how touchy these barbarian bastards can be about the honour of their women, so leave them well alone. Bring your hauls back to the chief's hut. Macro, you and the rest secure the compound and put sentries on the gate. We're going to be spending the night here, so I don't want any nasty surprises. We'll be marching back to the colony at first light.'

'Yes, sir.'

While Macro assigned the veterans to the search parties, Ramirus and Decianus dismounted and made their way into the chief's hut. The procurator's escorts led the horses to a rail beside the stable to feed and water them. As the search parties left the compound, Macro paced round the interior to assess the defences. The palisade, backed by an earth walkway, rose no more than eight feet at the highest point and was constructed from posts that would not have stood up to more than a few blows from a light battering ram. Worse still, the ropes binding the stakes had rotted in places, as had some of the stakes themselves. All the palisade was good for was to mark the boundary of the compound. Only the gates and the low timber towers on either side were in good condition. In any case, if the detachment was called on to defend this ground, they could not hope to cover the entire circumference.

As he returned to the gate and climbed the tower on the right to look out over the settlement, he saw that the sun had reached the horizon and the daylight was fading into a blue hue over the winter landscape. Shadows were gathering between the walls of the huts and pens. From across the settlement, he could hear the cries of anger and despair as the search parties went about their business. As he gazed to the south, in the direction of Camulodunum, he thought longingly of Petronella. For the first time since they had left the colony the previous day, he was starting to doubt the wisdom of choosing to volunteer for the detachment. The simple punishment of a small native settlement was turning into a bitterly resented and risky enterprise, and he would rather not have any part of it. But he had chosen this, and he had to live with it now.

A shout broke into his thoughts and he turned towards the stable. At the opposite end to the entrance, a figure was sprawled in the snow. One of the veterans was fighting off two men, while a third sprinted for the palisade.

CHAPTER FOURTEEN

'Fuck!' Macro hissed. He jumped off the walkway and sprinted towards the scene, joined by those men who had been patrolling the stable. He thrust his arm out to the two veterans guarding the doors. 'Not you! Stay in position, damn you!'

By the time he had reached the far end of the building, the guard still on his feet had wounded one of his assailants, while the other had moved back to the broken planks that had been taken out of the wall. The third man had reached the palisade and scrambled up and swung himself over the top, dropping out of sight. Macro drew up, breathing hard, sword raised as his eyes swept the scene. One of his men had been knocked down and was now stirring and struggling to get back on his feet. The other had pinned the wounded native up against the wall beside the small opening through which Macro could see the shadowy figures of the prisoners inside.

'What in Hades happened here?' he demanded.

'The bastards managed to get through the wall. The first one took Pollinus down before we could react. He ran off, but by then two more had got out.'

As the sentry spoke, one of the prisoners edged closer to the opening and Macro lashed out with his boot. He missed, and the man lurched back to a safe distance. Turning to one of the other veterans, he snapped an order. 'You, find something to block this. Something bloody heavy. Then check the rest of the building for weaknesses and block them too. Go!'

He turned back as Pollinus was helped back to his feet by his comrade. He was bleeding from a cut on the back of his scalp and swayed as he struggled to keep his balance. Macro spared no pity on him.

'What the bloody bleeding hairy bollocks were you two up to? You're veterans, the pair of you. Over twenty years in the army apiece and you let some barbarian sneak up behind you like you were a couple of pasty-faced recruits on their first sentry duty. You were lucky to get away with not having your throats cut. More's the pity. I'll be reporting this to Ramirus. Now get the fuck out of my sight and get that wound seen to.'

They scurried off towards the far side of the stable, and Macro replaced them with two of the remaining men. Then he caught sight of Ramirus at the entrance to the chief's hut and ground his teeth as he went over to report to his superior.

'What's the reason for all the shouting?' asked Ramirus.

'One of the prisoners escaped, sir.' Macro explained the circumstances briefly. 'I'd put those two jokers on a charge if they were still in the army.'

'But they aren't. Different standards apply for volunteers for reserve duties.'

'I know that, sir. But still, we can't have men endangering their comrades out here, surrounded by barbarians, a day's march from the nearest help.'

'I agree. I'll see to it that they aren't paid the bounty Decianus promised them.' Ramirus glanced towards the palisade where the prisoner had escaped the compound. 'There's no point in looking for the one who got away. He knows the ground and it's getting dark. Let's just hope he doesn't cause us any further trouble. I think it would be best if we doubled the watch tonight, Macro. I'll take command of the first.'

'Yes, sir.'

Both men turned to look out at the thatched cones rising up beyond the palisade, dark against the pale light that still streaked the sky close to the horizon. Above them the clouds had cleared and the first of the stars was twinkling in the dark heavens.

'It's going to be a very cold night.'

Macro nodded. 'At least there should be no more snow. We'll be able to make Tibullus's outpost well before tomorrow night, and get back to the colony the day after. All being well.'

Ramirus glanced at him with a questioning expression. 'You think it won't be?'

Macro chewed his lip, then shrugged. 'Who knows? Maybe I've served too long in difficult postings. I could be sensing danger when there isn't any. Like the procurator said, this is Roman turf now. We've beaten these people and they know it. They made a mistake over the tax collector and they're going to pay for it. Let's hope they don't make us repeat the lesson. That said, you know what these Britons are like. They have no love of Rome and they don't like to give in. Let's just hope they're smart enough to get over that.'

'Indeed.'

As night fell, the search parties returned laden down with their loot: baskets of jewellery and trinkets, furs, jars of wine and choice items of food to supplement the marching rations the veterans had brought with them. As the last man entered the compound, Ramirus gave the order for the gates to be sealed.

He cupped his hands together and blew into them before he

addressed Macro. 'Change the guard on the stables and get the rest of the men inside the hut. I want 'em well fed and rested for the march back to the colony. Best that they're as fresh as they can be if there's any trouble.'

'Yes, sir.'

'Same goes for you, Macro. Get some sleep.'

They exchanged a salute before Macro turned and strode off. The last of the twilight was fading and the men posted along the palisade were stamping their feet and rubbing their hands to keep them warm. As he ducked inside the chief's hut and let the leather cover fall back in place behind him, his cold skin was bathed in warmth from the large fire burning in a pit at the centre. The glow of the flames lit up the interior in a rosy hue. Close to the fire was a table at which Decianus sat as he went through the loot gathered by the search parties. He was selecting the items that would easily translate into value on the markets of Londinium, mainly items of gold and silver. Some pieces had jewels inlaid into the swirling patterns favoured by the Celtic artisans who had fashioned them. Rings, torcs, mirrors, ornately decorated daggers, brooches and combs were swiftly assessed and their value noted on the wax tablets in front of the procurator. Such work was beneath someone of Decianus's rank, and Macro imagined how much he must be smarting at the indignity of having to carry out clerical duties.

Macro undid his chin strap and removed his helmet, then located his marching yoke. Slumping down on one of the chief's furs, he took out some of the strips of dried meat Petronella had packed for him and began to chew as he considered the situation. The natives had not yet given them much trouble in response to the seizure of their property and their chief. That might well change when they saw the Romans drag their leader off the following morning. But there wasn't much they could do about it given their lack of proper weapons and the modest size of any band of fighting men they could field. Like the other tribes of these lands, there was only a small warrior caste. The rest were farmers whose only experience of fighting was taking part in cattle raids against enemy tribes. They presented little danger to fifty hardened army veterans and the men of Decianus's escort. All the same, Macro felt a nagging anxiety stirring at the back of his mind, and he looked forward to returning to the safety of Camulodunum. As he chewed in a steady rhythm, he shook his head and muttered reproachfully, 'Shit. I'm getting as twitchy as Cato in my old age.'

Most of the off-duty veterans had removed their armour and were sitting in their tunics and cloaks around the fire as they indulged themselves in the food and wine they had seized from the natives. The interior of the hut filled with good-humoured banter and laughter as jugs of wine were passed around. For a moment Macro was tempted to join them, but then he recalled Ramirus's instruction and conceded that he would rather not be nursing a hangover come the dawn. Nor, for that matter, would the other men. He stood up and made his way over to the fire.

'That's enough wine for tonight, lads.'

There was a short lull before one of the men holding a jug laughed and made to raise it to his lips.

'Put that down!' Macro shouted.

At once the hut fell silent and all eyes turned towards him. Macro placed his fists on his hips and leaned his head forward slightly. The man with the jar half lowered it and forced a smile. 'Oh, come on, Centurion. We've earned this. Have a drink with us, eh?'

'I said put it down,' Macro responded firmly, and gestured

to another group who were sharing two more jars. 'You too. I want all the wine taken over there by the entrance. Do it now!'

'Wait a minute, boys!' the first man called out. 'This is our wine. We found it, and by Jupiter's cock we are going to damn well drink it.'

There were a number of cries of support, and Macro knew he must act quickly before his authority was challenged any further. He sprang towards the man and snatched the jar from his hands, hurling it into the heart of the fire. It shattered against one of the logs and there was a loud hiss and a burst of steam as the wine splashed onto the flames.

'You bastard!' the man cried, and made to get up. Macro leaned forward and slammed his fist into the side of his jaw, and he collapsed into a heap at the centurion's feet.

He stepped back and glowered round at the other veterans.

'When I give an order, you fucking obey it. I don't give a shit if you have been given your discharge tablets. We're in the reserves, all of us, and that means we live under army regulations any time we are called on to serve again. Right now, we're two days' march from our base. We're surrounded by people who'd like nothing better than to cut our heads off and use them to decorate their doorposts. So far, no one's given us any trouble, but we have to keep our wits about us until this is over. You can get drunk when we get back to Camulodunum. But not now. If I catch any man the worse for wear, then as Dis is my witness, I will have him stripped naked and left behind for the natives to deal with. Is that clear?'

He looked round, daring any of the veterans to defy him. The man he had felled rolled onto his back, blinking as he groaned. No one else moved.

'I want every drop of wine over by the door, now!' Macro bellowed.

Those holding the jars stood up to do as they were told. One man, furthest from the fire, flicked his coat over an unopened jar at his side, but Macro's sharp eyes caught the movement and he turned to stare at the man, tilting his head to one side. At once the would-be miscreant snatched up the jar and followed the others to the door. When all the jars were in place, Macro paced over to the entrance, drew his sword, and smashed each one in turn, leaving the contents in a puddle around the shards of pottery. There were gasps and angry mutters from some of the veterans as he sheathed his blade.

'Finish what you are eating and get to sleep,' he ordered. 'You need all your strength for the march home. There'll be a change of watch halfway through the night. I'll be the duty officer and I'll have all of you who had wine jars in your hands. Starting with you.' He pointed to the man who had tried to conceal his looted wine. 'I'll also have him, on the ground. What's his name?'

'Torpilius,' a voice responded.

'Torpilius, then. When he comes round, you tell him.' Macro paused a moment, and then made his way over to Decianus. 'You'd do well to get some rest as well, Procurator.'

Decianus nodded towards the wine and spoke softly. 'Was that necessary?'

'Let's hope we don't have to find out.'

Macro returned to his yoke and removed his sword belt, armour and boots, then set about bolstering up his sleeping mat before lying down and covering himself with his cloak and one of the chief's finely cured furs. He lay with his back to the wall and through half-closed eyes looked over towards the men around the fire. They finished their meal quietly before moving off singly and in small groups to find themselves a place to sleep. He glanced last at Decianus, who was still reckoning up the value of their haul, then closed his eyes. Within a few breaths he was fast asleep.

Macro and the other veterans of the second watch were roused with a firm shake by the man sent by Ramirus. Dressing quickly, he left the hut and was immediately in the icy grip of the freezing night. Overhead the sky was clear and the stars glittered like specks of molten silver. Ramirus was waiting for him on the tower to the right of the gate.

'I'll bet you don't miss night watches like this,' he grinned. 'Feels like my nuts have frozen.'

Macro half nodded, half shivered, feeling the tremor go all the way down his spine. 'Anything happen?'

'The locals have been quiet as lambs. Almost. I've heard some movement, but it's most likely someone stepping outside for a quick piss. The winters of Britannia play havoc with your bladder when you get on in years. Apart from that, nothing to report. Any trouble in the hut? I heard a commotion at the start of the watch.'

Macro explained, and his superior nodded in approval before taking a last look at the roofs of the settlement. 'Right, I'm off. If there's any sign of trouble, send for me at once. We'll take no risks given the mood of that lot out there.'

'Yes, sir. Sleep well.'

He climbed down and made his way across the starlit compound to the hut. There was a brief glare of light as he swept the cover aside and ducked inside, then all was dark again. Macro stood still for a moment, straining his ears, but the only sounds from outside the palisade were the occasional howls of dogs or snorts of pigs or cattle, the muffled cries of infants, and once a brief, angry exchange between two women. Nothing to concern him then, he decided. He pulled the folds of his neckcloth up to cover his jaw and descended from the tower to make his way around the defences, ensuring that the sentries stayed awake and vigilant.

The rest of the night passed peacefully, and as the first glimmer of the coming dawn creased the horizon, Macro sent a man to wake the others. Shortly afterwards, they emerged from the hut, many moving stiffly as they adjusted their marching yokes. The last to emerge were Decianus and his escorts, carrying saddlebags filled with the valuables looted from the local people. When the main body of veterans was formed up, Ramirus gave the order for Macro and the second watch to fetch their yokes from the hut. The last of the men to make ready to march were those who had been detailed to guard the stables.

Opening the stable doors, Macro gestured to the natives inside. 'Out!'

They emerged from the warm fug scented by horse sweat, straw and dung. Several of the veterans ushered them over to the compound gates and drove them outside into the settlement. All except the chief, whose hands were bound before the other end of the rope was fastened to the saddle horn of one of the procurator's escort. The old man tried to stand proudly, but the cold was too much for him and he could not stop shivering.

'Torpilius!'

'Yes, Centurion?'

'Go into the hut and find the prisoner some furs.'

When the veteran returned, the chief glanced at Macro and silently nodded his thanks as he wrapped the covering over his cloak.

Ramirus eased himself up into his saddle and looked round at his small command to make sure they were ready to march. Now that the four men of the escort were carrying valuables, they, together with Decianus and his prisoner, took their place halfway along the column. The camp prefect looked to Macro. 'Time to go.'

Filling his lungs with the chilly air, Macro coughed before he gave the order. 'Detachment, advance!'

With the centurion at their head, the veterans marched out of the gate. There was no sign of the men who had been freed from the stable. Indeed, there was little sign of any life as they made their way past the huts. The main route through the village wound one way and then another. A movement on the periphery of his vision caused Macro to glance to his left, and he saw several men in cloaks moving parallel to the column before they disappeared behind a hut. He made to reach for the handle of his sword, and then thought better of it. If there was trouble, he would be able to draw the weapon quickly enough. To do so now would only make him look unduly nervous in front of the other veterans.

The route curved round another cluster of huts and the edge of the settlement lay ahead. But where the open country should have been, the way was blocked by a solid mass of tribesmen, some of whom wore armour and carried shields and the long swords favoured by the native warriors. They stood in silence a hundred paces away, shrouded in wisps of exhaled breath.

Macro glanced over his shoulder. 'Camp Prefect to the front!'

Ramirus trotted his horse to Macro's side and quickly surveyed the blocking force. 'I feared things were going too easily. There must be at least two hundred of them.'

'What are your orders, sir?'

'We keep going. Bluff it out like we did yesterday.'

Macro felt a drip of condensation tickle his nose, and he

sniffed. 'I don't think they're inclined to give way this time, sir.'

'No, but let's keep moving.'

The detachment cleared the village and approached the waiting natives at a steady pace. When they were no more than ten paces away, a figure stepped forward and raised his spear in an unmistakable gesture for the Romans to stop. It was the same tribesman who had blocked their path the day before and then supported the chief as he came out of the hut.

'Halt!' Ramirus ordered, and the men behind him took a half-pace and stopped. The camp prefect turned. 'Guide! To the front!'

Cardominus trotted forward warily.

'Tell that rascal to get that rabble out of our way.'

The guide translated the command, and at once the men behind the warrior shouted angrily and brandished their weapons until their leader turned to them and bellowed and they fell silent again. He turned back to the guide and gave his response.

'He says we are to release their chief, leave the valuables your soldiers stole from them and surrender your packs, weapons and horses. Do that and he will permit you to leave without any harm.'

Ramirus's eyebrows rose as he turned to Macro. 'The balls of this one!' But before he could reply to the warrior, Decianus spoke up from his position halfway along the column. His voice was shrill and angry and carried clearly in the cold air.

'How dare he? Tell him to get out of our way, or it'll be his chief who suffers.'

Cardominus translated haltingly, and the warrior raised his chin defiantly but made no effort to move. Instead he repeated his demand and added a further comment. The guide turned to

Decianus with a nervous expression. 'He says we must do as he says or he will kill us all.'

'Does he, by Jupiter, Best and Greatest.' The procurator's voice was filled with contempt, and he drew his sword. 'You tell him that unless he clears his rabble from our path, we'll deal with them the same way we deal with the rancid old stick he calls his chief.'

Edging his horse alongside the old man, Decianus raised the sword. He paused a beat, waiting for the warrior and his followers to disperse, and when there was no sign that they would do so, he gritted his teeth and plunged the blade down into the prisoner's neck, driving it deep into his torso.

The chief's jaw snapped open and he let out an astonished groan. Then his knees buckled and the blade came free with a sucking noise, blood pulsing from the wound. He writhed briefly on the ground before letting out one last gurgling sigh and then lying still amid the crimson spatters on the crisp white snow.

Macro felt the blood chill in his veins. 'What the fuck?' he muttered.

CHAPTER FIFTEEN

For an instant, both sides were frozen in shock. Macro was the first to react, throwing his marching yoke down before readying his shield and drawing his sword.

'Packs down! Close up!' he roared.

The veterans grunted as they dropped their yokes and raised their shields, swords ripped from their scabbards and held at the ready. Ramirus wheeled his mount round to confront the procurator. 'Why in bloody Hades did you do that?'

A sneer fixed on Decianus's face. 'They were never going to let us pass, you fool!'

The leader of the tribesmen let out a cry of anguish and anger that was picked up by his followers as they shook their weapons at the Romans. Then a war cry burst from the lips of a man directly in front of the detachment, and he charged forward, raising an axe above his head. He wore a simple tunic and brown leggings over soft leather sandals. His hair was held back off his face by a headband, so Macro could see the hatred and terrible anger straining his features.

Bracing his legs, Macro pushed his shield forward and readied his sword to strike. At the last moment, the native sidestepped him and swung his axe down with all his might onto the veteran to his left. The edge of the axe blade shattered the crest of the Roman's helmet and drove down through his skull almost to the jawline. The sides of the helmet burst outwards in an explosion of blood that sprayed those close by as the impact drove the veteran down onto his knees. A look of feral triumph was etched on the native's face as he gritted his teeth and worked the axe from side to side before it leaped free and the body collapsed onto the icy track.

Behind the warrior, his comrades let out a savage roar and charged the head of the small Roman column, weapons raised to strike, cloaks and furs swirling behind them.

Macro swivelled on the balls of his feet and threw his weight from the shoulder as he punched his short sword into the axeman's side, driving through his flesh and bursting through his ribs into his vitals. The impetus of the strike threw the man back, and he stumbled and fell, pulling himself free from the blade as he tumbled onto his back. There was no time to finish him off, and Macro lifted his shield and stepped nimbly back into the front rank of the detachment. The veterans closed up on either side, presenting an unbroken shield wall to their attackers. The Roman who had been felled by the axe spasmed once, twice and then went limp at Macro's feet just as the first of the natives slammed into the shields of the front rank.

Long years of training and campaigning had prepared the veterans to brace themselves, leaning forward slightly to absorb the blow of the charge and standing their ground before they punched their shields back into their enemy's faces and struck at their reeling foes with their swords, cutting cloth and piercing flesh. So wild was the charge and so eager were the natives to avenge their fallen chief that those following on pushed their helpless comrades onto the points of the waiting Roman swords. Macro felt his blade pierce soft tissue, and he thrust it home and twisted it from side to side before ripping it free and striking again quickly to complete the kill.

As he reset his feet, he glimpsed wild tattooed faces and flying locks of hair surging past on either flank as the head of the Roman column was swiftly enveloped by the shrieking tribesmen. The air around him filled with the rasps and grunts of those locked in combat as they pressed up against both sides of the shields and struggled to wield their weapons and find a gap through which to strike. The greatest danger to the Romans was the overhead blows of axemen, and so they tried their best to keep their shields up and heads down so that the hafts of the axes struck the metal trim and brought the strikes to a jarring halt.

The veterans had formed a tight box around the five horsemen and the native guide. Cardominus had drawn his long sword and raised it to strike any of the natives who managed to break through the shield wall, but for the moment the Romans held their ground as the enemy surged round and surrounded the detachment. A quick glance over his shoulder showed Macro that another veteran had been struck down and dragged into the interior of the formation. Ramirus dropped to the ground and drew his sword as he snatched up the fallen man's shield and made ready to fill the first gap in the line. Behind him, Decianus glanced round anxiously.

'We'll ride for help!' he called. 'Stand aside there!' He slapped the flat of his sword on the shoulder of the nearest veteran and kicked his heels in to make the horse push the man aside. 'Escort! Follow me!'

As he forced his way out of the formation, the natives scattered before the snorting mount and the Roman wielding his sword wildly. His men followed him, cutting to right and left with their longer swords. The first three quickly broke free of the skirmish and galloped off behind the procurator, but the last man was too slow and fell victim to the natives, who had swiftly recovered from the shock of the mounted men charging through their ranks. One of the tribesmen levelled a sturdy spear and thrust it into the horse's throat. The beast reared in agony and its rider desperately fought to stay in his saddle, but he was grabbed by the sleeve of his tunic and hauled off onto the ground. Instantly the natives swarmed over him, hacking at his body with their swords and axes while spearmen buried the points of their weapons in his torso.

The three survivors galloped after Decianus, pursued for a short distance by a score of the natives before the latter gave up and shouted insults at the fleeing Romans. Only when they were a safe distance from the action did the procurator and his men rein in briefly, surveying the scene before they rode off over a low rise and out of sight.

Ramirus moved through the narrow formation. 'Macro! On me!'

'Get ready to close the gap,' Macro ordered the men on either side. He stabbed out with his sword and slammed his shield into the warrior to his front, driving the man back onto his comrades. Another stab found its target and tore a shallow wound in the man's thigh. Macro quickly withdrew two paces and the veterans edged together.

'Seems like our procurator has a jellyfish for a spine,' Ramirus said bitterly. 'If we get out of this, I'll be sure to pay him a little visit in Londinium.'

'I might just join you for that,' Macro replied. 'But right now we have a more immediate problem.'

Both men glanced round as they weighed up the situation. There were three wounded men sitting on the ground inside the formation and a second man lying dead, his face smashed to a bloody pulp by a spear thrust. One of the wounded had been handed the reins of Ramirus's mount to keep the beast under control. The other veterans were holding their own behind the shield wall, keeping their shields up and only striking their swords at viable targets, as they had been trained to do many years earlier. The losses on the other side were far heavier, Macro noted. Through brief gaps between the shields he could see the native dead and dying surrounding the Roman formation. A thirst for revenge and raw courage were no match for good equipment and the finest military training in the known world, and the proof of that lay on the bloodstained snow beyond the shields.

'They won't keep this up for long,' Ramirus decided.

'No. But they won't be willing to let us escape. They'll harass us all the way back to the outpost and maybe beyond.'

Ramirus nodded. 'I fear so.'

The fighting around them began to slacken as the natives drew back one by one, chests heaving from their exertions and flecked with the gore of their fallen comrades. Then, seemingly all at once, the fighting was over and a gap of some ten paces opened up between the two sides. The air was filled with swirls of exhaled breath and the steam curling up from the sweat of hot bodies.

Ramirus detailed three men to help the wounded, and then gave the order to continue advancing along the track with their shields raised. As he called the time, loudly enough to be heard above the jeers and angry cries of the natives, the veterans trudged forward, watching their opponents warily over the rims of their shields. Macro resumed his position at the head of the formation. He had conducted such withdrawals a few times during his years in the army and well knew how exhausting they were. The effort of keeping shields to hand and the constant vigilance, interspersed with fighting off frequent attacks, wore men down as much as any pitched battle. More troubling was the slow pace that such a situation imposed on the Romans. A fully laden legionary could easily cover fifteen to twenty miles a day, but a man – even only carrying his armour and weapons – forced to march in close step, making sure that the integrity of the formation was maintained, would manage barely half that pace. Some ground could be made up if the enemy held back a sufficient distance for the Romans to open up into marching order, but they would be fortunate to reach the greater safety of the outpost before sunset. At night their progress would be far slower as they struggled to keep heading in the right direction, and the initiative would pass fully to their pursuers, who would be able to prepare surprise attacks under the cover of darkness.

From the grim expressions on the faces of the men closest to him, Macro knew that they too had grasped the danger they were in. What had begun as a routine punitive expedition two days earlier had now turned into a struggle to survive, and the odds against the veterans were not encouraging. As long as they had the strength to keep up with their comrades and sufficient numbers to maintain the formation, they had a decent chance of making it out alive. That was the hope they must hold on to.

'Chins up and keep in pace, lads!' he called out calmly. 'Let's show those barbarian bastards what proper soldiers look like!'

The fifty men of the detachment slowly progressed away from the settlement, leaving their loot and marching yokes behind them. Seeing the chance to retrieve their possessions and return the favour to the Romans by looting their abandoned yokes, more than half of the natives immediately rushed forward to pick over the spoils. A few of the veterans glanced back and hesitated at the prospect of losing prized items of kit, before they were nudged on by the men beside them. The more stalwart of the natives stood with their leader as he shouted angrily at those who had broken away. He had been left with too few to continue the fight, and Ramirus grasped the opportunity at once. 'Marching order! Advance!'

The veterans let their shields drop as they sheathed their swords, many running with blood, and shifted into a column of two, with the wounded and the horse taking their place halfway along the formation. With Ramirus occasionally calling the time, they stepped out along the track, whose course was barely discernible beneath the smooth folds of freshly fallen snow. Looking back, Macro could see some of the tribesmen scurrying back towards the huts with their loot, even as their leader cajoled them to join the others waiting to give chase. Their lack of discipline was one of the reasons the Celts had nearly always fared badly against professional Roman soldiers. Whether it was looting or taking heads, Celtic warriors could not resist a hunt for trophies as proof of their exploits, putting posterity above the needs of the moment. So much the better for Rome.

In line of march, the detachment was able to increase the pace considerably. They reached the rise where they had last seen Decianus, and saw that the procurator and his escort were already a couple of miles ahead, a group of barely discernible specks against the snow. A moment later they entered a forest and were lost to sight. Macro felt a surge of anger at the man's cowardice in abandoning his comrades. It was a long time since Decianus had served in the army, and now he was just another minor aristocrat on the make, filled with a sense of entitlement and judging those beneath him to be an expendable resource. If ever Macro and Ramirus cornered the procurator, they would give the coward the hiding he deserved, whatever the consequences.

They marched on, covering another mile before they caught sight of the first of their pursuers. Macro was puzzled by the natives' delay in chasing down the detachment, but as they drew closer, he saw that some of them had fetched bows from their huts, as well as light hunting javelins. With their leader urging them on, they swiftly closed up on the rear of the column, snow spraying from their heels as they came on at a steady trot. When they were no more than fifty paces behind, the leader swung his spear out to the side and the tribesmen swerved to the left of the compacted snow in the wake of the Romans. Plunging through the deeper undisturbed drifts alongside the track, they gradually drew level with the marching veterans.

Seeing the danger of letting the enemy get between the detachment and the outpost, Ramirus increased the pace of his men to a quick march. Macro felt his heart beating faster under the strain, and he breathed heavily as he strode on through the calf-deep snow. For another half-mile the two forces advanced neck and neck, shouting the occasional insult at each other.

'Save your breath!' Ramirus bellowed. 'No more calling out!'

As they neared the forest, it was clear that the veterans were going to reach the narrow mouth of the track passing through the trees first, and the native leader halted his men and snapped out a brief series of orders in a rasping voice. Macro saw some of the tribesmen string their bows.

'Beware arrows!' he shouted in warning. 'Raise shields!'

The weary veterans lifted the cumbersome shields and angled them towards the threat as they continued at the same pace, drawing ahead of their enemy. Macro could not help a grim smile at the leader's miscalculation in going to the left of the detachment. Had he gone to the right, the Romans would have been forced to waste a moment shifting their shields to their sword arms. A quick volley, followed by a charge, would have forced them to stop and fight. As it was, the first arrows to reach the column glanced harmlessly off the broad curved shields. Most of the shots, loosed in haste by men struggling to recover their breath, passed over the Romans or dropped short. There was a sharp whinny from the horse as an arrow struck its rump close to the tail. The beast reared up, then lashed out with its hind legs as the closest men scurried out of range.

'Drive it out!' Ramirus shouted. 'Now, for fuck's sake!'

One of the men darted forward and struck the horse on the hindquarter with the flat of his sword. It lurched forward, and the men opened ranks, allowing the animal through the gap, snow bursting into the air around its hooves as it bucked and kicked in pained torment. As it approached the tribesmen, they ceased shooting and leaped aside to avoid being trampled.

The greater danger to the Romans now made itself apparent, as several tribesmen carrying hunting javelins closed in and took careful aim before releasing the deadly shafts with their barbed iron tips. The heavy missiles struck home with a far more forceful impact, splintering the surface of shields so that the points burst through to the other side. Those that glanced off presented just as much danger; one of the veterans close to Macro, less nimble than his companions, was struck in the shin, the javelin slicing through his long breeches then striking bone before its energy was spent. He stopped abruptly as he clenched his teeth together to bite off his cry of pain.

'Halt!' Macro ordered before those following ploughed into the wounded man. He dropped back and grounded his shield before kneeling beside the casualty.

'Macro! What the fuck are you doing?' Ramirus shouted angrily as he came storming forward. Then he saw the spear shaft dangling from the man's leg. 'Shit. Deal with it quickly and then get the men moving again.'

Macro nodded as he inspected the wound. The calf bulged where the head of the spear had not broken through the flesh. He clicked his tongue, knowing what he must do. He had been wounded by a barbed arrow some years before, and recalled the procedure the surgeon had used. There was no way to extract the head through the entry wound without causing even more damage and loss of blood. The surgeon had had access to equipment and was able to extract the arrowhead in the calm of the fort's hospital. Macro had no such luxury. He drew his dagger and held it up to the veteran.

'Laenas, isn't it?'

The man nodded.

'This is going to hurt, but it's the only way. Ramirus, hold the shaft still close to the entry wound.'

The camp prefect grasped the slender length of wood as Macro sawed through it. Laenas tilted his head back and shut his eyes, a keening cry straining his throat. Around them arrows and javelins continued to strike home. As soon as he had cut through the shaft, Macro glanced up. 'Brace yourself, brother. On three.'

Laenas nodded.

'One . . .' Macro thrust the remaining length of the shaft into the wound. The barbed head burst from the calf, blood pouring out with it. He pushed until the barb had cleared the flesh, and then quickly hooked the blade of his dagger behind it and drew the short length of wood through the wound and out the other side. He let the blood-slicked shaft drop onto the snow as he reached up with his spare hand. 'Give me your neck cloth!'

Laenas did as he was told, and Macro tied the cloth tightly around the veteran's leg. 'That's the best I can do until we reach the outpost.'

Ramirus looked at the dressing doubtfully. 'Can you stand?' he asked Laenas.

The veteran tested his weight and his eyes rolled up in agony. But he glanced at his superior and nodded. 'I'll do my best to keep up, sir.'

'You'd better. I'm not going to lose any more men.' Ramirus turned to Macro. 'Get back to the head of the column and give the order to move off. I'll take care of Laenas.'

Picking up his shield, Macro edged his way forward, wiping the blood from his hand on the hem of his tunic. 'Detachment! At marching pace, advance!'

The column moved forward again and gained the edge of the forest. The enemy kept pace with them, but the barrage of missiles slackened as they exhausted their supply of javelins and arrows. As the bare trees and undergrowth closed in on either side, Macro felt safe enough to lower his shield. He stepped to one side of the track and waved the men on before he sought out Ramirus.

'If you keep the men moving, sir, I'll take charge of the rearguard.'

'Very good.' The camp prefect nodded.

Ramirus handed Laenas over to another of the veterans and strode to the front of the column. Macro waited for the other men to pass before he fell into step at the rear as the last of the veterans entered the forest. Behind them the track was clearly marked by the snow packed down under their boots. The dark shafts of arrows and javelins rose from the ground at a variety of angles. Already the tribesmen were rushing forward to salvage their undamaged missiles. That would delay them for a short time, Macro reflected. Long enough for the detachment to get some distance ahead. The trees on either side would afford some protection from the enemy's arrows, and the narrowness of the track would limit the front on which they could attack. He thought back to the previous day when the column had passed through the forest. There was perhaps three or four miles of woodland before they reached the far side, and then another six or seven miles to the outpost. Mostly open country with few choke points to help the veterans. From the far side of the wood they would be subject to bombardment and harassing attacks almost all the way to the outpost. Until then, though, they would be safe enough, and could use the opportunity to keep the pace up and buy the time they desperately needed to reach safety.

Macro took a last glance at the enemy, still retrieving their missiles, then turned and broke into an easy trot to catch up with the rear of the column.

CHAPTER SIXTEEN

'It's no good, sir, I can't go any further on this leg,' Laenas explained to Ramirus and Macro, wincing as he finished speaking.

Ramirus sighed in frustration. 'You're going to have to keep going. We can't stop.'

'I know that, sir, but look . . .' Laenas gestured towards the dressing Macro had tied around the wound. The cloth was drenched and his lower leg was streaked with vivid courses of blood. 'I haven't the strength to go on, sir.'

'Yes, you bloody well have!'

Laenas shook his head.

'We'll get you out of here. I swear I will not be the one to tell your missus we left you to die when we return to Camulodunum.'

'I don't envy you that job.'

They shared a brief smile, and Macro grasped the close ties enjoyed by the veterans and their families at the colony.

Laenas lowered his voice as he continued. 'The other men are tiring already. If they have to carry me, they'll be done in. You'll only be condemning them to share my fate, sir. Let me stay here. I'll buy you a little time at least. And I'll go out standing on my feet while I still can.'

Ramirus hesitated, and Macro saw the pained expression on his face as he made ready to protest. Then his shoulders slumped fractionally and he reached out a hand. The two men clasped forearms.

'Farewell, brother. I'll see you again in the shades of the Underworld.'

'First round is on you, sir. You owe me one for this.'

'It'll be an honour, brother.' Ramirus nodded and turned to catch up with the others, striding along the narrow track.

Laenas looked at Macro. 'Just wish I'd had time to get to know you better, Centurion. I served in the Second Legion for a few years at the end of my enlistment. It was after your time, but they still spoke about you.'

'Not too badly, I trust.'

Laenas chuckled, then his face creased in agony for an instant before he continued. 'You were something of a legend to the lads who knew you. It's a pity for both of us that this moment is all we will ever share.'

Macro felt a slight tightening of his dry throat. 'Well, I won't forget you, brother. Now show those barbarian cunts what the men of the Second are made of.'

'Trust me, I will.'

Macro patted him gently on the shoulder and marched away. As he rejoined his comrades, he glanced back and saw that Laenas had taken up a position in the middle of the narrow track. He had set his shield down and was leaning on the trim as he favoured his injured leg. His sword was in his hand and he tapped it against the trim in a light, easy rhythm as he waited for the enemy to appear. Macro resolved to make an offering to Jupiter in the man's name when he returned to Camulodunum, in the hope that Laenas was accorded the honour due to a hero of Rome when he joined his ancestors in the Underworld.

Then he caught himself and smiled. *When* he returned to Camulodunum. Not if.

'That's the spirit, Macro my lad,' he muttered to himself.

The track curved around the edge of some marshy pools now covered with ice and snow pierced by the dark tracery of bare undergrowth. Laenas was lost from sight and Macro briefly pictured him standing alone, waiting for his end, before he turned his attention to the veterans ahead of him.

'Pick up the pace, damn you! Look at those bloody gaps. Move yourselves!'

The men marched on in silence, accompanied by the chink of loose equipment, the crunch of snow and ice underfoot and the sound of laboured breathing. The quiet was broken now and again by Macro and Ramirus as they urged the veterans on. A quarter of a mile or so after they had parted from Laenas, Macro thought he heard a shout, and paused a moment to look back, straining his ears. A faint chorus of cries, the faintest clink of metal on metal and the thud of a blow landing on a shield. The distant sounds carried clearly on the crisp air for a few heartbeats before there was a ragged cheer of triumph, and then quiet.

'Farewell, Brother Laenas.'

All morning the sky had been clearing, and by noon, as far as Macro could estimate the time, there was not a cloud in the sky and the sun shone brightly to the south. They had emerged from the forest and the landscape opened up around them. Ahead of them lay the hoofprints of Decianus and his escort, a constant reminder of the procurator's cowardly betrayal. They passed a native farmstead not a hundred paces from the track. Smoke rose from the opening at the top of the hut, and a man in furs scooped up a pair of young children and disappeared inside as the Romans marched past. Macro considered setting fire to the farm to provide a warning signal to the outpost, but decided that it would delay the detachment for too long. Besides, Decianus and his men would have reached the outpost by now and raised the alarm. There would be no benefit in depriving the farmer and his family of their shelter.

At that moment, he saw their pursuers again, hurrying along the track behind them as they emerged from the forest. They had not closed the distance as quickly as Macro had expected given the heavier kit of the Romans. But the veterans were used to forced marches, having trained for them regularly during their time in the army, and the tribesmen were mostly farmers. The handful of warriors amongst them were hardened fighters to be sure, and man for man as courageous as any legionary, but their raw physical strength was easily matched by the tough stamina of the veterans. Already there were noticeably fewer of them in the vanguard, and the stragglers stretched out behind them. The longer the Romans could keep up the pace, the better the odds if it came to a fight, Macro calculated.

As the tribesmen drew closer, two men separated from the group and trotted across the snow to the farmstead. When the farmer emerged, there was a brief exchange as the two men gestured towards the fleeing Romans. The farmer briefly ducked back into his hut before reappearing with a shield and spear, and the three ran to join the band pursuing the veterans. The sympathy for the farmer and his family that Macro had felt shortly before evaporated in an instant, and he wished there had been time to torch the farm after all. It was a harsh thought, but when the prospect of death hovered close at hand, there was little kindness to be spared for those who chose to be his enemy.

'Get up! On your feet, you fool!'

Macro was snapped out of his thoughts, and he looked up to

see Ramirus standing over a man who had sunk to his knees beside the track, his chest rising and falling as he gasped for breath. The small column kept moving, the men pacing past their exhausted comrade glancing at him with pity in their eyes.

Ramirus grabbed the man's wrist and tried to haul him to his feet, but without success. He released his grip and slapped him on the cheek guard of his helmet. A light blow, but one hard enough to sharpen his weary senses.

'Stay here and you will die.'

The veteran gritted his teeth and struggled to his feet, raising his shield and stumbling into position near the rear of the column. Macro could hear the dry rasp of his rapid breathing and the soft moan as he took each step. He endured another mile before he tripped over some object in the snow and fell, sprawling in a drift beside the track, his shield landing close beside him. One of his comrades fell out to help him.

'Leave him!' Macro snarled through dry lips. 'He's done for. Keep going.'

The veteran hesitated, then did as he was ordered. Macro, holding up the rear of the formation, was the last to pass the stricken man, and he hissed one word as he trudged by.

'Fool.'

The man was propped up on his elbow, his cloak and armour plastered with powdery snow. He regarded Macro with an utterly resigned expression and responded in a flat tone. 'So it goes, brother.' Then, with a soft exhalation, he sank back into the drift and stared up at the sky.

The veterans marched on with leaden feet, their limbs aching with exhaustion. Macro looked around, searching for a familiar landmark that would allow him to calculate the distance to the outpost. He knew it could not be more than five miles away by now; no more than two hours at their current pace.

They should reach it well before sunset. Not so far then, he encouraged himself. The gradient of the track increased as they climbed a low ridge. Looking back from the crest, he saw the tribesmen reach the soldier lying in the snow. He did not make any effort to resist, and their leader barely paused as he thrust his spear into his enemy's throat and continued the laborious chase.

On the far slope of the ridge, Macro lost sight of the tribesmen, and when they reappeared on the crest, he saw them break into two groups. The leader and eighty or so of his men hurried after the Romans, while the rest followed more slowly. As before, the leader angled away from the track in order to bypass the Romans, but this time no attempt was made to bombard the column with arrows and javelins. Instead the group pulled in front, then headed back onto the track and steadily increased their lead.

It was obvious to Macro what their intention was. The first group would find favourable ground to block the advance of the Romans, while the tribesmen following up would attack from the rear. There was nothing Ramirus could do about it, short of abandoning the track and attempting to find a different route to the outpost. That risked blundering around the winter landscape as night drew in. The men were already exhausted and cold, and such a measure might deal a fatal blow to their sinking morale. It was better to stick to the track and attempt to fight their way through. The tribesmen would be just as weary, and the force that had marched ahead of the column were lightly armed and could be beaten off before the second group reached the scene. Despite his growing exhaustion, Macro began to believe the worst was now behind them and safety was within their grasp.

As they gained one painful mile after another, the sun slowly slipped towards the horizon. Then there was a shout from the front of the column.

'The outpost, sir! I can see the tower.'

Macro increased his stride and made his way to Ramirus's side at the front of the column. Sure enough, the watchtower was outlined against the sky, and a moment later they could make out the surrounding palisade, no more than two miles away now.

'Almost there.' Ramirus grinned. 'One last effort, boys!'

They marched on another mile before someone attempted to sing the opening lines of a popular crude marching song. A handful of others joined in before the first man dissolved into a coughing fit.

'Call that singing?' Macro scoffed, desperate to raise their spirits now that safety was so close. He picked up from where the man had stopped, belting out the lyrics in his tuneless barrack-ground voice as he leaned forward and planted one foot in front of the other, following the tracks left by the tribesmen.

'. . . and for a silver sestertius a day,
Did Messalina every man in Rome lay.
Senators, equites and plebs too,
Paid their coin and joined the queue.
Every man in Rome, down to the last runt—'

'Sir! Look there!'

The words of the song died in Macro's throat as he looked up. Ahead of them the track passed between another expanse of frozen marshland and a wood composed of fir trees before it turned towards the outpost, now no more than a mile away. In the fading light of the winter afternoon, Macro could see the makeshift barricade of hewn branches, trunks of small trees and thickets of gorse that stretched across the narrow strip of open ground between the woodland and the marsh. Behind it stood the enemy, jeering and shouting challenges as they caught sight of the approaching Romans.

Ramirus raised his spare hand and gave the order to halt.

'Oh shit,' panted a man close behind Macro. 'Now we're fucked.'

The camp prefect turned to look at his men as they lowered their shields, some of them resting their forearms on the trim as they caught their breath.

'Macro, with me,' Ramirus said quietly. He led the way forward until they were out of earshot, then stopped and surveyed the enemy's position. 'We're going to have to fight our way through, and quickly, before the rest of those bastards catch up.'

Macro nodded and cleared his throat. 'Best not wait a moment longer then. Give the men something to do before their spirits sink any lower.'

'Quite.' Ramirus clicked his tongue and turned to the veterans. 'One last obstacle between us and the outpost. Shouldn't take much effort to push it aside. Close up and draw swords. Wounded to the rear. The rest in five ranks.'

The men moved slowly into place and Macro knew this would be the last effort that could be asked of them. They were done in, but it was fight or die and the outcome depended on them bringing the guts and determination of their years in the army to this last fight. He could already see the tribesmen coming into view over a low rise less than half a mile behind.

'Shields up!' Ramirus barked. Macro dropped back into the first rank and adjusted his grip on his shield and sword before the camp prefect continued. 'At the command . . . advance!'

The first line moved forward over the disturbed snow of the track, making for the centre of the barricade. The four remaining lines followed at intervals to avoid any bunching up. Each man held his shield raised, blade resting against the side, point towards the enemy. The only sound from the Roman ranks was the soft crunch of snow underfoot and the heavy breathing of the most exhausted amongst them. As the marsh and trees loomed on either side, they were forced to close up to fit the width of the track. A dark shaft leaped up from behind the men lining the barricade, then another.

'Arrows!' Macro shouted in warning.

Without slowing down, the men lifted their shields still higher and angled them to deflect the missiles. The first few fell short, and then, as the Roman lines came within range, one struck the boss of a shield with a piercing clatter. More followed in a steady barrage as the gap shrank. Twenty-five paces out, the first of the javelins inscribed a shallow arc and punched low through the shield of the man to the right of Macro. At once he hacked at the slender shaft before using the pommel of his sword to batter the stump back through the splintered entry hole.

They were close enough now for Macro to make out the savage expressions of the men waiting for them beyond the barricade. The air was filled with their insults and war cries.

Ramirus began to beat his sword against the side of his shield to the rhythm of their pace, and Macro joined in, followed swiftly by the other men, until a loud metallic rattle rose to challenge the din of the enemy. The noise, together with the sight of the wall of shields approaching, unnerved some of the tribesmen, and they ceased shouting and eyed the Romans anxiously. There was an explosive gasp from the rear as one of the wounded was struck high in the chest by a javelin, the point punching through his collarbone and bursting out through the back of his neck. He staggered to the side and went down on his knees, fighting for breath with a gurgling noise as blood filled his throat and began to drown him.

The missile barrage died down as the last of the retrieved arrows and javelins was used up. Ten paces from the barricade, Macro could see just how flimsy a defence it was, given the rushed effort that had been forced on the enemy.

'Sheathe your sword, Macro. We'll need to pull that apart.'

Keeping their shields up, the officers attempted to start pulling the barricade apart. On either side the veterans warded off the points of spears thrust at them over the makeshift defences. The advantage was with the enemy, as the Roman swords were too short to reach the tribesmen. The rear lines of the detachment had halted, waiting to take the place of any casualties at the front.

The first trimmed length of a fir tree came away and was manhandled to the side of the track while Macro and Ramirus began to wrestle with one of the smaller branches. Grunting and cursing, they managed to free it, then Ramirus paused and looked at Macro.

'This is taking too long. We need to work round the flank.'

'Left or right?'

He glanced towards the marsh. 'I don't know if the ice will hold.'

Macro nodded. 'To the right then. I'll take ten of the men.'

'Be quick about it.'

The last comment was uncalled for, but Macro realised it was an unguarded moment that revealed just how desperate his superior thought the situation had become. He pulled back and called on the men from the rear of the formation.

'We're going to cut our way round to the right, lads. On me!'

He plunged in amongst the trees and quickly came up against a mixture of gorse and brambles. He started slashing at the obstacles, trampling them down and doing his best to ignore the thorns and spikes that snagged his clothing and tore at his exposed skin. The other veterans of his squad joined in on either side. They had not cut their way more than ten feet into the thicket when the enemy realised their intention. Their leader drew back and hurriedly shouted an order, and a group of tribesmen surged forward and began hacking their way towards the Romans.

'Bloody fools!' Macro chuckled. 'Don't they realise they're doing our job for us? If it's a fight they want, then we are the boys for it. Right, lads?' His men gave a ragged cheer and renewed their efforts.

With a series of vigorous slashes, Macro cleared the last tangle between him and the enemy and then stamped it down before moving into the gap, ready to battle the first native who dared to test his courage. There was no shortage of contenders; at once, two men with axes and bucklers surged forward.

Then there was a bellow of indignation and they were shouldered aside by a heavily muscled man wearing a thin cloak over long leather breeches. In his right hand he wielded a long sword with a handle fashioned to look like a man with splayed arms and legs. His hair was arranged in two dark plaits, with a third taking care of his straggly beard. His eyes blazed with hatred and excitement as his mouth opened wide to roar his battle cry. All this Macro took in within a heart-beat as he went into a slight crouch to ready his balance and lifted his right arm fractionally so that his sword was able to move freely.

The warrior wasted no time in sizing up his opponent, the undergrowth crackling beneath his hide boots as he swung his sword in a gleaming arc at neck height. Despite the ferocity of the attack, it was easy enough for Macro to counter. He raised his shield, twisting the handle slightly to adjust the angle so that the blow glanced off it. With a loud thud, the blade swept over his head in a blur, and Macro twisted as he instinctively punched his sword forward to where his opponent's torso should be. He felt the point make contact, but the warrior was already stepping away and recovering his own sword for another attack. Only a flesh wound, Macro cursed, as he marvelled at the man's speed on his feet, despite his size. The long sword whirled over his head and came round again, diagonally this time. Macro's reactions were marginally slower than his opponent's, and there was no time for any clever play with his shield as he thrust it out to take the blow. With a shattering crash, the sword cleaved the trim in two and cut almost six inches into the shield itself, almost far enough for the end of the blade to connect with the top of Macro's helmet. He even felt the sigh of air on the bridge of his nose from the sword's passage.

The fates had spared him by the span of an inch, and now the initiative was with Macro. Before the warrior could wrench the blade free, the centurion thrust the shield out to one side, threatening to tear the sword from his opponent's hand. With a hissed curse, the native clung on. That was his fatal mistake. He lost his balance just enough to prevent any nimble footwork, and Macro lunged forward and threw his weight behind a thrust to the warrior's throat, cutting deep into the soft tissue under his chin and severing the blood vessels there. He felt the slight jar as the point grated into the base of the skull, then twisted the blade both ways before tearing it free amid the spurt and spray of blood from the gaping wound.

For a beat the warrior seemed impervious to the mortal injury, taking a step to the right in order to recover his poise and return to the attack. It was only as he made to bellow another war cry but choked on a gush of blood instead that he realised he was dying. The look of rage on his face instantly switched to one of utter surprise.

Even dying men could be killers, and Macro did not give him the chance to prove the adage. He slammed his shield into the warrior's chest and knocked him back into the roughly trampled brambles, the long sword dropping. Then he sheathed his own sword and stooped to pick up the warrior's weapon. It was heavier and more unwieldy than a gladius, but for the same reasons it was perfectly suited to his needs, and he made short work of the twisted bundles of brambles between him and the far side of the barricade. The two tribesmen who had been pushed aside by the dying warrior now regarded Macro with fear and awe, and he brandished the sword in their faces as he bellowed, 'Gerrout of my fucking way!'

They backed off, snagging against the thorns, then turned to flee, almost heedless of the scratches they suffered to get away from the wild Roman who had defeated their champion. Macro glared round at the other tribesmen, but none seemed keen to challenge him, and he waved the other men of his squad forward.

'Keep going, lads. Cut us a path through this thicket and the fight is ours.'

The veterans went to work with a fresh will, slashing and hacking at the undergrowth and fighting off the more courageous of their lightly armed opponents who attempted darting attacks. Soon, only a thin screen of brambles remained between the Romans and the men defending the barricade. Macro drew back momentarily to assess the handiwork of his party. A route ten feet wide had been cleared enough for more men to follow up.

'Ramirus! We're almost through!'

He heard the camp prefect order the rear lines to follow Macro, and they hurriedly picked their way through the trees and crushed undergrowth and cut their way through the remaining screen before attacking the tribesmen in the flank. As Macro emerged onto the track, he saw the first of the enemy turn and run away from the barricade. Those who stood their ground were faced with the ferocity of the reinvigorated Romans, out to wreak destruction in return for the arrows and javelins they had endured over the previous hours. As more Romans spilled out of the trees and brambles and charged home, some of the tribesmen realised that their escape route was cut off. The only choice left to them was to fight on or take their chances fleeing across the frozen marsh.

Indeed, as he cut down an axeman, Macro caught sight of one of the enemy scrambling through the frost-covered reeds on the other side of the track and running out across the smooth snow covering the ice. More turned away from the fight to follow him, while their leader raged at those who had deserted their position and urged the remainder to hold their ground. Ramirus and the men still with him had managed to open a gap in the barricade, and now passed through in single file to add their weight to the Roman onslaught.

Dusk was approaching and the sun was already low enough in the sky for the trees to cast long shadows. Attacked on two sides now, and with the prospect of being cut off from the track, the tribesmen backed towards the marsh, more of them melting away all the time, until only their leader and a small knot of men, no more than twenty in all, fought on.

'Finish them!' Ramirus shouted above the thud and clatter of blades and shields. 'Quickly!'

Macro glanced back across the barricade and saw the second group of tribesmen rushing along the track, desperate to join the skirmish and swing the advantage back to their side. Now that he was free of the brambles, he had no need for the long sword and no wish to return it to his enemy, so he turned and threw it as far as he could into the brambles, then drew his gladius once again and rushed towards the enemy leader. His way was blocked by a warrior carrying a large round shield and wielding a long spear in an overhand grip. The leaf-shaped head of the spear darted out and back, keeping Macro at bay. He used his own shield to block the strikes while he waited for a chance to charge inside the reach of the spear and attack the man with his gladius. Around him more Romans were attacking the remaining tribesmen, driving them towards the marsh.

At last the natives' nerve broke in the way that instantly transmitted itself amongst men on the losing side in a fight, and suddenly they were all fleeing for their lives. Macro's opponent made a last desperate thrust against the centurion's shield before he dropped the spear and turned to run.

The leader stood his ground to the end, teeth gritted in bitter frustration, before three veterans piled into him at once. He managed to parry the first blow before being sent reeling by a shield blow in his side, straight onto the sword of the Roman coming in from the other direction; then all three were stabbing at his body and face as he fell to his knees, arms raised in a futile attempt to protect his head. It was all over in a few heartbeats.

Before Macro could register any sense of triumph, there was a dull creaking rumble from the direction of the marsh, and then a sudden crackle of breaking ice accompanied by a shrill cry of terror. He saw three of the fleeing tribesmen drop as if their legs had been cut from beneath them, disappearing into the marsh until only their heads and frantically waving arms appeared above the snowy mantle. There were other cries of alarm as more of the ice gave way under the burden of the men attempting to flee across it. The lucky ones found themselves floundering waist deep in the stinking black water. The less fortunate sank into deeper stretches and desperately tried to claw their way out onto solid ice. Some managed it, but others, weighed down by heavy cloaks and furs, disappeared beneath the surface, leaving only a swirl amongst the jostling plates of shattered ice.

Some of the Romans were moving down from the track onto the edge of the swamp in hot pursuit of the fleeing enemy.

'Stay back!' Macro bellowed. 'Stay off the ice, you bloody fools!'

His voice carried clearly enough, and the veterans stopped and withdrew to solid ground, breathing hard, chests swelling and shrinking as they gulped at the cold air. Around them the track was littered with the bodies of the dead and wounded; mostly their enemies, but several Romans amongst them.

Ramirus was staring back across the barricade. The second group of tribesmen were no more than two hundred paces away, and had broken into a dead run now that their prey was close. 'Get the wounded up and get moving!' he shouted. 'Make for the outpost!'

The surviving members of the detachment quickly gathered up their injured comrades and abandoned the dead and dying before trotting off in a loose formation along the track in the direction of the outpost. The enemy who had fled the barricade scattered ahead of them. Macro could see at once that his comrades were too weary to reach the outpost before the relatively fresh group of tribesmen caught up with them.

He turned to Ramirus. 'We have to delay the enemy. Give me four men and then get out of here.'

Ramirus hesitated for an instant, then nodded and turned to join the others half running, half staggering along the track toward the outpost.

Macro turned to the remaining veterans and singled out the four he wanted before sending the rest on their way.

'Block the gap in the barricade,' he ordered, before setting down his shield and reaching into his sidebag. His fingers brushed aside the remains of the food Petronella had packed for him a few days earlier and found the small tinderbox that the more resourceful soldiers counted as an essential piece of their kit. The brambles and gorse that had been cut and trampled around the end of the barricade were dead, and he prayed they might be dry enough to burn easily. The dead pine branches that had been added to the barricade to thicken the defences should also combust readily.

Using his sword, he pulled together a small heap of twigs and limbs of pine and kneeled down beside them before carefully sliding the lid of the box open and setting it in place on the ground. Taking up the stone, he worked it steadily against the finely serrated length of iron, and in a moment, the first sparks darted onto the thin sheets of lightly charred linen. A tiny red glow appeared, followed by a wisp of smoke, and then the first flame spread across the linen. He needed a taper and some kindling, and looked around frantically. Spotting the plaits on the warrior he had killed earlier, he snatched up his sword and hurriedly sawed through the tightly woven lengths of hair, offering up the frayed ends to the tiny flame. The hair sizzled and smoked, emitting a foul odour, then the flame caught, assisted by whatever oil the warrior had worked into his hair.

Macro looked up and saw that the enemy were much closer. Coiling the plaits under the edge of the heap of kindling, he puffed gently. The flame flared and burned more fiercely, and with a crackle and hiss the fire spread swiftly to the sprigs of pine and dried undergrowth. Quickly Macro heaped more brambles and gorse onto the hungry flames, wincing as thorns tore at the palms of his hands. In the gathering dusk, the fire gleamed brilliantly and cast a red hue over the disturbed snow on the track. Snatching up his tinderbox, Macro snapped it shut and stuffed it back in his sidebag before retrieving his shield. Then he turned to the other men, who had done as much as they could to repair the barricade in the brief time available. 'Go!' They hurried off to catch up with their comrades.

The enemy were now no more than a hundred paces away. The flames were spreading quickly, eagerly consuming the dry vegetation, and the pine branches burned violently with a wild roar. The flames were starting to work their way along the barricade and spread into the edge of the forest. Already Macro could see the first of the enemy slow down as they approached the blaze. He raised an arm to protect his face from the withering heat, then, nodding to himself in satisfaction, he turned and trotted away.

He moved as fast as his exhausted, aching limbs allowed, pushing himself on as his lungs burned with the strain. Soon he caught up with the stragglers from the Roman detachment and cajoled them into picking up the pace as they drew closer to the outpost.

Some of the enemy who had earlier fled the barricade were now emboldened by the strung-out veterans and closed in to attack individual Romans, so that they were forced to fight a running battle up the rise to the crest of the hill upon which the outpost had been constructed. Looking back, Macro saw that almost the entire length of the barricade and the edge of the treeline were ablaze, casting a ruddy glow over the ground on either side. Dark figures were still struggling to extricate themselves from the marsh. Beyond the flames stood the second group of tribesmen, washed in the lurid firelight, their long shadows wavering across the snow behind them.

A sudden clatter of weapons from nearby caused him to snap round, and he saw two of the enemy attacking Ramirus a short distance further up the slope. Macro surged forward as one of the tribesmen grasped the rim of the camp prefect's shield and tore it aside so that his companion could thrust his spear at the Roman's unprotected chest. Ramirus gave an explosive gasp as he doubled up.

'Bastards!' Macro managed to roar as he charged forward. The man holding the spear was about to strike again, but turned instinctively towards the shout. Macro targeted him first, slamming his shield into his side and sending him flying into the snow, then turned to slash at the tribesman still holding Ramirus's shield in one hand and an axe in the other. The warrior let go of the rim and stepped back to evade the gladius before swinging his axe. Macro gave ground, and the axe head hissed harmlessly through the air. Then he charged forward before his opponent could make a back-swing cut and punched the guard of his raised sword into the man's face. He went down and lay sprawled in the snow, eyes rolling. Macro turned back to the first tribesman, who had sat up and was reaching for his spear. Stamping his boot down on the shaft, he pointed his sword at the man as he shuffled back in a panic.

'You. Fuck off out of it,' he panted.

No translation was needed, and the native scrambled to his feet and fled.

Macro turned to Ramirus. The camp prefect was fighting

for breath as he swayed on his knees, a hand clasped over his breast. There were still enemies on the slope and no time to waste. Macro dropped his shield and sheathed his sword, then lifted Ramirus to his feet and reached round him to grasp the belt on his far hip. Ramirus let out a groan and slipped his arm over Macro's shoulder, and they began to climb the last hundred yards towards the outpost. The gate had been opened, and Tibullus and his men had emerged to help the shattered veterans over the last stretch to safety.

Clenching his jaw, strained breath hissing through his gritted teeth, Macro staggered up the bare slope, half dragging his superior with him. There were only a handful of veterans ahead of them, and as they approached the fort, several of the tribesmen made a final rush to try to cut them off. A sharp order from Tibullus brought his men trotting forward, and the natives veered away, running a short distance before stopping to hurl insults.

'Here, sir. Let me help!' Tibullus supported Ramirus from the other side. In moments they were across the ditch, through the gate and into the safety of the outpost. As the last of the auxiliaries followed them inside, the gate was shut and secured by the locking bar.

Macro eased Ramirus down onto the ground and bent over, gasping for breath. Around him he could hear the groans and wheezes of the survivors of the detachment. He forced himself to straighten up and look round. The others were slumped about the interior of the palisade wearing shattered expressions. A few, the fittest of them, remained on their feet staring vacantly. Ramirus was sitting, propped up by the auxiliary kneeling beside him. Macro could see no sign of bleeding from any wound, and realised that the point of the spear had failed to pierce the camp prefect's mail cuirass. Even so, the blow had driven the air from his lungs and must have bruised or broken some ribs.

'How are you doing, sir?'

Ramirus glanced up and chuckled before his face creased in agony. He swallowed. 'Oh . . . just fucking fine,' he replied in a strained tone.

Macro forced a grim smile. 'I'll think twice before I accept another invitation to join you on any more little expeditions like this. I'm done in.'

Ramirus nodded, then reached up and grasped Macro's hand. 'Thank you, Macro. I owe you my life. Same as the other lads here. We won't forget it, brother.'

CHAPTER SEVENTEEN

'Any sign of them?' asked Ramirus as he struggled painfully onto the platform of the watchtower. He stood still for a moment, breathing gently as he clasped his bruised chest. Macro had effectively taken command the previous evening as the camp prefect had been incapable of moving at the time. After the gate had been closed, the enemy had felt emboldened enough to approach the outer ditch to hurl small rocks over the palisade, though a few javelins from the auxiliaries had caused them to scurry down the slope out of range.

As night fell, Macro had seen that the veterans were fed and the wounded treated before he organised the watches for the night. Tibullus took the first, while Macro settled in the tower room and fell instantly into a deep sleep, before being roused in the middle of the night. Since then he had been keeping watch over the surrounding landscape and doing the rounds of the palisade to ensure the sentries remained alert. Now, as dawn crept over the eastern horizon, he was still tired, and his muscles ached abominably.

'Nothing, sir. There was some movement during the night down by the fire, but that's all. Looks like they've slunk off back to their settlement.'

Both men looked down towards the blackened remains of

the barricade and the patch of woodland that had been burned to the ground during the night. Thin trails of smoke rising into the pale light showed where embers still smouldered. To the right there were dark expanses in the smooth snow covering the marsh where the ice had broken. There were very few bodies visible, and Macro assumed the tribesmen had retrieved as many of their fallen as they could find before they withdrew back along the track. Some of the remaining bodies were Roman, and they would need to be taken back to Camulodunum for their families to carry out the burial rites, once Macro and Ramirus were sure it was safe to leave the outpost.

Ramirus coughed lightly and asked the question that Macro had been expecting.

'What's the butcher's bill?'

'We lost one of the wounded during the night, so twelve dead all told. Eight wounded. One of those looks like he won't last long. Four missing. They'll probably be down there on the slope.'

Ramirus shook his head sorrowfully. 'Half the detachment were casualties then. Fuck. There'll be a lot of grieving widows and orphans when we get back to Camulodunum. That bastard Decianus has got a lot to answer for. Did Tibullus see him?'

'Yes. Four riders passed by the foot of the hill and then turned west.'

'West?' Ramirus frowned.

'My guess is that he feared the reception he was going to get at Camulodunum and decided to make for Londinium instead. Either way, he didn't see fit to tell Tibullus what had happened.'

'Bastard.'

'Quite so. He'll need dealing with later on. Right now, we have to get back to the colony.' Macro let his thoughts move on to the wider consequences of what had occurred. 'I imagine the governor is not going to be happy about this. There'll have to be a reckoning with the natives. They can't be allowed to get away with killing a tax collector and then attacking us. That's going to cause even more grief.'

'What do you mean?'

Macro rubbed his eyes, sore from the strain of keeping watch through the darkness. 'The governor will have to make an example. Most likely he'll execute the ringleaders and some of the elders of the tribe. He may even burn their settlement down. That will encourage other tribesmen to pay their taxes, but it's more than likely to stir up resentment and fire up those troublemakers who still haven't accepted that Britannia is part of the Empire.' He sighed heavily. 'The gods only know what this will lead to. If I were you, sir, I'd be thinking about getting the colony's senate to vote on improving the defences at Camulodunum. The place is wide open to attack at the moment.'

'I know. I'll see what can be done. But I doubt we're in any danger. There's a big difference between taking on a small detachment and the full strength of the veterans at the colony.'

'I hope you're right.'

There was a brief silence before Ramirus forced a grin. 'Anyway, I feel a bit safer knowing we have a man of your calibre joining us at Camulodunum.'

'Ah, that makes me feel all warm and woolly inside, sir.'

They shared a laugh, but then Ramirus's expression changed. 'I mean it. Your actions last night saved many lives, including mine.'

'That's what brothers in arms do. And before you get too used to my company, I should tell you that I'm intending to spend most of my time in Londinium, rather than the colony.'

'That's a pity. If you ever change your mind, you'll always

have comrades you can rely on in Camulodunum.'

'I appreciate that. Truly.' Macro turned to scan the surrounding country for any sign of the enemy, but all he could see were the smoke trails of distant farmsteads and a small group of men and women foraging for firewood. 'I think we should recover our dead, sir. If you'd give the order.'

It was a tacit surrendering of authority now that the camp prefect was able to resume command of what remained of the detachment. Ramirus looked at him for a moment before he nodded. 'Carry on then, Centurion Macro.'

They recovered three of their dead and searched an hour longer before giving up any hope of finding the last man. Meanwhile, stretchers had been improvised for the injured who could not walk or keep up with a marching pace. When the much-reduced column was ready to leave the outpost, Ramirus reassured Tibullus that those at the colony would be ready to march to his aid at once should he have cause to raise the alarm by lighting the signal beacon.

The cold weather of the previous month seemed to have broken, and the temperature was warm enough to start melting the snow. The surface of the track had been frozen hard when they had marched out to avenge the tax collector, but now the boots of the veterans churned it into a dirty slush as they made their way home. For the first few miles Macro kept a wary watch on his surroundings, but there was no cause for alarm. As they passed a farm shortly after midday, a farmer waved a greeting at them, and Macro responded in kind, relieved that they had passed into friendlier territory as they drew closer to Camulodunum. They had to take brief rest breaks every few miles to relieve the men burdened by the stretchers, and so they did not reach the colony until dusk.

Word of their approach went swiftly around the small community, and by the time they reached the gatehouse, a modest crowd had gathered. Most were curious onlookers, but the wives and sweethearts of the men who had marched out searched the ranks of weary soldiers for signs of their loved ones. There were cries of relief as women rushed forward to embrace their menfolk, and growing anxiety on the faces of those who scurried down the line then back again before they grasped the truth that their man would not return. Some cried silent tears of grief, while others sobbed inconsolably before they were gently led away by their friends.

Macro looked for Petronella but could see no sign of her anywhere in the crowd, nor amongst those watching proceedings from further off. With a growing sense of concern, he asked Ramirus for permission to be relieved and hurried off to the room they had been allocated in the headquarters building. The light was fading as he opened the door and peered into the dim space.

'Petronella?'

There was no response from the bed in the far corner, and now Macro began to feel the terrible ache of dread knotting his guts. He noticed that her best cloak had gone, as well as the closed-toe leather boots she preferred to wear. He hurried over to the colony's administration office and found a clerk still there, hunched over a large wax tablet as he etched figures onto the surface by the light of the thickly smoking tallow candle.

'You remember me? Centurion Macro? My wife and I arrived a few days ago.'

'Indeed, sir.'

'My wife is not in our quarters. Do you know where she is?'

'Yes, sir. Londinium.'

'Londinium? Why the hell has she headed back there? Did she leave a message for me?'

'Yes, sir. She said to tell you that she was needed urgently and that you were to follow her. A man with a cart came to fetch her. His name was Ven . . . Den . . .'

'Denubius?' Macro prompted.

'That's it. Yes, sir.'

'Did she say *why* she was needed urgently?'

'No, sir. But she said that you must follow her as soon as possible.'

'That's it?' Macro was starting to lose his patience. 'What else?'

The clerk thought a moment, then shook his head. 'That's all I can recall.'

Macro growled. 'Fat lot of fucking good you are. At least you can tell me when she left the colony.'

'The same morning the camp prefect led the detachment out.'

Four days then, thought Macro as he turned away and left the office. Four days. That meant she must have reached Londinium already. He suddenly felt very afraid for her. What if the emergency was something to do with Malvinus or one of the other gangs? What if they had attacked the inn? Or worse, done harm to his mother? And what if Petronella was now in similar danger. She had a tongue and a temper on her that might well get her into trouble, and he would not be there to protect her. The more he thought about it, the more agitated he became. Despite his terrible weariness, he resolved to set off at once. But first he needed a horse, and food and wine to sustain him.

Hurrying back outside, he found Ramirus trying to console a small group of weeping women. Some had children with them, too young to grasp the gravity of their loss, and they clung to their mothers, crying out of shock at the release of raw emotion on display.

'Ramirus, a word,' said Macro as he strode up.

'When I am finished here,' the camp prefect replied tersely.

'No, sir. I need to speak with you at once.' Macro hoped he would not have to stoop to reminding the other man of the debt he owed to him.

Ramirus gave a grunt and nodded before turning back to the women. He spoke gently. 'Forgive me. I'll only be a moment.'

The two men moved a short distance away and Ramirus glared at Macro. 'This had better be important. Those are the wives of men I called friends. Make it quick.'

Macro explained what the clerk had told him, and that he had resolved to start for Londinium that night, as soon as he could find a horse and rations.

'Even if I could get you a horse, it'll be dark before you can set off. You'd do better sleeping tonight and leaving at first light.'

'I have to go now,' Macro insisted. 'My wife or my mother, or both of them, could be in danger. They are the only family I have, sir. For pity's sake, help me.'

'All right. You can draw rations from the quartermaster's stores. As for a horse, I lost my best mount in yesterday's action. All I have left is a mare and her foal. But there are far better horses to be had at the imperial couriers' station. I'd try there. You'll find them in the stable yard behind the headquarters block.'

'Thanks, I'll do that.'

Ramirus gave him a sympathetic look. 'I hope the urgent situation you spoke of has already resolved itself. Good luck, brother.'

Macro nodded and hurried away, breaking into a trot as a rising sense of panic gripped him. Having helped himself to enough food for the journey and stuffed it into his sidebag, he made his way to the stable yard. The official in the red tunic of the courier service listened sympathetically, but when Macro had finished, he shook his head.

'Nothing doing, sir. The horses are for couriers and official messages only. I can't let you have one.'

Macro's first impulse was to grab the man by the throat and squeeze the life out of him until he relented. But that would be to incur the severest of penalties inflicted on those who abused the courier service. The least he could expect for the offence would be banishment from Britannia, and that would not help either Petronella or his mother. Then a thought struck him.

'Wait! You say the horses are for official messages.'

'That's right, sir.'

'Then I have an important message for the governor concerning the fate of the detachment. I'll be the one to make the report. So it's an official message. Now give me a bloody horse or I'll report you to your superiors. I'm sure they'll take a dim view of any man who causes such a message to be delayed.' Macro grasped the handle of his sword and half drew it with a menacing look. 'But that's nothing to what I might do to you.'

The official winced at the determined expression on the centurion's face, then nodded. 'Very well, sir. Come with me.'

He led the way into the stable reserved for the service and indicated a dark stallion in the stall nearest the arched doorway. 'He's the fastest. Take him. I'll give you a hand with the saddle and bridle, sir.'

Night had fallen by the time Macro was ready to leave. He climbed wearily into the saddle and took up the reins. The official handed him a small bronze plate with a length of chain running from each end.

'You'll need to wear this around your neck, sir. So that you can swap horses at the way station.'

Macro hurriedly slipped the chain over his head and nodded his thanks before tugging the reins round and walking the animal out of the courtyard and towards the road that led to Londinium. It was just possible to follow the route by the loom of the snow and the dull gleam of a crescent moon rising into the starlit heavens. It was difficult to resist the impulse to urge his mount to move faster, but it would be foolhardy to gallop in the darkness when the horse might easily stumble and fall. Better to wait until dawn to increase the pace.

After a mile or so, Macro turned in the saddle to look back at Camulodunum, which assumed the appearance of a dark stain against the dull snow. A handful of tiny flames – torches and braziers – flickered brightly like distant stars. It was seemingly peaceful from afar, but filled with lamentation this night, and he prayed that the violence of the last few days was not the harbinger of any wider conflict between the Romans at the colony and the surrounding tribes. There had been enough bloodshed over the last fifteen years, and the province desperately needed a period of peace to allow the Roman invaders and the natives to get used to living alongside one another.

However, Macro found that he was increasingly disturbed by the procurator's implication that there were many powerful people around Emperor Nero who were concerned by the amount of time and treasure the conquest of Britannia had already consumed. It seemed there was growing support for the notion of abandoning the new province, a prospect that filled Macro's heart with disgust. Far too many good men had died during the invasion and the campaigns that followed. If all they had fought for was cast aside, then their sacrifice would have been meaningless and there would be many back in Rome who would question the reliability of an emperor who was prepared to allow such a thing to happen.

As the horse followed the familiar route and Macro retreated inside his thoughts, he was tempted to close his aching eyes to rest them.

'Just for a moment,' he muttered to himself.

His heavy lids drooped and a warm comfort embraced him as his mind drifted aimlessly. He felt himself swaying, and woke just in time to stop himself toppling from the saddle. Then he was wide awake, cursing himself for committing the worst sin a soldier could be guilty of – falling asleep on the job. But even as he swore a silent oath to stay awake, he felt the appalling weariness steal over him again.

At length he could bear it no more. Dismounting and crossing to the side of the road, he bent down and scooped up a handful of snow, rubbing it on his face. The icy cold seemed to burn his skin even as it quickened his mind, and he applied a second handful. Feeling better for it, and more alert, he knew he must find a way to stop weariness creeping up on him once more, so decided to walk alongside the horse holding the reins. That way he could keep the leaden exhaustion at bay for a while at least. He forced himself to think about every step, counting each pace as he led the horse on into the bitter cold of the night. Every so often he would forget which number he had reached and had to start again. It was hard to keep his thoughts focused, and his mind wandered freely in between circling back to his anxiety about the reason for Petronella's sudden recall to Londinium.

Several hours after he had set off, a cold wind rose up. As it moaned and sighed through the bare branches of the trees growing alongside the road, Macro thought he heard voices from time to time and stopped to see if he was being followed. But of course there was nothing. Who else would be mad enough to be abroad at night in the depths of winter? As the wind strengthened, clouds closed in overhead and blotted out the stars and the moon, and light powdery crystals fell from the sky, whisked into his face as he plodded along beside the horse. Though it was cold, the constant motion kept his body warm, and regularly changing the reins between hands so that he could warm them alternately in his armpit kept his fingers from freezing.

At one point he passed within shouting distance of a farmstead and paused, tempted by the notion of seeking shelter until dawn. However, anyone roused from sleep by a stranger in the night might be tempted to stab him with a spear first and ask questions later, particularly in light of the trouble caused by the attack on the tax collector. So he trudged on, fighting off the urge to stop and sleep.

As dawn broke, he halted. Putting some oats into the horse's feed bag, he left it to eat as he climbed to the top of a hillock next to the road. From the crest, he squinted into the breeze and saw a handful of farms and a couple of villas in the distance, but nothing recognisable to help him gauge how far he had travelled. He made his way back to the horse, replaced the feed bag in the pannier and climbed back into the saddle with a strained groan.

'Come on, you brute. We've got ground to make up.'

He urged the animal into a canter and took the middle line down the barely visible contours that marked the road. As the sun rose, the breeze began to moderate, and fluffy ribbons of cloud scudded across a clear sky. Where the cloud was thickest, brief flurries of snow followed, but when the sun was out,

Macro basked in the little warmth it shed and began to feel reinvigorated.

He rode at a steady pace and reached the way station of the imperial courier service just before noon. Like many such places in the various backwaters of the Empire, it comprised a roadside inn with a small yard at the back for the use of the service. Macro slid from his mount and presented the badge on the chain around his neck, demanding a hot meal, a drink and a remount. There was only one other horse in the stable, a chestnut mare that looked inferior to his original mount, but at least it was fresh. Macro hurriedly gulped down some stew while the innkeeper who ran the way station saw to the saddling and provisioning of the mare.

He instructed the innkeeper to rouse him after a couple of hours, then curled up and fell asleep in front of the fire. He stirred as soon as the man touched his shoulder, and rose stiffly before making his way outside to mount his fresh horse. He was soon on his way again, his stomach full and his body warmed through by the inn's fireplace. Though the mare was a little skittish at first, it soon settled into a steady trot for mile after mile. The passage of wheeled traffic as well as many hooves and feet had compacted the snow and clearly marked the route. The going was easy and the mare proved to have far more stamina than Macro expected.

As dusk approached, the road ran along a low ridge for a few miles. Away to the west, Macro saw the late-afternoon sun gilding the broad ribbon of a river and the tracery of narrow waterways that fed into it. This, he was certain, was the great River Tamesis, upon whose banks the rapidly expanding town of Londinium was constructed. Not so far to go then, he encouraged himself.

The sun set, bathing the western horizon in a band of gold

that turned by stages to fiery red and then a velvet purple that would have graced the finest of the emperor's togas. The coming of dusk forced him to slow to a walk, and it was not until late in the night that he reached another gentle ridge and saw Londinium a few miles ahead, delineated by the flicker of torches and other fires lit to give warmth and illumination to the densely packed streets of the rapidly expanding town.

He followed the track along the edge of the town to where the governor's headquarters rose up, dominating the surrounding buildings. He presented his plaque at the gate leading into the compound before dismounting and entering the open area in front of the main structure. Handing his mount over to one of the native stable boys, he gave the report drafted by Ramirus to one of the clerks and then left to make his way to the Dog and Deer, anxious to find Petronella and discover the nature of the emergency she had alluded to before he allowed himself to sleep.

The streets were dark, occasionally lit by pools of light from cheap tallow candles still burning as they illuminated inn signs. Muffled figures and small groups of men were still abroad, and Macro regarded them cautiously as they passed by. With no local law enforcement on the lines of the urban cohorts of Rome, there was little to deter muggers and small bands of robbers, other than a watchful eye and a good sword.

As he approached the crossroads where the inn was situated, he slowed down and scrutinised the streets on either side, but there was no sign of anyone keeping a watch on the place. Slipping into a narrow alley between two shops, he made his way round to the yard at the rear of the inn and eased the gate open before pausing to listen. There was a commotion from the direction he had just come from as a pig started squealing and then abruptly stopped. He waited a moment longer, but there was no sound from the inn, and he crept across to the back door, his right hand closing round the handle of his sword. Despite his earlier tiredness, his mind was clear and his senses strained to pick up any sound, movement or even smell that might betoken danger.

Trying the latch, he managed to edge it up a short distance before it gave a soft squeak and would not move any further. He increased the pressure, but it was clearly fastened within.

'Shit,' he whispered softly, and ground his teeth for an instant before he accepted he had no choice but to announce his presence to whoever was within. Raising his hand, he lightly rapped his knuckles on the door three times, then waited for a response. His heart was beating faster and he felt the muscles in his limbs tense up, ready to act. There was no reply from inside, and he rapped again, louder this time. He heard the faintest sound of shuffling beyond the door before a woman's voice sounded in a coarse whisper.

'Who's there?'

'It's me.'

'Macro?' Then again, louder, 'Macro!'

A bolt rattled aside, and then the latch jumped as the locking pin was snatched out and the door swung inwards. Before Macro could react, a shape leaped from the darkness of the corridor beyond, and hands grasped the wool of the cloak covering his shoulders and pulled him close.

CHAPTER EIGHTEEN

'Oh, Macro!' Petronella sighed. Her lips clumsily grazed his stubble before finding his, and she kissed him hard before pulling back suddenly. 'Thanks be to Jupiter, Best and Greatest, that you are safe!'

She dragged him across the threshold before shutting the door and securing the latch. Inside it was not quite dark, and Macro could see the loom of a light from the kitchen door, outlining Petronella's body as she took his hand and led him to where the cooking fire still burned, warming the room and providing a rose-hued illumination. A sudden snorting from the far corner made him turn quickly and half draw his sword. Then he saw Denubius curled on his side on top of a sleeping mat. He wore a dressing around his head, and a sword lay on the floor beside him. Macro sighed and let his own blade slide back into the scabbard.

'What's happened, Petronella?'

She indicated the small table with a pair of stools at the far end of the room. 'Sit there.' Then she sat opposite and looked at him with a strained expression. 'They've taken your mother. And the boy.'

'They?'

'Those thugs. Malvinus's men. The day after we set off for

Camulodunum. Denubius said they came shortly after dawn, just as the inn opened for business. They demanded to know where you were. Your mother refused to tell them, so they beat it out of Denubius, the poor old sod. Then they took your mother and Parvus, and told Denubius to pass on a message to you.'

'Go on,' Macro urged.

'They said . . .' she paused to recall the details she had been told, 'they said that if you wanted to see her and the boy again, you'd better return from Camulodunum as swiftly as possible and meet Malvinus at the bathhouse the first morning after you get back. If you fail to do this, he'll make sure their bodies are discovered floating face down amongst the cargo ships using the wharf.'

'The fucking bastard,' Macro growled. Thoughts of the violence he would like to inflict on Malvinus flitted through his mind, each image more bloody and agonising than the one before. He pushed them aside as he spoke again in a furious undertone. 'What does he want with them?'

'What do you think? He offered you a job. He gave you ten days to accept and you ignored his deadline. You made him lose face, so he had them abducted after the tenth day had passed. This is his way of forcing you to beg him for their lives and a second chance to accept his terms. He needs to humble you and he knows that you'll do whatever he says to keep them alive. And if you turn him down again, he'll kill us all. Macro, I'm afraid.'

His tired mind thought over what she had told him. 'You're right to be afraid. I had hoped that Malvinus would not dare to harm a former centurion of the Praetorian Guard, but it seems I was wrong.'

She looked at him earnestly. 'What are you going to do?'

'I don't have any choice. I'll have to go and see him and ask him to spare their lives. If that means I have to agree to work for him, what else can I do?' He gave a helpless shrug. 'The bastard's got me by the balls, well and truly.'

'What if you agree to do what he says and then, once your mother and Parvus are released, we all leave Londinium? We could go to Camulodunum.'

'That's not far enough. He'd send his thugs after us the moment he tracked us down. Besides, I'm not sure how safe we'd be there either.' He briefly outlined what had happened to the detachment sent to avenge the tax collector, omitting any details that might upset her unduly. At the end, she embraced him and murmured in his ear.

'Don't ever put yourself in that kind of danger again. I can't bear the thought of losing you, Macro.'

'Believe me, I'm doing my best to stay out of trouble. I can't help it if others just won't leave me be.'

'Then what if we left Britannia completely?'

'We could do that.' Macro closed his aching eyes and rubbed the lids gently. 'But that would mean losing almost everything: the inn, our property in Camulodunum and anything else Mum has invested in. We'd just have what's left of my savings. We could get by on that for a while, but after that? We'd be broke.' He blinked and took a deep breath. 'But we're not going anywhere. I'll be damned if I let a cock-sucker like Malvinus drive us out of our home. I'll do what he says for now, but I'll find a way to get back at him, no matter how long it takes.'

'What about the governor? Surely he'd put Malvinus in his place if he knew what was going on.'

Macro shook his head. 'The governor's seldom in Londinium, so I'd have to go through the chain of command to get a message to him. And that means going to Decianus Catus to ask for help. I don't think that's a meeting either of us is going to enjoy. After the way he abandoned me and the lads to our fate, I doubt he'll lift a finger to help us. He'd rather see me dead so I wasn't around to talk about his cowardice. No, we're on our own. I'll have to give in to Malvinus. There's no other way.'

'Oh, Macro, I'm so sorry.'

'Not your fault.' He smiled reassuringly. 'We'll get through this and things will get better. You'll see.'

'I hope so.' She didn't sound convinced.

'In the meantime, I need some sleep. Come and keep me warm . . .'

Late the next morning, Macro woke suddenly from a dream where he was being chased through a snowy forest by a pack of painted barbarians. He sat up with a start, and for a moment his surroundings seemed unrecognisable. Daylight shone through the narrow gap where one of the shutters had been left open. The bed was empty beside him, but there were none of the usual sounds of this time of day. No conversation and laughter from the morning customers in the inn. No high-pitched chatter from the prostitutes as they turned up for the day's business. But thankfully there were smells of cooking drifting upstairs from the kitchen.

He put on his boots and then took a clean tunic from his kitbag. He paused as he looked at his sword belt and scabbard. It was tempting to take it with him, but he did not want to be seen to be ready for a fight when he went to meet Malvinus. Instead he took his dagger in its sheath and tucked it into the small of his back beneath his broad leather belt. Then, picking up his cloak, he made his way downstairs.

He found his wife sitting on a stool in front of the counter in the bar. She had a fired clay cup in her hands and was swirling it round in her fingertips when she caught sight of him entering the room. She gave him a nervous smile.

'Sleep well?'

Macro smiled back and nodded before he sniffed. 'Sausages?'

'I've set Denubius to work in the kitchen. You need a good meal.'

In truth, Macro did not feel hungry. The prospect of meeting Malvinus had robbed him of his appetite; he just wanted to get the matter over and done with. He cleared his throat. 'I'll eat when I get back. I haven't got time now.'

'You're going to go through with it then?'

'I have to. But I should be safe enough. Malvinus is hardly going to make any trouble in a public bathhouse.'

'I hope you're right. Just promise me that you'll be careful, and if there's the slightest sign of danger, you'll come straight back here. Promise me.'

'I promise I'll be careful.'

She sighed with relief. 'Then agree to what you have to and come back with your mother and Parvus, safe and sound. I'll be waiting.'

He turned and strode towards the door, pulling the cloak around his shoulders and making sure that it fell over his belt and covered any sign of the dagger. Slipping the locking pin, he lifted the latch and swung the door inwards. Light flooded in from the street, and there was a blast of cold air as he stepped outside and closed the door behind him.

He looked both ways. The street was busy as people squelched through the grimy slush. As he glanced towards the junction, a sudden movement caught his eye. A scrawny youth dressed in rags jumped down from the wall of the yard. He looked directly at Macro for an instant, then turned and dashed across the street, disappearing into an alley that led in the direction of the bathhouse.

'Looks like they'll be expecting you, Macro old son,' the centurion muttered grimly to himself.

He set off, striding up to the junction and then turning towards the bathhouse, taking an alley parallel to the one the youth had run into. He had expected that the inn would be watched for signs of his return. No doubt he would also be followed as he navigated his way across the heart of the town. Glancing back at the heavily muffled figures in the street behind him, he wondered which of them was trailing him on the orders of Malvinus. Not that it mattered. The gangster wanted him alive for the time being, so Macro felt he was safe at least until their meeting. After that, however . . .

Above him, the sun was shining in an azure sky streaked with skeins of dazzling white clouds. After the bitter cold and snow of recent days, Macro would normally have relished being abroad on such a fine morning, but today he could not shake the icy grip of fear that tingled the hairs on the back of his neck. Not so much for himself. If it came to a fight, he felt confident he could deal with one or two of Malvinus's heavies. No, it was his mother and Parvus he feared for. If they were still alive, they remained so on the whim of a ruthless leader of a criminal gang. Macro had little doubt that Malvinus was quite capable of sending someone to their death without any qualms if it was in some way good for his business.

As he approached the bathhouse of Floridius, he saw the youth emerge from the entrance in the company of a burly man with a heavy club swinging from a leather loop on his wrist. The man tossed a silver coin to the boy, who glanced at Macro then dashed off and disappeared into an alley. Macro didn't recognise the doorman from his previous visit, but he nodded a greeting as he passed by and entered the lobby. The slave, who was also different to the one who had served him before, hurried forward to present him with a bath sheet.

Macro raised a hand. 'Won't be needing that. I shan't be staying long. Is Malvinus here?'

'Y-yes, master. He's in the warm room.'

'He already knows I'm here, doesn't he?'

The slave refused to meet Macro's gaze and bowed his head as he gestured towards the changing rooms. 'That way, master.'

As he passed through the arch and saw that all but the last of the pegs was empty, Macro felt an anxious chill slither down his spine. He had come here to seek the release of his mother and Parvus, even if that meant agreeing to be one of Malvinus's men. At the same time, it was likely that he was walking into a trap, but what else could he do? He cursed himself for not having the sharp wits of his friend Cato, who would surely have found a better way to handle Malvinus. Instead, all Macro had was some small comfort in the feeling of the dagger in the back of his army belt.

When he entered the warm room, he saw Malvinus lying on a massage table, a dark-featured young man working his thumbs into the oiled flesh of the gangster's shoulders. The next moment, two men stepped out from either side of the doorway and barred Macro's way. They were dressed in tunics and heavy boots, and both wore a sheathed dagger hanging from the side of their belts.

'Easy, lads.' Macro smiled. 'I'm here on business and your master is expecting me. I can't imagine he's waiting for anyone else, since we seem to be the only customers here. So it looks like our meeting won't be interrupted.'

Malvinus had not shown any indication that he was aware of

Macro's presence, and one of his men glanced over his shoulder. 'Malvinus. This 'un says he's expected.'

Macro detected the sly amusement in the man's tone, and realised that the details of this encounter had already been worked out. Malvinus raised his head and then rolled onto one side before propping himself up to look at Macro. The masseur pulled the sheet up to cover his client's groin, and stepped back from the table.

Malvinus gave a vague wave at their surroundings. 'I'm not a customer. I own this place. Floridius fell behind with his payments, then it was a case of hand the business over to me and stay on as manager, or take a swim in the Tamesis with a millstone tied to his feet. Centurion Macro, I'd like to say it's a pleasure to see you again, I really would. When we last met, I made you the offer of a position in the Scorpions. I take it that's why you're here.'

'Offer?' Macro sniffed. 'Is that what you call it?'

'I was endeavouring to show you some respect by putting it that way. But you chose not to honour me with a reply. Instead you abandoned Londinium and slipped away. Your mother tells me that you made for Camulodunum.'

'How is my mother?'

'She's fine. I'm a businessman, not a monster. She's been taken care of and hasn't come to any harm.'

'And the boy?'

'The little mute? He's with Portia. Though I can't see why you'd bother to take a wretch like that under your wing.'

'He's prepared to do an honest day's work. That's more than can be said for present company.'

There was a tense pause, during which the only sound was the faint hum of voices from outside. Then Malvinus eased himself up and swung his legs round to sit on the edge of the table. His dark eyes gleamed like polished ebony. 'Be careful, Macro . . .'

'We're here to talk about the deal you offered me. Let's get it over with and you can let my mother and the boy go.'

'Fair enough.' Malvinus snapped his fingers. 'Search him, boys.'

The two men squared up to Macro, watching him closely, shoulders slightly hunched and ready to spring at him in a heartbeat. Macro raised his hands in line with his shoulders and smirked. 'Watch how you go, lads. Not too much touching. I'm not the kind who likes overfamiliarity.'

The larger of the pair chuckled. 'Funny man. I'm looking forward to seeing how tough you really are.' His right hand dropped to grip the handle of his dagger while he gestured to his companion. 'See to him.'

Stepping forward, the second man expertly patted down the front of Macro's tunic and breeches before working his way up the rear. As he reached his buttocks, Macro blew him a kiss and winked. 'Easy, you dog. We haven't been properly introduced.' It was a desperate attempt to distract the man from his belt and the dagger hidden there, but to no avail. He felt the man's hands run along the top of the belt and then stop as they reached the small of his back. The thug glanced up, a warning look, and tugged the dagger and sheath free before stepping away and holding it up for Malvinus to see.

'Is this how you come to negotiate with me?'

Macro lowered his hands and shrugged. 'Best to go prepared for any eventuality, I always say.'

'Really? I can assure you, Centurion, it is better not to carry a weapon when it is not needed than to have one and cause offence, and therefore have possible need of it.'

Macro frowned. 'Now you've lost me.'

Malvinus beckoned to the man holding the dagger, who crossed the room and handed it to him. He briefly examined the sheath before drawing the blade and testing the edge carefully with his thumb. Then he rested the dagger on the palm of his hand as he scrutinised the workmanship of the ivory handle. 'Nice weapon.'

'Thank you.'

'In different circumstances, I'd offer you a fair price for it.'

'It's not for sale.'

'How right you are. I think I'll keep it. Consider it a small payment on account.' Malvinus's expression hardened. 'I'm very disappointed in you, Macro. What did you think bringing a weapon to this meeting would achieve? All it's done is to offend me and cause me to regard you with suspicion. A reasonable man might think you were intending to do me harm. How do you think that is going to help your cause?'

'I don't particularly care, Malvinus. I'm only here to agree to your terms. Free your hostages and I swear to serve you. On my honour.'

Malvinus smiled thinly. 'You'll be glad to know that they have already been set free. The order was given the moment you entered the bathhouse. I imagine they'll be making their way back to the Dog and Deer as I speak.'

Macro felt a surge of relief at the words, followed at once by doubt and suspicion. 'I'm not sure I believe you.'

'No?' Malvinus's lips twisted into a cruel grin as he raised his right hand and addressed Macro in a mocking tone. 'I, Malvinus, swear before the gods and those present that I speak the truth . . . Satisfied?'

'Why release them first?'

'Because they have served their purpose. I don't need them any more. I only needed them to make sure you came back to

Londinium and gave yourself up to me. And here you are, like a lamb to the slaughter.'

The truth hit Macro like a blow to the guts. It was a trap. It had been from the outset. The realisation caused him to freeze for an instant, and that was his mistake. He sensed a blur of movement from the side, but before his eyes could swivel to it, there was a burst of dazzling white as he was struck violently on the temple. He felt giddy as the room spun around, the white sparks quickly fading. Then he felt nauseous, and retched. Another blow, this time from behind, halfway down his back, right over his kidneys. The agony was instant. The first man slapped him hard on the cheek, and Macro reeled, staggering as his sense of balance crumbled. A rough shove between the shoulder blades sent him down onto his knees. He was too dazed to think straight, and swayed as he blinked and shook his head to try and clear his mind. A figure loomed in front of him, fist bunched and drawing back to strike.

'Stop!' Malvinus commanded. He hopped down from the table and tucked the bath sheet tightly about his waist before approaching his victim. 'You refused me, Macro. No one refuses me. You challenged my authority and people got to hear about it. The rumour on the street was that a retired centurion had put Malvinus in his place. That sort of thing damages my reputation, and in my line of work reputation is everything. I have to be feared. People have to know that they must obey me without question or face the consequences. So I have to make an example of you. It's nothing personal, you understand. In fact, I happen to admire your courage and integrity. But such qualities are irrelevant in my line of work. So it's just business, Macro. Remember that. Any thoughts you have of revenge will only make the situation worse for you. Do you understand?'

Macro's head had cleared enough for him to grasp the gist of what Malvinus was saying. He blinked to try to stop the spinning sensation in his head, then coughed painfully and clutched a hand to his ribs as he took a breath. 'Fuck you.'

Malvinus's expression soured. 'Have it your own way, fool. You know what to do, lads. Give it to him, but don't forget, I promised our friend that he wouldn't be killed or crippled. Not too badly crippled, at least. I'm done with him. Teach him a lesson and then take him home.'

Malvinus took a last look at Macro, gave a mocking wave farewell and turned away, making for the doorway into the hot room. The masseur waited until he had passed before falling into step a short distance behind him. Macro glanced from side to side at the two thugs clenching their fists as they shaped to strike.

'Let's do 'im good, Sirius. Like the boss said, eh?'

A fresh blow snapped Macro's head to the side, and was followed by a kick to his stomach. He folded over and immediately threw up, vomiting down the front of his tunic before he could direct it elsewhere. He fell onto his side and tried to protect his face as he was subjected to a relentless assault of kicks and punches that battered his body so that each fresh blow was agony. He felt one of his fingers break as a boot crushed it against his skull. He tasted blood in his mouth and felt the sticky flow over his tongue and teeth as he coughed and spat to keep his throat as clear as he could. He had no idea how long the beating lasted, and finally there came a point where the pain of the blows was so great and so relentless that the ground beneath him seemed to dissolve into a bottomless dark chasm, and he felt himself falling and falling until he finally blacked out.

* * *

'Where is he?' Portia demanded. She and Parvus had reached the inn shortly before to be embraced by Petronella and Denubius. There were tears of relief briefly, before Portia looked for her son.

'I thought he'd be with you,' said Petronella. 'Weren't you there when he went to meet Malvinus at the bathhouse?'

As Parvus sank down onto a stool and stared at the floor, the old lady shook her head. 'We were being kept in a dark storeroom somewhere. They'd kept us there for days. When they opened the door, I thought they were going to kill us. But they just dragged us into the street and told us to go home. So where's my son?'

'He was told he had to swear to follow Malvinus in order for you to be set free. Perhaps he's still talking with him,' Petronella responded hopefully. She turned to Denubius. 'Go and keep an eye on the bathhouse. See if you can find out where my husband is. See if . . . See if there's anything you can find out about him at all. Go!'

'Yes, mistress.' The elderly retainer grabbed his cloak from a hook behind the bar and hurried out of the inn.

Petronella stood at the door looking both ways along the street, trying to pick out Macro's characteristic stocky shape, but there was no sign of him. She closed the door and went to sit with her mother-in-law and the boy to wait for news.

After an hour or so, she was too anxious and restless to sit still. Instructing Portia and Parvus to wait inside, she left the bar and made her way down the corridor to the door leading out into the yard. It was close to noon and the sun was gleaming brightly off the snow still heaped about the open space. The gate was half open, and she swore under her breath at Denubius's carelessness. As she began to cross the yard to close it, she heard a low groan that made her turn with a start.

Slightly to one side of the gate, a dark heap of material moved, and then a blood-streaked arm rose up with a clawed hand at the end of it, one finger horribly misshapen. Her first thought was that some drunken derelict had got into a fight and chosen to sleep it off in the yard. As she approached, the shape turned slowly towards her to reveal a face ravaged by cuts and bruises. Her nose wrinkled in disgust as she saw the man's puffy lips part, then a familiar voice croaked, 'Petro . . . nella . . .'

She clasped both hands to her face in horror.

CHAPTER NINETEEN

As soon as she heard the scream, Portia shot to her feet and turned towards the yard. Parvus, who had been sweeping the floor, turned as well. The old woman scurried round the counter and down the corridor as fast as she could go, the boy close behind. As they reached the kitchen door, Denubius appeared on the threshold. 'What in Hades was that noise?'

'Outside,' Portia responded, brushing past him. 'Now!'

As they burst through the door, they saw Petronella on her knees in the snow, bent over a bloodied form on the ground. Portia realised immediately what had happened. She dashed over to Petronella and kneeled beside her, feeling her heart twist in agony as she stared down at her son. His face was disfigured and covered with smears of blood and cuts that oozed yet more blood. Beneath the gore, his skin was bruised and his eyes, nose and lips were swollen. As she ran her hands over the rest of his body, searching for further wounds and broken bones, she felt her grief turn to a raw sadness for her son, and then fear for what might become of him even if he recovered from his injuries.

Then her native pragmatism took over and she snapped out a string of orders to Denubius and the boy to clear a space in the bar and put a mattress down. As they hurried off, she turned to Petronella and took her hand.

'Listen to me. We have to get him inside and get him warm. The gods know how long he has been lying out here. He'll be chilled to the bone. I need you to be brave, Petronella. It's going to hurt him when we move him, but we haven't any choice. Do you understand me, girl?'

The younger woman pressed her lips together as she nodded.

'Good. Stay here while I fetch some cloaks.'

While she was gone, Petronella held Macro's head in her lap and stroked his hair as shallow breaths rasped from his throat. His right eye opened fractionally and stared up at her, then the corners of his mouth lifted in a faint smile and he managed to whisper her name again.

'Shh. Don't talk. Save your strength, my love.'

Portia returned, running across the yard, and dropped one of the cloaks beside her son, slinging the other over her bony shoulders. 'We must move him onto that. You take his shoulders, I'll take his feet.'

They took up position, and Portia looked at Petronella. 'Ready? Together then . . . Now.'

Though Macro was a short man, he was solidly built, and the women had to strain with all their might to move him over onto the cloak. The task was made no easier by Macro groaning in agony as they shifted him. When it was done, he slumped back, his battered face creasing up as he fought to control the pain. Portia quickly placed the other cloak over his torso, and then each woman took a corner of the cloak beneath him and began to drag him across the yard to the back door of the inn. Just as they reached it, Denubius emerged, and with his help they were able to move Macro down the corridor and onto the mattress in the bar, where Parvus was feeding kindling onto the small flames he had stirred into life.

'Denubius, heat up some water in the kitchen and bring it to me. Petronella, fetch me some linen. We're going to have to cut it up to clean his injuries.'

'We should send for the garrison's surgeon,' Petronella suggested.

'No,' Portia replied firmly. 'I know him. The man's an incompetent drunk. We'll deal with this ourselves.'

The inn remained closed that day, the shutters and door securely bolted. It took Portia and Petronella all morning to clean Macro's wounds before covering them with dressings. For most of that time Macro was unconscious, but now and then he stirred and cried out in pain as his mother dealt with the more serious cuts. She worked by the light of the fire, which Parvus kept feeding to ensure that the room was heated. Petronella assisted by wringing out bloodstained cloths and handing Portia fresh strips cut from one of her linen stolas.

The skin on Macro's brow and cheeks had been torn open by some of the more vicious blows. Portia examined the wounds briefly and glanced at Petronella.

'I'm going to have to sew these up. It's going to hurt. You'll need to keep his head still while Denubius and the boy hold his shoulders down.'

Fetching her workbox, she squinted as she threaded a needle with some fine twine. When everything was ready, she leaned over Macro and spoke gently. 'Son, I'm sorry, but I need to put some stitches in your face. You'll have to hold still.'

'Had worse . . .' Macro responded with a weak grin. 'Just be . . . quick.'

'I'll do my best.' She glanced at the others. 'Here we go.'

Petronella felt his muscles go taut and then tremble as the needle pierced his flesh, causing further blood to flow. Portia worked steadily. When she had tied the last knot, she set the needle down and stroked Macro's hair, now matted with sweat. 'We've done all we can for you, my boy. You need to try and rest for a bit, and when you wake, I'll make you something hot to eat.'

He tried to say something, then shook his head gently from side to side.

'Hush now. Just do as your mother says.'

She took a fresh length of linen and soaked it in the water bucket before wringing it out and placing it over his brow and eyes to cool and comfort him, while Petronella held his hand and tried to keep her concern from overwhelming her. As daylight faded around the edges of the shutters and the door, Denubius picked up a cudgel from a low shelf and took position near the front of the bar in case anyone tried to get in. Parvus stoked the fire, then went to the kitchen to prepare a broth while Portia and Petronella watched over Macro as he slept fitfully.

'Why did they do this to him?' Petronella asked softly. 'He was going to agree to work for Malvinus in order to effect your release.'

Portia was silent for a moment as she thought it over. 'I doubt the boy and I were ever at risk. It was Macro they were after. We were just dangled like bait to lure him into the trap. Malvinus wanted to make an example of him to show those in Londinium what happens to people who attempt to defy him. Once word gets round, everyone will think twice about crossing Malvinus and his gang. No one will want to risk being beaten like . . . like this . . .' She clasped her hands to her face, and a sob tore from her throat as her shoulders trembled. 'My poor, poor boy.'

Petronella shuffled over and placed an arm round the old lady, squeezing her gently as she tried to find some words of comfort, but none came and they sat in silence. At length, as night fell outside, she cleared her throat softly.

'Do you think he'll recover?'

'Hard to say. He's been beaten to within an inch of his life. But they've been careful to leave only bruises and cuts, as far as I can see. They wanted him to live so that people could see their handiwork and be afraid. Besides, I doubt Malvinus would want anyone to trace the murder of a Roman centurion back to him and his gang. That would have landed him in very deep trouble . . . the bastard.'

'What if he decides he wants to finish the job once the lesson has run its course?' asked Petronella. 'Even if he's wary of murdering a former Praetorian, he may decide to just make Macro disappear. Macro will be in no position to defend himself for at least a month, maybe longer. He's not safe here. We need to find somewhere else he can recover. Somewhere Malvinus can't get at him so easily.' She paused and thought a moment. 'That's not the only problem. Once he's on his feet again, he'll want revenge. Just like I do. If I get the chance, I'd like to put my hands round Malvinus's throat and make him die slowly. That's what he deserves.'

'Yes, that's what he deserves,' Portia agreed. 'But we can't do anything about that now. Our revenge will have to wait until we have the means to do something. In the meantime, we need to protect Macro.'

'We could take him to the colony,' Petronella suggested. 'The veterans would protect him, and they're tough characters. He would be safer there. Besides, he saved the life of the senior man at Camulodunum. Ramirus is his name. He owes his life to Macro from what I understand. He'll take care of us.'

'Good.' Portia nodded thoughtfully. 'It would be wise to keep him there for as long as possible. He needs to rest and recover from his wounds. My worry is that as soon as he is well enough to stand up, he'll want to come back here and wreak havoc on Malvinus and his men. Do you think you can persuade him not to? A little time to think might make him realise that this is a fight he can't win as things stand.'

Petronella shook her head tiredly. 'You know Macro. He'll want revenge for this, and I doubt there's anything that can stand between him and what he is determined to do.'

'That's what I'm afraid of. Next time Macro confronts him, Malvinus won't be satisfied with delivering a beating. He'll want his head.' Portia closed her eyes briefly and winced at the thought. When she spoke again, her voice was strained and tears glistened in her eyes. 'He's been trouble from the moment he could walk. Fighting with the other kids from the insula. Cheeking the men from the urban cohorts and leading them a merry chase through the alleys of Subura. Then, when he was older, he was a lady's man. Despite being short, he has a certain rough charm, I suppose.'

'I can vouch for that.' Petronella smiled as she looked down at his battered features.

'I was afraid he'd get some local slapper pregnant and be forced to take the girl on. Luckily his father and I dodged that javelin. But despite it all, I'd never have had it any other way.' Portia touched his cheek tenderly.

'So why did you abandon him?'

She looked at Petronella sharply. 'So you know about that? I'm not really surprised that he told you. But it's not as simple as the way he no doubt related it. The man I married was a dullard. Ironically, he ran an inn as well. But we barely scraped a living due to his incompetence with money. We often went short. There were days we couldn't afford to eat if we were to pay the rent. He was never going to change and I could see myself spending the rest of my days scratching a living in a back street of Rome. I wanted more out of life than that.'

'What woman doesn't? But—'

'But what? Are you going to say we have to put our duty as wives and mothers first? Before any dreams we might cherish?'

Petronella pursed her lips. 'Something like that.'

'That was not for me when I was younger. But I was patient. I waited until Macro was old enough to fend for himself and didn't need me any more. That's when I met a man who promised me a better life. He was a marine centurion from the fleet at Ravenna. We met while he was on leave in Rome. He was handsome and he had enough money to keep a wife in comfort. So I went with him back to Ravenna. Don't think it was an easy decision. It was hard to leave Macro behind.'

'But you did so all the same.'

'He was fifteen. He could handle himself. We'd have parted company a few years after that in any case, when he joined the Second Legion up on the Rhenus frontier. It was blind chance that we ran into each other later on, but I am glad we did. I'd never expected to see the man my little boy grew into, and I'm proud of how he turned out. The gods have been kind to give me a second chance, and I aim to make the most of it. I hope you understand, but I don't give a shit if you don't.'

Petronella could not help laughing. 'He's your son all right, and no mistake.'

'Yes, he is . . . and your husband. We're both lucky to have him.' Portia clicked her tongue. 'Which makes it all the more irritating that he got himself into this mess. If anything good comes out of this, I hope it's that Macro will grasp that he has responsibilities and needs to look after his old mother and his young wife.'

'I don't think you need much looking after. You're a hard one, Portia.'

'Maybe. But I've had to be in order to survive. I'm old now, though, and I'm glad Macro chose to retire to Britannia.'

Petronella leaned closer. 'What about your man over there?' she whispered.

'Denubius? He's good for some things, but he ain't the sharpest arrow in the quiver. He hasn't the nous to run this place alone when I'm too old to do the job. You and Macro make a good team. When the time comes, I'll be happy to know that the Dog and Deer is in your hands.'

It was the first time she had shown any appreciation of Petronella's ability, and the latter smiled in gratitude.

Macro stirred slightly and licked his lips gingerly. 'Glad to . . . hear it, Mother,' he muttered.

Portia scowled at him. 'You were listening?'

'Every word.' He tried to smile. 'Don't . . . seem to have much . . . confidence in my . . . common sense.'

'None at all, my boy. So count your blessings that you have Petronella to keep you in line.'

'Oh? Sounds to me . . . as if you two are like . . . peas in a pod . . . May the gods spare me.'

After Macro had been fed some stew, he fell into a deep sleep. As his snores echoed off the walls, Portia made preparations for him to be taken to Camulodunum. The poor condition of the road and the basic nature of the carts and wagons available in Londinium meant that he would suffer terribly if he had to travel by the land route. So, escorted by Denubius carrying a torch, she went to the wharf and secured some berths on a coaster that was due to make the short voyage to Camulodunum the following day. That night, they prepared a handcart to carry him down to the wharf, along with warm cloaks and furs to keep him warm on the coaster, where he would have to remain on deck as the hold would be filled with cargo.

As Petronella prepared her own bag for the journey, she noticed that Portia had made no effort to do the same.

'Are you staying here?'

'Of course. This is my home. The inn won't run itself.'

'It's not safe for you to stay. Not for a while. Close the place down. Denubius and Parvus can watch over it until we return.'

Portia shook her head. 'I'll be fine. It was Macro they were after. They've made their point, and as long as I pay them what they demand, they'll leave me to get on with it. After all, it's just business to them. They want the inn to make money so they can feed off it.'

'And what if they come looking for Macro again?'

'Then I'll tell them you've left Britannia and returned to Rome.'

'They won't believe you. They might try to get you to talk.'

'Are you suggesting they'd torture an old lady?' Portia sniffed. 'I doubt they'd sink that low. If they did, I don't think it would do their standing much good in Londinium.' She reached out and cupped Petronella's cheek. 'I'll be fine. Don't you worry about me. Just get my boy to safety and look after him until he's back on his feet. Then we'll worry about what happens next. Now finish your packing and get some sleep. Denubius and I will take turns to keep watch through the night. I'll wake you as soon as there's enough light to see our way to the wharf. There shouldn't be more than a few people on the streets at that hour, so you'll be able to slip away without anyone noticing.'

Petronella considered pressing her to join them, but it was clear from the old lady's tone that her mind was made up, and there was little chance of her changing it. 'You take care of yourself, Portia. I'll send you a message when we reach the colony, and I'll report on his recovery.'

'Make sure you entrust any letters to someone you can rely on. If they were to fall into Malvinus's hands . . .'

'I understand. I'll be careful. I can handle myself well enough.'

Portia could not help a small smile of amusement. 'I can believe it. Macro landed on his feet when he found you, my girl. And I'm grateful for that. Now, let's get another mattress so you can lie next to him. You'll need a good night's sleep to see you through the next few days.'

A mist formed over the Tamesis during the last hours of the night and drifted into the town, providing good cover for the small party pushing the handcart along the frozen streets and alleys as they made for the wharf. The master of the coaster was waiting there for them and helped carry Macro aboard and lay him down on a bedroll in the stern, where he would be marginally more sheltered from the elements. Once he had been covered with a cloak and a thick sheepskin, Portia knelt down and kissed him on the forehead. Macro took her hand and squeezed it feebly.

'I'll be back, Mother . . . Then we'll make those bastards pay.'

'Yes, we will. When we're good and ready, eh?'

She stood quickly and gave Petronella a brief hug before treading lightly across the boarding plank and returning to Denubius, who was standing by the cart.

The master gave the order to his two crewmen to cast off

the mooring lines and ready the sweeps. Using the portside oar to shove off, he took his place at the tiller and called the time as his men worked the oars and eased the coaster out into the glassy flow of the river. Standing close to Macro, Petronella gazed towards the wharf, where the two figures were already growing indistinct in the mist. Just before they disappeared, she raised her hand to wave farewell, and then they were gone, swallowed up by the mist, together with the ships moored along the river front and the town beyond. All that could be seen was the ghostly grey that closed round the ship like a funeral veil.

CHAPTER TWENTY

When the coaster reached Camulodunum, Ramirus arranged for Macro and Petronella to have the best accommodation available, the former legate's house opposite headquarters. It was reserved for dignitaries visiting the colony, but since the rapid expansion of Londinium had eclipsed the status of the former provincial capital, the house was seldom in use. After Petronella related the details of the attack on Macro, Ramirus posted two veterans to guard the house day and night, and put out the word for the colonists to be on the lookout for any strangers asking questions about him.

As the days passed, Macro's injuries began to heal. The bruising on his face and body slowly faded and the wounds that his mother had stitched together became livid scars to add to the faded ones he had acquired during his army years. One day a month later, Petronella carefully removed the sutures and handed him a polished brass mirror. He surveyed his battered features and sucked in a breath. 'I ain't going to be getting work as a studio model for any sculptors, that's for sure.'

'I don't think there was ever much chance of that.'

He handed the mirror back to her and eased himself onto one elbow as Petronella prepared a fresh dressing for a cut on the side of his head. 'Malvinus's lads did a pretty thorough job. I can hardly move or take a piss without being in agony. I was a fool to go into that bathhouse alone.'

'You did it for your mother and Parvus. If you hadn't put yourself in danger, who knows what Malvinus would have done to them? Anyway, there's no point in kicking yourself for that now. What matters is making sure you recover and get your strength back.'

'Yes, sir.' Macro gave a mocking salute before his smile faded. 'And when I'm ready, there'll be a score to be settled.'

Petronella paused in winding the strip of linen around his head. 'We'll see about that when the time comes.' She gave the dressing a sharp tug before tying it off.

'Ouch! Was that necessary?'

'If it reminds you of what that kind of foolish comment leads to, then yes.' She examined the dressing, tilting his head from side to side, then gently pushed him back down until his head rested on the bolster. 'Malvinus had you beaten to within an inch of your life. A sensible man would heed such a warning and not go seeking the chance for a second helping.'

'I'll be better prepared next time.'

'Prepared or not, you are one man against his many. That only points to one outcome and I'll not let that happen. I swear it, Macro.'

Their eyes met and he could see that she was serious. He puffed out a breath in frustration. 'I'll find a way.'

She rolled her eyes as she cleared away the old, stained dressing and bundled up the fragments of the stitches into a bit of cloth, then stood up and regarded him with a stern expression. 'If you try to defy me on this and go after Malvinus single-handed, I will have nothing further to do with you. Whether I love you or not.'

'And do you love me?' he teased.

'Of course I do!' she cried angrily. 'Why do you think I'm telling you this?'

'But this is the Macro you love. Don't ever change. That's what you once told me.'

'Well, I was wrong, wasn't I? I want you to change now. I want you to be smart enough to know what's good for you. And for us. Is that too much to ask?'

Even as she said it, Petronella realised the comment was unwise, and she quickly continued. 'All I'm asking is that you think about the situation carefully and don't do anything rash when you have recovered.'

He considered this and then nodded. 'Fair enough.'

The darkest days of winter had passed, and each evening the light endured a little longer. The snow melted soon after they arrived, and only a few drifts beyond the reach of sunlight remained, while the ground, frozen iron-hard, reverted to glutinous mud. There were days when the sun shone brightly from a clear sky and the temperature was just warm enough for Macro and Petronella to spend a few hours in the small courtyard of the legate's house. Years before, someone had set out some flower beds and planted small hedges to demarcate them. These had been largely neglected recently, so while Macro rested on the couch that had been set up for him, Petronella set to work tidying the beds with a view to planting some flowers and vegetables come spring.

Macro tried to convince her that she was wasting her time, since they would be leaving the house as soon as he had recovered. 'We were only given this place as temporary accommodation.'

'You could always make an offer to Ramirus and the colony

senate. Name a price to buy it. They're hardly getting any use out of it, and I dare say the senate would welcome the extra silver in the colony's coffers.' She looked round the courtyard with a fond expression. 'It would make a fine home for us to grow old together in.'

He could not help smiling at her enthusiasm. 'You've got it planned out to the last detail already, haven't you?'

'Almost, my love. Now that I've had a chance to see the rest of the colony and some of the country around it, I can tell it's a peaceful place.'

'Let's hope it stays that way. All right, I'll have a word with Ramirus. Sound him out and see if the colony might be willing to sell the place to us.'

She grinned and hugged him before he winced and she let him go. 'Oh! I'm so sorry. Are you all right?'

'I'll live.'

Every few days, Ramirus would pay a visit to check on Macro's progress. As they drank their way through the jar of wine he always brought with him, the conversation would turn to the affairs of the colony, including the consequences of the action at the Trinovantian settlement.

'Will the procurator be sending out another punitive expedition?' asked Macro as they sat in the courtyard late in February. Thanks to his weakness, he still felt the cold more than he was used to, and sat with a blanket over his legs and a thick cloak around his shoulders.

'It's out of his hands, and a good job too,' Ramirus replied. 'The governor has ordered a full cohort of auxiliaries to do the job. They marched past the colony yesterday, and I had a quick word with the prefect in command. Seems that word got back to Londinium about Decianus riding off and leaving us to deal with the shit he stirred up. His name is mud as far as the governor is concerned.'

'That's something, I suppose,' mused Macro as he cradled the silver goblet in his hands. 'Let's just hope the old boy has enough clout back in Rome to get Decianus dismissed from his post before he causes any more trouble.'

'Too right. He couldn't have made a better job of causing trouble if he'd been sent here to do that in the first place. It does make you wonder.'

'Bollocks to that. There's not much doubt about it. Looks to me like Decianus is here to squeeze as much treasure out of the province as he can just in case the emperor decides to give the order to withdraw his troops from Britannia.'

Ramirus's eyes widened. 'Do you think Nero would really do that?'

'He might.'

'But . . . but that would be madness. The Senate wouldn't stand for it.'

'The Senate ain't so powerful as it once was. The real power is with the emperor now. And the army. I'd say the real concern for Nero is how the army reacts if he gives the order to pull out. There have been mutinies over lesser grievances.'

Ramirus frowned. 'If he tries that here, it's more than likely mutiny is what he'll get. The lads of all four legions, and the auxiliaries, have earned this province. They've shed blood and lost friends for the cause. If Nero jacks it in, then it's all been for nothing. I'll tell you now, if what you suspect is true, the lads here in the colony won't stand for it. I just hope you're mistaken.' He refilled his goblet and stared down into the wine as he continued. 'This is dangerous ground, Macro, either way. It's best not to talk about it until there's some firm evidence. We wouldn't want to be accused of stirring up the shit.'

'No.'

Ramirus lifted his goblet and drained it in one go before setting it down sharply with a satisfied sigh. 'Ah, that's good stuff, that is. I'd better be going, before I get in my cups and earn myself a good ear-bashing from the wife.'

'You're married? I had no idea.'

'You never asked.'

'Well, you never mentioned a wife before, and I've never seen you with her.'

'She's not one for mixing with the other women at the colony. My Cordua is a local girl. I say local – she's one of the Iceni. A daughter of one of their nobles. Speaks decent Latin – learned it from a Roman trader who was permitted to settle on their land. I'd best get home. One of her relatives is coming to stay for a few days, and it would be wise of me to be sober when she arrives with her husband and their retinue.'

He stood up and nodded to Macro. 'I'll see you again in a few days, after our visitors have gone.'

The following day, Macro was sitting with Petronella in front of a fire in what had once been the legate's office. Since the fortress had given way to the colony, the room had been turned over to entertaining, and couches were arranged on three sides of the fireplace, with a low table set in the space between them.

The sound of the door to the front yard opening, followed by footsteps and muted voices from the atrium, interrupted his thoughts. Petronella paused and lowered her sewing as she glanced round in the direction of the voices.

A moment later, there was a knock at the door. When it opened, Ramirus stood on the threshold. 'Hope I'm not disturbing you, my friends.'

Macro turned on his side and propped himself up on an

elbow. 'Not at all. I hadn't expected to see you again until your guests had left the colony.'

'As it happens, my early return is down to our guests. We were talking about our recent action against that rebellious element of the Trinovantes, and I mentioned your name. It seems they know you from several years ago, not long after the invasion.'

Macro was puzzled. 'They know me?'

'That's what they say, and they asked me to take them to you. So here we are.'

With an amused smile, Ramirus stepped aside and beckoned to those waiting in the corridor. There was a rasp of leather-soled sandals, and then two figures entered the room. The first was a frail-looking figure who appeared to be in his sixties. The woman with him was considerably younger, and locks of red hair framed her bold if not beautiful face. She wore a faintly nervous expression, but her mouth lifted in a smile as her gaze met Macro's.

As soon as he recognised her, Macro's eyes widened. 'By all the gods! Boudica!'

'Centurion Macro.' She smiled back uncertainly. 'Or have you been promoted since we last met?'

'I'm no longer in the army.'

She stepped closer, a surprised look on her face. 'You look like you've been in the wars. Ramirus told us you had been attacked.'

'I'll recover,' Macro replied firmly.

'No doubt.'

'Ah, but where are my manners?' He sat up and gestured to Petronella. 'This is my wife, Petronella.'

She stood, and the two women sized each other up before Petronella smiled. 'Pleased to meet you.'

'Likewise,' Boudica responded warmly. 'It's good to see that someone has made an honest man of Macro.'

Macro looked past Boudica to the man still standing in the doorway. Now that he was focusing on him, he did look familiar somehow, but he couldn't place him. The Icenian was gaunt, and his flesh hung on his bones like washed-out linen rags. Deep-set eyes gave a watery glint, and his thin strands of hair were tied back loosely behind his bony shoulders. As Macro stared at him, the man began to cough, grimacing as the fit racked his frail body. Boudica hurried to his side and placed an arm around him, muttering something soothing in their tongue.

Once he had recovered, she helped him to a stool and eased him down. He smiled weakly at Macro and spoke in broken Latin, his voice as reedy as his frame. 'We meet again, Macro. Is good.'

Realisation struck Macro. 'Prasutagus?'

The Icenian nodded, and a smile flickered on his bloodless lips. 'You know me still.'

Now that he recognised Boudica's husband, Macro was horrified by the transformation. When they had last met, some years before, Prasutagus had been a huge, muscled warrior at the peak of his power. The two men had fought alongside each other against a sinister Druid sect. He was a champion of his people, and his reputation was known across the tribes of Britannia. It had come as little surprise that he had been named as king by the tribe's council of elders when the previous ruler had died. Now only a shadow of the former man remained.

There was a pained look on his face as he read Macro's reaction to his appearance, and he cast his gaze down in hurt and shame.

'I sick, Macro. I die soon.'

Macro reached over and gently grasped his forearm, wincing as his fingers closed round skin and bone. 'My friend. I am so sorry.'

There was a moment's sad stillness before he looked back at Boudica. 'I expect we have much to catch up on. Let's have some food and drink and talk.'

'I'll see to that,' Petronella offered.

Once she had disappeared into the corridor, Boudica arched an eyebrow. 'I take it you have told her about me, then?'

'She knows about you, yes.'

'All about me?'

'Enough to guess the rest.'

Boudica reflected briefly. 'She greeted me warmly. I like her. She has a generous spirit.'

'Oh, she has plenty of that!' Macro laughed. 'So what are you doing here in Camulodunum?'

'We're on the way to Londinium,' Boudica explained. 'We have matters to discuss with the governor. The crops failed last year and the people of our tribe are hungry. The Iceni can't afford to pay taxes this year, so we've come to petition the governor to defer the taxes until after the next harvest.'

Macro sucked his teeth. 'Good luck with that. After that business with the Trinovantes, the governor will be determined to make an example of anyone who doesn't cough up.'

'But what can he do if we have nothing to pay him with?'

'You don't want to know.' Macro saw the pained look on her face and decided to change the subject. 'What else do you need to speak to him about?'

'We need to draw up a will for my husband.'

Prasutagus nodded. 'Must make Boudica, our daughters safe.'

'Safe?' Macro frowned. 'Safe from what?'

'Rome,' Boudica answered for him. 'Who else?'

'What do you mean?'

'We know what you Romans are like. You don't like to deal with women in positions of power. When Prasutagus dies, it is likely that the council of elders will confirm my rule. While our tribe will be happy to accept that decision, I doubt Rome will be quite so willing. Besides, there have been rumours that your governor intends to annex the lands of the Iceni. I have heard that is what happens to many kingdoms who have signed treaties with Rome. You call them "client kingdoms". They are like the clients of your aristocrats in Rome. Is that not so?'

Macro reflected on her accusation. She was right about how the system worked between individuals in Rome, and more worryingly, she was right about the fate of many minor kingdoms that had traded the protection of Rome in the present for their future independence. The Iceni tribe might well be in the same danger.

'You think that writing a will may protect you from that?'

Prasutagus sighed. 'I hope. I leave my kingdom half to my queen, half to emperor. I ask him to protect my people. My family. Iceni are loyal to emperor.'

'Not all of them,' Ramirus pointed out. 'Some took it into their heads to rebel against us a year or so ago.'

'They rebelled against us too,' Boudica protested. 'It was our warriors who helped to put the rebels down.'

'I know. But to many Romans, the sins of one part of your tribe will be taken as being the sins of the whole tribe. Whatever the truth of it. There will be some in Londinium who consider the Iceni unreliable at best. You may not get what you want out of having a will drafted.'

Prasutagus stirred angrily. 'I give my word. I give the honour of Prasutagus. The Iceni and Romans are friends.' He frowned as he groped for a stronger word. 'Allies. Honour of Iceni is good. The honour of Rome – the same? Or lie?'

'Rome is honourable,' Ramirus insisted.

Macro was not so sure of that principle as he once used to be. Long years of service had revealed many occasions when Rome had not acted with honour, much as it pained him to admit it. He was not convinced that the governor would agree to the will that Prasutagus proposed. Even if he did, his approval might easily be overturned by the emperor on the advice of his advisers, or even on a whim. Macro sighed softly. There was nothing he could do about imperial machinations. What mattered more to him was the friendship of old comrades. He reached for the wine jug Petronella had brought in, and filled the cups before raising his in a toast.

'To my good friends and allies who fought at my side. May the gods watch over us all and see that our plans and ambitions come to fruition.'

As they ate and drank, the conversation turned to lighter matters and reminiscences of the mission they had shared to rescue hostages from the clutches of the Dark Moon Druids. At length, as dusk gathered outside and Petronella came in to light the oil lamps and build up the fire, Macro yawned.

'Boring you, are we?' Boudica chided.

'Sorry. I'm still feeling weak. Perhaps we can continue our reunion tomorrow?'

'No. Not tomorrow. We need to settle our matters in Londinium as soon as possible. We'll be leaving the colony in the morning.'

'Ah, that's a pity. Another time then.'

Boudica stood up, along with Ramirus and Prasutagus. The latter was unsteady for a moment and reached out to his wife for support until the giddy spell had passed. Then the three of them made for the door. Boudica paused there and looked back at Macro.

'Take care, old friend.'

'*Sa*,' Prasutagus added in agreement. 'Be strong.'

'And you too. Wait, there's one thing, before you go. Can you take a message to Londinium for me?'

Boudica and Prasutagus exchanged a quick look, and he nodded.

'Who is the message for?' asked Boudica.

'My mother. Her name is Portia. You'll find her at the Dog and Deer inn on the street of the fullers.'

She repeated the location. 'What's the message?'

'Tell her that we are safe, and that I am well and hope to recover soon.'

Boudica looked him up and down and clicked her tongue. 'A lie then. You don't look well. Is that all?'

'All that she needs to put her mind at rest.'

'I'll see that she gets your message.'

'Thank you. And ask her to let me know how things go with her when it is safe to send me a reply.'

Ramirus closed the door behind them and Macro turned to his wife. 'What did you make of our Iceni guests? You seemed to have formed something of a bond with Boudica.'

'We share a discerning taste for the right man.' Petronella's smile faded. 'Such a pity that her husband is so ill. He must have been an impressive figure once to have won the hand of a woman like that.'

Macro nodded as he recalled Prasutagus in his prime: a fearless warrior with the strength of an ox. Now he was almost unrecognisable as the towering man he once was. Death was reaching out to him and would claim him very soon. The thought of it made Macro shiver, and he felt a sudden wave of gratitude that he himself would recover from his injuries and, if the gods were kind, share many more years with Petronella.

Reaching out impulsively, he took her hand. 'I love you with all my heart. I will always love you. In this life and the next.'

She gave him a look of surprise. 'Why, Macro, that's the nicest thing you have ever said to me.'

He thought a moment and nodded. 'Yes, I thought so. Almost eloquent.'

'Cato would have been proud of you.' She smiled, then leaned forward to kiss him and embrace him carefully.

'Cato . . . I miss the lad. Especially now, when I need his advice more than ever.'

CHAPTER TWENTY-ONE

Day by day Macro's strength grew and the bruises that had discoloured so much of his body began to fade. The bones in his broken finger knitted back together gradually, and the livid red and purple of the cuts and stitched wounds grew pink and white and resolved themselves into scars that he would carry with him for the rest of his life. As he recovered, the worst of the winter months passed by. The days began to grow longer, while showers of rain were interspersed with fine clear days with cool breezes that obliged Macro and Petronella to wear thick cloaks as they walked slowly around the boundary of the colony. After nearly a month in bed, his legs felt weak and trembled if he tried to walk any further than a mile, or climbed more than one flight of stairs. He cursed his weakness and gritted his teeth in frustration as he forced himself on.

Ramirus brought him some crudely fashioned iron weights from one of the colony's blacksmiths to help him tone the muscles in his arms, and he went at it until he was covered in sweat and could take no more. All the while Petronella looked on with growing concern as it became clear that this was not merely an effort to aid recovery. Macro harboured a deeper motivation that was not hard to guess at.

Sometimes Ramirus brought his wife with him when he

came to visit, and she did her best to communicate with Petronella in her faltering Latin. Despite that obstacle, the two women quickly formed a bond, to Macro's relief. The other Roman women of the colony were coolly formal to both of them, despite the fact that they were married to senior army officers. Once Petronella overheard a group of them discussing 'the barbarian bitch and the freedwoman', and returned to the house in a cold fury and on the verge of tears.

'How dare they treat us like that?'

Macro tried to answer in a soothing tone. 'It's just the way of army wives in small garrisons and colonies when they haven't got much else to keep them busy.'

'Really? Well, bollocks to them! I'll not be made to feel small. Not when my husband's a decorated centurion. I'll show them. We'll have the finest house. The best clothes. And we'll buy wines and tableware from Gaul. Then, if they still look down their long noses at me, I'll shove their noses down their throats and they can choke on them.'

Macro laughed. 'I believe you would!' Then he raised his eyebrows in surprise and touched his chest gently.

'What is it?' she asked in concern.

'It's gone. There's no longer any pain when I laugh.'

Her expression broke into a smile of delight. 'Now there's progress! We'll have you back to your old self before you know it.'

As the first days of spring arrived, Macro exercised in the courtyard garden and then took a walk in the afternoon, sometimes with Petronella alone, sometimes in the company of Ramirus and Cordua. One such day, as puffy white clouds glided overhead on a stiff breeze, the four of them were walking through the countryside that surrounded the colony. The fear of native violence had receded following the harsh suppression of the Trinovante settlement. The ringleaders had been executed, and half of the younger men had been conscripted into an auxiliary unit. Property had been seized; the chief's hut and the other buildings he had owned had been burned to the ground and his cattle and pigs slaughtered. After a month of concern, there was no sign that the action had provoked any wider rebellious sentiment, and those living in the colony relaxed their guard and continued to live as they had before.

As the men strode a short distance ahead of their wives, Ramirus turned to his companion. 'I have some news for you. Good news.'

'Oh?'

'I put your proposal to the council at yesterday's session. They voted to allow you to buy the legate's house. There was some haggling over the price that should be set, but I pointed out that there were some in the colony who owed you their lives, and that the price should reflect that.'

Macro felt a twinge of concern as he made himself ask the necessary question. 'And what do you want for the place?'

'I got them down to ten thousand denarii, if you give up your plot of land within the colony. A bargain, I think you will agree.'

He was silent for a moment as he considered the proposed arrangement.

'What do you think?' Ramirus prompted.

Macro stopped and turned to face the camp prefect. He spat on his hand and held it out. 'I think we have a deal.'

They shook to set the seal on the arrangement, and then Macro turned to announce the news to Petronella as she and Cordua caught up with the two men. At once her jaw dropped and her full lips parted in surprise. 'Thank you. Thank you. I . . . I don't know what to say.'

'I'm sure you'll think of something,' said Macro. 'You usually do.' He took his wife's arm in his. 'Come, let's get back and share a jar of wine to celebrate.'

The four of them turned towards the colony, some two miles away. Clouds were rolling in from the east, and a fine grey veil was suspended beneath them.

'Rain,' Petronella sighed. 'Come, let's be quick about it.'

A sharp crack and boom of thunder heralded the downpour just as they reached the edge of Camulodunum. People were hurrying for shelter, while traders in the marketplace packed their wares into baskets and drew goatskin covers over them to protect them from water damage. As the first drops fell, there was a brilliant flash of light in the heavens, and a vivid white bolt appeared half a mile or so away and was gone in an instant. There was the briefest delay before their ears were filled with a rolling crash of thunder that ended with a deep percussive boom. The rain slashed down from the sky in earnest, hissing through the air. Ducking their heads instinctively, the four broke into a trot as they made for the gateway leading to the yard at the front of the legate's house.

There were two large four-wheeled covered carts to one side. A man in a dark cloak that whipped around him in the wind and driving rain was busy unharnessing the mule teams.

'I'll deal with this,' said Macro. 'You three get inside.'

As they dashed through the fine silver rods of rain, skirting a large puddle that was already forming, Macro hurried over to the mule driver.

'Who are you?' he demanded. 'And what are these carts doing here?'

The man turned and bowed his head quickly. 'They belong to my master, sir.'

'Where is he?' Macro was irked by the thought that anyone would take such a liberty as to park these carts right outside his home.

'Inside, sir. With the rest of them.'

Macro was about to demand more information, but a fresh burst of dazzling light lit up the yard in white and dark shadow, accompanied by a deafening roll of thunder. He turned away and ran to the entrance of the house, feeling the first trickles of icy rain running down his skin as the water penetrated his cloak and tunic. Dashing through the doorway, he drew up, chest working hard as he looked at a group of shadowy figures on the far side of the atrium. More lightning slashed across the sky above in a flickering series of brilliant flashes that flooded the atrium with illumination.

Opposite him, he saw Ramirus and Cordua to one side, and Petronella on her knees hugging a young boy. Beside them stood a dark-haired woman Macro did not recognise. At her side, with his arm around her shoulders, was Prefect Cato, the closest friend Macro had ever known during his army career. Tall, in his early thirties, with a spare physique, he had dark curly hair and a white scar crossing his face diagonally from brow to cheek. One noticeable feature had been added since the last time they had met, a year earlier: a scar over Cato's left eyelid.

As the thunder died away, Macro held his arms wide and cried out his greeting with unalloyed happiness. 'Fuck me if it ain't Cato!'

His friend grinned back. 'Not the greeting I had been expecting. A simple "nice to see you" would have been better, especially in front of my son and my new lady.'

Macro hurried forward and clasped forearms with his former commander. 'By all the gods, lad, it's good to see you!' He turned his attention to the dark-haired woman at Cato's side. 'And who is this?'

'Claudia, say hello to Centurion Macro, lately of the Praetorian Guard. Don't be put off by his tough exterior, because he's just as tough on the inside.'

She smiled. 'I've heard so much about you, Centurion. Not all of it bad.'

Despite the expensive cut of her stola and the gold clasp on her cloak, there was a trace of the Subura neighbourhood in her accent, and Macro realised that she was not the daughter of an aristocratic household. Before he could size her up any further, he felt a small hand grab his own and give it a yank. He looked down to see Cato's son beaming up at him.

'Uncle Macro, I've missed you.'

Macro squatted down so that his face was level with Lucius's and held him at arm's length as he looked the boy over. 'You've grown, little man.'

'I'm not little any more.' Lucius pouted.

'You've still got some growing to do.' Macro made a fist and tapped him lightly on the shoulder. 'Keep going at this rate and it'll be you bending down to be at my level.'

Lucius smiled with pride. As Macro stood up, a large dog with a shaggy coat and a scarred lump where one of his ears had once been came racing in from the courtyard garden and jumped up, large paws braced against Macro's chest as he gave the centurion a lick across his face.

'Ah, Cassius, you still have the foulest breath. I don't know why you keep this beast, Cato.' Macro grimaced and pushed the dog down before giving it an affectionate pat on the head.

There was one other member of Cato's party in the atrium: a thin man with a gleaming head that looked like a barely fleshed-out skull. His deep-set grey eyes crinkled at the edges as he met Macro's gaze, though there was more cool scrutiny there than good humour. The two men regarded each other warily for a moment. Before he had joined Cato's household, Apollonius had been a spy in the service of a governor of an eastern province. He gave away very little information about himself, which caused Macro to regard him with a degree of mistrust.

'Apollonius.' Macro nodded. 'Still haunting Cato's shadow, I see.'

The thin lips widened marginally. 'I thought I'd take the opportunity to see Britannia before I died.'

'I am sure that both of those can be arranged.' Macro turned back to Cato. 'What am I thinking? You must be cold and hungry and . . .' He felt a sudden twinge of shame at having failed to introduce the camp prefect and his wife, and now he beckoned to them. 'Ramirus, this is Prefect Quintus Licinius Cato, my former commanding officer. Ramirus is the ranking officer of the colony. And this is his wife, Cordua.'

Cato regarded them closely for a moment before exchanging a nod with Ramirus. Macro read his expression accurately. 'Always the wary one! Put your worries to one side, brother. Ramirus can be trusted. Now then, let's find something to eat, get sat down by the fire and catch up.'

Lucius sat on the ground, both hands clasping one end of a worn neck-cloth as Cassius worried the other end and tried to wrestle it from the boy's grasp. Macro and Petronella were on a couch to one side of the fireplace, while Cato and Claudia sat opposite, with Apollonius reclining alone on the remaining couch. Ramirus had tactfully bowed out of the reunion and escorted his wife back home before the group settled down to talk. The remains of a light meal lay on the low table between the couches.

'What are you doing here?' Macro began. 'And what happened to your eye, lad? When we left you in Rome, you were about to take up a command in Sardinia. Easy roads, I thought.'

Cato sucked in a breath. 'Far from it. Ended up having to put down some brigands in the middle of an outbreak of a pestilence that ravaged the island and the men under my command. It might have done for me too, were it not for Claudia taking care of me.'

She flushed slightly and shook her head. 'You exaggerate.'

'I don't think so.' Cato tapped his brow above the scar. 'Later I was wounded in the eye during the fighting. I'd hoped it would mend, but it's still a bit blurry and painful from time to time. I had to wear a patch to protect it for a while.'

Lucius looked up. 'He looked like Hannibal, Uncle Macro.'

Macro could not help laughing, and after a beat, so did Cato. Self-consciously.

'I saw a physician there who examined it and said it should recover in time. That was before he sold me a pot of expensive ointment that reeked of piss and didn't seem to help much. I threw it away shortly after we left for Britannia.'

Macro sat up. 'And how did you end up coming here?'

'Long story. The short of it is we took ship to Massilia, went by road across Gaul and sailed to Britannia from Gesoriacum. When we reached Londinium, we made straight for your mother's business and she told us what had happened and where to find you. We came straight here.'

'Much as I am pleased to see you, it's a bastard of a journey to undertake at this time of year just for a social call.'

Cato's expression became serious. 'It's rather more than that, brother.'

'Indeed it is!' Apollonius chipped in. 'Far more exciting and dangerous, I'd say. Quite an adventure in itself.'

Cato shot him an irritated look before he continued. 'The truth of it is, we had to get out of Rome in a hurry.'

'Trouble?'

Cato nodded. 'You recall that before taking up my command, I was tasked with escorting the emperor's former mistress to Sardinia when Nero sent her into exile.'

Macro thought a moment and nodded. 'That's right. We saw her in the imperial box that day at the races. Nice looker, as I recall. What was her name again?' He frowned as he tried to remember, but it was Petronella who got there first.

'Claudia Acte . . . Although her hair was blonde at the time.'

'That's it!' Macro snapped his fingers and then did a double-take as his eyes widened. 'Shit . . . it's you.'

'Quite.' Apollonius smiled in amusement. 'What a small world we live in.'

'How in Hades did you . . .' Macro began, and then shook his head in bemusement as he started to grasp the enormity of the situation. 'Jupiter's balls, Cato. What have you got yourself into? The emperor's mistress and an exile? How the fuck did that happen?'

Cato cleared his throat and nodded meaningfully towards his son in an effort to get Macro to tone down his language.

'It began after we reached Sardinia. I couldn't leave her behind when the campaign against the brigands was over, so she came back to Rome with me under a false name.'

'But Cato, she's an exile. It's a death sentence for her to return to the capital.'

'I know. That's why I reported that she had died from the pestilence.'

Macro clasped a hand to his temple and closed his eyes.

'Didn't you stop to think what would happen to you when they discover she's still alive?'

Claudia coughed gently. '*She* is in the room. I tried to dissuade him, Macro. Truly. I said we should part company.'

'Obviously you didn't try hard enough, my lady.'

'It was my choice,' Cato interrupted sharply. 'We kept her out of sight at my house. I swore the household to secrecy, but there are always visitors, guests and tradesmen. I realised I could not keep her hidden for ever. Even with dyed hair and going under the name Claudia Junilla, there was a danger that someone would recognise her. So we left Rome for the small farm I inherited from Senator Sempronius. We were there for a few months while I settled my affairs and made preparations for us to come here. I needed to find somewhere as far from Rome as possible, amongst people I could trust to keep our secret. I haven't registered our arrival with the procurator's office in Londinium. No one knows who we are and what our business is. I aim to keep it that way for now.' He looked from Macro to Petronella with a guilty expression. 'I'm sorry. Now it puts you at risk as well. But I couldn't think of anywhere safer for Claudia.'

Macro considered this for a moment, and then smiled wearily. 'I'm glad you came. We'll keep your secret, and keep you safe. You have my word on it. Right, Petronella?'

He looked to his wife, who shrugged and sighed. 'I might have guessed your retirement would turn out to be anything but peaceful and quiet. But we'll keep your secret, Master Cato. I'll always be in your debt for giving me my freedom.'

'Not after this,' Cato replied. 'It's me and Claudia who will be in your debt.'

Apollonius clapped his hands together. 'That's all very well, but how long do you think you can keep this up? At some point there will be a new arrival to the province from Rome who may recognise Claudia. Then what?'

'We'll deal with that if it happens,' Claudia answered. 'I've done what I can to change my appearance. We will remain in Britannia until Nero dies and we can return to Rome.'

'Brilliant.' Apollonius nodded cynically. 'Quite brilliant. I *am* impressed. As I have been telling you two for the last few months, you're going to have to come up with something better than that.'

'It's the best chance we have,' Cato replied. 'We've got away with it so far.'

'It will be interesting to see how long this deception plays out,' mused Apollonius.

'Aren't you forgetting something?' said Macro.

'Oh? And what would that be?'

'You're part of it. Have been from the moment you joined Cato's household. You're in danger as well.'

'Of course I am. But I simply cannot resist the urge to see how it ends. This has all the qualities of a cheap melodrama. As such, it is irresistible.'

Macro rolled his eyes. 'Mad. You're all mad. And now you've made us part of the madness. By the same token, as you have heard from my mother, you may not be as safe here as you think.'

He briefly explained in his own words what had happened to him in Londinium, and outlined the ongoing danger posed by Malvinus and the other gangs.

'So I'm not sure which of us presents the greater danger to the other right now,' he concluded. 'We're both in hiding.'

'But we can help each other,' Cato responded.

'We always have. From the very earliest of days after you joined the Second Legion as a green recruit.'

Cato smiled briefly at the memory, then fell silent, thinking over Macro's account of the situation in Londinium.

'There may be a way to deal with Malvinus,' he said eventually. 'Him and his rival. Listen . . .'

CHAPTER TWENTY-TWO

Ramirus opened the door to the legate's office and beckoned to the men waiting in the atrium. They filed in and formed a loose group along the wall opposite Macro and Cato, who were standing behind the desk. In front of them lay an opened set of wax boards and a stylus. Apollonius was sitting on a cushioned stool in the corner of the room, inspecting his fingers and using the fine point of the thin-bladed dagger he carried to pick out the dirt from underneath his nails. When the last of the men had entered, Ramirus closed the door and stood in front of it. Macro examined their faces by the sunlight streaming in through the open shutters that overlooked the courtyard. Most were familiar from the desperate retreat from the Trinovante village. The others were unknown to him, but they seemed like good men – solid and not too old for the task that lay ahead of them.

It was two days since Cato's arrival, and the plan of action he had laid out was ready to be put into effect. At first Macro had had a few reservations – if the scheme failed, many of the men would be hunted down and killed, and it was unlikely that Macro's mother or her business would survive. It was only when Apollonius chipped in to ask if Macro could come up with anything better that he relented. Submission to the criminal gangs was the only other option. In Macro's view of the world, that was never going to happen.

Now he cleared his throat and eased his shoulders back. 'Thanks for coming, lads. I know you're all volunteers and you'll be looking to get stuck into the enemy, but this is going to be a battle unlike any you are used to. It's going to take brains as much as brute strength, guile as much as courage, and patience as well as aggression. I won't lie to you, this is going to be dangerous. Our enemies aren't facing us across a battlefield; they could come from any side, at any time, and will happily stab us in the back if they get the chance. We'll be living on our toes until this is over. It'll be a fight to the finish with no quarter asked or given. Those we are up against are hard bastards who fight dirty. I'll warn you now that some of them are former comrades in arms, but they lost the right to be regarded as such the moment they sold their souls to the criminal gangs in Londinium. When it comes to a fight, we cannot show them any mercy. Is that understood? In their way they are as much an enemy of the Empire as any barbarians, and it's fallen to us to deal with them now that the governor has sent every available soldier to join his campaign in the mountains. It's not the kind of warfare we are used to, but make no mistake, we are still fighting for Rome.'

He studied the faces opposite, looking for any sign of dissent, but saw nothing but calm determination in their expressions. He nodded. 'Good. Now it's time to introduce the man who will be in command.' He indicated Cato. 'This is Prefect Quintus Licinius Cato. Some of you may have already heard of him. He's between postings and may be here for a while yet, unless his standing improves in Rome. Cato's one of us. He's not the spoiled brat of a senator, nor some upstart son of a fat merchant or tax farmer. He's earned his promotion every step of the way. I should know; he started out as an optio in my century back when we served in the Second Legion. I've seen him out-fight and out-think every enemy we have ever faced together as he led us to victory. I have complete trust in him. If any man can outwit and destroy our enemy, it is Cato.' He paused, and then stepped aside respectfully. 'Sir?'

Cato nodded his thanks, then moved out to the side of the table and regarded Ramirus and the others before he spoke. He had long since learned the value of a short silence before addressing his men, and of speaking softly enough to force them to keep still and quiet in order to follow his words.

'Macro is very generous in his praise, and I will do what I can to live up to what he says. Of course, that's made somewhat easier by my lack of aristocratic background and the incompetence and entitlement that tends to go with it.'

Some of the veterans chuckled, while others smiled. The value of a brief moment of humour at the start of an address was another thing Cato had come to appreciate. It put the men at their ease and allowed them all to share a common bond. He waited until the smiles had faded before he continued.

'Centurion Macro is not wrong about the challenges facing us. It's going to be dirty work. Cloak-and-dagger stuff. You know the risks. But it's for an honourable cause: to right the wrong that was done to our brother in arms, Macro. We will also fight to clear the streets of Londinium of the corruption and oppression of the criminal gangs. Rome has come to these lands to bring civilisation and the rule of law. That is what we stand for. It is the ideal we soldiers have fought to uphold. So we fight for the honour of Rome itself.

'Before I go any further, it's only fair to offer you all a chance to back out now. I won't hold it against any man who decides he wishes to have no part of this. If you do decide to march with us, then you'll give your name to Macro and swear an oath to see this through to the end, come what may. Otherwise, you are free to go and no one will think any the worse of you.' He indicated the door. 'Anyone want to leave?'

He paused, but no one moved.

'Very well. Thank you. Are there any questions before we proceed?'

A bald-headed veteran with a wiry frame raised his hand.

'Yes?'

'What's in it for us, sir? Aside from putting down the scum who attacked Macro? And that business about honour.'

'Isn't that enough?'

'Of course, sir.' The veteran looked slightly sheepish. 'No one fucks up a veteran from the colony and gets away with it.'

'But . . . ?' Cato prompted.

'Well, sir, I've heard rumours that we'll get a share of the silver and other loot we take from the gangs. At least, that's what I heard Centurion Macro was promising.'

Cato looked sidelong at his friend. 'Is this true?'

'Spoils of war, lad.' Macro shrugged nonchalantly. 'Once we've done in their previous owners, all those denarii are going to need new homes to go to.'

'I see.' Cato pressed his lips together and frowned slightly as his shoulders drooped in resignation. 'Very well. Spoils of war it is.'

There was a ragged cheer from the other side of the room. He gave them a moment to enjoy the prospect of riches before he coughed and held up his hand to silence them.

'Brothers. The oath . . .'

The veterans stood to attention and raised their right hands, and Cato began, pausing intermittently to allow them to repeat the words after him. 'We, veterans and brothers in arms, swear by Jupiter, Best and Greatest . . . that we will obey the orders of those placed over us . . . that we will fight and never falter . . . until our foes are vanquished . . . and until we are released from this oath by final victory or defeat and death . . . This we freely swear . . . If we should fail to honour our oath . . . may Jupiter and every god we acknowledge . . . strip us of our flesh and grind our bones . . . and make carrion of our remains . . . This is our oath. So swear we all.'

As the last voice died away, he indicated the wax tablets. 'This is the written oath. Sign your name, or make your mark in turn.'

He picked up the stylus and carefully marked his own name in the space at the top beneath the legend 'Commander'. Straightening up, he handed the stylus to Ramirus and then Macro to add their names before calling forward the veterans one at a time. A handful could write; others either pressed a ring seal into the wax or made a distinctive mark beside which Cato filled out their name. The last to sign was a muscular giant of a man named Herennius. Cato nodded approvingly. 'Glad you're on our side.'

Cato closed the tablet and handed the slates to Ramirus. 'When we're done here, have this placed in the colony's strongroom. There'll be fair shares for those that live, and the families of those who don't.'

'Yes, sir.'

Cato clasped his hands behind his back as he faced the veterans again. 'You are bound to my word of command now, brothers. My first order is that you keep every detail of our enterprise a secret from here on. No word of our band must leave this room. You may tell your families only that you are joining a hunting party, which is true after a fashion, or whatever story satisfies or silences their curiosity. But you must not reveal our true destination. There is to be no mention of Londinium or our intention to destroy the criminal gangs. Nothing. Understand?'

The veterans nodded and muttered their assent.

'Very well.' Cato relaxed his expression. 'At first light tomorrow, we'll be leaving Camulodunum in three parties, commanded by myself, Ramirus and Macro. My section will set out first. Ramirus follows at noon, while Macro and his men will be travelling to Londinium by barge. When we reach the town, we'll proceed in twos and threes to the warehouse owned by the centurion's mother. That way I hope we won't attract any unwanted attention before we concentrate our forces. The warehouse will be our base of operations. The only kit you take with you is your swords and daggers. No army cloaks or tunics are to be worn. We must not let anyone think we are soldiers.' He indicated one of the veterans who had grown his hair long and sported a beard. 'I see that some of you have made a head start in going native . . .'

There were grins and a few mocking comments made by the other veterans.

'That's for the good. The rest of you need to follow his example. I don't want to see any shaved faces or freshly cropped hair. We have to fit in with the other civvies so that no one looks at us twice in the streets. If our enemy gets any inkling of our presence and what we're up to, then the battle is lost.' He fixed them with a steady look. 'That means no loose talk, and no drinking until the job is done.'

There were some groans and muttered protests.

'Quiet!' Cato snapped. 'Brothers, I've served long enough to know how much we soldiers like a drink. And I know how often that leads to exchanges of words and fights. There'll be time for that once we've completed our mission, and I'll be happy to buy the first round for every man here. Until then, no drinking. Any man who defies that order will be sent straight back to the colony to face the dishonour reserved for oath-breakers. There will be no share of the loot Macro spoke of for any who let us down. Not one sestertius. Am I clear?'

He let his words settle in their minds and then continued. 'Once we're in position, we'll be ready to strike the first blows. I'll brief you on the overall plan then. If all goes as I hope, the gangs will tear each other apart, and once that happens, we'll clean up the survivors and put an end to those criminal bastards. That is all. Dismissed!'

The veterans left the room, eyes bright with anticipation of the action to come and the prospect of acquiring loot to ease their retirement. Cato was struck by how many of them were grey-haired or going bald. Many had scars and some moved a little more stiffly than he would have liked. But they were hardened veterans to a man and their experience and toughness more than compensated for their onset of years. If – more likely when – it came to a fight to win control of Londinium's streets, he would rather have such men at his side than any others. Particularly the likes of Macro and Ramirus, who had worked their way up from the ranks through courage and tenacity.

His gaze swept over to Apollonius, who had risen from his stool and put his nail file away. The former spy regarded the last of the veterans to leave the room with the mocking smile that Cato still disliked, even though he had long since got used to it.

'Prefect Cato, I simply cannot wait to hear the details of your plan when we reach the comfort and security of the warehouse you mentioned. We are not even thirty strong and somehow you propose to overthrow the gangs of Londinium. I have to say, I am much looking forward to learning what your intentions are.'

'We?' Cato smiled. 'I take it you will be standing with us when the time comes.'

'Of course.' Apollonius affected a hurt look. 'Do you really think I'd be willing to miss out on your escapade?'

'I wondered. You tend to prefer the role of observer to participant, unless you are forced to act. No one is making you come with us on this venture.'

'True. However, it will be different to the usual run of soldierly activity I have been involved with while attached to your small retinue. This sounds more like my kind of work.'

'Work?' Macro sniffed with derision. 'Is that what you call snooping and back-stabbing?'

'That is what spies do, Centurion. And right now my skills are precisely what is needed given the nature of what is to come.' Apollonius flashed a smile. 'Now all this breathless talk of action and secrecy has all but overcome me. I need a drink to calm my nerves.' He strolled off at an easy pace, leaving the room and turning in the direction of the kitchen.

Macro stared after him with a sour expression. 'I can't say that absence has made my heart grow any fonder as far as that smug bastard is concerned. I don't trust him, Cato.'

'Maybe you don't. Just be grateful that he is on our side.'

Macro gave him a sidelong look. 'For now.'

'For now,' Cato conceded. 'Don't try to antagonise him. He has skills we may need. He is good with a knife and he's one of the smartest men I have met. That comes with its own burden. Those with brains tend to be regarded with resentment and suspicion by others, particularly if they make no attempt to hide their intelligence.'

'Not only does Apollonius make no attempt to hide it, he rubs your face in it.'

'Quite.' Cato thought briefly before he continued. 'So far

he has not let me down, and he's got me out of some tight corners. So I have learned to live with his awkward manner. And you need to as well. I can't afford to have men at each other's throats. All right?'

Macro sucked in a frustrated breath. 'As you wish, lad. You're in charge.'

Cato smiled. 'It's like old times, then. The odds are stacked against us. Our enemy is ruthless, and we're going to have to get by with courage, determination and raw luck.'

'That, and having a good blade in our hands and the will to use it.' Macro grinned. 'I could get used to this kind of retirement. But for the love of the gods, don't ever tell Petronella I said that.'

'Going away?' Lucius frowned from the other side of the low dining table as the small group finished their evening meal. Petronella gestured to the serving girl to clear the platters and bowls away, and Macro looked on in quiet amusement at his wife's easy assumption of authority. Born into slavery before being freed only a few years ago, this was the first time Petronella had experienced being the mistress of her own household. It filled his heart with pleasure to see her in this new role.

Cato nodded and dabbed some garum from his chin as he replied. 'Macro and I have some business to deal with in Londinium. We'll return as soon as we can, I promise.'

'Business?' Apollonius repeated archly. 'Is that what we are calling it?'

Cato gave him a warning look. There was no need to go into any details that might alarm his son. The spy shrugged and continued cutting up the gristle in his bowl and tossing chunks to Cassius, who snapped them out of the air, licking his chops with a long pink tongue as he waited for a follow-up titbit.

'What are you and Uncle Macro going to do in Londinium?' asked Lucius. 'Will it be dangerous?'

Cato hesitated, then decided the boy was old enough to be told some details. 'It might be. But mostly for the bad people who get in our way.'

'Oh . . .'

'Look here, lad,' Macro intervened. 'Your dad and I have always come through any trouble unharmed in the past, haven't we?'

Lucius made a face and pointed to the fresh scar over his father's eye. Cato could not help laughing. 'Good point. I'll do my best to make sure I keep safe from harm.'

'Please do,' said Claudia. She smiled faintly, but the concern in her voice was obvious. 'Come back to us safely, Cato.'

He nodded. It was not the first time he had left behind a woman he loved as he marched into danger. But he was aware that things had changed. In the early days, he and Macro had had no one to worry about them as they marched to war. Their only family was the brotherhood of soldiers. Other men who shared a bond even closer than siblings in civilian families.

Now Cato was a father, and from the outset he had felt a love for his son that was as deep as it was unanticipated. He had come to understand what his own father had felt for him, and felt a burden of shame that he had not appreciated that while the old man was still alive. And there was Claudia, a spirited woman with an intelligence and resourcefulness that he admired. Though they had met less than a year ago, Cato was convinced that she was the woman he would spend the rest of his days with. Perhaps they would make their home here in the new province. Maybe even here in the colony where his best friend was already putting down roots. Britannia would be at peace just as soon as the last of the tribes and nests of Druids still holding out realised the futility of defying Rome. In Cato's estimation, it seemed reasonable to assume that it would all be over within a year. He just prayed to Fortuna that he would be alive to see it and to settle down with his family, his love and his friends.

'Claudia, I'll be back. I have everything to live for now.'

'I know.' She kissed him.

Lucius caught Macro's eye and discreetly put his finger in his mouth and mimed a gagging motion. Macro had just helped himself to a large swig of wine, and now he snorted the liquid out through his nostrils as he choked on his laughter. Petronella looked at him with concern and whacked him on the back. 'You are a bad influence on that boy.'

Cato turned to his son, forcing himself not to smile. 'I saw that. Look here, you are the man of the house while Macro and I are away. That means you must look after Claudia for me, and do whatever Petronella tells you to.'

Macro wiped his nose and cleared his throat, wincing at the stinging sensation in his nostrils. 'Your father's right, lad. Petronella wears the breeches in this household and it's a brave man who forgets it. Do as she says, eh?'

Petronella narrowed her eyes at the boy and they shared a mischievous smile.

'I'd offer a toast to home, hearth, family and friendship,' Apollonius announced, 'were it not for the centurion's drinking problem.'

'Bah.'

It was a fine moment, Cato mused. The six of them shared a bond of happiness, and even the edgy tension between the spy and Macro had eased. It was a memory he was determined to cherish, particularly in view of the peril facing the three men. If they failed, he had little doubt that the leaders of the crime gangs would not be satisfied with their heads alone. If they were anything like the gangs of Rome, they would first murder those who defied them, and then their women and children, to serve as a warning to the poor unfortunates over whom they exercised power.

CHAPTER TWENTY-THREE

Macro scratched his stubbly jaw. 'You sure you don't want to take the dog?'

Cato shook his head as he leaned over to gently stroke Cassius's neck. The huge beast leaned against his master's thigh and opened his mouth in a wide yawn. Steamy breath swirled around his maw in the rosy glow of dawn. Even though spring had come, the air was cold and crisp, and there was a slight frost on the tufted grass growing outside the colony's main gate.

'We don't want to attract any attention, and Cassius is the kind of dog that makes heads turn. Ugly as sin, aren't you, boy?'

'There's no denying it.'

Cassius looked from man to man and happily wagged his stump of a tail at the sound of his name.

Cato slipped the leash over the dog's neck and handed the end to Macro. 'Just in case he tries to follow me.' Then he picked up his marching pack, gave Cassius a final pat on the head and met Macro's gaze. 'I'll see you in Londinium three days from now, gods willing.'

'My lads and I will be there, any river pirates notwithstanding.'

'From what I've heard, they'll be giving you a wide berth.'

'If they're wise enough to have learned their lesson.'

Cato nodded as he glanced past Macro towards the roof of the legate's house rising above the surrounding buildings. He had said farewell to Claudia and kissed Lucius, who was still asleep, before leaving the house, as he did not want there to be any display of emotion in front of the veterans he was about to lead into battle.

There was a beat, and then the two friends clasped forearms before Cato turned away from the colony and gestured to the waiting veterans to follow him. There were seven of them, dressed in simple cloaks that had seen better days. Each man carried a small pack with some spare clothes wrapped around their weapons – sturdy thumbsticks or light javelins. If anyone questioned their purpose for being on the road, the story would be that they were making for Londinium to buy hunting gear and dogs. A common enough sight at this time of year as people emerged from their winter quarters with an appetite for fresh meat. Ramirus and his party had loaded a small cart with cured sheepskins to allow them to pose as traders taking their wares to the market at Londinium. With luck, the teams would meet up at the warehouse without attracting the attention they would have received if they had marched into the town together as one large band. The criminal gangs had plenty of informers on the streets and drinking at the inns in order to pick up on potential opportunities or threats. It was vital to the success of the plans brewing in Cato's head that the enemy did not grasp the danger posed by his men until it was too late.

As Cato's party set off at a steady pace along the road to Londinium, Cassius strained at the leash and whined softly. Macro watched them until they were out of sight, then clicked his tongue. 'Come on, boy.'

They returned to the legate's house to complete his packing. Petronella had neatly folded some spare clothes and placed them in his sidebag. She had also prepared some hardtack and fresh loaves of bread to feed him on the short voyage upriver to Londinium.

It was the first time since before his beating that Macro had carried his weapons and a pack, and he still felt some stiffness and aching from his injuries. Drawing his sword, he tested its weight, then gave it a few experimental swings and thrusts. He felt relieved that the motions came easily and with no more than a twinge of pain at the extremity of each action. That would improve as he exercised his body each morning, he mused.

'Are you ready for this?' asked Petronella as she wrapped her arms around him.

'As I'll ever be.'

'That's not encouraging. I should have told Cato to wait a little longer, just to be sure.'

Macro shook his head. 'I've been waiting long enough. It's time to make Malvinus pay for what he did to me. Him and his crew need to be cleared off the streets like the scum they are. Oh yes, I'm ready for it.'

Petronella chewed her lip, then sighed. 'It's pointless me telling you to be careful, isn't it?'

He broke the embrace. 'Where are the others? Lucius and Claudia?'

'He's still asleep. She's in her room. I thought I heard her crying a while back.'

'Then say goodbye to the boy for me. And tell Claudia that I'll look out for Cato as best I can.'

'She'll appreciate that.'

They stood staring at each other for a moment before

Macro clicked his tongue. 'I'll be going then.'

He turned and strode across the atrium towards the entrance of the house, and stepped out into the courtyard, where the veterans of his group had assembled. Petronella followed him to the door and stopped at the threshold.

'Let's be off, lads.' Macro marched past them, making for the arch on the other side of the courtyard. 'We need to catch the morning tide if we want to make the voyage as quick as possible and get back on dry land. I've had my fill of fucking around in boats, I can tell you.'

There were some cheerful voices raised in agreement as the men hefted their packs and followed Macro out of the gateway and into the street, and then they were gone, only the fading crunch of their boots on gravel enduring for a moment longer before they were lost against the sounds of the colony stirring into life.

Cato and his men made good time as they strode out along the road to Londinium. The sky was clear and there had been no rain for several days, so the ground was firm. Blossom – white, pink and yellow – adorned the trees, where vivid green leaves were budding, and either side of the road the grass was brightly speckled with daisies, buttercups and dandelions. Birds filled the air with their song, occasionally drowned out by the raucous cries of nesting crows from the treetops, where they flapped about like scraps of black linen caught on a stiff breeze.

Despite what lay ahead, Cato was in a good mood, his spirits lifted by the vital energy of the natural world around him and the warmth of the sunshine. Behind him the veterans chatted happily, now and then breaking out in laughter or raising their voices in an old army marching song. They had served together in the same legion, the Twentieth, and the song was one that was not known to Cato, so he could not join in. Not that he would, since he maintained that an officer, especially one of his seniority, needed to preserve a little distance from those he commanded. These men had volunteered to follow him and Macro into a fight that was not their own, and that was something of an extra burden over and above the usual concerns of a commander leading soldiers into battle. But such thoughts did not weigh heavily on Cato. It would take them three days to reach their destination, and until Londinium was sighted, he resolved to enjoy the journey, amiably greeting fellow travellers heading the other way, and those they overtook.

As the light began to fade, they approached a wayside inn, half of it still under construction. But there was a large covered hall where travellers could drink and eat, and plenty of room to bed down around the fireplace once tables and benches had been dragged aside. As Cato and his men entered, the chubby innkeeper gave them a friendly wave from behind the counter before he scurried over rubbing his hands on his apron. He had the cropped hair of a former soldier, and his Latin was spoken with a heavy accent that Cato judged to be from Germania. A retired auxiliary, most likely, he reasoned.

'Looking for warm wine, hot food and a comfortable spot to sleep for the night, gentlemen?'

'You've read my mind.' Cato grinned. 'That'll be what we're after. As long as it's any good.'

'Good enough for royalty, sir.' The man puffed his fat chest out. 'Had the king of the Iceni and his entourage stop here the other day on their way to Londinium. Didn't hear any complaints from them, even if they was barbarians, sir.'

'Sounds like a recommendation.'

'Any horses with you, sir?' the innkeeper asked, hopeful of some extra income from feed and stabling.

'Just me and my friends here.'

'Fair enough.' He did a quick calculation. 'Fifteen sestertii for the group then, sir. In advance.'

Cato took out his purse and counted out the coins as he placed them in the innkeeper's hand. The latter swept them into the pocket on the front of his apron and waved the veterans to two tables and benches next to a group of five men already sitting by the fire. They set their packs down and unfastened the clasps of their cloaks, stretching and sighing with weary satisfaction before they took their seats. As soon as they were settled, the innkeeper waddled over with a wooden tray of plain samianware goblets. He returned a moment later with two large jugs, one for each table.

'Stew will be ready shortly, sir. My kitchen boy's just heating it up.'

'Fine. Thank you.' Cato took charge of his table's jug and filled all the cups before setting it down. 'We covered a fair distance today. If the weather holds, we'll make quick time to Londinium.'

The men settled to their drinking and quiet conversation in the comfortable warmth radiating from the logs burning in the hearth. With a cup of the warm, albeit parsimoniously diluted, wine inside him, Cato felt a glow of well-being, and had closed his eyes in contentment when he heard the scrape of a bench on the flagstone floor beside him.

'Excuse me, friend . . .'

He blinked his eyes open and stirred stiffly, turning to see a man from the group of strangers leaning towards him. He had a shock of brown curly hair and the flattened nose of a boxer, together with the requisite bulk under his dark green tunic. The studded leather bracers on his arms added to his pugnacious appearance. Just above the top of the bracer on the right arm

Cato could make out a tattoo depicting the claws of an insect. The man smiled in a friendly manner as he continued. 'Are you lads from the colony?'

Cato nodded, and felt a cold prickle on his scalp as he scrutinised the man and his companions more closely. 'What's it to you?'

A slight frown creased the boxer's brow. 'No need to take that tone with me, friend. Just asking a polite question.'

The weariness of a moment earlier was gone, and Cato was alert, his heartbeat quickening as he forced himself to appear calm. It was possible the man's curiosity was harmless enough. He inclined his head in apology.

'Sorry, I'm just tired. Didn't mean to sound rude. No offence meant.'

'None taken,' the man said in an easy tone. 'So?'

'We're from Camulodunum,' Cato agreed, before adding his cover story. 'Heading for Londinium to buy hunting gear.'

'Ah, then you'll be wanting Salvius. He owns a smithy on the corner of the main market square. No one makes better boar spears or hunting arrows.' The man jabbed his thumb towards his chest. 'Tell him Festinus sent you.'

'All right, thanks. I'll be sure to look him up.'

'You won't be sorry.'

Cato nodded slowly. 'What about you? Are you making for Londinium?'

'No. Going the other way. We're looking up an old friend in the colony. Arrived there a few months back. Used to be a centurion in the Praetorian Guard before he was discharged. Lucius Cornelius Macro. Don't suppose you know him, by any chance? Only it would help to know where to find him now, rather than wasting time asking about.'

'I'll have to think about it,' Cato replied. 'What does he look like?'

'I was hoping you could help me with that.'

Cato's throat felt dry and his body tensed up. He cleared his throat and shrugged. 'I thought you said he was an old friend.'

'Sure, from some years back, when I lived in Rome.'

'Oh, I see.' Cato affected a yawn as he reached for the wine jug and began to top up his goblet.

'Do you know him then?' the man pressed.

'I think I know who you mean.' Cato turned to the veterans. 'Oi, Severus, this lad's looking for Macro.' He kept his tone light, but his eyes widened to alert his men and he bunched his spare hand into a fist and made a slight gesture towards the other group. 'Do you know where he can find the centurion's house?'

Festinus switched his attention to Severus. Cato clenched his jaw, tightened his grip on the jug's handle and drew a sharp breath. Then, with an explosive movement, he slammed the jug into the side of the boxer's head. It shattered in a burst of clay shards and dark liquid, and Festinus fell off the bench, landing on his hands and knees.

'Get 'em!' Cato yelled, just as the innkeeper emerged from the kitchen door carrying a steaming iron pot by its wooden handles.

'Dinner, gents!'

His words were drowned out by the sound of benches crashing back and a table overturning as the veterans surged towards the other men. Cato was still holding the handle of the shattered jug, and now used the jagged edges as a knuckleduster as he lashed out at the man seated next to Festinus. The latter managed to throw himself back, and the improvised weapon merely grazed his cheek. The other gang members were already on their feet and drawing their daggers. Cato cursed his decision to keep his men's weapons in their marching packs. He punched at the second man again, this time catching him on the side of the skull. The jagged edges of the handle gouged through hair and skin before grating on bone. The man tumbled back, taking the table with him and sending platters of food and cups of wine flying. The handle broke in two and Cato threw the remaining piece aside.

'Watch out, lads!' he warned. 'They've got blades.'

It came too late to save one of the veterans, who took a thrust deep into his side as he threw himself at the nearest gang member, wrapping his hands about the man's throat before headbutting him.

Cato went after Festinus, who had scrambled a short distance away on all fours and was now rising to his feet as he snatched out his dagger. There was no time to think, and he charged into the boxer instinctively, using his momentum to knock him down. The dagger slipped from Festinus's fingers and flew across the floor into the shadows on the other side of the room. Both men scrambled up quickly, and Festinus lowered himself into a slight crouch, fists raised ready to protect his face or lash out. Cato too made ready to fight as Festinus edged forward, moving lightly on the balls of his feet. His right fist shot out towards Cato's face, and Cato ducked to one side just as the real blow landed in his ribs, a powerful punch delivered from Festinus's shoulder. He gasped as air was driven from his lungs and stepped back quickly, ready to ward off the next attack. The boxer moved in, head lowered as he jabbed and punched, and Cato was forced to take the blows he could not block, knowing that he was dangerously outmatched by his enemy. His leg brushed up against something and he glanced down to see a stool. Stooping to snatch it up, he was just in time to block a punch with the top of it, and there was a loud crack.

'Shit!' Festinus stepped back, cradling his bloodied knuckles, teeth gritted in agony as he glared at Cato. 'Going to fucking die for that, soldier!'

But Cato felt more confident now he had the stool firmly in hand, ready to block any new attack. He stepped forward and swung it at the boxer's head. Festinus raised his fists and pivoted on the balls of his feet to deflect the blow. As he began to move, Cato raised his right boot and stamped the nailed sole into his opponent's kneecap, feeling flesh and bone give under the impact. With an animal howl of agony, Festinus sank to his knees. Cato swung the stool again, catching him on the forearm, then again, this time smashing into the boxer's shoulder. A third blow struck him on the head; Festinus's eyes rolled up and he fell onto his back, legs and arms thrown out.

Satisfied that his opponent was out of the fight, Cato turned to the others and saw that the man whose head he had laid open was staggering towards the counter at the back of the room, blood pouring from his scalp. Half blinded, he collided with the innkeeper, and the scalding stew splashed over his raised hands and face, causing him to cry out in shock and stumble into a doorpost, knocking himself senseless. Two of Cato's men were down on the floor, bleeding from knife wounds, along with one of the gang members, whose head had been caved in. The rest of the veterans, armed with fire pokers and some of the other stools, had cornered the last two gang members, who faced them with daggers raised, ready to strike. The innkeeper turned and dashed out of the room with a surprising turn of speed given his size.

Cato drew a deep breath and called out to the men backed into the corner. 'Give it up! You're outnumbered. You can't fight your way out of here. Drop the blades.'

They hesitated a moment before the larger of them growled, 'Fuck you.'

His surviving comrade was a nervous-looking younger man. Cato saw the dagger wavering in his hand, so directed his order to him. 'Drop it, or have it beaten out of your hand. The fight's over, boy.'

There was a brief hesitation before the youth tossed his dagger on the ground at Cato's feet and quickly stepped away from his companion.

'Coward,' the man snarled. 'Bloody coward!' He opened his mouth to speak again, but Cato's swiftly thrown stool caught him squarely in the face and slammed his head back against the plastered wall. He groaned as he slumped to the ground, the dagger falling from his fingers. The fight was over only moments after it had begun, and the sounds of ragged breathing and the soft crackle and hiss of burning logs sounded unnaturally loud as the men in the room were still for a few heartbeats.

Cato took a deep breath and surveyed the chaos around the fireplace, then issued his orders to his second in command, Optio Catillus. 'Find something to bind the prisoners. Hands and feet. Then take 'em into the yard behind the inn. I'll see to our wounded.'

The two veterans who had been stabbed were helped to a bench close to the light of the fire, and Cato helped them strip off their tunics. One had a flesh wound on his shoulder where the blade had passed through the muscle without hitting bone. Painful, but needing nothing more than stitches and rest to ensure a good recovery, provided the wound did not go bad. The other man, Silenus, had not been so fortunate. He gritted his teeth and winced as he took his bloodied hand away from his stomach to reveal a wide cut where the blade had gone in deep and torn through his guts. Blood and fluids spilled from the puckered flesh around the wound. Cato had seen similar injuries before and knew that the odds were firmly against the veteran recovering. In most cases the wound became foul-smelling within a few days and the victim died in agony.

'Not good, eh, sir?' Silenus smiled grimly.

Cato did not reply, but glanced up at the innkeeper, who had reappeared in the kitchen doorway and was looking round the room nervously. 'You. Get me some water and some clean rags. Quickly.' He turned his attention back to Silenus. 'We'll do what we can for you.'

'You can't do much, sir. You'll have to leave me behind.'

'I know.' Cato nodded to the other casualty. 'The two of you are going back to Camulodunum.'

'I'm not going anywhere, sir. I can't walk and I don't want to lie on the bed of a cart either.'

Cato could imagine the extra agony that would result from the jolting and juddering as the wheels of a cart bumped along the rutted road surface. 'Very well. You'll stay here until you recover.'

'Or I don't.'

Cato patted him on the shoulder and stood up as the innkeeper returned with a bucket and some rags. As he set them down, Cato addressed him. 'We'll need a needle and some thread.'

'My wife would know where that is, sir.'

'Then go and get her.'

'I can't. She's visiting family in Londinium.'

Cato gritted his teeth in frustration. 'Fine. Then get this mess cleared up and bring us some more food and wine. Go.'

The innkeeper scurried back to the kitchen, and a moment later a boy emerged with a bucket and mop and set to work.

Cato dressed the wounds of the two veterans as best he could, then picked up one of the daggers and helped Catillus drag the bound prisoners outside, while the other men from his group restored the benches and tables to their original places around the fire.

When he had the five bound gang members arranged against the stable wall, he inspected them in the failing light. The man with the grievous head wound was still conscious and babbling softly, while his comrade who had been scalded had come round and was moaning in agony. Festinus and the gang member who had refused to surrender stared back sullenly, while the youngest of them looked terrified.

'As fine a bunch of cut-throats as I've ever seen,' Cato commented to Catillus.

'What do you want to do with them, sir?'

Cato scratched his jaw as if musing before he replied. 'A few questions first.'

'Ask away,' Festinus sneered. 'We ain't saying a bloody thing. Right, boys?'

Only the man next to him offered a supporting grunt. The youth said nothing and tried to stop shaking.

'Really?' Cato nodded slowly. 'We'll see about that.'

He approached them and squatted down in front of the man beside Festinus, then slammed the point of the dagger into the thug's leg, just above the knee. The man's jaw snapped open in shock, then he bellowed in pain as Cato twisted the knife left, then right, before pulling it out and wiping the blood on the hem of the man's tunic. He glanced at Festinus. 'Ready to talk?'

'Fuck off.'

'You're a hard man, I can see that. A boxer once, by the look of you.' Cato decided to work on the man's vanity. 'Your face seems familiar. Did you ever fight in Rome?'

'Eight years back. In front of the emperor himself. Old Claudius gave me a gold torc after I became champion.'

'I remember now.'

Festinus chuckled. 'I suppose you remember his wife sucking me off too? You fucking idiot. I've never been to Rome in my life. You reckon you can play me? Who do you think you are dealing with here? I ain't going to spill my guts. Not to you, not to anyone. I swore an oath of silence, by Dis himself. So sod off with your questions.'

'I see.' Cato shifted the handle of the dagger into an underhand grip, steeling his nerves for what he must do in order to persuade the man to talk. 'You might not spill your guts, but someone else will.'

He thrust the blade into the stomach of the man next to Festinus and savagely sawed it across before tearing it free. Greasy grey intestines bulged through the torn cloth of the man's tunic. His eyes clenched shut, he rolled his head around, his mouth stretched wide as he screamed. At the end of the row of prisoners, the youth's head lurched to the side and he vomited. Festinus flinched away from his stricken companion, and Cato leaned towards him, this time wiping the blade on the boxer's tunic, right under his chin.

'You'd better be ready to talk now.'

Festinus was shaken but recovered quickly. 'What's the point? We're already dead men. Ain't that right?'

He was trying to sound brave, but his tone betrayed desperate hope. That was something Cato could play on. 'Maybe not. Depends if you tell me what I need to know.'

Festinus made no response.

'Why were you looking for Macro?'

'Why do you think? It weren't no social call. The boss had a change of plan and wanted him seen to. Him and his wife.'

'Malvinus sent you?' Cato was struck by a sudden fear. 'What about Macro's mother? Portia?'

'What about her?'

'Have you harmed her?'

Festinus shook his head. 'What for? As long as she runs her business and pays up, why would we kill the old hag? We just need to make an example of Macro so no one else dares to ask Malvinus to cut them some slack.'

Cato's mind was briefly filled with images of what might have happened if Festinus and his crew had reached the colony. He forced such thoughts aside. There were more questions he needed answers to.

'How many men does Malvinus have behind him?'

Festinus stared back defiantly, lips pressed together. Cato stood up and regarded him coldly. 'You'll answer me or I'll cut the eyes out of one of your men.'

Festinus's gaze darted towards the youth, and a brief look of terror flitted across his face.

'The boy then.' Cato paced towards him, and the young man shrank back and shook his head.

'No!' Festinus shouted. 'Spare him!'

Cato paused. Now that he looked more closely, he could see the resemblance between the boxer and the youth. Handing the dagger to Catillus, he returned to Festinus. 'You'll tell me everything I want to know. If you refuse, or I get the slightest feeling you are lying to me, I'll order my optio to take out your son's eyes then cut him up piece by piece. Do you understand?'

'I'll talk. Just don't harm the boy. Give me your word you'll let him go and I'll tell you everything.'

Cato was still for a moment. 'Fair enough. You have my word that I'll not harm him if you tell me what I want to know.'

Festinus's shoulders slumped. 'Ask, then.'

'How many men does Malvinus have?'

'There are fifty or so of us enforcers. Besides the informers and lookouts.'

'Are you all armed?'

'Just the enforcers.'

'What about weapons, armour? What do you have?'

Festinus's head bowed in shame as he continued to give up the information. 'We carry daggers and clubs in the town, but Malvinus has an armoury. Mostly auxiliary kit he bribed a quartermaster for.'

'Where is this armoury?'

'In the wood store behind the bathhouse he owns. Floridius's place. It's hidden in a chest under the logs.'

'Good. Now then, where do we find Malvinus if he needs to go to ground? Not his main house. Somewhere more secret.'

Festinus glanced up. 'What do you mean?'

'Don't play dumb with me!' Cato snarled and stabbed a finger towards the youth. 'Tell me, or your son is going to have to feel his way back to Londinium.'

'All right! There's a bakery in the next street to the bathhouse. The Bread of Bacchus, it's called. Or something like that. Malvinus has a safe house behind it. If there's trouble, he can go there with his bodyguards and lie low.'

'Is it fortified in any way?'

'I don't know. I've never been there. I just overheard one of his guards talking about it one night when we were drinking. That's all I know. I swear.'

Cato grasped the boxer's heavy jaw and forced his head up, then stared into his eyes for a moment. 'I believe you. That's all I need.'

Festinus sighed with relief.

Cato turned to Catillus. 'Cut their throats. We'll bury the bodies at dawn.'

'What?' Festinus started. 'I told you everything.'

'So you did.'

'What about my son? You gave your word.'

'That's true.' For a moment, Cato considered sparing the youth, but he could not afford to risk having him escape and return to Malvinus. Besides, if the fight had gone the other way, he could have expected no mercy from Festinus's men. 'I said I would not harm him and I won't. Catillus will do the job instead.'

'You bastard . . . you fucking bastard!' Festinus spat at him.

'Be honest, if our positions had been reversed, would you have spared any of us? As for your boss, Malvinus, that's your genuine bastard. He feeds off the livelihoods of others, and he lured my best friend into a trap and had him beaten to within an inch of his life by thugs like you . . .' Cato paused and shook his head as it dawned on him. 'By you. That's why Malvinus sent you to track him down in the colony, because you'd recognise him.'

He turned to Catillus. 'Kill him last.'

The optio hesitated. 'Sir, I—'

'He would cut your throat in an instant if he had the chance. We'll show him the same standard of mercy. If you haven't the stomach for it, you can stay here with the wounded men. I can't have a man at my side if I cannot rely on him to kill when necessary. There are no prisoners in the war we are about to fight. There is only victory or death. The only choice is whose death. Ours, or theirs? Understand me?'

Cato stared hard at his subordinate, searching for any remaining glimmer of doubt, or worse, moral defiance, that meant he could not depend on the optio to do the grim work that would be required of him in the coming days. It would be the dirtiest conflict Cato had taken part in during his long years of soldiering, and any victory would be without fanfare or awards for courageous service; merely relief at the removal of the blood-sucking parasites bullying the people of Londinium.

Catillus swallowed and nodded as his expression hardened. 'Yes, sir.'

'Good. If it makes you feel any better, see to it that you do it quickly and cleanly. But do it you will. I'm going back inside.'

As Cato strode towards the door at the rear of the inn, he heard the youth scream with terror and Festinus plead for his son's life. Something clenched tightly in the pit of his stomach, and he knew it for what it was: misplaced pity. He pushed the feeling aside and left Catillus to carry out his grim task.

CHAPTER TWENTY-FOUR

Three days later, towards dusk, the barge carrying Macro and his squad moored alongside the wharf just short of the long bridge that crossed the Tamesis to a low island on the south side of the river. It had taken twice as long as he had expected, thanks to contrary winds and rough water along the short stretch of coast between the Camulos river and the mouth of the Tamesis. A steady rain had been falling most of the afternoon and the cobbles of the wharf were slick and gleaming, as were the tiles on those of the town's buildings that were not thatched or shingled. Both he and his men were soaked through and hollowed out by seasickness. As they stepped ashore, the solid ground seemed to sway, rise and fall beneath their boots. Shouldering their packs, they trudged along the busy wharf, threading their way through the gangs of stevedores and piles of cargo being loaded onto or unloaded from the vessels moored alongside.

Macro found the lane on which the entrance to the warehouse lay and led his party up a narrow thoroughfare with a foul-smelling drain running down the gentle incline towards the river. They passed a beggar at the intersection just before the modest gateway set into a high wall streaked with grime. As Macro made for the timber gate, the beggar rattled a dagger against the side of his mess tin and cried out loudly for alms. The centurion spared him a brief glance and recognised the veteran's face as that of one of the men who had marched with him to the Trinovante village months before. Having him play the part of a beggar to keep watch on the street was a wise precaution, Macro decided. He tried the iron ring on the gate, but it refused to shift and he realised it was locked from inside. He rapped sharply just below the narrow grille. It shot to the side at once and a pair of eyes scanned him and his men briefly before it closed again and he heard the sound of a heavy beam being removed from the other side. The gate swung open and one of Cato's men, Optio Catillus, waved them through before closing it behind them and slipping the sturdy wooden bar back into its iron brackets.

Macro found himself standing in a small yard facing the entrance to the warehouse, where two large doors led onto the storage space beyond.

'We'd begun to fear the worst, sir,' said Catillus. 'We expected you to arrive before us.'

Macro explained the reason for the delay before nodding towards the warehouse. 'Are Cato and Ramirus and their men here, then?'

'Yes, sir. Though not all the men made it.'

Macro frowned. 'How's that? No, never mind. Let's get out of the rain first and then Cato can explain.'

Catillus ushered them into the warehouse and then returned to his post by the gate. Inside, Macro saw that the men who had already arrived had made themselves at home. The flagstone floor was raised a foot above the ground on stone pylons to keep the goods stored there dry. It looked to have been swept, and the walls were lined with sleeping rolls and blankets and the kitbags and weapons of the first two squads. Ramirus and Cato and their men were sitting on makeshift benches around two braziers, whose fires cast a cheery glow around the inside of the warehouse.

As faces turned towards the bedraggled men who had just entered the building, Cato stood up and approached Macro. 'I feared you had drowned, or fallen victim to those pirates you told me about.'

'Pirates? Pfft. I could eat those pansies for breakfast. As for drowning, I thought we might at one point. Then I remembered how furious Petronella would be with me if that happened and thought better of it. Anyway, we got here. Now we need to dry out and get something warm inside us. What's the food and wine situation?'

Apollonius sauntered up. 'I see your priorities are as constant as ever, Centurion.'

'Spare me the droll humour, spy.'

Cato smiled at the ongoing light friction between the two men and turned towards the veterans around the braziers. 'Make space there for our comrades!'

As the light faded in the barred slit windows high up on the warehouse walls, Macro stripped down to his loincloth and draped his wet tunic and spare clothes over a wooden frame improvised from a small stack of timber in the far corner. His men did likewise while their comrades prepared a meal, stirring gruel in a large iron pot suspended by a chain from an iron tripod arranged over one of the braziers. Several buckets and pots collected rainwater that had worked its way through cracked tiles in the roof, and every so often one of the men emptied them into a large water butt beside the doors. The warehouse might not offer the comforts of home, but there was a gratifying familiarity to being cooped up with fellow soldiers on campaign again, and Macro felt his spirits rise accordingly.

Cato and Apollonius ladled gruel into three mess tins and came to sit with him.

'Here you go.' Cato handed him one of the tins. 'Get that inside you.'

Macro took his spoon from his pack and all three ate in silence for a moment as the rain rumbled lightly on the tiles overhead.

Macro finished first and set his tin down between his feet. 'So, from what you say, we're two men down before we've even got started.'

'True, but by the same token, Malvinus is five men down,' Apollonius pointed out. 'The trouble is that he can afford the losses more easily than we can.'

'How are we going to take him on then? Not forgetting that we have the other gang to deal with as well.'

Cato grinned. 'There's a saying that seems appropriate to our situation: my enemy's enemy is my friend.'

Macro frowned. 'So you think we should stir the shit up and then side with one of the gangs? When the fighting is over, we're still going to have to sort out our new friends.'

'No, that's not what I'm thinking. Except for the first part. We will certainly be stirring the shit, but our enemy's enemy is going to be our friend without realising it.'

'Fine, now you've really lost me. What the fuck are you talking about, lad?'

'I'm saying that we need to cut down the odds against us. The gangs have far more men than we do, which makes any frontal attack on them a risky enterprise. Even if we were to destroy one of them, we'd have too few men left to finish the job with the other.'

'So how do we adjust the odds, then?'

'We get the gangs to do that for us. If they go for each other, then we'll be ready to take on the survivors.'

'And why would they go to war just to fit in with our needs?'

'That's the beauty of it. They won't even know we're involved. Not until it's too late. Let me show you something.' Cato stood up and crossed to the rear of the warehouse, where there were two piles of clothing. He picked up a garment from each and returned to his companions, holding two tunics up for them to see. 'I got these from the market while we were waiting for you to arrive.'

Macro examined them briefly. The tunics were cheaply made, worn and stained in places. 'Can't say I'm impressed with your choice of wardrobe, lad. Besides, we've all brought along spare clothing. I'd take these back and get a refund.'

'Look again and tell me exactly what you see.'

Macro sighed, weary of Cato's game-playing. 'All right. I'll humour you. Two tunics. One green and one black.'

Apollonius slapped his thigh and chuckled. 'I get it. Interesting strategy, Prefect Cato.'

'I don't get it,' Macro growled. 'Someone care to explain what's so bloody interesting about these tunics.'

'Gang colours,' Cato responded. 'Green for Malvinus and his men. Black for Cinna's lot. What do you think would happen if a group of men dressed in Malvinus's colours ambushed the other side's enforcers? I don't think such an action would be taken lightly. We already know that Cinna's men tried to steal Malvinus's business when they pitched up at Macro's inn. And you know what the gangs are like back in Rome – always ready to shed a little blood if they feel they're shown any disrespect or hostility. So we strike at each gang's interests disguised as their rivals. Like I said, we stir up the shit, our “friends” set about knocking seven shades out of each other, and when it’s over, we emerge from the shadows and finish off whatever is left of the gangs.’

Macro pondered this for a moment. ‘My enemy’s enemy, eh? I like the sound of it. I’d pay good money to watch Malvinus and Cinna go head to head while the whole town enjoys the sport.’

Apollonius clicked his tongue. ‘Of course, if they were to discover what we were up to, the chances are that they might settle their differences and come for us. That I’d like to see not so much.’

‘It’s a risk,’ Cato conceded. ‘However, as things stand, we lack the numbers to take on either gang, so I don’t see we have much choice. That’s why we’re going to have to pick our targets and the timing of our attacks carefully.’

‘If we are going to do it your way, then best to do it at night,’ suggested Apollonius. ‘Or during the hours of dusk. And it might be an idea to conceal our faces. We use cloaks with hoods, or scarves, or better still, masks.’

‘Is that necessary?’ asked Macro. ‘After all, our men’s faces aren’t known in the town.’

‘What if they run into the same people more than once and their faces are remembered? What if they are seen in different colours by the same witness?’

‘That’s easily resolved,’ said Cato. ‘We earmark specific groups of our men to play the part of each gang. Furthermore, we keep them off the streets so they don’t show their faces and give the game away.’

Apollonius glanced at Macro. ‘It occurs to me to ask if your mother knows of our presence in her warehouse.’

Cato shook his head. ‘Portia doesn’t know, and it’s safest for all of us that it stays that way.’

'That won't be much comfort to her if Malvinus turns up and starts asking her if she knows anything about the men sent to Camulodunum to kill Macro. From what I understand of him, he is not the type to ask questions politely.'

Macro glowered. 'If he lays a finger on her, I will smash every bone in his body before I kill him. Do you think she's at risk, Cato?'

'I can't say she isn't. But she is in less danger if she knows nothing about our plans.'

'She should be warned,' Macro insisted. 'She should be told to leave the town until this is over. She should have come with me to the colony.'

'Maybe,' Cato agreed. 'But it's too late for that now. If she was to suddenly leave, where would she go?'

'Camulodunum, most likely.'

'Precisely. And that's where Malvinus will go looking for her. If his thugs don't catch up with her on the road and drag her back here, they'll track her down in Camulodunum, along with Petronella, Lucius and Claudia.'

'So are you saying it's a choice between saving my mother, or my wife and the rest of them?'

'No. It's your mother, or your mother and the rest of them.'

'Quite the quandary, isn't it?' Apollonius commented as he regarded Macro with an ironic expression.

Macro rounded on him. 'This is my family we're discussing, you cold philosophising bastard. If you think there's anything funny about the situation, then perhaps you and I should step outside to talk it over.'

'Why on earth would we do that? It's raining. Besides, you'd only do yourself an injury, or oblige me to do it for you.'

'Big talk for a scrawny streak of piss,' Macro sneered.

Apollonius's habitual thin smile faded and his lips flickered with what looked to Cato like irritation. He knew the spy well enough to know how deadly he could be in a fight, and he feared for Macro. Moreover, they had already lost three men to injury and could ill afford any more.

'That's enough!' he snapped. 'There's to be no fighting within our ranks. I'll not have you two do our enemy's work for them.' He moved between them and glared defiantly at each man. 'If either of you takes this any further, I'll send you both back to the colony until the job is done here. Do I make myself clear?'

Macro nodded and grumbled something indistinct.

'Ineluctably so,' Apollonius confirmed.

'Good. I have known you both long enough to value your qualities. You're good men to have at my side, so spare me your childish intolerance. I expect you to work together in the coming days and be ready to guard each other's back.'

As he spoke, Cato was aware that the other men in the warehouse had fallen silent and turned to look in their direction with curious, and in some cases anxious, expressions. He was acutely aware of the need to give the impression of unity amongst their leaders, and he breathed calmly and spoke again in a lower, more measured tone.

'It's time to talk about our first move. We need to strike at one of the gangs to spark off the conflict between Malvinus and Cinna. It would be best if the target was something that caused as much personal affront as possible. Something that would compel them to respond in kind in order to defend their reputation. From what I've gleaned since I have been out on the streets, neither man has a wife or family, so we can't hit them on that front. It has to be something else they value. Any ideas?'

Apollonius shrugged. 'I know even less about this benighted frontier town than you do, Prefect.'

‘The bathhouse owned by Malvinus,’ Macro suggested. ‘I’ve been there twice. I nearly didn’t survive my second visit. It’s an upmarket place catering to merchants and senior officers and officials. Malvinus is a regular and it’s clear he’s proud of the place. Be a shame if anything was to happen to it.’

Apollonius’s eyes glinted eagerly at Cato. ‘You told me that Malvinus’s man said there’s a cache of weapons hidden at the bathhouse. We could destroy that as well. Two slaps in the face for the price of one. I would imagine our gangster friend will be incandescent when confronted with the blazing ruin of his prized property and the loss of his arms chest.’

Macro smiled to himself. ‘What I would give to see the bastard’s face when that happens . . .’

‘Quite.’ Cato nodded. ‘You’ll get your chance to avenge what he did to you before this is over, brother. I promise. So then, the bathhouse. Are we agreed?’

Macro nodded at once. Apollonius thought a moment before he responded. ‘I believe it serves our purposes admirably. When the smoke fills the sky over Londinium, word will spread to everyone in the town that Malvinus has been humiliated. He will be out for blood immediately he hears it was the work of Cinna’s men.’

‘Concerning that,’ Cato interrupted. ‘It might be best if we weren’t too obvious about it. We need to make sure that the blame for the attack is firmly attributed to Cinna, and that we do nothing to give our real identity away. It’s going to take some careful handling as the conflict escalates. Equally, we have to make sure that the fighting is contained enough that the garrison doesn’t get drawn in to restore order and drive the gangs underground for a while. They’ll only re-emerge once the pressure is off and we’ll be back where we started. They have to be destroyed once and for all.’

'I shouldn't worry about the garrison,' Macro sniffed. 'They're most likely to be under orders to guard the headquarters complex so that Decianus can sleep at night. I dare say he's living in fear of finding himself on the wrong end of a veteran's sword, given the way he left us to die a few months back.'

'Decianus?' Cato frowned. 'Decianus Catus?'

'That's the man.' Macro noticed Cato's thoughtfulness. 'Why? What's he to you?'

'How long has he been in Londinium?'

'He took up the procurator's post shortly before Petronella and I arrived.'

'Then he could be the same man who was procurator in Sardinia when I was campaigning there last year.'

'Small world.' Macro shrugged. 'So?'

Apollonius sighed. 'So, he knows about Claudia Acte being sent into exile on Sardinia. Cato reported her death from the pestilence when he returned to Rome, so how do you think Decianus is going to react if he visits the colony and recognises her? He'll wonder how the dead former mistress of the emperor has miraculously returned to life in Britannia. That sort of thing might go without question within the Judaean cult that worships Yeshua, but I dare say Decianus is going to be a little harder to satisfy.'

'Oh.' Macro grimaced. 'I see.'

Cato pressed his lips together briefly. 'Given what happened to the detachment of veterans from the colony, Decianus won't be returning to Camulodunum, so Claudia is safe as long as she remains there. As for me, I'll have to do my best to make sure our paths don't cross.'

'It's not the biggest of towns, lad. Keep your head down.'

'I will. In the meantime, our work begins at first light tomorrow.'

CHAPTER TWENTY-FIVE

Two days later, Macro was sitting beneath a cloudless sky outside a small canteen along the street from the entrance to the bathhouse. It was late in the afternoon and the sun bathed the customers of the canteen in a warm glow. The season had taken a definite turn and the daylight stretched out into longer, languid evenings, drawing more people onto the street to enjoy the change in temperature after the damp, cold months of winter and early spring. Around him the other customers were chatting happily as they drank watered wine and ate stew from plain bowls with spoons that chinked and clattered against the sides.

Cato sat opposite him on the end of the bench closest to the street. Each had a cup of wine, and they made small talk while they waited, so as not to arouse suspicion. Neither had shaved since leaving Camulodunum, and while Cato's jaw was lined with dark stubble, Macro already sported a thick beard that did much to conceal his features. Anyone who might have seen him visit the bathhouse before would be hard pressed to recognise him now, in his grimy worn tunic and cloak and scuffed boots.

'There he is.' Cato nodded discreetly towards the bathhouse.

Macro turned and saw Apollonius striding up the street towards the canteen. His face still had the sweaty glow of a man recently emerged from a steam room. His beard had been neatly trimmed, and he was dressed in a black tunic beneath a grey cloak with a fine fur collar. He would easily pass for a successful merchant. He drew up opposite the canteen and glanced back to make sure he was not being watched. Then he crossed the street, swerving around a large heap of manure that had fallen off the back of a cart, and sat down on the stool at the end of the table.

'Well?' Cato enquired quietly.

'Four armed men guarding the complex. Two patrolling outside. One on the gate and another on the reception counter. There are also at least ten slaves: cleaners, masseurs, fire tenders and a clerk and manager. The last of the customers was dressing as I left. They'll be closing up for the day as soon as he's done.'

'How are the men armed?' asked Macro.

'Daggers and clubs. I didn't see any other weapons.'

While Apollonius had been scouting the inside of the complex, Cato and Macro had ambled around the outside, mixing with the other people on the streets and alleys that bounded Malvinus's prized business. Besides the customer entrance, there was a gated arch for deliveries and a small door in the rear wall that Cato guessed was used for more discreet visitors to the bathhouse.

'Did you get a good look at the layout?'

Apollonius nodded. 'I took a wrong turning inside the main block and then the storage rooms before I encountered one of the slaves. I played dumb and said I had lost my way. Then I told him I would be fascinated to see the workings of a hypocaust system. I flattered his pride and was rewarded with a brief tour of the wider complex before we encountered a guard who put an end to that. But I saw as much as I needed to and have it all stored up here.' He tapped his head.

'Then let's get back to the warehouse. We'll strike as soon as it's dark. Come.'

Cato stood up and took a few coins from his purse to pay for the drinks. Macro paused long enough to drain his goblet, and then the three of them stepped into the street and made their way towards the junction of the road leading down to the port district. As they approached the turning, Macro saw the sign of the Dog and Deer hanging from its bracket at the next corner and drew up.

'I should check on my mother. She'll be worried that she hasn't heard from me.'

'Macro . . . brother,' Cato began gently. 'We can't go to the inn. She'll recognise us, and if any of Malvinus's mob are keeping an eye on the place, they'll know we're in Londinium and the cat will be out of the bag. Come now, let's go.'

Macro did not move. 'We could try the yard at the back when no one is looking. I just want to make sure she's not in any trouble.'

'She will be if we fail to get rid of the gangs,' said Apollonius. 'See reason, man. We can't risk being found out.'

'Easy for you to say. She's not your mother.'

'Very easy for me to say, as I never knew my mother.'

Macro turned towards him with a cynical smile. 'Why does that not surprise me?'

Apollonius's eyebrows twitched. 'Ouch.'

'That's enough,' Cato intervened. 'We haven't got much time. Let's go back to the warehouse, plan the attack and get the men ready.'

* * *

The weather was warm enough for the streets to still be busy when the trumpet note sounded the second hour of the night. By the light of a three-quarter moon, groups of young men and sailors roamed from one inn to the next in various stages of inebriation, talking and laughing loudly and making lewd comments to any woman unfortunate enough to be passing by. In amongst them was a band of ten men in black tunics, covered by brown cloaks just in case they ran into any genuine gang members. Cato led the way, with Macro and Apollonius on either side of him. They picked their way along the street towards the bathhouse, steering clear of the other groups in order to avoid any exchange of insults or challenges.

They were close to the corner where the bathhouse sat when a youth staggered out of an alley into their path and vomited across Apollonius's chest.

As the men drew to a halt, the spy looked down at his front with a deadpan expression and muttered, 'How droll.'

Macro stared at him, then burst out laughing. 'I thought that kind of shit only happened to me. Ah, Apollonius, my friend, that look suits you.'

The youth retched a couple of times, then spat to clear the residue of vomit from his mouth and rounded on Apollonius, swaying unsteadily. By the light of the moon, Cato could see that he was well built, with a bovine expression on his face that might have been the result of intoxication but was more likely to be inherited. He looked Apollonius up and down with a sneer. 'The state of you, mate.'

'In no small part due to your contribution, my friend.' Apollonius smiled politely. 'Now if you would kindly step from our path so that we might go our separate ways in peace.'

'You what?' The young man shook his head uncomprehendingly. 'You taking the piss? Is that it? You taking the piss out of me then?' He bunched his fists and staggered forward to confront the spy. 'Give me some money, or I'll lump yer, streak of piss that you are.'

'It's all piss with you, it would seem.' Apollonius frowned. 'Step aside now.'

The youth grinned stupidly. 'Make me.'

'With the greatest of pleasure.'

In a blur of motion, the spy grabbed him by the shoulders and rammed a knee into his groin. He followed up with a headbutt to the nose. The youth staggered back, one hand on his nose, the other on his crotch. Apollonius followed and pushed him back into the mouth of the alley he had emerged from, where he fell back onto the flagstones with a pained grunt.

The spy dusted his hands off. 'Witless oaf.'

'Nicely done,' Macro said grudgingly. 'You might start growing on me one day.'

Cato strode past them and spoke in an undertone. 'We've work to do.'

He led them to the corner of the bathhouse complex. The arched entrance in the wall surrounding the complex was guarded by two men standing to one side, talking quietly as they passed a wineskin between them. Ramirus and his section were waiting in the glow of lamplight outside an inn fifty paces down from the junction. They would act as the reserve, and would only intervene if the alarm was raised or more of Malvinus's men arrived unexpectedly. Leading his men across the junction, Cato followed the wall until they reached the alley that ran along the rear of the complex. A row of dingy shops and homes lined the opposite side. Little light penetrated the narrow route, and there were no other people in sight, which suited Cato's purpose as he made for the small doorway set halfway along the wall. He paused as he reached for the iron ring in the middle of the weathered iron-studded door and tested it. The door shifted very slightly on its hinges before coming up against the bar on the far side.

'Too much to hope for,' Cato muttered before turning to his men. 'We're going to have to go over the top. Herennius, to your place.'

A burly veteran came forward and stood braced against the wall as another man, slim and nimble, climbed up and stood on his shoulders, easing his fingers up the rough plaster towards the line of tiles running along the top. His fingers brushed a loose tile and a fine shower of debris fell on Cato below so that he had to blink it away and rub his eyes. Once the man had a good grip on some secure tiles, he hissed, 'Ready.'

Herennius moved his hands from the wall and gripped his comrade's ankles. With a light grunt, he thrust upwards, and the other man pulled himself up onto the top of the wall.

'Got it. You can let me go.'

'Can you see anyone?' asked Cato.

'No, sir. We're safe, sir.'

'Over you go then.'

The man swung his legs over before lowering himself down the far side of the wall. Cato heard him drop to the ground. There was a brief delay, then a soft scraping and some rattling as the bar was eased out of its brackets. Then the door swung open on slightly squeaky hinges and Cato ushered his men inside before closing it and ordering the locking bar to be replaced.

'Cloaks off,' he instructed, reaching up to undo the bronze clasp on his own garment and shrugging it from his shoulders. The others followed suit, and one of the men gathered the cloaks into a bundle and tucked them under his arm.

There was a faint red glow around the shutters of the slaves' quarters at the rear of the main building, and the sound of voices came from within. Elsewhere, all seemed still. Cato pointed. 'Apollonius, your group takes care of the slaves. Wait outside until one of them emerges. That'll be your cue to go in and keep them quiet until I send word that we have started the fire. After that you can release them.'

Apollonius nodded, and turned to beckon to the three veterans of his party. They padded across the compound and took up position along the side of the wall close to the door.

Cato gestured to the remaining men, who were carrying sidebags containing kindling boxes and tapers. He had reckoned on a ready supply of oils and other flammable materials being available within the bathhouse to prime the fire.

'Follow me.'

He made for the rear of the building and peered around the corner, towards the far wall of the complex. A figure was walking slowly away from him, right arm bent and slightly out. It was a pose he recognised well, that of a man resting his hand on the pommel of a sword. At least one of the enemy was better armed than Apollonius had reported. Cato felt a twinge of amusement. It seemed the spy was fallible after all, and when this night was over, he would enjoy puncturing his self-assurance. The faint smile faded from his lips as he eased himself back and faced his men.

'There's one man on this side of the bathhouse. Take him down quietly, Herennius.'

The giant unslung a club from his belt and crept around the corner, keeping close to the wall as he moved slowly to make sure that his army boots made as little sound as possible on the gravel that covered the ground. Ahead, Cato saw the guard approach the corner, and he felt tension tighten his throat. All now depended on whether he rounded the corner or turned and retraced his steps, in which case he was almost certain to spot Herennius. As the man stepped past the end of the wall, he was illuminated by the glow of a fire or brazier on the far side of the bathhouse, which bathed the right of his body in a red glow, stark against the grey shades of moonlight. Then he stopped, stretched his shoulders and rocked his head from side to side to ease his neck, and turned back the way he had come.

Even though there was no danger of him being seen, Cato held his breath and froze, sure that the man would raise the alarm at any moment. Herennius had already grasped the danger and dropped into a low crouch beside a log pile by the arched entrance leading to the chamber containing the hypocaust's furnace. He pressed himself into the wall and kept quite still as the guard resumed his beat. Reaching the end of the log pile, the man stopped again and yawned widely, tipping his head back. The dark form of Herennius burst from concealment and crashed into his side, sweeping him off his feet and sending him several feet through the air before he crashed onto the ground. He let out an audible gasp, but the veteran was on him before he could even think of shouting in alarm. Cato saw Herennius's club rise and slash down again and again, as he knocked the man senseless then caved his head in.

'On me,' Cato ordered, and hurried towards the two men. By the time he reached Herennius, the giant had stopped beating his fallen foe and stood over him breathing hard, blood dripping from the knotted wood that formed the head of the club. Cato crouched down by the guard and heard the harsh grunts as the man breathed his last, his body trembling violently. Then the movement suddenly stopped and he went limp with a long, soft sigh. Cato rose. 'He's gone. Good job. Get the body into the furnace room and then catch us up.'

Herennius nodded. He tucked the club into his broad belt and swept up the inert form, throwing him over his shoulder before carrying him towards the archway.

Cato waved the rest of the men on, leading the way to the far end of the wall. Peering around the corner along the front of the bathhouse, he saw the entrance some twenty paces away. The two guards were now standing just inside, close to a lit brazier, the bulge of their swords clearly visible underneath their cloaks. One was tossing some logs onto the blaze as the other stood facing the other way, warming his back.

'Ready, boys,' Cato whispered. 'Move slowly, but be prepared to rush them the moment I give the word.'

The man building up the fire had tossed the last log on and gone to stand opposite his friend, reaching out for the wineskin that was proffered. The way he was facing, he would surely see the attackers as they rushed forward. Cato waited a moment, willing him to turn away, but he didn't shift from his position. The two men continued talking in relaxed low voices, oblivious to the party of raiders nearby. Cato felt the tension building inside him. A noise from behind caused him to snap his head round and raise his club ready to strike, but it was only Herennius rejoining them.

There was an outburst of shouting from the street, and a moment later two men stumbled through the archway, swinging punches at each other as they bellowed slurred insults. The bigger of the two guards dropped the wineskin and strode towards the brawlers, grabbing one by the collar of his tunic and wrenching him away from his opponent before dumping him on the ground.

'What the fuck do you two think you're playing at? This is Malvinus's place. You know what that means.'

Even though the interlopers were drunk, they were not so

drunk that the name didn't strike fear into their hearts, and they hurriedly gathered themselves up and staggered towards the archway, watched by the guards.

This was his chance, Cato decided, and he beckoned to his men. 'Let's go.'

They rounded the corner of the building and spread out, clubs tightly gripped and ready to strike. They were only ten paces away when the nearer of the guards heard them and turned. By the glow of the flames in the brazier Cato saw his eyes widen in surprise, and he froze for an instant before his hand swept his cloak aside and grasped the handle of his sword. The blade was halfway out of the scabbard as Cato sprinted the last few paces and swung his club at the man's sword hand, crushing his knuckles with a dull crack. His grip loosened and the sword slid back into the scabbard with a metallic click, then he staggered backwards, and threw his arms up as Herennius slashed his club at his head. Two blows smashed into his arms before a third broke through and crunched against the crown of his head. His jaw snapped shut and blood spurted from his nostrils, then his eyes rolled up and he folded over and slumped to his knees. Herennius gave a disdainful snort as he kicked him onto his back.

The other guard had faster reactions than his comrade and had time to draw his sword and shout over his shoulder towards the entrance to the bathhouse. 'Alarm!'

Three of Cato's men closed round him, striking out with their clubs while dodging the wild slashes of his sword. One of the veterans was too slow and grunted in pain as the guard's sword ripped open his forearm. His companions backed off a pace, anxious not to be wounded. The guard took advantage of their hesitation to shout another warning.

'Stuff this!' Herennius thrust his comrades aside and lunged towards the guard, who raised his sword to parry the giant's club as it arced towards him. The blow was so powerful that the blade was knocked from his hand with a shrill ring, clattering down close to the brazier. Herennius followed up with a body charge, sending the guard flying onto his back, the impact driving the breath from his lungs in an explosive gasp. Then, snatching out his dagger, he leaned down and thrust it into the guard's eye, driving the blade into his skull and twisting it from side to side before ripping it free. He paused to make sure the man was dead before wiping the blade clean on the guard's tunic and sheathing his weapon. Then he moved to the brazier and picked up the sword.

Cato's pulse was racing, and he swallowed to get rid of the tacky sensation in his mouth before he issued his orders.

'Get the bodies out of sight. Over there by the wall where they can't be seen from the street. Ancus and Nepos, put their cloaks on and take their place guarding the archway.'

While the guards were dragged away, Cato turned towards the entrance to see if anyone in the bathhouse had responded to the warning cry. No one emerged from the dimly lit atrium, and there was no sound other than the voices of the revellers in the inns along the street, and others that seemed to come from somewhere further off. Once the two veterans had taken their places beside the brazier, he led Herennius and the others towards the entrance. They approached from the side, and Cato led the rush into the room, where the last of the guards was sitting on a stool behind the counter, a woman on his lap, her nipple in his mouth. Her breast dropped away as the guard's startled gaze took in the armed men rushing towards him. Abruptly he shoved her off his lap and snatched his sword from its scabbard on the floor beside the stool.

The woman shrieked and rolled away as the guard sprang to

his feet. Cato reached him first, thrusting the head of his club into the man's chest and feeling the blow land solidly against his breastbone, winding him so that he strained for breath. He still managed to deflect Cato's follow-up blow, the edge of his sword splintering the shaft of the club. Cato hurled the stump at the guard's face, momentarily distracting him so that he never saw the sword thrust from the side as Herennius slammed the point of his captured blade into the man's midriff, tearing through flesh and the vital organs within. He stumbled back, tripping over the stool before collapsing beside the woman, his sword still gripped in his hand. He tried to raise it, but Cato leaped forward and stamped his heel on the man's wrist, and he released his grip. The woman stared at the mortally wounded man who had been groping her just a moment before, and opened her mouth to scream.

'Don't!' Cato snapped at her.

She froze, mouth gaping, then swallowed in fright and raised her hands in front of her face, as if that would protect her. 'Please don't hurt me. Please, sir . . .'

'Herennius, take her outside. Tell Ancus to keep her with them until we get the fire started. Get some tapers lit and bring them back to me. The rest of you, this way.'

He led the men into the changing room and indicated the piles of sheets and robes on the shelf. 'Shove those under the foot benches. We'll start the fire here and then get another one going in the storerooms.'

He left them to get on with their preparations. Recalling the diagram detailing the layout of the bathhouse prepared by Apollonius, he made his way back to the atrium and through the narrow doorway into the short corridor beyond, with storerooms on either side. He located the room with the oil jars, and another with wooden clogs and brooms that would make for perfect kindling. He was about to return to gather some of his men to prepare another fire when he heard voices from beyond the door at the end of the corridor.

Approaching cautiously, he grasped the handle on the latch and eased it up as he drew his dagger. Slowly pulling the door open just enough to peer into the warm room beyond, he saw that it was lit by a series of stands carrying oil lamps. Around the interior were at least twenty figures, male and female, some energetically engaged in sex while others sat or lay on couches, spent from their exertions. Wine jars and the remains of a meal were scattered around. He was about to push the door closed when one of the men lying on a couch close by turned and saw him. Their gazes met through the gap between the door and the frame, and the man frowned and then looked relieved.

'Fuck me, I thought you was Malvinus.'

Cato made no reply, too surprised to respond. Had Apollonius missed the presence of these people, or had they arrived after he left?

The man swung his feet over the side of the couch and stood up. 'Wait a moment, who the fuck are you?'

CHAPTER TWENTY-SIX

Cato slammed the door shut, dropped the latch back into its bracket and threw his weight against the timbers as he abandoned his club and drew his dagger. He jammed the blade into the gap behind the latch and forced it down to wedge the bar in place. An instant later, the latch budged slightly as someone on the far side of the door tried to open it. Cato pressed down harder on the dagger as he sensed more force being applied. The voices in the warm room were much louder now as others reacted to the shouts of the man behind the door. Suddenly the wooden surface leaped against Cato's shoulder.

He turned his head to shout. 'On me! On me! Get in here!'

The door lurched again and his blade slipped and nearly came out from behind the latch. Hunching his shoulder, he pressed down on the handle, gritting his teeth as he strained to keep the door closed.

He heard footsteps rushing up behind him and glanced back to see Herennius. 'Take the dagger and keep the latch jammed!'

The veteran took his place and pressed his bulk against the door as he closed his meaty fist around the handle of the dagger. Cato hurried to the nearest storeroom, but he could find nothing heavy to pile up against the door. The same was true of the other storerooms, and he cursed under his breath. 'Hold them back!' he ordered Herennius.

'I'm bloody trying to, sir!'

Running back through the atrium, he smelt smoke. He glanced towards the changing-room door and saw the flicker of flames there. Outside, he found Ancus and his companion guarding the woman. 'Ancus! Get down the street to Ramirus. I need him and his men here at once. Run, man!'

Back inside, he stopped at the door of the changing room and saw the men there steadily feeding the small fires they had lit. Smoke curled up into the curved ceiling overhead, and one of the veterans was already coughing. He told the man to go down to the hypocaust furnace and get a fire going in the underground chamber using the wood stocks outside, then ordered the rest to follow him as he rushed back down the corridor to aid Herennius.

The giant was straining against the door, boots scrabbling for purchase on the flagstone floor. The dagger had fallen from the latch and lay at his feet, and the men on the far side were gradually gaining ground. Before Cato could reach him, he lost his footing, and the door opened far enough for the first of Malvinus's men to squeeze through. He swung a fist at Herennius, catching him a glancing blow on the jaw that seemed to enrage rather than harm the huge veteran. But there was nothing he could do to stop the men from forcing him backwards.

Cato drew up. 'Fall back, Herennius!'

The giant snarled with frustration and gave one last shove before he stepped back. He blocked another jab before unleashing a punch of his own, which smashed into the nose of the first man to step through the gap, slamming his head back against the corridor wall with a dull crack. He was quickly thrust aside by one of his companions as Herennius turned away and ran to join Cato and the other veterans formed up across the corridor. The door swung open fully and smashed against the wall as Malvinus's thugs surged through in various states of undress. A handful wore tunics, but most were stripped down to loincloths, and one was naked. All of them, however, were armed with a mixture of daggers and swords.

With his dagger in one hand and a club in the other, Cato braced his boots and bent his knees slightly in readiness to move quickly. 'We have to hold them until the fire takes, lads.'

'We won't let you down, sir,' said Herennius.

A large man with a scarred face and an empty eye socket shouldered his way through the gang members and brandished an iron-studded club in Cato's direction. 'You're Cinna's men. What the fuck are you doing here? You break the peace now and Malvinus will have every last one of you nailed to the walls of the bathhouse.'

Cato did not reply and the veterans stood silently, ready to fight. Then, by the dim light of the oil lamps, he saw the one-eyed man frown, tilt his head back marginally and sniff. 'You bastards . . . The cunts are burning the place down! Get stuck in, boys!'

He raised his club and charged, and his men surged after him. The veterans were outnumbered at least two to one, Cato realised. Unless Ramirus and his squad came quickly, they would be overwhelmed and cut down and the fires put out.

Pushing all thought aside, he focused on the men running towards him. The leader pulled his right arm back when he was no more than three paces away and then swung his weapon with ferocious strength at Herennius. The giant leaned back just in time and the nailed head swished by and struck the wall, shattering the plaster in an explosion of flakes and dust. The attacker's momentum carried him into another veteran, and the two men began to grapple, trying to wrestle one another to the floor.

Cato could spare them no further attention as he threw his club aside, drew his sword and faced his enemy with two blades. He feinted with his sword at the nearest opponent, a red-haired youth with swirling tattoos on his face – a native recruit to Malvinus's gang. Like Cato, he was armed with a short sword, and he frantically swiped at Cato's blade to beat the point away from his face. The Celt possessed no discernible skill with the weapon, either because he was used to the longer blades of his people, or because he was the type who thought simply wielding a blade made him tough. But Cato was no frightened civilian, and fifteen years in the army had made him into a formidable warrior. He feinted again, with the dagger this time, and the youth swerved away, opening himself up to a thrust from the sword that punctured the smooth skin of his toned stomach. His jaw sagged as the impact drove the breath from his lungs. Instantly the will to fight vanished, and he looked down with a stupefied expression as Cato ripped the blade free and stabbed his dagger at a slight angle into the Celt's armpit. The shock of the first blow had gone, and now the youth howled in terror as he staggered back, blood gushing from both wounds.

At once, another man took his place, older and more wary. He stood off a little and sized Cato up for an instant before holding his dagger out and going blade to blade with Cato's sword. Instinctively Cato stabbed with his blade, but the gang member's reactions were finely honed, and he caught Cato's wrist in a powerful grip and stopped the thrust before it had gathered any momentum. The two men stood face to face, straining to break the other's lock and press home a fatal strike.

Suddenly Cato wrenched his arm back, and his opponent dipped slightly towards him, enough to bring his face within reach. Cato whipped his head forward and cracked the crown against the man's brow. The gang member was dazed and blinking, but still in sufficient control of his wits to keep his grip on Cato's wrist. With a flick of his hand, Cato disengaged the sword and punched the guard into the man's jaw. He swayed back a step, and then there was a metallic glimmer as Herennius's sword swept past Cato and tore into the man's throat.

There was a brief opportunity for Cato to glance to both sides. One of his men was still wrestling with the rival leader, pressed up against the side of the corridor. The other veteran was lying face down on the floor, blood pooling around his head. The youth Cato had dealt with was slumped against the wall a short distance away, while another gang member was falling back nursing a crushed and misshapen hand. Three of them against eight. Where in Hades was Ramirus? Cato thought furiously.

The enemy leader managed to free his club and twist his wrist savagely to deal a blow to the veteran's temple. The iron studs tore at the flesh, the impact stunning Cato's man long enough for a second attack that shattered his skull, spraying blood up the wall behind him.

'Get back!' Cato ordered his remaining comrade as he backed away, sword raised and sweeping from side to side as he dared his opponents to attack him.

Herennius snorted with derision, his eyes staring madly. 'Not until I've dealt with that fucker.'

He turned on the enemy leader and the two men sized each other up as Cato continued to retreat. 'Herennius, fall back. That's an order.'

'Save yourself, sir. I'm not leaving until this one's dead.'

The surviving gang members held back a short distance behind their leader, watching as the two large men seemed to fill the width of the corridor. Cato took advantage of their hesitation and turned to hurry towards the doorway leading into the atrium. His movement broke the spell.

'What you waiting for?' the leader bellowed at his men. 'Help me deal with this big bastard, then see to that one ratting out!'

Cato paused mid stride and gritted his teeth. 'Ratting out . . . Fuck that.'

Even though he knew it was his duty to put the mission first, something deep inside him rebelled at the idea of leaving the foolhardy Herennius to die alone. His fighting blood was already up, and now he turned round, took a deep breath and muttered to himself. 'Gods preserve me, I'm turning into Macro.'

He let out an animal roar and charged back into the fight. Every face turned towards him, shocked expressions dimly illuminated by the lazy ripple of the oil lamp flames.

Herennius broke the spell, thrusting his sword at the leader, who threw himself back amongst his men to avoid it. The veteran pounced forward and lashed out with his fist, knocking a man's head to the side. The leader recovered his balance and cried out in an attempt to rally his men, 'For Malvinus!' then thrust his club into the veteran's midriff. As Herennius staggered to a halt, winded, Cato rushed up and hacked at the club, knocking it out of the leader's hands, then turned his blade towards a man lunging at Herennius with a thin-bladed dagger, causing the attacker to recoil.

'Sir, look out!' Herennius gasped.

Cato felt a blow to his left forearm and looked down to see that he had been stabbed a few inches above the wrist. He felt his fingers spasm, and his dagger dropped to the floor. Malvinus's man tore the blade free and made to strike again, but Cato stepped away just in time, sweeping his sword in a flat arc to discourage any other attackers. But the enemy's leader was not the kind to run from a fight. He snatched a sword from one of his men and hurled himself at Cato, hacking in a wild flurry of blows that gave Cato no chance to riposte. All he could do was hang on grimly, parrying and deflecting one blow after another. At the edge of his vision he was aware of three men piling into Herennius and stabbing at him with daggers as he went down and curled up on his side, hands raised to protect his head. There was nothing Cato could do to help him, and now he cursed his earlier impulse as he was forced back down the corridor.

He heard noises behind him, boots pounding across the tessellated floor of the atrium, and then heard Ramirus's booming voice as he called out to his men. 'Get stuck in, lads!'

The veterans piled into the corridor, clubs and daggers at the ready as they surged forward to support Cato. The enemy leader snarled in frustration, then disengaged and backed off. Behind him, the rest of Malvinus's men turned and fled back towards the warm room, fighting each other to get through the doorway as they tried to escape. Their leader glanced round and spat in contempt before he reluctantly joined them.

Ramirus drew up at Cato's side. 'Thank the gods we got here in time.'

Cato stabbed a finger towards the far end of the corridor. 'Go after them. Kill them all. We can't let any escape. Go!' He stood aside as Ramirus and his section charged past and poured through the door into the warm room. The women still inside started screaming as fighting raged across the couches, benches and tables.

A deep groan drew Cato's attention, and he saw Herennius roll slowly onto his back, legs bent. His arms, hands and body were covered in stab wounds, and blood smeared his exposed flesh and stained the ripped material of his tunic. Cato lowered his sword and kneeled beside him. Herennius reached out a trembling hand, and Cato clasped it tightly, feeling the tremors shaking the veteran's body. With his spare hand, he cradled Herennius's head.

'Should have fucking obeyed the order.'

'Yes, brother.'

'And you shouldn't . . . have come back for me.'

Cato smiled gently. 'What else was I going to do?'

Herennius's eyes rolled up into his head as his face screwed up in agony for a moment.

'I'll get you out of here,' said Cato. 'And see to your wounds.'

'I'm done in, sir. Finished . . . Survived three campaigns against . . . the Germans, another here in Britannia, and it ends . . . in a bloody back corridor of a provincial bath-house . . . Fuck my luck.'

Cato shrugged. 'That's the way it goes, brother. But we'll remember you.'

'See that you do well by my little Camella . . . Promise me.' His grip tightened painfully.

'I swear it.'

The grip relaxed and the veteran's face looked almost restful. He licked his lips and pushed feebly at Cato. 'Go. Help Ramirus and his lads . . . I'll wait here.'

Cato eased the veteran's head back onto the floor and picked up his sword before rising to his feet. He nodded a farewell to Herennius, then ran through the door into the warm room. At once his ears were assaulted by the terrified screams of the women amid the crash of furniture and the clatter and scrape of blades. Pausing for a beat to take stock, he glanced round the room. It was no more than ten paces square, and still held much of the warmth from the hypocaust system even hours after the furnace had stopped being fed with fuel. A short time ago, Malvinus's men had been enjoying a party in the company of several of the town's prostitutes, including a couple of catamites. Now they were fighting for their lives while the other partygoers had backed into the far corner and stood in a tightly packed group. There were bodies sprawled on the floor, but Cato could see that almost all of Ramirus's men were still on their feet as they closed in around the leader and the last of his men. Another of the gang members was kneeling behind them, working away with a dagger as he enlarged a vent low on the wall.

Cato cautiously approached the prostitutes, halting a sword's length away from them as he pointed to the door with his wounded hand. 'Go!'

They flinched at his raised voice, but none of them moved from what they seemed to think was the safety of the corner.

'The bloody building's on fire,' Cato continued urgently. 'Cinna is only after Malvinus's men. You'll fry if you stay here. Go, damn you!'

He moved to one side and brandished his sword at an over-painted woman. She shrieked before bolting for the door, and at once the others fled after her.

When Cato turned back to join Ramirus, only the one-eyed leader was still on his feet, lashing out with a long sword he had taken from one of his men and keeping the veterans at bay. Behind him, the man who had been widening the vent was now wriggling into it feet first.

'You find Malvinus!' the leader called over his shoulder.

'You tell him it was Cinna's men. Move!'

The man eased himself through and disappeared from sight.

Ramirus and one of his men had picked up a small table and tilted it over to form a makeshift shield, and now the camp prefect gave the order to charge using it as cover. The one-eyed man managed to get one blow in, splintering the edge of the table before it slammed into him and drove him back, pinning him against the wall. Ramirus snatched out his dagger and stabbed his enemy twice in the face before the point found the eye socket and he punched it up into the skull, twisting it from side to side. The man thrashed about briefly before suddenly going limp and collapsing.

Ramirus shoved the table aside and pulled the leader away from the vent, then pointed to one of his men. 'Sandinus, go after that bastard and finish him off.'

A waft of hot air, reeking of woodsmoke, came from the opening.

'No,' Cato ordered. 'Let him go.'

'What?' Ramirus turned to him with a confused expression. 'Why?'

'You heard him.' Cato gestured to the fallen leader. 'He called us Cinna's men. That's what Malvinus needs to hear. Let him go.'

Ramirus was breathing hard, still keyed up by the skirmish. He swallowed and nodded, forcing himself to calm down.

Cato glanced round. 'Most of the furniture will burn nicely. Pile it up and set it alight. Then get your men outside.'

'Yes, sir.' Ramirus hesitated. 'What about our dead?'

'Leave them. Just take the wounded and get 'em back to the warehouse as quickly as possible. Stick to the alleys. I'll join you there with my men once we've got some witnesses to see our colours.'

Ramirus acknowledged the orders with a curt nod and Cato left him to deal with starting the fire while he made his way to the changing room to check the progress of the blaze there. Thick smoke was already drifting into the atrium, and as he approached the archway leading to the changing area, he saw flames roaring up from the piles of robes and sheets his men had heaped into four pyres inside the room. He nodded with satisfaction and returned to the storerooms, where he picked up two jars of oil. Back in the warm room, he handed them to one of Ramirus's veterans who was busy piling furnishings into a heap. Another man had got a small flame lit using his tinderbox and was blowing lightly on the smoking wood shavings he had used to encourage the flames to take.

Mindful of the other fire already burning fiercely, Cato gave the order for Ramirus to get his men out, and they followed him back down the corridor, past the bodies and pools of blood. He paused as he reached Herennius, but the giant veteran was already dead, a pained expression fixed on his features.

When they reached the atrium, Cato had to shield his face as he hurried past the changing room and into the cool night outside. Ramirus and his men were already dispersing, mingling with the crowd gathering in the street. More men came running from the corner of the main building, and Cato caught sight of Apollonius and the men assigned to keep the slaves quiet.

'Any trouble?' asked Cato.

'None. They were as meek as lambs. I let 'em go once I heard the commotion. Don't worry, I primed them with the message – told them this was Cinna's doing. Said there was going to be one crime king in Londinium when it was all over, and it wasn't going to be Malvinus. I think they believed it.'

'Good.'

There was a crashing noise, and both men turned towards

the bathhouse. Cato watched as a section of the roof above the changing rooms collapsed and flames licked up into the darkness. More smoke and flames appeared around the eaves of the warm room, and the edge of the building close to the furnace glowed against the dark sky. There was a sudden roar as the blaze spread to the oil in one of the storerooms. A raging red glow illuminated the interior of the wall surrounding the complex and lit up the faces of the crowd that had gathered in the street to witness the spectacle.

'Time we left,' said Apollonius.

Cato nodded. 'Get the men out the way they came in. Then back to the warehouse. Ramirus and his section will make their own way there.'

'What about you?'

'I'll follow on. Go.'

The men trotted off around the corner of the building, leaving Cato standing alone before the conflagration. Timbers burst with sharp reports, and there was a dull roar and clatter as more of the roof fell in with a fresh explosion of sparks. He slowly turned to face the crowd packed into the gateway and the street beyond. There was mostly shock in their faces. Some looked on in awe, mouths agape, all of them brightly illuminated by the fire. But all they could see of Cato was his dark shape outlined against the flames. He raised his hands and shouted to be heard above the din of the blaze.

'By order of Cinna! Let all of Londinium know that Malvinus is finished!'

He stepped forward and waited a moment, long enough to be sure that many would see the colour of his tunic, then he turned and followed Apollonius.

CHAPTER TWENTY-SEVEN

The following morning, the smoke still rising from the charred ruins of the bathhouse was visible across the town, and the air of the surrounding neighbourhood was thick with the choking stench of burning. The damage done was mainly within the walls of the complex, but the thatch on a number of nearby buildings had caught fire as burning debris fell on their roofs and set them alight, and only swift action had prevented the flames from spreading any further. Not that that was much comfort to those whose homes and businesses had been pulled down and the remains doused with water from a nearby culvert.

Nor was it much of a distraction to the four men in black tunics and cloaks who strode down the street where the town's tanneries were concentrated. Thanks to the edict of a previous governor, who had wanted the sickening odour of the businesses concentrated in one area, as far from headquarters as possible, an area had been set aside for them downriver of the wharf and one street back from the Tamesis. A ditch ran from the street down to the river, fed by a diverted stream that sluiced away the tanneries' waste. Even so, the ghastly smell rising from the ditch was a daily affront to those living on either side.

The men approached the entrance to one of the yards, where teams of workers prepared the carcasses, hoisting them up onto wooden frames where iron hooks were fixed to their limbs to spread them out and make the work easier for the men who gutted the dead animals before removing their hides; a skilled job carried out by hardy individuals wielding very sharp knives. The skinners focused on their work as the four gang members entered, and pretended not to notice their visitors nor question why they had come to the premises. The same men came to see the owner every month, two of them holding the handles of a small chest that was always somewhat heavier when they left and moved on to the next business that fell within the purview of Cinna's protection racket.

On this particular day, the visit was conducted in the usual manner, despite the palpable tension as a result of the attack on Malvinus's bathhouse. The leader of the group, a slender, dark-haired man with an amiable expression, smiled broadly as he held his arms wide in greeting and approached the owner of the business, who sat on a stool outside the tiny office where he kept his records and the strongbox in which he safeguarded his takings.

'Friend Gracchus! How is your business going this fine day?'

Gracchus, a paunchy man with wild grey hair and a stained leather apron, rose stiffly, his manner wary and resentful. 'Can't grumble, Naso. Enough work to keep me going.'

'Delighted to hear it. Yet despite this being my regular collection day, you seem somewhat surprised to see me.'

Gracchus indicated the dark smudge against the clear sky above the smouldering bathhouse ruins. 'Word is that your lads torched Malvinus's place last night. They say he'll be coming for you.'

'If that's what they say, then they are completely mistaken, friend. We had nothing to do with it. Too many fires break out in this ramshackle town of ours. I've a good mind to petition the governor to set up a firefighting force to deal with such a scandalous state of affairs. After all, decent taxpayers like yourself deserve to be properly looked after by the powers that be, eh?'

Naso glanced up at the clear sky and sighed. 'Warm weather for the time of year. What would you say to offering me and my men something to drink? Thirsty work doing the rounds and lugging that chest with us.' He looked at the other man steadily, and there was a beat before Gracchus nodded. He took a cloth out of his apron pocket and dabbed his forehead as he turned to a small boy carrying two pails of blood across the yard.

'Lupercus. Put those down and bring us some wine and cups. Quick about it, lad.'

The boy did as he was told, disappearing through a door that led into the house attached to the tannery.

Naso sauntered over to the stool and sat down, leaning back against the wall and folding his arms as he tilted his face to take advantage of the sunlight. 'Ah yes, a fine day indeed . . .' He sat up abruptly. 'What am I thinking? Where are my manners? Do have a seat, Gracchus. We can have a friendly chat over the wine before me and my boys go on our merry way.'

'I've got a lot of work on today; haven't got much time to spare.'

Naso's face became expressionless and his voice was flat as he repeated, 'Haven't got time?'

Gracchus shifted uneasily and glanced round. Spotting an empty wooden tub nearby, he hurried over to fetch it and set it down, upturned, near Naso, then sat heavily.

Naso smiled, leaned over and slapped the tanner on his fat knee. 'There! That's better! You and me, sitting in the sunshine having a nice chat over a cup of wine – when that little streak of piss comes back with it – just like a couple of old mates, eh?'

'If you say so,' Gracchus replied guardedly.

'So, what's new in the world of Gracchus?'

'New?'

'Yes, new,' Naso responded slowly, as if he was addressing an idiot.

'What do you mean?'

He rolled his eyes theatrically. 'Let's see. Your young wife, for example. How is her pregnancy going? You must be looking forward to having a new member of the family to employ in the business as soon as they can walk.'

'Pregnant?' Gracchus looked confused. 'She's . . . she's not pregnant.'

'Not pregnant?' Naso frowned.

They were interrupted by a heavyset woman with round red cheeks emerging from the house carrying a small amphora under one arm and some leather beakers with handles on a length of twine. The boy came after her with a basket of small loaves of bread. Naso regarded her with a raised eyebrow as the refreshments were set down between the two seated men.

'Are you certain she's not expecting a child? From the look of her I'd say it might even be twins.' Then he slapped his forehead. 'Oh, I see it now! You must be right, Gracchus. She's not pregnant, just fat, like a tub of lard.' He roared with laughter, and his three men joined in.

Some of those working in the yard risked a glance towards the unhappy scene. Gracchus's wife blushed, and shot a pained look at her husband, appealing for support. He shook his head and gestured to the house. 'Leave us, my dear.'

As she turned away, Naso lurched towards her and slapped her hard on the rump. She uttered a cry and scuttled to safety with a wounded expression that betokened some harsh words between herself and her husband the moment Naso and his men left.

'Don't do that again,' Gracchus said through clenched teeth.

Naso had pulled out the stopper from the amphora and was pouring himself a cup of wine. He froze at the comment. 'Are you threatening me, old man?'

Gracchus looked down at his booted feet and spoke quietly. 'Just don't treat her like that. That's all.'

Naso slowly rose to his feet, all trace of his former mocking mirth gone. 'Why, Gracchus, I thought we were friends.'

In a sudden burst of motion, he hurled the wine in the cup into the tanner's face, then threw the jar against the wall above his head. It burst into fragments, and the explosion of wine splattered the plaster and drenched Gracchus's head.

'We're not welcome here, boys. So we'll be leaving just as soon as this fat fuck has paid up.' He kicked Gracchus. 'Move!'

The tanner rose into a crouch, head hunched down, and hurried into his office. There was the nervous rattle of a key being fitted to a lock and turned, followed by the faint squeal of hinges, then a pained grunt before he emerged carrying a strongbox. He set it down and opened the lid, and Naso counted out the coins into his own chest.

'. . . forty-eight, forty-nine and fifty. That's your monthly dues paid up, and let's say, another ten for our cleaning bill.' He indicated a splash of wine on the hem of his tunic. 'Close the box and let's be on our way, boys.'

He rose and led his group towards the gateway leading into the street. As he approached, a group of men in green tunics and cloaks spread out across the opening. Their heads were covered by the hoods of their cloaks, and they wore neck cloths over their mouths. There were five of them. A tall man in the centre, with a short, bulky individual to his right and a thin man to his left. Two solidly built men of medium height flanked them.

Naso and his men stopped dead. Clearing his throat, Naso made an open-handed gesture of greeting. 'My friends, what is the meaning of this? We're just going about our business. This tannery is on our turf, as agreed by our boss and yours. So if you don't mind, I'd like to kindly ask you to fuck off out of it before Cinna finds out you're threatening the peace.'

'Swords,' the man in the centre said quietly. There was a short chorus of rasping metal, and Naso found himself faced with a row of gleaming short swords handled by men who knew what they were about and looked determined with it.

'Put the chest down, drop your weapons and walk away,' the man continued.

Naso's bravado of a moment ago, and the swaggering manner in which he had bullied Gracchus, instantly fell away, and his sharp mind grasped that his life and those of his men were in the gravest danger. Not just from the men of Malvinus's gang standing before them, but also from Cinna, who did not take kindly to those who failed to return to their master with the monthly takings fully accounted for. More than one miscreant had paid the price by being garrotted before being found floating face down amid the shipping on the Tamesis.

'Boys, we'd better do as the man says.' He turned to his comrades, discreetly plucking a throwing knife from the scabbard concealed beneath his belt. He glanced at each of his men so that his intentions were clear, and then spun round and hurled the blade at the chest of the man in the middle of the line.

The weapon flashed across the yard and there was no time for a warning shout, but with reactions so quick Naso scarcely believed it possible, the man jerked to one side. At the same time, his sword shot up to block the knife, and there was a metallic ring as it spun through the gateway and clattered off a thick beam of wood running above the shop on the opposite side of the street.

As soon as the blade had left his fingers, Naso's hand had moved in a swift blur to the short sword concealed beneath his cloak, and now he wrenched it free, shouting to his men, 'Get stuck in!'

Yelling as savagely as he could, he led the charge at the line of Malvinus's men, knowing that he must either emerge victorious or go down spitting defiance in the face of his enemy. The tannery workers were scrabbling to get as far from the gateway as they could, dashing into the house or the storerooms and sheds arranged around the edge of the yard. Naso picked the man who had given the orders, mindful of his lightning evasion of the throwing knife. If he could only strike him down, maybe that would knock some of the courage out of his followers and so even up the odds a little.

His opposite number stood feet apart and knees slightly bent, sword angled out from the hip and spare arm raised to help balance his body. An experienced fighting man, but then so was Naso, before he was flogged and thrown out of the Ninth Legion for stealing another man's purse. He knew well enough how frightening it was to be on the receiving end of a charge. He was running as fast as he could when he felt his sword parried aside, but before his opponent could get the point of his weapon turned inward to impale him, their bodies collided in a mutually winding thud that caused Naso's jaws to snap shut with a jarring clash of teeth. He tasted blood in his mouth, and the sweaty odour of the other man filled his nostrils. The impact swept the man off his feet and carried him back a couple of paces before his legs gave way, taking Naso with him so that both of them fell into the foul trickle of sewage and cadaverous fluids flushed out of the tanneries.

Both men retained their grip on their weapons as they desperately scrambled back to their feet in a bid to be first to strike the next blow. Once again Naso was surprised, and not a little impressed, that his opponent was poised, blade ready, at exactly the same time as himself. Both were still for a moment, senses alive to every sound, any hint of a sudden movement as they weighed each other up.

'You're good.' His lips lifted in a tight grin. 'Which legion?'

They were close enough now that he could see the slight milky tint in the other man's left eye, and the scar that crossed his face. He was so focused that he was barely aware of the sounds of the other men fighting a short distance away. His opponent made no reply.

'Like I said, you're good. But I'm better!' As he spoke the last word, he sprang forward, thrusting at the other man's midriff. Their swords clashed and held, and he tested his strength against his opponent's blade and sensed the firmness of his arm before withdrawing his sword and quickly switching angles to slash diagonally at the man's shoulder. Once again his blade was intercepted, but this time his enemy surged forward, swivelling so that his left hand shot out and grasped Naso's sword arm at the wrist and thrust it down, causing him to momentarily lose his balance.

At that instant, Naso knew he was finished, even before the point of the sword pierced his side, just under his ribcage, and drove up at an angle into his vitals. His eyes widened and his mouth gaped in stunned surprise as he felt the air bursting from his lungs, and then at once the horrible sensation of blood welling up inside so that he could not breathe. One twist, then another, and the man tore the blade free and shoved Naso off his feet so that he fell back into a sitting position, legs splayed, arms to the side, sword slipping from his fingers. His breaths were laboured as he looked at the man standing over him.

'Better, eh?' the man sneered. 'The Ninth Legion never were up to much, brother.'

'Wait . . . who . . . ?'

His enemy ignored the question and turned toward the entrance of the yard. Naso saw that all his men were down, and the short member of Malvinus's squad was finishing off the last of them with a sword thrust to the throat before turning to his leader.

'What now, lad?'

'Take the chest and let's get out of here.'

The men who had been on the flanks picked up the rope handles at each end and lifted the chest between them as easily as if it had been filled with goose down. Guarded by the short man and his thin companion, they left the yard and moved down the street in the direction of the wharf. Naso suddenly felt very cold and tired. His strength was fading and darkness was edging in at the periphery of his vision. The enemy leader stood at the entrance to the yard and called out clearly, 'Malvinus sends a warning to all those dogs who serve him and anyone else who offers him support!' Then he turned away.

Naso knew his life was almost spent, but there was one thing he would know before the shades claimed him. 'Who . . . are . . . you?'

The man turned back and smiled. 'I guess you'll never know.'

'Wait!'

But it was too late. His enemy had trotted after his companions and Naso could not summon up enough breath to call after him. The last thing he saw was the green blur of the man's cloak before darkness shrouded his vision. He managed to half raise a weak fist in a final defiant gesture, then he toppled onto his side and his blood mingled with the stinking fluids trickling down the street towards the river.

CHAPTER TWENTY-EIGHT

Two days had passed since the attack on Cinna's men. Cato rapped the signal on the gate of the warehouse and waited briefly while the locking bar was lifted to let him into the yard. It was late in the afternoon, and the yard was in the shade of the neighbouring warehouse. The day had been unseasonably warm, and the air was still and stifling as clouds hung stationary in the sky, threatening a downpour. Pigeons were strutting and flapping on the ridge of the roof, and the raw cry of gulls circling above the ships in the river was clearly audible, which only emphasised the unusual quiet that lay over the town. Most of the inns had closed their doors once the fighting between the gangs had started, and there had been a number of tit-for-tat raids before the situation had developed into running street battles: groups of men laying into each other with brutal intensity and no thought of quarter being asked nor given.

Macro had been sitting with Apollonius, sharing a wineskin as they waited for Cato, and now they stood up and approached him.

'How is it out there?' asked Macro.

'Messy. Plenty of bodies on the street and roving groups of Malvinus's men. I've seen a lot less of Cinna's lads. Either it's going badly for him, or he's ordered them to go to ground while he regroups.'

'Not sure if that's good or bad news,' said Apollonius, frowning. 'We'd hoped the gangs would whittle each other down to the point where we could take them on and finish the job. If Malvinus wins the day soon, the odds will be against us.'

'Quite.' Cato nodded, gesturing to the wineskin in Macro's hand. 'May I?'

Macro passed it to him, and they stood in silence while he tilted his head back to slake his thirst on the watered wine. He lowered the wineskin and returned it to Macro before wiping his lips on the back of his hand. 'Needed that.'

'What about the garrison?' Macro scratched his bearded chin. 'Any sign of them getting involved?'

'No,' Cato responded. 'I spoke to the duty optio on the headquarters gate. Told him I was a discharged veteran and asked why they were sitting on their hands. He said they're under orders to defend the compound. Decianus won't let any of them out onto the streets to try and restore order. Small wonder; there's few enough of them, and they're mostly old sweats and inexperienced youngsters. Not front-line troops at any rate. The governor's taken the best men to fill out the ranks of the auxiliary units for the campaign against the Druids and what's left of the Silures and Ordovices.'

Apollonius clicked his tongue. 'The governor's not going to be terribly pleased when he hears that Decianus sat back and let the gangs take over the streets. When word of that gets back to Rome, I dare say the boy Nero is going to take a dim view of it. I wouldn't want to be in the procurator's boots.'

'That's a matter for a later date,' Cato responded. 'Has Ramirus come back yet?'

Macro shook his head.

The camp prefect had taken his section out in Malvinus's colours to keep stirring up conflict. He was also tasked with scouting the district where the gang's boss had his lair to gather intelligence on the number of men still available to Malvinus. Cato had already stealthily scrutinised the exterior of the fortified compound Malvinus operated from. Some years before, the gang leader had taken over an abandoned building site outside the boundary of the initial settlement at Londinium. The owner, a wealthy wine trader, had died after a brief sickness, and his wife had abandoned the new province she had never developed an affection for and returned to Gaul, selling the site to Malvinus at a knockdown price. He had quickly appreciated its potential, on a rise overlooking any approach, and had also shrewdly anticipated the continuing rapid expansion of the town and the value that would add to his new acquisition. He had completed the original villa, adding as many refinements as his budget allowed, and then surrounded it with a high wall with a walkway running around the interior and watchtowers at each corner. Instead of the planned simple gateway, a substantial gatehouse had been added. In short, the final structure looked more like a fortress than a home, and therefore presented a challenge to Cato and the small force he commanded.

'We have to keep provoking Malvinus and Cinna and get them to kill off more of each other's men before we can strike.'

'Or we need to bolster our numbers,' said Macro. 'We could send a man to Camulodunum and appeal for reinforcements.'

'It might be several days before they reach Londinium. That's assuming any more men would volunteer to join us. I think the crisis will come before they can be of any use to us.' Cato gently rubbed the palm of his hand on his scarred eye as he considered the matter. 'If there was a way of getting Decianus to deploy his garrison, we'd stand a far better chance. We may need his help after all.'

'You could appeal to him in person,' Apollonius suggested. 'Although I imagine he will be surprised to find you here in Britannia. And if he starts snooping and discovers that you brought Claudia Acte with you . . .'

There was no need to complete that line of thought, Cato mused. Claudia would be charged with breaching the terms of her exile to Corsica and put to death. A fate that might equally be applied to Cato for enabling her escape from Sardinia, in defiance of the emperor's will.

'I'd rather not have to appeal to Decianus,' he conceded. Then another, happier thought struck him. 'There is someone else who might help us. It's an outside chance but worth trying. After all, they've fought with us before and may well be willing to honour that memory.'

'Who would that be?' asked Apollonius.

Before Cato could reply, the three of them heard footsteps rushing along the street outside, approaching the entrance to the warehouse.

Macro turned to raise the alarm, but Cato grabbed his arm. 'Wait.'

They could hear the crunch of nailed boots on the cobbles. The men were close enough that they could even make out laboured breathing. An instant later, the gate shook as someone hammered on it with their fist. Instinctively Macro and Cato reached for their swords and made ready to draw them. There was a pause before the knocking came again, this time giving the signal that indicated a friend.

Apollonius reacted first, hurriedly lifting the locking bar, and Cato pulled the gate open. The first of Ramirus's men squeezed through the gap even before the gate began to swing wide. Cato saw the flecks of blood on his face as he stumbled into the yard. Three more men followed him, waved inside by Ramirus, before the camp prefect himself stepped off the street and the gate was quickly sealed again. One of the men sank down to sit a short distance away, while another two doubled over, gasping. Ramirus swallowed and leaned a hand against the wall beside the gate as he tried to catch his breath.

'Where are the others?' Cato asked. Two men were absent from the group Ramirus had taken onto the streets at first light.

'Gone . . . One dead for sure . . . The other's missing.'

'What happened?'

Ramirus held up a hand. 'A moment . . . Can't breathe.'

He forced himself to draw several deep breaths and cleared his throat before he could speak in a dry rasp. 'We were on Cinna's turf, close to the market square, looking for some of his men to take on. That's when we ran into a band of Malvinus's lot on the hunt for the opposition. They saw us first so there was no chance to avoid them. I had no choice but to try and bluff our way past. But their leader barred the way. He said he didn't recognise us as part of the gang and demanded to know what we were doing in their colours.'

The words made Cato's heart sink. There was always a chance that his plan would be discovered, and now he and his men were in even greater danger.

'What did you do?' Macro asked.

'What could I do?' Ramirus replied. 'I ordered my men to fight it out. We had the upper hand and would've won, but another group came upon us from a side street. I could see we had no chance of taking on both groups, so I gave the order to retreat. We had to fight our way clear first, and that's when Helvius copped it. He was too slow to outrun the enemy, and three of them caught up and cut him down. Vibenius was a few paces ahead of him and turned to help, but it was too late. That's when more of the enemy appeared from a side street between us and cut him off. I shouted to him to run for it and make his own way back here.'

'Here?' Apollonius raised an eyebrow. 'You shouted our location?'

'The fuck I did,' Ramirus responded sharply. 'What kind of bloody idiot do you take me for?'

'Now that you ask—'

'Not now. Be quiet,' Cato snapped. He cocked his head towards the street outside, but there was no sound of pursuit. He relaxed his strained senses and took a calming breath. 'Doesn't sound like you were followed.'

'We weren't. I made sure we ducked down alleys and kept changing direction.'

Cato sucked his teeth. 'You'd better be right. If either gang finds us, we've had it.'

'What do we do now?' asked Macro.

Cato rubbed his brow gently as he considered the developing situation. 'Let's give Vibenius a chance to get back to us. We'd better keep out of sight for a day or so. After Ramirus's encounter, we can be sure that Malvinus is going to be thinking hard about the men his lads ran into. If we're lucky, he may pass it off as a group of opportunists using his gang's colours as cover to do some looting while the streets are quiet.'

'We'd have to be very lucky for that to happen,' said Macro.

'There's one other thing to consider,' Apollonius mused. 'What if Vibenius is captured? If he blunders into Cinna's fellows, they'll likely kill him, no questions asked. On the other hand, if Malvinus's men run him down, they'll be sure to question him about what he's up to. Then it's down to how tough a man he is.' The spy turned to Ramirus. 'He's your man. You know his quality. How long do you think he'll hold out if Malvinus tortures him?'

The camp prefect did not hide his disdain at the question. 'Vibenius? I'd trust him with my life.'

'No doubt that's all very well on the battlefield, but do you trust him to keep his mouth shut?' Apollonius tilted his head slightly to one side. 'It's not the same thing. It takes a very different type of courage.'

Ramirus's lips twisted into a sneer. 'And how would you know?'

Apollonius smiled faintly as he replied. 'Because I have tortured enough men in my time to know what I am talking about. With a minimum of tools, I guarantee I'd be able to persuade Vibenius to sell out his own mother in a matter of hours.'

There was an icy certainty in the spy's tone that left Ramirus in no doubt about the truth of his words. He swallowed and cleared his throat before he responded. 'Vibenius is tough. He'll not give in to torture. You have my word.'

'Your word?' Apollonius's smile took on a mocking aspect. 'That's all the reassurance a man could require, I'm sure.'

'I've had enough of this,' Macro intervened, turning to the spy. 'You may be good with weapons but all that amounts to is stabbing people in the back or doing men harm when they are powerless to fight back.'

'You do me an injustice.' Apollonius's lips lifted slightly in a cold smile. 'It's not just men I have tortured . . .'

Macro bunched his hands into tight fists. 'You haven't earned the right to smear the reputation of honest soldiers.'

'That was never my intention. I merely wished to ascertain the degree to which Vibenius is likely to resist torture.'

Cato gave an exasperated sigh. 'Quiet, all of you. I will not allow this kind of discord. Our situation is precarious enough without you going at each other. If Vibenius doesn't get back to us before nightfall, it might be that he is holed up somewhere, waiting to make his move. If he doesn't return by dawn, the chances are he's already dead, or will be soon. Even if he has been hunted down by one of the gangs, let's hope that he went down fighting.'

'But there's still a risk he might be taken alive,' Apollonius countered.

Cato waved a hand around the men in the warehouse yard. 'It's all a risk. We knew that when we began this. The outcome is never certain when you go to war.'

'Still, there are risks you can foresee, as well as those you can't. Vibenius knows where we are, but we don't know where he is. We don't know if he has been made to talk.'

'*If* he is still alive, and *if* he has been captured.'

'Granted. But if he has fallen into enemy hands, it would be dangerous for us to remain here.'

'There's nowhere else we could go without drawing attention to ourselves. All we can do for now is stay alert. I need time to think . . . Macro, I want a lookout posted at each end of the street to watch the approaches. They're to raise the alarm at the first sign of trouble.'

'Yes, sir. I'll see to it now.'

They exchanged a brief nod before Macro strode towards the entrance to the warehouse and disappeared within. Cato turned to Ramirus.

'You'd better see to yourself and your lads. Get something inside 'em and then make sure they rest.'

The camp prefect ordered his men to follow him, leaving Cato and Apollonius alone in the yard. Cato stared into the mid distance for a moment, weighing up the possible dangers implied by Vibenius's failure to return.

Apollonius gave a light cough. 'Sestertius for your thoughts.'

Cato rolled his head to relieve the tension in his neck. 'We're in trouble. I hadn't expected Cinna to back away from confronting Malvinus. Unless we can stir the shit up enough to force him to come out from cover and get his men back into action against his rival, we're not going to have enough men to finish the job. I may have to go and plead our case to Decianus after all. Even though his men are second rate, they might tip the balance in our favour.'

'They might,' Apollonius responded doubtfully. 'Earlier, you mentioned someone else who might help us.'

'That's right.'

A rumble of thunder interrupted him, and both men looked up at the sky. The clouds were starting to move very slowly as the faintest of breezes stirred the oppressive heat in the yard. Cato made a decision. 'Before I speak to Decianus, I'm going to pay a visit to some old friends. I can't guarantee they'll help us. There's no good reason for them to. But they may be our last chance of getting out of this alive.'

CHAPTER TWENTY-NINE

The distant growl of thunder barely registered with Malvinus as he stood, legs apart and arms folded, surveying the charred ruins of the bathhouse. Where his most prized possession had once stood lay a jumble of blackened masonry, the seared skeletal remains of timbered buildings and cracked and shattered roof tiles. Several of his men were picking their way across the site looking for anything of value that could be salvaged. Now and again they prodded at something with their clubs or levered back bricks or pieces of wood to further expose a potential find. Most of the ruins were still too hot to touch, and it was slow and uncomfortable work that soon had them sweating freely. Some risked brief glances towards their master in the hope of detecting some sign that he had decided there was no longer any purpose in continuing the search, since nothing had been recovered so far. The destruction of the bathhouse and the ancillary buildings was all but absolute, and only the wall that surrounded the complex still stood.

Malvinus glanced towards a line of bodies lying on the ground just inside the entrance from the street. Several were barely recognisable as human, having been roasted by the intense heat in the heart of the blaze. Skin and clothing had burned away, fat had dripped off and all that was left was seared sinew and bone, twisted into hideous shapes by the flames. Only one body, at the end of the line furthest from the entrance, had not been damaged by fire. He was part of the group of slaves that Cinna's men had spared and set free once the flames had taken hold. Malvinus recalled how they had trembled when he had arrived at the scene, far too late to organise any attempt to tackle the blaze. Instead he had stood back from the stinging heat, jaw clenched, eyes narrowed as he regarded the slaves by the bright red glow of the flames.

He had demanded to know precisely what had happened, and the scant details had unfolded from the lips of the slave who had been chosen to speak for his comrades. A youth, scarcely more than a boy. Maybe the other slaves had picked him in the hope that his innocence might make his words more convincing. Maybe they had thought his appearance might appeal to what small measure of mercy still flickered in the heart of their master. Either way they had been mistaken. Malvinus had flown into a rage when the youth's account stumbled to a stuttering halt. Snatching a club from one of his bodyguards, he had battered the boy to death, ceasing the savage rain of blows only when there was little recognisable that remained of his features. The other slaves had been taken away to have their fate decided later. The rage burning inside Malvinus's heart demanded their deaths, but his shrewd businessman's head realised that would be a waste of assets at a time when he would need labour and silver to rebuild his cherished bathhouse. He already envisaged doing so on a scale to rival the best establishments across the sea in Gaul. The slaves, who he never wanted to see again lest they become walking reminders of what he had once lost, could be sold for a decent price. For the moment their lives had been spared.

Unlike the lives of Cinna and his followers, Malvinus

reflected as he swatted away a horsefly from his forearm before it could bite. He had gathered his men from across the town and divided them into teams to destroy Cinna's property and track down and butcher every man of his that could be found. The task would have been easier with the swords and military kit that he had stockpiled, but his armoury had been consumed in the blaze and now lay buried beneath the hot rubble. Even if it was possible to retrieve it, the chances were that little of any use could be salvaged. That meant that even though Malvinus had more men than his rival, they were not so well armed, and the street battles that had raged across the intervening two days had been evenly balanced in terms of casualties and damage caused.

This afternoon, reports had reached Malvinus from his teams scouring the streets that Cinna's men had disappeared, and now he was pondering what had become of them. It was unlike Cinna to duck a fight. There had to be another reason for him to pull his men back. What that might be, Malvinus could not yet decide.

'Boss!'

He stirred and drew himself out of his coldly determined train of thought to see Pansa marching in off the street at the head of a small procession of his men, two of whom had pinioned the arms of a man in the colours of the Malvinus gang. There were scratches and cuts on his exposed flesh, and one eye was swollen. But he still managed to carry himself well enough, Malvinus observed, with the kind of haughty demeanour typical of a soldier.

Pansa halted his gang and waved the men holding the prisoner forward.

'Who is this?' Malvinus demanded. 'I don't recognise him.'

'That's the point, boss. I didn't either when me and the lads came across him and his mates. Didn't recognise any of 'em, even though they was in our colours. None of my boys has seen them before either. When I challenged them, they put up a fight before we saw them off. We killed one, and this one did a runner before we finally caught up with him and knocked him down.'

Malvinus inspected the man briefly. 'Looks like you knocked him down quite a few times.'

'He did put up a bit of a struggle before we beat some sense into him, or out of him, that is.' Pansa grinned. 'I thought you might want to speak with him, boss, and ask him about this.' He plucked at the prisoner's green tunic.

'Indeed.' Malvinus nodded as he regarded the man thoughtfully. 'Better start with your name.'

The prisoner lifted his chin defiantly and pressed his lips together.

Malvinus laughed softly. 'I can see you're a soldier, my friend. Or at least you were. From the look of you, I'd say you are old enough to have served your career out. Were you in the auxiliaries?'

A fleeting look of contempt passed over the man's face.

'A legionary then.' Malvinus pursed his lips. 'I thank you for your service to Rome, friend. My name is Malvinus, in case you didn't know. I suspect you do, though. Which is why you are wearing my colours. But we'll get to that later. First I'd like to know your name, soldier. It can't do you any harm to tell me that at least. What do you say?'

The prisoner considered this for a moment and then shrugged. 'My name is Gaius Vibenius. Former optio of the First Cohort, Fourteenth Legion.' He glanced sideways at Pansa. 'You might want to remember that, friend, so that you know the name of the man who is going to kill you as soon as he gets his hands round your throat. You and that greasy little cunt you work for.'

Pansa's grin disappeared instantly and he shot a look at Malvinus, who gave a nod. He stepped up in front of Vibenius and growled an order at the men on either side. 'Hold him up.' Then, fishing around in his sidebag, he took out an iron knuckleduster and fitted it over the fingers of his right hand, clenching them gradually to settle the weapon in his grip as comfortably as possible. He tested it a few times by punching the air at his side before he turned to face Vibenius and gave him a fresh grin. 'Ready to learn some manners, friend?'

The veteran opened his mouth to reply. 'Do your worst, fu—'

Pansa slammed his fist into Vibenius's stomach, just below the ribcage, driving the breath from the veteran's lungs in an explosive and agonised gasp. He followed up with several more blows before stepping back. Vibenius hung forward in the grip of the men on either side. He groaned, retched, and then vomited onto the ground at Pansa's feet, splattering the gang member's boots with stinking gobbets.

'Charming,' Malvinus said drily. 'I think he could use another lesson in manners, Pansa. Nothing fatal. Nothing that will prevent him from speaking when he needs to. Just something painful.'

'Yes, boss.' Pansa stepped up and grabbed a fistful of the prisoner's hair in his left hand, yanking Vibenius's head up so that their eyes met. The veteran stared at him, then gritted his teeth at a fresh wave of pain surging out from the area of his torso that Pansa had worked over.

'Let's get some Falernian flowing,' said Pansa. He drew his other fist back and delivered a carefully weighted blow to the side of the veteran's head, above the ear close to the hairline, gouging the scalp. At once blood ran from the wound, seeping through Vibenius's hair before dripping from his brow onto his cheek and from there onto the breast of his tunic, staining the green wool.

Vibenius let out a low groan, then swallowed, forcing words out through his gritted teeth. 'Going to . . . kill you.'

Malvinus clicked his tongue. 'How disappointing. Seems like it's going to take longer to mend our soldier friend's uncouth manners than I thought. Again, Pansa.'

His henchman landed another blow in the same place.

Malvinus waited a moment for the veteran's dazed senses to recover. 'I have every respect for our soldiers, retired, serving or dead. Rome wouldn't be the master of the known world but for their brave service, and I wouldn't be master of Londinium's biggest gang. So in a way, I owe everything I have to the likes of you, my dear Vibenius. Which is why it pains me to let my friend Pansa treat you this way. I'd rather we just talked.'

He paused and waited for a response, but when the veteran remained silent, he sighed wearily and continued. 'You are probably thinking that this is a test of your loyalty to your friends and your loyalty to Rome above that. All your beliefs about who you are and what is important are being placed on the line, and you think that to be a good soldier you must keep your mouth shut. Let me tell you something, Vibenius. All of that is a pile of festering bollocks. The emperor and the politicians tell ordinary blokes like you that to go out and die for Jupiter, Best and Greatest, and the honour of Rome is the sweetest pleasure of your short lives. It ain't. It's bloody and it's frightening, and the only reason you are sent out to do or die is because some prick in the Senate wants to play the patriot in front of the mob, or some wealthy businessman wants to make a profit out of the blood shed by men like you. Or both of those things. You are just living tools to them, to be used until you are broken and then thrown onto the rubbish heap.

'That's something I learned long ago. I'll cry out "Long live Rome!" with the rest of them, but I owe nothing to Rome, the emperor or any fucking aristocratic politician. I'm living my life for me, and it pays off. Look where your loyalty and years of good service have got you. A shitty stretch of boggy land attached to a backwater military colony at the arse end of the Empire. You're only still on your feet because my men are holding you up, and your face looks like a butcher's block. You deserve better than this, Vibenius. You don't owe anything to Rome or the army you once served in. Or the comrades who abandoned you and ran for their lives. You owe it to yourself to save yourself and be rewarded.'

He patted the prisoner on the shoulder. 'Now then. There's a few things you must tell me and then this will all be over. I'll have my surgeon dress your wounds. We'll get you a nice fresh cloak and a purse filled with silver, and stand you a few drinks before we send you on your way. If you really want to, you can choose to rejoin your friends. How does that sound?'

Vibenius looked up. His mouth opened slightly and there was a dry rasping noise as he tried to speak.

'What's that?' Malvinus edged closer.

Vibenius tried again, and Malvinus dipped his head to try and make out the words. The veteran suddenly spat on Malvinus' cheek, and a grin split his bloodied face as the gang leader backed off with a look of disgust, wiping the back of his hand across his cheek. The reptilian glint returned to his eyes as he addressed Pansa. 'Do what you have to. But get the truth out of him. Be sure he knows that he is going to die one way or another and the best he can hope for is a quick death if he gives us the information we need. If he tries to be brave,

I want you to teach him just how much torment that entails. Frankly, I don't think he's got it in him to last more than a couple of hours at your hands.'

Pansa smiled. 'Trust me. I'll show him, boss.'

'I'm going to get a drink across the street. Report to me once you're done here.'

It was less than an hour before Pansa appeared at the doorway of the inn Malvinus had forced to open up to provide him with wine and food. Every so often he had heard a cry of agony or a loud groan from beyond the bathhouse wall as Pansa went about his work. His henchman was wiping his bloodied hands on a rag as he entered, and there were specks of blood on his face and exposed skin.

Malvinus swallowed the mouthful of pie he was chewing and wiped the crumbs from his lips. 'Well?'

'He said he wasn't one of Cinna's men.'

'I guessed as much,' Malvinus responded archly. 'So what's a fucking veteran doing in my colours? I imagine the others you found with him were also veterans.'

Pansa nodded. 'He gave that up too. There's something else. One of my lookout boys was here the night the bathhouse was burned down. He reckons he saw our man Vibenius fighting alongside the men that torched the place.'

'Well, well.' Malvinus scratched his cheek. 'Looks like we've got more of 'em to worry about than just the group you encountered. I don't like the look of this.' He frowned for a moment, deep in thought, before he continued. 'They were wearing Cinna's colours when they attacked my bathhouse. Wanted me to think Cinna was behind it so that I would go to war with him. It's pretty clear now that they've also been using our colours to stir things up with Cinna.'

'Why would they do that, boss? And who are these bastards?'

'A new gang, perhaps. Stirring the shit to weaken me and Cinna before they move in strength to finish the job.'

Pansa raised his eyebrows. 'I ain't heard anything about any new mob setting up in Londinium.'

'Me neither. But someone's playing both ends against the middle here and I want to know who, and where to find them. And then I'm going to take great pleasure in having you break every bone in their bodies before you cut their fucking throats.'

'Yes, boss.'

'Did you get anything else out of Vibenius?'

Pansa shook his head. 'He clammed up after he coughed up what I just told you. I hit him a couple more times, then he upped and let out a deep groan and keeled over. Dead as a post. He was a tough old bird, but I guess his heart wasn't as strong as it used to be.'

'A pity. We need to know where his companions are hiding. We can get our street kids to work sniffing them out. Tell 'em there's five hundred sestertii and a place in the gang for the one who finds Vibenius's friends.'

'Yes, boss.'

'Meanwhile, I need to speak to Cinna. Put the word out on the street that I want to speak to him. When he responds, let him know I'm offering peace and want to meet in person. Somewhere neutral and safe for both of us. Temple of Ceres on the south bank. I'll be waiting for him at dawn tomorrow. Tell him I'll be alone and he's to come by himself.'

'Alone, boss?' Pansa frowned. 'Is that wise?'

'Of course it fucking ain't. That's why you and ten of your best are going to be hiding in the reeds around the temple. If I give the shout, you come running. Otherwise stay out of sight. I'll tell Cinna that we've both been played by a third party.

We've got to stop the fighting. The hunt for Cinna's men is off and we leave his property alone. That should demonstrate my good intentions. He'll want peace as much as I do. He'll also want to take his revenge on those scheming little shits who have set us at each other's throats. So we'll work together to track 'em down, then we'll kill 'em all. And when that's over, we'll turn on Cinna and do the same to him.' Malvinus smiled coldly at the prospect. 'It's an ill wind and all that. Vibenius and his mates will have done us a nice favour at the end of the day.'

CHAPTER THIRTY

As darkness enfolded Londinium, Macro and Cato pulled dark cloaks around their shoulders, strapped on their sword belts and streaked their faces with soot from the braziers in the warehouse. Apollonius lowered his sling, with which he had been engaged in target practice against a battered sack of gravel in the far corner of the yard. He regarded them with none of his usual detached wry amusement as they stood by the gate leading out into the street.

'I should come with you. Safety in numbers and all that.'

'It's not necessary. We're trying to pick our way through the streets without drawing attention. Two's company, three's a target. Besides, you've already played your part,' Cato pointed out. Two hours earlier, the spy had left the warehouse to track down the inn where the Iceni king and queen and their retinue were staying while they waited to petition the governor. Paulinus was still far to the north, preparing his forces for the campaign he aimed to unleash on the remnants of the tribes and their Druid leaders still resisting over the summer months. He would not have heard of the outbreak of violence on the streets as yet. Cato estimated that it would be another day at the earliest before a message could reach him, and another three to four days before he could return to Londinium with enough mounted men to restore order. Anything could happen in that time.

He refocused his attention on Apollonius. 'Stay here. If Malvinus or Cinna discovers where we are, Ramirus will need every able-bodied man to defend the warehouse. And you, my friend, have proved how able-bodied you are time and again.'

'One thing to stab a man in the back,' Macro muttered under his breath. 'Quite another to take him on face to face.'

Apollonius glanced at him. 'Did you say something, Centurion?'

Macro smiled. 'Only that I'm glad you are on our side. For now . . .'

'So am I, and so I am.'

Cato lifted the locking bar and slid it aside just enough to allow one of the gates to open, wincing as the heavy iron hinges let out a dull protesting squeal. There was enough light from the stars and a half-moon to see some distance along the street in both directions, but there was no sign of movement, nor were any torches or lamps lit in the brackets mounted on the walls. Which was all to the good, he mused.

'All right, let's go,' he said softly.

He led the way out and Macro followed before the gate was closed behind them and secured with a dull thud. Cato turned left, heading west along the warehouse-lined street. Prasutagus and his retinue had taken all the rooms in an inn on the opposite side of the street to the governor's headquarters, half a mile away. It should not take long to cover the distance. As long as they did not run into any of the gangs patrolling the streets.

He led the way towards the crossroads at the end of the line of warehouses. There was little sign of life as they paced along, keeping to the shadows as much as they could. Once in a while they would hear the low exchanges of people who dared not draw attention to themselves. Towards the end of the street they came across a warehouse whose gates had been shattered by a wooden beam that still lay amid the splintered remains.

'Do you think this was done by someone looking for us?' asked Macro.

'I don't think so. Look.' Cato pointed through the opening. In the gloom they could just make out opened crates and scattered baskets surrounded by shattered pottery and rolls of cheap cloth. 'Looters, most likely. Could be one of the gangs, or just locals taking advantage of the fighting.'

At the corner of the junction, they paused. A wide avenue stretched out to the right and left, but Cato sought a more discreet approach to the inn where the Iceni royal party was accommodated. On the opposite side, a lane led into the district that catered for the passing trade of ships' crews and the less affluent visitors to the town. The narrow route was lined with inns, brothels and flophouses where, for a cheap price, a customer could get a place to sleep for the night on a worn bedroll. More dubious establishments could be found in the narrow alleys that led off the lane.

Only days before, the area would have been thriving, with lamps and greasy tallow candles illuminating the drinking places and carousing couples in a lurid red glow. Now it was dark and quiet. Only twice did Cato and Macro come across other people. The first was trying to lever open a shop's shutters with a length of timber, but he dropped it and ran off the moment he became aware of the two men stealing towards him. The second was a drunk, propped up in an arched doorway to an inn, his snores alerting them to his presence long before they saw him.

There were corpses, too. A man sprawled face first in the drain running down the street; and a short distance further on, several more men lay in a small open area around a public well. All had been stripped of their clothes, and their bodies gleamed dully, like unpainted marble statues. Cato could make out the wounds in their flesh, washed clean by the rain that had fallen briefly the day before. He stopped and squatted by one of the corpses, lying on its side, and lifted the cold flesh of the forearm so that he could better see a mark on the skin. A tattoo depicting a scorpion's head was clearly visible just below the elbow.

'Malvinus's man,' he muttered as he stood up.

Macro examined the other bodies briefly. 'All of them are.'

'We must be on Cinna's patch. That's why the bodies have been left here. Malvinus's men daren't retrieve them. And they serve as a warning to the locals. This is what happens to those who oppose Cinna.'

'Nice.'

They moved on with renewed caution, winding their way through the district until they came across another broad avenue leading up from the river, which Cato judged would lead them close to the walls of the governor's headquarters. Keeping to the side of the street as before, they made their way into a more prosperous part of town, where there were modest townhouses in the familiar Roman pattern – imposing doorways between rented shops facing the street. Ahead, Cato could make out the crenellations of the headquarters wall.

'We're close,' he whispered to Macro. 'The place is called the Red Boar.'

'Good. I could use a drink. All this creeping around has given me a thirst.'

They found the inn easily enough, as it was the largest of such establishments either man had seen in Londinium. It was one of the few buildings with an upper storey, and was built on three sides surrounding a large yard. Judging from the musty odour, there were stables within where the horses and mules of wealthier clients were stalled. Cato gently tested the gate to the yard and was not surprised to find that it was locked. The doors of the drinking hall were locked as well.

'How in Hades are we going to get in?' Macro growled. 'Anyone would think they wanted to keep new customers at bay.'

'Or protect the ones they already have. Come, there must be some way inside.'

They made their way around the outside of the inn until they heard the sound of voices from within; men speaking a native tongue. At the end of the wall was a small drain leading out from the stables, and Cato stopped beside it. 'We can get in here.'

Macro sniffed the acrid odour rising from the drain. 'In that muck? Fuck off.'

'There's no other way without arousing too much attention. We can't afford to bring down one of the gang's patrols on us while we argue with the innkeeper. I'll go first.'

Cato took off his cloak and sword belt and rolled them into a bundle that he handed to Macro. 'Pass it to me when I'm through, together with your kit.' Then, dropping to his knees, he examined the drain more closely. It was scarcely more than eighteen inches in height, and sewage trickled steadily out into the street. Gritting his teeth, he lowered himself to the ground and began to wriggle forward on his elbows. He tried to keep his face above the acrid stench, but could not avoid splashing it as he progressed. Mercifully, the drain was only two feet in length, and as soon as he could, he rose into a crouch and reached back into it. 'I'm through. Pass me the bundles.'

A moment later, after a considerable amount of difficulty

and cursing, Macro pulled himself through and clambered to his feet.

'Getting too fucking old for this sort of bollocks.' He spat to one side.

'And rather too round, it would seem.' Cato grinned in the darkness as he slipped his sword belt over his head and put his cloak on. 'Retirement appears to agree with you, brother.'

'If only I'd known that retirement would entail crawling through shit, I might have re-enlisted instead. If Petronella could see me now . . .'

'Be thankful she can't.'

Cato looked round the interior of the yard. The main building of the Red Boar stood opposite, and a tallow candle smoked in a bracket next to a large doorway. Glimmers of light marked out the edges of shuttered windows on either side, and he could hear voices, laughter and some drunken singing from within.

'That's the place,' he decided. 'Let's do this slowly. I dare say in our current state those Iceni warriors might be inclined to cut us to pieces before asking questions.'

'They can try.' Macro flipped his cloak over his shoulder to expose his sword.

'Best cover that for now.'

'What if we need them at the ready?'

'Let's hope we don't. Come.'

Cato glanced round the yard to make sure there was no one else in sight, then approached the door and eased the latch up. He paused for a moment to take a calm breath, then gently pushed the door inwards. At once a waft of warm air, scented with woodsmoke, sweat and millet beer, washed over him, along with the din of laughter and voices competing to be heard.

Prasutagus's retinue was made up of a score of his finest warriors. Big men, powerfully built, with simply braided hair tied back, swirling tattoos visible on their exposed skin and wearing woollen breeches and tunics with blue stripes woven into the material. They were in the prime of life, and a handful wore gold or silver torcs around their necks as proof of their valour in battle. As the nearest of the warriors turned towards the two men standing on the threshold with streaks of filth on their clothing and faces, they fell silent and lowered their beer mugs. Within a few heartbeats, all was quiet, save for the hiss of the logs burning in the fireplace in the centre of the room.

Cato saw a man take a step towards the hooks on the wall where the warriors' weapons were hanging. He raised his hands, palm outwards. 'Peace. We've come to speak with Prasutagus.'

The warrior snorted with contempt and quickly reached for his sword, drawing it in one fluid movement. At once the other Iceni warriors followed suit and formed a rough arc around the two Romans.

'So that's how it is.' Macro nodded grimly as he grasped the handle of his own sword beneath his cloak.

The man who had been the first to arm himself shouldered his way through his comrades to confront Cato.

'Who you?' he demanded.

'Friends of your king, Prasutagus, and his wife.'

'Friends, pah!' The warrior spat at the ground in front of Cato's boots. 'You Romans. No friend of Iceni.' He stepped closer, and his nose wrinkled in disgust. 'You smell like pig.'

Macro took a half-step forward. 'I've just about had enough of this.' He made to draw his sword, but Cato grasped his wrist tightly.

'What is the meaning of this?' a woman's voice called out to them from the far end of the hall. Some of the warriors turned towards her, and there was a swirl of movement before a tall, solid woman with red hair emerged from their ranks and frowned at the sight of the filthy men standing just inside the doorway. A moment later, her eyes widened in surprise and she let out a roar of laughter.

'By Andrasta, what brings you two here, covered in what looks very much like shit?'

Boudica stood her warriors down and led Cato and Macro to a table at the end of the room. There was a fur-covered bier behind the table where Prasutagus lay on his side, his skin looking pale even by the glow of the flames in the brazier set up nearby to keep him warm. More furs covered his body, and his head was propped up on a linen bolster. He gave a thin smile in greeting as he recognised the two Romans, and took Boudica's hand as she sat beside him. She called out to the innkeeper to bring them some food and beer.

A short time later, Cato and Macro were hunched over a washing tub scrubbing the filth from their exposed skin as food and beer were placed on the table for them. Macro leaned forward to smell the beer and pursed his lips in grudging approval.

'It ain't Falernian, but . . .' he took a healthy swig from the mug and set it down with a contented smile, 'it'll do nicely.'

Boudica turned to Cato. 'So, what is the meaning of this? You two turn up in the dead of night, covered in shit. That can only mean trouble. Are you here to warn us of danger, or ask for help?'

'The latter.' Cato briefly outlined the situation, concluding, 'We need your men to fight with us. It may be the only chance we have of winning the day and coming through this alive.'

Boudica exchanged a wary glance with her husband before

she responded. 'Why ask us? Why not go to the procurator and ask him for help? He has twice as many men at his command.'

Macro laughed harshly. 'Twice as many maybe. But not even half as good as your lads. Though it pains me to say it.'

Prasutagus nodded with pride. 'True. Iceni warriors. Much better than Roman soldiers.'

'Some Roman soldiers,' Macro said firmly.

'*Sa!*' Prasutagus reached over and gave Macro a feeble punch on the arm, then his face wrinkled in pain and he slumped back against the bolster and closed his eyes. Boudica stroked his brow tenderly and muttered softly to him in their native tongue before she spoke to Cato again. 'The procurator?'

Cato shook his head. 'Decianus is a coward. He won't risk putting the garrison out on the streets to try and restore order. He knows he's outnumbered.'

'Then he could do with the support of you and your men to take on the gangs. Why not put that to him?'

Cato shifted uneasily. This was the question he had feared she would ask. 'I can't risk asking him. He doesn't know I'm in Londinium.'

Boudica arched an eyebrow. 'And why is that a problem?'

'The reason I returned to Britannia is to lie low for a while. Let's just say that Decianus would be surprised to see me here and might make trouble for me by referring the matter to the emperor and his advisers back in Rome.'

'Then Macro can speak to him on your behalf.'

Macro made a face. 'That's not possible either. There's bad blood between me and the procurator. He'd sooner see me dead so that I can't tell anyone how he abandoned me and some other men after he'd stirred up trouble with the Trinovantes.'

Boudica's expression became hostile. 'So I heard. Seems

your procurator is the kind of man who leaves nothing but trouble in his wake. When Prasutagus and I went to ask him to defer the taxes for our people until the next harvest, he refused. We told him of the hardship his decision would cause and warned him that there is already plenty of discontent amongst our people. It's not just the taxes. There's the matter of the demand for recruits from our tribe to fill out the ranks of your auxiliary cohorts. Who is going to provide for the families of the men who are pressed into service? He didn't seem to care. Worse, he said that if the taxes aren't paid when they are due, he'll have the governor send the legionaries in to force the issue.'

'I doubt Paulinus will be happy with that,' said Macro. 'He's got his hands full preparing the army to march on the Druids and their allies. He won't take kindly to any delay in launching his campaign.'

Cato saw a calculating expression cross Boudica's face. She thought for a moment before she continued. 'It seems you are depending on our help. Without our men, you are lost.'

There was no denying it, Cato mused as he nodded.

'In which case, if we throw our lot in with you, we shall want something in return.'

'What did you have in mind?'

'Deferring our taxes by a year, and an end to pressing our young men into military service.'

Cato took a sharp breath. 'I have no authority to make any such agreements. That is a matter for Decianus, or the governor.'

'But they're not here. You are. I want your word that you will present our case to the governor in person, and do whatever you can to persuade him to agree. Promise me that, and we will fight with you.'

'I can't guarantee that I will have any influence with Paulinus.'

'I understand. But you have won an enviable reputation amongst your people. Your opinion carries weight. More than that of a barbarian king and his wife,' she added bitterly. 'Give me your word that you will speak for us, and that will satisfy me and Prasutagus.'

'Very well. I give my word.'

'Swear it.'

'I swear, by Jupiter, Best and Greatest, that I will do as you require.'

She regarded him closely for a moment, searching for any sign of insincerity, and then nodded. 'Very well, the Iceni will fight at your side. But will your men and ours be enough to overcome the gangs?'

'Our best chance is to strike at them in the next few days. If we fail to do that, or they unite against us, I fear we may be defeated.' Cato considered the forces in play for a moment before he continued. 'Despite my hopes of completing the job without help from the garrison, the situation has changed. I know that Decianus has ordered his men to remain in the headquarters compound, but if we can provoke him into action, then the balance will tip in our favour.'

'And how do you propose to do that?'

Cato smiled. 'We must hit him where it hurts his kind most. I'll send word to you when we are ready to strike.'

CHAPTER THIRTY-ONE

The dawn mist lay thick across the river and the reeds growing along the south bank opposite Londinium. Only the masts of the ships moored and at anchor were visible to Malvinus as his horse made its way along the bridge, the clop of hooves echoing off the thick timber planking. There were very few people abroad that morning, and the handful he passed on the bridge glanced at him warily and hurried aside. Under any other circumstances he would have made the brief journey across the Tamesis on foot. He disliked horses and only ever rode them out of absolute necessity. This morning was such an occasion. Malvinus – always a wary man fully conscious of his surroundings – needed to be able to make a quick escape at the first sign of danger.

Ahead he could see the vague shapes of shrub- and tree-covered hummocks that made up the landscape for some distance along the far bank. The bridge angled down slightly, and a moment later the planking gave way to a gravelled ramp as he reached the far shore. A figure stepped out from the toll collector's hut and stood in his path, then just as quickly hurried back inside as he recognised Malvinus.

The cool air was quite still, and tiny beads of moisture glistened on his cloak as Malvinus pulled it more closely about his shoulders. He gave a gentle tug on the reins and steered his mount onto the left fork of the routes leading away from the bridge, heading across the small islet towards another bridge that carried the road onto higher ground. The Temple of Ceres stood a short distance beyond; an ill-defined block of grey with a pitched roof looming up no more than two hundred paces away. There was a wavering orange gleam from the brazier in front of the temple that was kept alight night and day.

As Malvinus rode slowly across the short length of bridge, the hollow clop of his horse's hooves sounded again. It was accompanied by the cacophony from the frogs hidden amongst the tall reeds surrounding the spit of land upon which the temple had been built. He resisted the urge to look for any sign of Pansa and his men, who had crossed the river hours before to take up their hiding places. Much as he would have been reassured by the sight of them, Malvinus knew there was a good chance that Cinna, or one of his men, already had him under observation, and it would be foolish to be seen looking for his own followers.

Once he had crossed the bridge, he steered his mount off the road and up the narrow track that led towards the entrance of the temple precinct. Closer to, he could make out the low wall, no more than shoulder high, that surrounded the building. As he walked his horse slowly up to the entrance, a man emerged from the archway and took two paces out into the open. He swept back the folds of his cloak and placed his hands on his hips, at the same time exposing the handle of a sword.

Reining in ten paces away, Malvinus swung his leg over and lowered himself to the ground before tying the reins to a post a short distance from the wall. Then he turned to face the man.

'Cinna, my friend, why the sword? It breaks my heart that you have so little faith in my promise of safe conduct. I did not come here to fight with you. Just to talk. Let's leave the swordplay to another time, eh?'

'Faith in promises is best left to fools, Malvinus.' Cinna patted his scabbard. 'The only faith I put much store in is cold steel.'

Malvinus raised his hands as he slowly approached the entrance. 'Oh, such times! Such customs! What has the world come to, brother, when two men of business such as we cannot trust each other?'

He stopped a good two sword lengths away and briefly scrutinised his surroundings.

'If you are looking for my men, you're wasting your time,' said Cinna. 'They got here long before your lads showed up and have been keeping their heads down. If there's any treachery, it'll be your boys who are most likely to come to grief.'

Malvinus felt a chilly sensation at the base of his neck, but forced himself to smile to conceal his unease. 'Very well then. Let's get down to business. You want to know the reason I have asked you to meet me.'

'I was told you wanted to discuss making peace. Which, frankly, comes as a great big fucking surprise, since you caused the bloodbath in the first place.'

'Ah, but it wasn't me. That's what I've come to tell you.'

Cinna gave a derisive snort. 'Bollocks.'

Malvinus chuckled lightly. 'I expected that sort of response. Tell me, Cinna, why would I start a war between our gangs? What could I possibly have to gain from losing so many of my men and damaging my hold over the turf I control? It is going to take me some time to restore my position to what it was before this conflict started. You've fared even worse, I imagine, given that you have withdrawn your men from the streets.'

'No sense in losing any more of them than I have to,' Cinna responded curtly. 'I've enough left to take you down with me. That said, I've been asking myself the same questions about you. Why would Malvinus behave in such a fucked-up fashion, unless he was playing a very long game and taking the hit now in order to clear out his rival and win control of the entire town?'

Malvinus sucked his teeth. 'I'll not deny that had occurred to me. Just as it has occurred to you. But as things stand, you are strong enough to fatally weaken me if I attempted such a strategy now. So I can assure you that I would not be so foolish as to start a war.'

'Then who did? Discordia her bloody self? It was your bastards who carved up my men at the start of all this.'

'Just as I once thought that the burning of my bathhouse was your work.'

'Nothing to do with me.'

'I know. I believe you. And I'll tell you why. Some of my lads came across another group dressed in our colours while they were hunting for your boys. We managed to take one of 'em alive and had a little chat with him. My first thought was that he might have something to do with some little scam you were running, but it turns out he was a bloody veteran from the colony at Camulodunum, and chances are his mates were also veterans.'

Cinna frowned. 'Veterans? What are they fucking doing getting mixed up in our line of business?'

'That's what I asked myself. More to the point, why would they want to stoke up a conflict between us?'

Cinna stroked his chin. 'Could be that some third party wants us to take each other out of the game.'

Malvinus nodded. 'Quite. That's exactly what's going on.

So it's up to us to put our differences aside and join forces to track down and kill the bastards who started this nonsense. I've got my snouts on the streets looking for them right now. It's only a matter of time before I discover where they are hiding. And when I do find them, I thought you might like to be in on the kill. Then we can get things back to the way they were.'

'In on the kill?' Cinna's features twisted into an expression of cold, cruel hatred. 'Fuck that. I want to see those cunts die a lingering, painful death so that they have plenty of time to understand the error of their ways. And then I'm going to track down their women and kids and do the same to them.'

Malvinus took two steps towards his rival and held out his hand. 'Spoken like a true businessman. Do you agree to making peace with me, then?'

Cinna thought for a moment, scrutinising the other man, then nodded as they clasped hands. 'Peace it is.'

'Good. Let's call our men out from their hiding places. I expect they've had quite enough of being cold and wet. They'll have worked up an appetite for making someone pay for their discomfort and the loss of their comrades. Frankly, if I was a man who had any use for pity, I'd spare a few crumbs for the scum skulking in their lair over there.' Malvinus gestured across the river, where the mist had cleared just enough to reveal the roofs and trails of rising smoke that marked the sprawling expanse of Londinium.

Cinna snorted and spat on the ground. 'They'll die like rats. Every last one of them.'

It was late in the afternoon when Apollonius returned from scouting the streets. Cato knew that he was the bearer of worrying news the instant he saw the anxious expression on the spy's face.

'What's happened?'

'The word's out that Malvinus and Cinna have declared a truce.'

'Shit . . .' Macro growled.

'They must have discovered our ruse,' said Cato.

Apollonius nodded. 'There's a price on our heads, and every lowlife and street urchin is out looking for us. I caught one not far from here and got the truth out of him before giving him a hiding and sending him on his way.'

Cato chewed his lip briefly. 'We haven't got much time. If we're going to see this through, we'll have to strike at them first thing tomorrow. Either that, or escape from Londinium before we're caught. If we leave tonight, there's a good chance we can get back to the colony. There's safety in numbers there. I doubt even Malvinus would have the balls or the men needed to come after us when we're surrounded by veterans.'

Macro's forehead creased. 'You're not thinking of giving in to those bastards, are you?'

'No chance. We've started the fight. I'm not for walking away from it. It's Ramirus and his men I'm thinking of. This isn't their struggle. They're volunteers, Macro. Most have families waiting for them back in Camulodunum. We owe it to them to give them a choice now the odds have tilted against us.'

Macro nodded slowly, and looked to Ramirus. 'The lad's got a point. You've done right by us this far, but it ain't fair to ask you to do any more, unless you and your boys are willing.'

Ramirus's expression darkened. 'Like the prefect says, we volunteered. We owe you our lives, Macro. There's one thing that all soldiers know. We look out for each other. We watch each other's backs, and that means we ain't fucking running from this fight with our tails between our legs. We're staying until it's over, one way or another. And that's final.'

Cato could not help a slight smile at the prickly pride of the legions. He had had little doubt about Ramirus's decision, but it would have sat uneasily with his conscience not to have given the veteran the chance to decide for himself and his comrades.

'Thank you, brother.' He nodded. 'I'll send word to the Iceni to join us here before dawn, and we'll attack at first light.'

'Attack who?' asked Apollonius. 'Malvinus or Cinna? We can't take them both on at the same time.'

'We'll attack Malvinus,' said Cato. 'I have a plan for someone else to deal with Cinna.'

'This is madness,' Ramirus protested later that night once Cato had explained his plan. The two men were sitting around the warehouse brazier with Macro and Apollonius. 'You brought us here to fight the criminal gangs that are plaguing Londinium. Now you want us to become one of them.'

'Extreme situations require extreme measures,' Cato responded. 'That's an aphorism that almost every soldier learns to embrace at some point, brother. We need Decianus to order his men onto the streets to take on Cinna's gang, however that is achieved. We've already lost several good men fighting for the cause. I don't want their deaths to be in vain. Nor those of us who will fall when the final battle with Malvinus and Cinna comes in the morning.'

'Yes, but stealing the governor's treasury?'

'We're not taking it all. Just enough to provoke Decianus into action. We make it look like the work of Cinna's gang, just like we did when we burned the bathhouse down.'

'And how are we supposed to get into the treasury?' Ramirus demanded. 'It's right under the headquarters building, and guarded at all times. The moment we try anything, the guards will raise the alarm and we'll have the entire garrison down on us. It's madness.'

'Not if we do it right. The garrison is the problem, so we need to make sure their attention is elsewhere when we go for the treasury.'

'How do you propose to do that?' asked Macro.

'The fire at the bathhouse got Malvinus's attention. There's no reason to suppose that another fire won't do the same for Decianus.' Cato drew his dagger and scratched a rough diagram on a stone slab on the warehouse floor. 'The headquarters building is here. The barrack blocks between there and the wall are being used as storerooms now, so there's little chance of running into anyone once we get over the wall. That won't present a problem, since the defences have been neglected for years. The ditch has been filled in places and sections of the wall are crumbling.

'Once the diversionary action begins, all eyes will be turned away from the wall on this side.' He indicated the opposite side of the old fort complex and tapped the point of the dagger close to the line of the far wall. 'This is where the stables are. There's a hay store between the wall and the stables. If a fire is started there, it'll go up in flames quicker than you can boil asparagus. There'll be a panic, and the garrison will be needed to save the horses and fight the fire. Setting the fire is your job, Ramirus. Pick some good men to go with you. We'll all be wearing the colours of Cinna's gang. We just have to make sure that we're seen and reported to Decianus. Once he discovers we've raided the treasury, he'll stop at nothing to get the money back and teach Cinna a lesson.'

'What about the men guarding the treasury?' asked Macro. 'How are we going to deal with them?'

'If it's the same set-up as in every other army headquarters building, there'll be four of them. Two at the top of the stairs, and two outside the underground chamber. You, me and Apollonius can handle them. I don't want them hurt if we can avoid it, but we have to get hold of a decent amount of silver. If it comes to a fight, we have to be ready to put them down without killing them.'

Macro clicked his tongue. 'I don't like the sound of that. They may be the scrapings of the army, but they're still soldiers. Brothers in arms.'

Cato nodded patiently. 'Like I said, we'll try to avoid harming them. But we have to be ready to if we want Decianus to move against Cinna.'

'I suppose so.'

Apollonius leaned forward slightly and fixed his gaze on Cato. 'Assuming all goes to plan, what happens to the silver we take once the fighting is over?'

'We'll deal with that if and when the time comes. For now we need to get the raiding party organised.'

The spy nodded slowly. 'All right then. When do we go?'

'As soon as it's dark.' Cato looked out of the warehouse entrance. The late-afternoon shadows were already stretching across the yard. Sunset was no more than an hour off. He turned back to the others. 'It'll work, gentlemen. It has to. Otherwise there's every chance that by this time tomorrow, all of us will be dead.'

CHAPTER THIRTY-TWO

News of the truce between the gangs had spread quickly through the town, and the more courageous businesses had reopened, so that there were more people on the streets than had been the case over previous days. Cato and the others made their way through Londinium in twos and threes in order not to draw undue attention. They wore old cloaks over their black tunics to make sure that they were not picked out as gang members. Hidden beneath the folds of the cloaks of Ramirus's men were the materials they needed to set the diversionary fire. Cato had a length of rope wound about his middle, and all the men carried concealed weapons. Mindful of his wish not to harm the soldiers of the garrison unnecessarily, Cato had ordered the men to bring clubs instead of swords, in addition to daggers, cord, and strips of cloth to serve as gags if needed.

As they approached the front of the old Roman fort that had served as the province's administrative headquarters for several years, the two parties separated. Ramirus headed towards the street that ran outside the western wall, while Cato, Macro and Apollonius followed the line of the largely abandoned ditch to the opposite corner, where the ground fell away. The slope was covered with small huts, closely packed together, along with enclosures for sheep and pigs. Here the ditch had been filled in with rubbish and rubble from sections of the battlements that had collapsed or been pulled down after being judged unsafe. Making sure that they were unobserved, Cato led his party along what was left of the ditch until they reached the blocked-up gate halfway along. A short distance beyond that, he found what he was looking for: a stretch of wall where rubble formed a slope leading up to the gap above.

'Let's get up there,' said Macro.

'Wait, there's one last thing.' Cato crept away towards the nearest huts. After a few moments, there was a soft rumble of wheels and he returned with a small handcart he had taken from outside a pigsty. Apollonius and Macro smelled his approach even before he emerged from the shadows.

'What in Hades is that for?' asked Macro.

'We'll need it for the treasury chests,' Cato explained as he parked the cart at the rear of the nearest hut. 'Let's get onto the wall and wait for Ramirus to get the show started. I'll go first.'

He began to climb the rubble, scraping his knees and hands on the broken flint and other stones. As he reached the gap, he heard a distant shout from the far side of the compound. Then another voice, much closer – a sentry on the section of the wall that was still in use. 'Over there! Look. Fire!'

Cato pressed himself down into the rubble, his face brushing up against a clump of stinging nettles. He winced, flinching away, and then lay still, his heart beating fast. He heard a brief exchange of words between the two sentries, followed by the scrabble of boots on gravel, fading swiftly as they moved away. He waited a moment, then rose slowly into a crouch and peered along the walkway either side of the gap, but he could make out no one in the darkness. Across the roofs of the barrack blocks and the headquarters building he could see a red glow on the far side of the compound, and could hear more shouting.

He turned back towards the ditch and called softly to the two dimly visible figures below. 'Get up here, quickly. Ramirus has lit the fire already.'

He heard Macro swear softly, and then there was the sound of shifting rubble and grunted breaths before the others joined him in the gap. A flame licked up into the night and illuminated a handful of men on the far wall looking on helplessly as more voices shouted across the interior of the headquarters compound.

'The timing's working in our favour, at least,' Cato conceded, then gestured to Macro and Apollonius to follow him as he slid down the turf bank behind the wall. On the ground, he paused and glanced round to make sure that they had not been seen. 'We'll leave the cloaks and the rope here.'

Drawing their clubs, they moved on, keeping to the sides of the barrack blocks as they worked their way towards the dark mass of the headquarters building. The main entrance was to the front, but from his earlier visit Macro knew that the wall of the courtyard at the rear had been knocked down to make way for an array of smaller buildings to accommodate the governor's staff. Reaching the side of the structure, they could hear the crackle of flames and the panicked whinnying of horses, as well as the shouts of the men tackling the growing blaze.

A bright glow stretched into the sky above the headquarters block as the three men stole along the wall to the rear. The office and stores buildings were quiet, and Cato led his companions to a small door leading into the headquarters. Pressing his ear against it, he listened for movement within but heard nothing. He eased up the latch and opened the door with the faintest of creaks, and the three of them crept inside.

From the powerful odour of woodsmoke and a rich, ill-defined aroma, Cato realised they must be in a kitchen. A faint glimmer of light outlined the door leading further into the building, and he groped his way towards it. Just before he reached it, he felt something snag on the sleeve of his tunic. There was a soft scraping sound of metal on stone, and an instant later a loud clatter as a pan struck the floor. He felt every muscle in his body leap in alarm, heart pounding as his ears strained for any sound that might indicate that his clumsiness had betrayed them.

There was a long silence before Macro let out a deep breath. 'Nice going, lad.'

Cato was glad that his look of shame was invisible to his comrades. He heard Apollonius chuckle lightly.

'You might want to let an expert lead the way, Prefect.'

'Shut up.'

He moved more cautiously towards the door and felt for the latch. Opening it fractionally, he looked out into the main corridor that stretched the length of the building. It was dimly illuminated by a handful of oil lamps that provided barely enough light to see by. The entrance to the crypt that had once held the pay chest of the legion that had built the fort and now served as the provincial treasury would be to their right. He drew the door inwards just enough to slip through the gap, then pressed himself against the wall as he glanced both ways.

'Clear,' he whispered.

Macro and Apollonius filed out to join him, and they moved as quietly as possible along the edge of the corridor. Some fifty feet ahead, the passage gave out onto a large open space. Brighter light glimmered off to the right, but there was no sign or sound of anyone else in the building, and Cato assumed that Ramirus's diversion had consumed the attention of almost every available person in the compound. Only those standing guard over the crypt were likely to remain.

He gripped his club more tightly and edged into the main hall. To the left lay the main entrance, one door of which was ajar. To the right was an arch that led into the sacred enclosure where the garrison's standard and the treasury were kept, along with the small altar dedicated to Jupiter and another standard carrying the image of the emperor. He heard a cough and a shuffling of feet, then silence again. He held his hand up to stop the others and whispered as loudly as he dared.

'I'll go in first. Follow my lead when you hear me shout. Ready?'

Macro and Apollonius nodded in the gloom.

Cato swallowed and drew a deep breath, then sprinted forward, rushing around the corner. As he had expected, there was the shrine behind which the standards stood in a wooden rack. In front of the altar was the opening to the flight of stairs leading down to the crypt. On either side stood two men from the garrison, armed with spears in addition to their swords and daggers.

'Fire!' Cato yelled, and thrust his hand back in the direction of the kitchen. 'The building's on fire!'

The guards looked startled and hesitated in challenging him as Cato continued to shout and gesticulate. Then Apollonius burst into view, with Macro at his heels also shouting, 'Fire!'

The guards looked past Cato towards the other men, and that was their undoing. Cato had drawn level with the man on the right, and now he swung his club into the back of his helmet. The guard lurched forward and stumbled onto one knee, holding tightly to his spear to try to steady himself. Cato swung again at his companion. The brief element of surprise was lost, though, and the second guard raised his spear to deflect the blow. He was lowering the point and making to thrust when Macro slammed into his side and sent him flying head-first into the corner of the altar. Macro stood over him and smashed his club against his helmet to knock him out. Apollonius ripped the spear from the hands of the other guard and kicked him in the chest, knocking him onto his back, then aimed the point of the spear at the man's throat.

'Don't move,' he snarled. 'Or I'll kill you where you lie.'

Cato stepped to the side of the crypt stairs to stay out of sight of the men below just as a voice shouted, 'Junius! What in Hades is going on up there?'

Cato indicated to Macro to take up position on the opposite side of the stairs, then cupped a hand to his mouth. 'The building's on fire! Get out!'

'Fire?'

There was a rush of footsteps and the clatter of a spear against the stone wall, then a helmet appeared as a man came rushing up the stairs. Cato waited until he was almost at the top before he struck the back of his helmet and snatched his spear from his hands. The guard stumbled over the last two steps and went down close to Apollonius.

The last guard's head appeared from below along with the angled tip of his spear, and Macro shouted, 'Here!' The guard turned towards him with a startled expression, and Macro thrust the head of his club into his face, breaking his nose. His helmet jerked backwards and he released his spear, which clattered back down the steps. He was about to try to retreat after it when Macro grabbed his arm and dragged him up and into the open, depositing him on the floor.

One man was out cold, the others dazed and moaning as Cato stood over them. 'Lie on your fronts! Arms straight out by your sides! Do it!' The man Macro had downed last responded slowly, and Cato kicked him. The guard spread his arms and lay groaning softly. 'If any of you moves, you'll get a spear between the shoulder blades. Stay still and you'll live.' He gestured to Macro. 'Bind them.'

Once the soldiers were secured and watched over by Apollonius, Cato beckoned to Macro and they descended the narrow flight of stairs towards the faint glow of lamplight from the crypt. At the bottom, the air was cooler and smelt damp and musty. The crypt was no more than ten feet by fifteen, and three sides were lined with shelves. Most of the space was taken up with scrolls and neat piles of sealed writing slates, but there at the back were at least ten or so small chests with sturdy iron handles at each end. Cato examined the nearest and saw that it was locked, as were those next to it. He decided there was no point wasting time trying to break them open. He went to lift the first, but it budged only a short distance before he gave up, so laden with coins was it. The next two were lighter and more manageable, and he nodded to Macro. 'These will do.'

'What about the rest?' Macro said wistfully.

'We can only take what we can manage to get away with. It'll be enough to shame Decianus into action.'

Upstairs, Cato ordered the three conscious guards to carry their comrade down to the rear of the crypt. As soon as they were out of sight, he pointed to the altar. 'Let's get it over the entrance.'

The three men threw their weight against the stone and it began to shift, grinding over the flagstones a short distance before coming to an abrupt stop and refusing to move any further.

'Wait,' Cato ordered, and went round to the other side. He saw that the foot of the altar had caught against a low stone lip beside the stairs. 'Shit.'

He returned to his position. 'Push against the top. Heave . . . Again . . .'

The altar slowly tilted forward and then overbalanced and crashed down across the staircase, leaving just a small gap, not large enough for a man to get through. The noise echoed off the walls of the chamber, and Cato felt sure that it must have been heard by someone.

He grabbed the handle of the nearest chest. 'We have to go. Apollonius, take the spear. Macro and I will carry the chests.'

'Hey!' a voice called out from the crypt. 'You can't leave us here! The fire!'

'You fool.' Apollonius laughed harshly. 'There is no fire. When your mates find you here, be sure to tell them it was Cinna who tricked you. Easy as taking honeyed cakes from a child.'

With Apollonius leading the way and Cato and Macro straining under the burden of the chests, they retraced their steps through the kitchen and out of the rear of the building. There was still plenty of shouting from the direction of the fire, but by the time they had made their way through the darkened barrack blocks to the gap in the wall, the rosy loom of the blaze was much reduced, and looking over the roofs, Cato could no longer see any flames. Apollonius abandoned the spear, and they retrieved their cloaks and used the rope to lower the chests down the rubble before loading them onto the bed of the small handcart. Then Cato heaped pig shit over them before taking up the handles of the cart and easing it into motion. Leaving Apollonius behind to watch the garrison for any sign of response to the theft, Cato and Macro hauled the cart away.

As he led the way back through the dark streets towards the warehouse, Cato allowed himself a smile at the thought of the procurator's reaction when he discovered the theft of the chests. Unless he moved swiftly to attempt to recover them and punish Cinna for his audacity, he would feel the full force of the governor's wrath when the news reached Paulinus. It was a good night's work, Cato told himself. He already had an idea how the stolen silver might yet be put to further good use. Provided he and his comrades lived to see that day.

CHAPTER THIRTY-THREE

Apollonius's face was flushed with excitement as he burst into the council of war being held in the light of the brazier burning in the middle of the warehouse. It was still an hour before dawn, and Boudica and her Iceni bodyguards had reached the warehouse shortly before. The tribesmen were gathered on one side of the interior of the building while the veterans sat opposite, the two groups regarding each other warily.

'He's already on the move!' Apollonius gulped a breath before he could continue. 'Decianus . . . I saw him lead the garrison out a short while ago. Followed him to Cinna's neighbourhood.'

'Ha!' Macro punched his fist into the opposite palm. 'Your plan worked, lad.'

Cato gave a curt nod as he briefly reflected on the spy's tidings. 'Then we need to strike now. There's no guarantee that the garrison troops are going to defeat Cinna, and we can't afford to have him drive Decianus off and come to Malvinus's aid.'

'What makes you think he'd do that?' asked Ramirus. 'Surely he'd be happy to sit back while his rival goes down?'

'That might have been true in the past, but things have got

to a point where the gangs either stand together or face defeat. Cinna's a former soldier. He will be sure to realise the danger. We need to crush Malvinus before they can unite their forces. There's one other thing. We need to let Decianus know that we're going after Malvinus. There's no longer any point in concealing our presence from him. Ramirus, have one of your walking wounded get a message to him. Tell him we're marching on Malvinus and to join us there once he has dealt with Cinna.'

As the camp prefect headed for his veterans, Cato turned to Boudica. The Iceni queen was wearing a leather jerkin with iron plates sewn onto it over a checked tunic. A sword belt was slung across her solid hips and a small shield was braced against her knee. Her red hair had been tied back and hung in a hastily arranged plait between her shoulders. 'Someone needs to remain in charge here and guard the injured, as well as the chests.' He nodded towards the cart with its reeking cargo of pig shit. He had told Boudica of its contents in order to explain how he had hoped to provoke Decianus into action.

'I'm not staying here,' she replied firmly. 'Choose someone else.'

Cato sighed with frustration. 'There isn't time to argue.'

'I agree. So choose another and let's be gone.'

'It'll be dangerous,' Cato persisted. 'I cannot in good conscience put the life of the queen of the Iceni in danger. Your king and your people need you. There is no place for a woman in battle.'

Her expression became fierce in the light from the brazier.

'How dare you?' she hissed through gritted teeth. 'Have you forgotten how Prasutagus and I once fought at your side against the Dark Moon Druids?'

'I haven't forgotten. But you were not a queen back then.'

'As queen, it is my duty to fight even more so than before. I will lead my men into battle, Prefect Cato, or I will order them to return to the inn.'

Cato grimaced, irritated with himself for unintentionally causing offence to the prickly Iceni woman. She was right to upbraid him. Barbaric as it might seem to Roman sensibilities, many of the native tribes of Britannia did not think it strange for women to fight alongside their men.

'Very well,' he conceded. 'We'd be honoured to have you fight with us once again. Right, Macro?'

The centurion grinned widely at Boudica. 'Absolutely. By the gods, I can think of nothing more likely to give Malvinus and his thugs the shits than the sight of you leading your lads in a charge against them. That's my girl!'

The last words had barely passed his lips before he realised he had made a mistake.

Boudica turned to him with a sad expression. 'I was your girl once. A long time ago, it seems. But we now belong to others. Best to keep your mouth shut, before you say anything else you may regret.' She forced a faint smile and then walked away towards her warriors, who gathered round expectantly as she approached.

'What was that about?' asked Apollonius, and arched an eyebrow. 'Some history there between you and our Iceni friend, I take it?'

'None of your fucking business,' Macro replied coldly.

'We need to go,' Cato intervened. 'Gather up your kit and make sure everyone has a strip of white cloth tied around their left arm. I don't want any friendly casualties.'

It was still dark as Cato led his combined force out of the warehouse yard and into the street. He carried a length of rope over his shoulder with a grappling hook on the end, ready to scale the stockade of Malvinus's compound. The veterans went first, followed by Boudica and her warriors. The gate was closed behind them by one of the walking wounded who had been left behind to watch over the injured men and the cart. They kept to the side of the street, in single file, moving as quietly as they could. Only the soft crunch of army boots and the faint padding of the Iceni's calfskin footwear sounded in the narrow thoroughfare.

The street ran parallel to the wharf, and Cato headed upriver, towards the compound Malvinus and his men had used as their base since the war with Cinna had broken out a few days before. Until the first hint of the coming dawn seeped over the horizon, only the stars and the wan gleam of a half-moon would light their way, and Cato's eyes and ears were strained as he picked his way forward cautiously. As they left the warehouse district behind them, the street became little more than a narrow alley between the thatched hovels and small businesses of one of the town's poorer districts, situated on low ground that flooded from time to time and where the drainage was poor even in summer.

Now and then he heard the sound of voices from within the buildings they passed, and once he saw two figures, a man and a woman, obviously copulating against the rear of an animal enclosure. As soon as they became aware of the line of armed men stealing by, they hurriedly disengaged, pulled down the hems of their tunics and scurried away down the nearest alley. A moment later, there was a faint cry as the woman stumbled and fell.

'It seems that the way of true love is ever strewn with obstacles,' Apollonius chuckled softly.

'Silence,' Cato hissed as they moved on.

Soon he sensed that the alley was climbing a gentle slope, and as they passed out of the buildings onto a patch of open grazing land, he made out the walls of Malvinus's compound on higher ground, a hundred paces ahead. He held his hand up to signal the others to halt and then lowered himself onto a knee as he scrutinised the approach to the compound. There was a lookout tower to the left of the gate, where a solitary sentry stood looking out across Londinium. From the relative scale of the sentry, he estimated the palisade to be at least twelve feet high. Enough to require ladders to scale it during any attack. That left the gate. If a man could climb that and drop within unobserved, it would be a simple matter of shifting the locking bar from within to admit the veterans and the Iceni warriors.

Looking back over his shoulder, he picked out Apollonius crouching at Macro's shoulder.

'Apollonius, on me,' he whispered.

The agent squatted beside him and Cato indicated the sentry. 'Can you get close enough to take him down with a slingshot?'

Apollonius stared silently for a moment before he spoke. 'Not an easy shot, to be sure. But I can do it.'

Cato was reassured by the man's confident tone.

'I'll need to be close to be sure of hitting his head. Close enough that he'll hear the sling when I spin it up to shoot, so I'll only have one shot before the alarm is raised.'

'If anyone can do it, you can.' Macro smiled encouragingly.

Cato indicated a cluster of huts some thirty paces from the gate. 'Close enough for you?'

Apollonius nodded. 'That'll do nicely.'

There was a chest-high post-and-rail cattle pen between them and the huts that would provide some cover as they crept closer to the gate. A thick tangle of nettles and thistles grew along the line of the pen that would help conceal the attackers.

Cato steeled himself, then moved forward steadily so as not to draw the sentry's eye. The others followed him, crouching low, until they were shielded from view by the huts. When the last of the Iceni was in place, Cato slipped the loops of rope over his head and let the grappling hook swing free.

Macro held out his hand. 'I'll tackle that once our boy has taken care of the sentry.'

Cato hesitated, but then conceded that Macro's powerful arms would allow him to scale the gate more easily. 'All right. Here.'

He turned to Apollonius and pointed at the sentry. 'You're up.'

The spy rose to his feet and reached into his small sidebag. Taking out his sling, he slipped the loop over the middle finger of his right hand. He pinched the knotted end and then felt for one of the cast-lead shots and seated it in the leather pouch. Then he stepped out from the line of huts, set himself up at an angle to the sentry tower and swayed the cords back and forth before swinging them up so that the sling was circling just above his head with a clearly audible whirring noise.

'If he does it, I'll stand him a jar of the best wine at the inn,' said Macro.

'Shh.'

Apollonius took his time to concentrate on the target and get the feel of the sling's momentum before he braced himself for the release. At the last moment the sentry seemed to lean forward against the wooden hoarding, as if listening attentively. In one flowing motion, Apollonius lowered himself slightly, took a half-step and snapped the cords forward, aiming through the pointed finger as he released the knotted end. The lead shot made a distinctive noise as it hurtled through the air for just over the time it took to snatch a breath.

The sound of the impact – a dull thwack – was clearly audible from where Cato stood. There was a strangled groan and the sentry swayed from side to side before suddenly lurching forward, hands clutching at his throat, and toppling forward over the front of the lookout tower, disappearing from view against the dark line of the palisade. Cato heard the impact as the man struck the ground, and instantly waved the veterans and warriors forward.

Dark shapes surged up the slope towards the gate with a light rumble of footsteps and panted breath. Cato found the sentry lying at the foot of the lookout tower, his head twisted at an impossible angle. Apollonius's shot had torn into the base of his throat, just above the collarbone; it was no wonder he had not been able to raise the alarm before he fell.

Macro waved the Iceni away to create some space as he swung the grappling hook and then launched it up and over the gate. A firm tug was enough to satisfy him that the iron prongs had a firm lodgement, then he began to pull himself up hand over hand, his boots scrabbling for purchase on the gate's timbers. At the top, he swung a leg up and drew himself up and over before lowering his body out of sight. Cato heard him drop heavily to the ground on the far side, and a moment later came the scrape of the locking bar shifting in its brackets. He noticed Boudica close by.

'Are you ready for this?'

'As any man,' she replied firmly.

'Remember, the men inside the compound are thieves and murderers and they'll fight like cornered rats.'

'And that's how they'll die.'

The locking bar stopped moving, and an instant later the gate swung inwards.

Cato gave the order as loudly as he dared. 'Draw swords!'

The veterans acted first, and the Iceni followed suit. Cato helped Macro push the gate back as the attackers swarmed into Malvinus's compound. Directly across the open space lay a large two-storey villa with a balcony running along the length of the upper floor. The sides of the compound were lined with storerooms on one side and what looked like barracks on the other. Lamplight glimmered from the windows of the main building, and Cato led the rush across the open ground, certain that they had caught the enemy completely by surprise.

It was then that he realised how silent it was within the compound. No sound of men talking. No laughter. No drunken singing. He slowed down and drew up ten paces in front of Malvinus's villa.

'Wait!' he called out in warning, raising his arms. 'Halt.'

Even as his followers responded to the order, there was a sudden commotion as doors swung open in front of them and on either side. Scores of men rushed out of the buildings, and a group raced to the gate and swiftly closed it before turning to face the raiders.

Cato felt a nauseous anxiety as he whirled around taking in what was happening. More men had appeared on the balcony, and he could see they were armed with bows and javelins. Before he could give any orders, a voice rang out across the compound.

'Don't move! Stay where you are!'

Men carrying torches emerged from the house, and more came out of the storerooms and barracks. Soon a ring of light surrounded the intruders.

'Where in Hades did all these bastards come from?' Macro growled. 'I thought we were supposed to be evenly matched in numbers.'

By the glow of the torches on the balcony, Cato saw two

men gazing down at them. One of them raised a hand in mock salute.

'Malvinus bids you welcome! As does my friend Cinna.' He indicated the man at his side. 'And you, I take it, are the little bastards who have been setting us at each other's throats these last few days . . .' He held up his arm to reveal his gang's tattoo. 'Bet you weren't expecting this sting in the tail.'

Even as Cato was listening to Malvinus's words, his mind was racing to understand how he could have walked into the trap. Why was Cinna here? He and his men should have been on their own turf, being dealt with by Decianus and the soldiers of the garrison. He felt a cold tremor of fear trace its way up his spine.

Malvinus gave a curt command, and the men along the balcony raised their bows and javelins and took aim at the veterans and the Iceni warriors.

'There is no escape for you!' he called out. 'You are trapped and outnumbered. Drop your weapons and surrender, or die where you stand.'

CHAPTER THIRTY-FOUR

As the ring of torches closed in, revealing more details of the intruders, Malvinus gripped the rail of the balcony and leaned forward with a gloating expression on his face.

'Ah, I see my old friend Centurion Macro! And who are these others, I wonder? Or are you in charge, Macro? If so, shame on you for recruiting those barbarian animals to your cause.'

'Fuck you!' Macro answered, as those on either side of him formed a tight knot, facing outwards.

Malvinus shared a laugh with Cinna before he continued. 'I imagine you are wondering why my good friend Cinna and his men are here? When I heard that men in Cinna's colours had claimed responsibility for last night's attack on the governor's headquarters, it did not take us long to realise why our enemies would want to provoke the procurator into action. We've seen through your plan to divide and rule, Macro. Now order your men to surrender.'

Cinna pointed down. 'Not all men, it seems. Who is your woman, Macro?'

Boudica took a half-step forward, drawing herself up to her full height as she sneered. 'I am Boudica, queen of the Iceni, and no Roman's woman!'

'Your barbarian woman speaks!' Cinna laughed. 'Oh, Macro, how could you think it was possible to defeat us with this rabble of old men and uncivilised scum?'

Apollonius edged closer to Cato and spoke in an undertone. 'What are we going to do, Prefect?'

Cato cleared his throat and spoke up. 'What's in it for us if we surrender?'

Malvinus turned his gaze to Cato. 'If you think we'll spare you all, then you are mistaken. The ringleaders will be killed here, tonight. The rest will serve as a useful reminder to the people of Londinium of the price of challenging the authority of my gang, and Cinna's. They will leave here alive, but their right hands will remain with the bodies of the ringleaders. Those are our terms. Accept them and lay down your weapons, or none will be spared.'

Macro spat. 'He's a stupid cunt if he thinks we'll allow that.'

Cato glanced towards Ramirus and Apollonius. 'You have a choice. If Malvinus is satisfied with the lives of me and Macro, you can live.'

'Big if,' said Ramirus.

Apollonius pursed his lips. 'And it all rather depends on how many they choose to define as ringleaders. Besides, though I am ambidextrous to a degree, I would miss the luxury of deciding which hand to use when I kill my enemies.'

Macro chuckled. 'For a snooty spy, you do have your moments.'

Apollonius tilted his head towards the Iceni warriors. 'What about our native friends?'

Cato looked at Boudica. 'What do you say?'

She hefted her sword. 'I say we kill as many of these vermin as possible.'

'Thank you.' Cato lowered his voice. 'When I give the

word, we'll charge for the gate. We might escape the trap yet.'

He was interrupted by a shout from the balcony as Malvinus took a step back and raised his arm. 'Surrender, or I'll give the order to cut you down. Which is it?'

Cato took a deep breath of the cool night air. At the same time, he thought he detected a smear of light along the sky to the east. Dawn was not far off. 'On me! To the gates!'

He spun round, and led the others towards the line of men advancing on them from the far side of the compound. At the same time, Malvinus roared an order from the balcony.

'Kill them! Kill them all! No prisoners!'

The archers and javelin men released their missiles, and two of the veterans and one of the Iceni went down, struck at short range from behind. Only Cato's swift order and the equally swift response it encouraged spared them more casualties. There was no chance for a second volley, as Malvinus and Cinna's men swept in on every side towards the smaller band racing across the compound.

Cato made for one of the torchbearers in front of him. His opponent stopped dead and readied the torch and the short sword he carried in his spare hand. Cato slowed and thrust at the man's midriff, causing him to swerve and at the same time slash out with the torch. Cato felt the heat of the flames sweep across his face as he lurched away, and the glare momentarily dazzled him. Sensing the counter-attack, he raised his sword to the horizontal and parried across his front, connecting with his opponent's sword with a shrill clang. Then, aiming where he estimated the centre of the man's torso should be, he thrust again, feeling the point strike home. He threw his weight behind the blow and surged forward, knocking into his enemy and driving him back. The torch brushed up against his right elbow, and he felt a momentary searing pain before he broke contact, stepped back and recovered his sword with a firm tug.

To his right, Macro had downed a man and now turned to face another. The charge towards the gate had been halted halfway across the compound, and now the veterans and Iceni warriors formed a loose ring amid the mass of the combined gangs. Cato stepped back into the ring and pulled Apollonius with him as the spy expertly slashed the throat of the opponent he had been duelling.

'Your sling.' Cato spoke urgently and pointed to the gang leaders still watching from the balcony. 'Take them down.'

Apollonius sheathed his sword and took out the sling, readying a shot as Cato cleared some space around them. He swung the cords up and whirled them around overhead before releasing them with a dull snap. This time the sounds of fighting drowned out the noise of the hurtling shot. An instant later, Cato saw Cinna's head snap backwards, and he tumbled out of sight. Malvinus glanced down at him in shock as Apollonius prepared another shot and took aim. At the last moment, the gang leader turned quickly and ducked to one side, diving through a doorway into the building and out of sight. The missile struck just above the door frame in an explosion of plaster.

'Shit . . .' Cato gritted his teeth. 'Still, one less of 'em to worry about.'

'One less isn't going to even the odds,' Apollonius responded as he shoved his sling into his bag and drew his sword again.

Cato quickly looked round and saw that his band, no more than forty in all, was outnumbered by at least three to one. Torches blazed and blades flashed red as they reflected the fiery gleam. The air was filled with the cacophony of battle: the clash, clatter and scrape of metal on metal, the grunted effort of blows delivered and wounds received and the constant roar of Iceni war cries as they laid about them with their long swords, hacking through limbs and shattering skulls. But even though the losses were heavier amongst the gang members, they were taking down the veterans and Iceni one by one. The end was almost certain, unless they could gain the gateway.

Cato cupped his spare hand to his mouth and called out, 'We must make for the gate! Stay on me!'

He thrust his way in between Macro and Boudica and hacked at the exposed arm of the man to his front. His foe nimbly recoiled, and Cato's blade cut through the air as he took a step forward and repeated the order. 'On me!'

Those on either flank pressed a pace towards the gate, and the band edged fractionally closer to safety. There was a howl of anger from further along the line, and one of the Iceni warriors was hauled out of formation by three of the enemy before a group of their comrades stabbed and hacked at him in a frantic blur of blows that drove him onto his knees and out of sight. Cato clenched his teeth and pressed on.

Little by little the shrinking formation battled across the compound. If only they had had shields, Cato thought bitterly. A tight shield wall would have kept the enemy at bay all the way to the gate. But there was no point in wishing for things he did not have. Progress began to slow as their numbers dwindled, and then he realised that they had ground to a halt, a scant ten paces from the gates. The enemy had blocked their only means of escape.

'We're stuck, lad,' Macro grunted as he lashed out at a tall figure in the black tunic of Cinna's men.

Cato beat aside a clumsy attack before he responded in frustration. 'We must try. Keep moving!'

He forced himself to take a step forward, and Macro and Boudica followed suit, the latter calling out to her surviving warriors in the Iceni tongue. They responded with a throaty cheer and advanced with her. The veterans to Cato's left also tried to force their way forward, but failed.

'Ramirus!' Cato shouted. 'Get your men moving!'

'He's gone,' said Macro. 'Cut down ten paces back.'

Cato swore under his breath as the slow advance came to a standstill again. No more than twenty of them were still on their feet. There was no hope of escape now. Even as the sky lightened, he knew they would all be dead long before the sun rose. He resigned himself to his fate and called out, 'Close up and stand your ground!'

The veterans understood the import of the order at once and grimly edged closer together, facing their enemy. Boudica and her Iceni warriors still bellowed their war cries, as if the fight was going in their favour. Cato caught her eye and shook his head sadly. She sniffed derisively and swung her sword at a bulky foe with a pockmarked face, laying open his arm from the shoulder to the elbow. He let out a harsh cry of pain and dropped his sword. Immediately she followed up with a cut to his head and sank the edge of her blade into the top of his skull, driving him down. Miraculously, he managed to remain on his feet, blood coursing from the deep cuts in his arm and head. A few paces further along, Apollonius was fighting alongside the Iceni and shouting as he imitated their battle cry.

A veteran tumbled back amid the small knot of defenders, clutching at a deep wound in his neck, trying to stem the flow of blood. A quick glance around the compound revealed that the enemy had taken far greater casualties than Cato's men, and he felt a sour regret at the thought that without Cinna's gang, they might have won the day, or at the very least fought their way out of the trap.

Ahead of him, the gates swept inwards and dark shapes

pressed through the opening, and he felt sick at the prospect of yet more thugs arriving to ensure the destruction of the desperate band of men who had defied the gangs of Londinium. An instant later, there was a shout of alarm from nearby, and then another shout, of panic this time, as blades clashed around the interior of the gate. Instinctively Cato's band and those they were battling drew apart and turned towards the gate.

There was a pause before Macro punched his sword into the air. 'It's the garrison! It's our lads!'

Sure enough, Cato could make out the oval shields and iron helmets of the auxiliaries, and there on horseback towards the rear, a bareheaded figure in a cape urging his men forward. The panic spread through the enemy as swiftly as fire sweeping through a field of parched grass. Many fled from this fresh peril, turning and running across the compound towards the presumed safety of Malvinus's house and the storerooms and barrack buildings. The stouter-hearted stood firm and hurled themselves on the auxiliaries.

'Come on!' Macro called out to those of the band who remained. 'Let's get the fuckers!'

He charged out of formation, directly towards the nearest of the gang members, a tall man armed with a hatchet. Macro made to thrust, but his opponent responded quickly, and the head of the axe smashed a numbing blow against the guard of Macro's sword that numbed his fingers, loosening their grasp. The sword slipped from his hand and left him standing helplessly as the axeman swung his arm up and back to strike the fatal blow.

'No!' Boudica shrieked. She threw herself forward and raised her buckler to take the blow, at the same time driving her sword into the soft tissue beneath the gang member's left armpit. An instant later, his axe smashed into her buckler, crushing the boss and splintering the wood, and knocking Boudica to the ground.

Her sword remained wedged between the axeman's ribs, even after she had lost her grip, and she lay helpless as he stood over her, weapon raised to deal out death to the Iceni queen.

Before Macro could intervene, another figure rushed in. There was a blur of motion, a grating crunch and the axeman stiffened as the sword point that had smashed through his teeth and throat burst out above the nape of his neck. He fell to his knees, gurgling horribly. Apollonius clenched his left fist in the man's hair as he wrenched his sword free, and then shoved him away, glancing anxiously at Boudica.

'She's injured, Macro. Get her to safety.'

Macro's right hand was still too numb to function, and he pulled her up with his left and heaved her onto his shoulder. Figures from all three forces were rushing across the compound or locked in combat, and he made for the corner of the nearest store shed, where they could shelter against the foot of the stockade until the fighting was over. He eased her to the ground and crouched before her as he drew his dagger with his left hand and stood guard.

Cato had seen the incident over the heads of the intervening men, and now that he was satisfied that his friends were safe, he hurried towards the auxiliaries still surging through the gate, arms raised to attract their attention.

'We're friendlies! Veterans from Camulodunum and Iceni allies!' He saw a crested helmet and approached warily. 'Centurion!'

The auxiliary officer turned to him, shield raised and sword poised ready to strike.

'I'm Roman,' Cato said. 'Prefect Marcus Licinius Cato.' He tapped the strip of white cloth on his arm. 'All of us wearing this are on the same side as you.'

'What the fuck are you doing here?' the centurion responded suspiciously.

'We're taking on the gangs. Same as you.'

The centurion's eyes narrowed in the faint light of the coming dawn. 'How do I know you're Roman? Could be a rival gang.'

'Do I bloody sound like one of them?'

The centurion stared back briefly, then shook his head. 'Not a chance.'

He turned and bellowed across the compound. 'The lads with white armbands are friendlies! Leave 'em be! They're on our side!'

Cato nodded his thanks and turned to race over to Apollonius, who was standing back to back with two Iceni warriors. He grasped the spy's arm. 'Come with me. Them too.'

They hurried over to Macro and Boudica, and Cato indicated to the warriors to remain with their queen, who was cradling her wounded shield hand, clenching her eyes closed as she fought against the pain. Then he turned to Macro.

'Are you up for some hunting?'

His friend frowned. 'What?'

'Malvinus. We need to find him. You ready for this?'

Macro flexed his right hand, sensing the feeling returning. 'Ready as I'll ever be. Ready enough to make that bastard pay for what he's done.'

Cato led his companions around the chaotic melee still raging across the heart of the compound. Parties of auxiliaries and veterans were forcing the doors of the barrack rooms and bursting in to cut down the gang members sheltering inside. The open ground was littered with discarded weapons and severed limbs amongst the bodies of the dead and dying, illuminated here and there by the garish light of discarded torches. Already the strengthening gleam of dawn made it possible to make out the details, and Cato's eyes scanned for any sign of the surviving gang leader as he and his companions made for the house. Malvinus was nowhere to be seen, and Cato guessed that he was preparing to make a stand with what remained of his followers.

The entrance to the house was sealed. The sturdy studded door made of oak was unyielding as Cato tested his strength against it briefly. He gave up and motioned Macro and Apollonius to follow him as he made his way along the front of the building, trying the shuttered windows. All were securely fastened, except for the last, where the wood was cracked at the point where the shutters met. Cato pressed his fingers against it and felt the rotten wood give fractionally.

'This will do us.' He looked around and saw a small bench further along the wall. Sheathing his sword, he looked to Apollonius. 'Give me a hand.'

They picked up the bench and returned to the window, where Cato took aim at the slender gap between the shutters. 'On three. One . . . two . . . three!'

The end of the bench smashed through the shutters and sprang the iron latch on the inside so that it fell and rattled across the stone floor within. At once Cato withdrew the makeshift ram and heaved it to one side before climbing through the opening. As Apollonius and Macro followed him inside and readied their blades, he looked round and saw that they were in a sleeping cell, ten feet across. The only furniture was a stool, a small chest and a simple low bed frame with a thin bedroll on top. He was about to cross the room when Apollonius caught his arm and nodded towards the corner of the bed, where a small foot was visible. The spy reached over and grasped the far side of the frame, then looked to the other men to make sure they were ready.

With a powerful wrench, he pulled the bed away from the

wall and turned it over. There was a shrill scream as a young girl, no more than thirteen or fourteen, clutched at the thin blanket that covered her body and flinched from the three bloodied men standing around her in the pale light coming through the shattered shutters.

Cato let out a sigh of relief and gestured for the others to follow him to the door and out into the hall that ran the length of the building. As they emerged, they saw gang members running from room to room, looking for loot to carry off with them as they attempted to escape. The sight concerned Cato, since it implied there might be another way out of the compound. He led Macro and Apollonius along the hall, not challenging any of Malvinus's men, who were in any case no longer interested in fighting. There was no sign of their prey on the ground floor, and when they climbed the stairs, they found only Cinna lying dead on the balcony and one other man besides, rifling through a chest outside a room at the end of the corridor. Cato charged up to him and kicked him to the ground before turning him over and presenting the tip of his sword to his throat.

'Where's Malvinus?'

The man trembled, small bronze coins slipping from his fingers as his hands opened in a pleading gesture. He shook his head in fright.

'Malvinus?' Cato pressed the point so that it made a pronounced dimple on the man's skin.

'G-gone. He's gone.'

'Gone? Where?'

The man pointed a quivering finger towards the back of the house. 'Rear door. Behind the stairs.'

Cato withdrew his sword and ran for the top of the stairs. 'Let's hope we can catch him.'

They pounded down the staircase and turned into the narrow space behind it, where a small door stood open, leading into a low tunnel. Cato ducked down to peer along it and saw that it gave out onto what looked like an animal pen that must have been erected against the rear of the compound.

'Come!' He stooped and made his way through the damp, dank air of the tunnel before emerging into the small enclosure. The doorway was well hidden by matting, onto which had been sewn green strips of material in the shape of leaves. They blended into the ivy that covered the rear of the house. The pen gate was wide open, and when they reached it, Cato saw at least a score of men running in all directions across the slope towards the hovels of Londinium's poor that surrounded the stronghold. In the pale light, it was impossible to know which of them was the man they sought.

'Shit.' Macro hesitated, glancing from one fleeing figure to the next. 'I can't see him.'

'Doesn't matter,' said Cato. 'I have a good idea where he'll be. It's time we paid a visit to the Bread of Bacchus.'

CHAPTER THIRTY-FIVE

It was daylight by the time they passed the blackened ruins of the bathhouse and turned into the side alley where the best of Londinium's bakers had their businesses. There was already smoke rising from some of the chimneys as the proprietors lit the fires of their ovens in readiness for the day's baking. Halfway along the street, Cato caught a waft of the homely smell of the first batch of bread cooking. There was a fleeting sense of the strangeness of normal life, and he wished that he could pause for a moment just to close his eyes and enjoy the aroma. Ahead, the alley curved to the right, and he saw a sign hanging over the entrance to a yard depicting a fat man with a wine jar in one hand and a large loaf of bread in the other.

A slight movement on the opposite side of the alley a short distance further on caught his attention, and he saw a boy sitting behind a pile of logs lean forward and look at them. Then he stood, and Cato saw that he was barefoot, dressed in rags and covered in grime. He stared at the three men for a beat, then ran towards the entrance to the baker's yard.

'Stop him!' said Cato.

He broke into a run, but already he could see the boy would reach the entrance first. The urchin dived round the corner just ahead of them, and they followed him. The entrance opened onto a cobbled area with raised flour stores to one side and a row of querns on the other. At the rear were two large ovens, where a man, stripped to the waist and sweating freely, was working a bellows to get the fires going. The boy had a ten-pace head start and was already halfway across the yard and making for a narrow passage to one side of the ovens.

Apollonius had drawn his sling and slipped a shot into it, and now he stopped to spin the cords and pouch overhead. There was no need for precise accuracy, and he let fly, sending the shot low so that it glanced off the ground not far behind the boy and struck him on the back of the calf. He tripped and fell face first with a shrill cry that was cut off as the impact drove the air from his small lungs. Cato and his companions caught up with him as the man at the ovens turned towards them with an angry expression.

'Here, what's going on?'

Macro rounded on him with the kind of ferocious scowl he had once deployed on recruits he had trained. 'You'll get back to your fires and keep your nose out of it, if you know what's good for you. Understand?'

The man wilted and returned to the bellows, working them hurriedly.

Apollonius had put away his sling and was kneeling beside the boy. He took the bony leg in his hand and quickly felt it. 'Nothing broken, but he'll be badly bruised for a few days.'

The boy tried to break free from the spy's grasp. 'Fuck you,' he gasped.

Apollonius affected a shocked expression as he pinned the boy down and clamped a hand over his mouth. 'Such language out of the mouths of babes!' He winced as his hand was bitten, and gave the boy a quick slap with his other hand before holding him down once more. 'No more of that, thank you.'

Cato leaned over the boy. 'Where's Malvinus?'

The child glared back defiantly. 'Suck my cock!' he muttered through Apollonius's hand.

Macro clicked his tongue. 'With that attitude and vocabulary, I'd say we are on the right track in finding our gang friends.'

Cato grasped the boy's leg where the slingshot had struck and pressed the red patch of skin so that he squirmed with pain. 'Tell me where Malvinus is, or I'll make it really hurt.'

The urchin shot an arm out and pointed to the passage. Cato glanced in the direction indicated. 'What's down there?'

Apollonius eased up on his grip enough to let the boy speak clearly. 'His place. The boss's place.'

'Is he in there now?' Cato pointed a finger. 'No lying or it'll be the worse for you.'

The boy nodded.

'Is he alone?'

He made no response.

'The truth, now,' Cato demanded, adding slight pressure to the injury, just enough to encourage a reply.

'Pansa's with him. And two more of his men. Let me go.'

'No chance. Apollonius, tie him up and gag him.'

'My pleasure.' Apollonius reached for his sling and used the cord to bind the boy's wrists and ankles before gagging him with the leather pouch.

While the spy secured his foul-mouthed prisoner, Cato cautiously entered the passage and followed it until it turned at a right angle. It was open to the sky, and there was more than enough light to see the cracked and damp-stained plaster on either side. The space was constricted enough that a man had to move down it at an angle. At the corner, he paused and glanced round warily. The passage was twice as wide here, and some six feet away there was a doorway with an iron grille set in it at head height. The door was open, and he could hear the sounds of voices and movement beyond.

He turned back to beckon to the others. Macro came at once, while Apollonius finished gagging the boy, then issued a warning to the fire tender to get on with his job and not attempt to intervene in any way. When he joined his comrades, the three of them stood ready at the corner.

'What's the plan?' asked Macro. 'Do we take 'em alive?'

'If possible. It would be good for the people of Londinium to have Malvinus tried and executed as a warning to any other would-be gang leaders.'

'And if he fights it out?' Macro continued hopefully.

'He dies.'

'Or we do,' said Apollonius. 'There are more of them than us.'

'True.' Macro grinned. 'But we're us, and that ain't so good for Malvinus and his boys.'

Cato waved them forward. 'On me . . .'

Sword raised and heart beating quickly, he paused at the threshold. On the other side of the door was a small, neat courtyard with a shallow pool in the centre. Neatly trimmed hedges, knee high, provided a boundary between the courtyard and a colonnade, and a handful of statues and Greek vases depicting mythical scenes were mounted on plinths in the alcoves along the walls. Two doors opened off to each side and a further passage opposite the door led deeper into the house.

'Nice hideout,' mused Macro. 'Very classy.'

'Shh.' Cato could not yet see anyone, even though the voices were more distinct now, and he was certain he could pick out the smooth tones of Malvinus from the direction of the passage. He led the way into the courtyard, Apollonius and Macro fanning out on each side.

They had got halfway across when a man stepped out of one of the side rooms holding a basket stuffed with clothing. He froze for an instant as he saw the three armed men, then he dropped the basket and shouted, 'Boss! We've got company!'

Macro was closest, and sprang over the low hedge to confront the man as the latter drew his sword. The pounding of footsteps on the flagstone floor heralded the arrival of Malvinus and the rest of his men, who raced out of the passage, weapons at the ready. The gang member facing Macro slashed at him, then reached for the handle of the decorated urn in the nearest niche to throw at his opponent.

'No!' Malvinus bellowed in rage. 'Get your fuckin' hands off it! It's priceless, you fool!'

His man recoiled in mortal terror of incurring his master's wrath and concentrated on Macro, who had lowered into a crouch. The two men tested each other's reactions with a series of feints.

In the open courtyard, Cato and Apollonius stood either side of the small pond facing Malvinus, Pansa and another man with the build of a prizefighter. Swiftly weighing up the situation, Malvinus dropped back as he issued the order. 'Kill them.'

The larger man charged towards Apollonius and rained down a sequence of furious blows with his sword as he forced the spy back. Cato was confronted by Pansa, who approached cautiously, a sly grin on his face. 'I take it you are the leader of the troublemakers?'

Cato made no reply, but lowered his body slightly as he balanced his weight, ready to move swiftly.

'After we've finished with you, we'll hunt and kill your friends, your women and your children,' Pansa continued, inscribing small circles with the tip of his sword, attempting to bait Cato into a rash attack. But the latter held his ground, merely staring back intently. Suddenly Pansa lunged, thrusting his sword out and throwing his weight through his shoulder as he pivoted at the waist. Cato dealt with it easily, parrying the blade aside with a sharp metallic clink. He made to riposte, but Pansa was light on his feet and got away easily, weaving from side to side.

'Too slow, soldier!'

They drew apart, and Cato spared a quick glance to either side. Macro was engaged in a frantic exchange of swords in the colonnade, while Apollonius was duelling with his far larger opponent, deftly deflecting each attack as the fighter growled with increasing frustration at the spy's lithe movements. Cato refocused on his opponent just as Apollonius struck the gang member in the thigh – neither a lethal blow nor a disabling one, but a bleeding wound all the same, and one that further enraged his foe.

At the same moment, Macro's enemy smashed the centurion's blade aside and launched himself forward, bringing them both down onto the flagstones at the foot of the plinth on which Malvinus's Grecian urn stood, leaving Macro trapped beneath his opponent. The vessel rocked slightly and the gang member instinctively reached up to steady it, giving Macro the chance to grasp him by the throat with his left hand, closing his fingers around his windpipe. The man wrenched his head back and broke away before angling his sword at Macro's face. There was just enough time for Macro to snatch hold of his wrist in a desperate attempt to keep the blade away from his eyes. His own sword was pinned down by his opponent and quite useless.

It would be a test of strength, and the other man had the advantage of being able to press down with his full weight against Macro's arm. The point edged closer, and Macro knew that he would not be able to last much longer in this unequal contest. Bracing one foot on the ground, he rammed his knee up into the man's groin, trying to drive him over and onto the ground. Instead, he landed heavily against the plinth and the heavy urn tottered and then toppled forward, crashing onto the back of the man's head before shattering on the flagstones. The man gave a groan and slumped onto Macro as blood ran through his hair and streaked his face.

'My urn!' Malvinus shouted in horror.

Macro gave a puff of relief and then gritted his teeth as he heaved the senseless body away and let the man slump to one side. Clambering back to his feet, he saw that Malvinus had vaulted the hedge on the far side of the courtyard and was making for the door. Cato saw the movement and shouted to Macro. 'Don't let him get away!'

'No fucking chance,' Macro snarled, turning to sprint after the gang leader.

'Looks like the boss has outsmarted you again,' Pansa chuckled. 'Your short friend will never catch him.'

'We'll see,' Cato responded.

Pansa struck at once, thrusting at his opponent's chest. Cato's sword came up to deflect the blow, just as the other man flicked his wrist to undercut, easily clearing Cato's blade before punching in towards his body. Cato lurched to one side, tripping over the edge of the pond and falling in, water bursting into the air around him. Pansa rushed towards him, sword raised to finish him off. Scooping his hand, Cato hurled water into Pansa's face. Instinctively, the gang member blinked and recoiled, and Cato snatched at his wrist and hauled him down so that Pansa too stumbled over the rim and landed with a splash. His hand struck the birdbath in the centre of the pond, and he lost his grip on his sword, which disappeared beneath the disturbed surface.

Cato recovered first, turning the gangster onto his front before putting a knee in the small of his back, then clenching his hands in the man's hair and thrusting his face against the tiles at the bottom of the pond. Pansa struggled frantically, bubbles bursting around his head as he clawed fruitlessly at Cato. His thrashing became desperate, water spraying up and splashing onto the surrounding flagstones, and after a series of violent convulsions, he went limp. Cato held his head under for a moment longer to be certain, and then released his grip.

Recovering Pansa's sword from the bottom of the pond, he stood up, ready to assist Apollonius, but there was no need. Malvinus's man was bleeding from several flesh wounds, and he swayed from side to side, lashing out feebly with his blade. Apollonius batted it away with contemptuous ease, then slashed at the tendons of his enemy's sword arm. The big man's fingers lurched and danced wildly as the sword dropped at his feet.

'It seems almost unfair to finish you off while you're disarmed, so to speak,' Apollonius said in an apologetic tone. 'But if our positions were reversed, I have no doubt that you would do this.' He stepped forward nimbly and thrust his blade into the man's throat, twisting it left and right before ripping it free with a gush of blood. Malvinus's man staggered back, clutching at the wound, until he was halted by one of the columns supporting the colonnade, where he slid down onto his knees as he bled out.

Macro's voice bellowed from the mid distance. Any words he might have said were incoherent, and Cato feared for his friend. He stepped out of the pond and pointed to the door. No words were needed. Both men sprinted after Macro and Malvinus.

* * *

A moment earlier, Macro had emerged from the narrow passage and seen Malvinus thrusting an axe into the fire tender's hand. The latter had just cut the bonds of the boy, who rose stiffly to his feet and stared at Macro with a feral expression before snatching the dagger from Malvinus's belt and limping towards the centurion with a wild shriek. Macro waited until the boy was within easy reach, then slapped him aside with a heavy blow that sent him flying into the wall. He slid down into an untidy heap, dazed and out of the fight. The fire tender brandished his axe with a trembling hand.

Malvinus turned to face Macro, breathing hard through flared nostrils. 'It seems a good beating wasn't enough. Should've fucking killed you when I had the chance.'

'Yes, you should have.' Macro gave an icy chuckle. 'Big mistake. Now you're going to pay for it.'

But instead of attacking Malvinus, he charged at the other man, bellowing as loudly as he could. As he suspected, the man hadn't a fighting fibre in his body, and swung his weapon back in an uncontrolled fashion so that the back of the axe head struck him on the rear of his own skull. His mouth opened wide as he let out a shocked grunt and collapsed.

Malvinus shook his head in contempt before facing Macro again. 'Just you and me then, Centurion Macro. Better say your prayers.'

'Save that for yourself.' Macro edged forward, watching for the telltale signs of attack. Malvinus remained motionless, sizing his opponent up.

'You won't be the first soldier I've killed. Nor the last.'

Macro sniffed. 'You're not the first grubby little street criminal I've killed.'

He heard footsteps behind him as Cato and Apollonius came rushing out of the passage, and called back over his shoulder.

'Leave him to me. The bastard is mine.'

Cato nodded and worked his way round with Apollonius to block off the entrance to the yard.

Macro smiled. 'No way out. My friend there says we should try to take you alive. So I'll let you choose. Take the coward's way out, throw down your sword and grovel on your knees before you're dragged off to beg the governor for mercy, or die by my hand.'

The gang leader spat at his feet. 'Malvinus goes on his knees for no man.'

'I hoped you'd say that.' Macro moved forward and burst into a charge, slashing at Malvinus's head. The gang leader swept his sword up to block the blow, then made a cut at his opponent's neck. Macro knocked the blade away, and the two men thrust and deflected in a series of loud clangs and scrapes of metal as each held their ground in the middle of the yard. Macro, veteran that he was, quickly sensed the strength and speed of his enemy and had to use all his experience and skill to save himself from a lethal blow. But almost imperceptibly, the tide began to turn against him. He was tiring more quickly than his enemy, and was forced to take a step back.

Malvinus's lips parted in a sneer. 'You're an old man, Centurion. Too old for this.'

Something seemed to snap inside Macro. All sense of control was lost as injured pride screamed at him to challenge the other man's insult. His lips lifted over clenched teeth and his expression twisted into a ferocious snarl of rage as he powered forward, bludgeoning Malvinus's sword and driving him back. He saw surprise, then fear in his opponent's eyes as the latter frantically defended himself. Then, with a last powerful blow, Macro hacked through the other man's wrist, and his sword spun through the air before landing beside one of the ovens. Blood sprayed from the stump, and Malvinus's jaw hung open slackly.

Macro stepped towards him. 'I may be old, but there's a reason why I've outlived you. I'm the better man.' He let his words sink in, then rammed his sword forward, the point tearing through the material over Malvinus's breast before ripping open his flesh, shattering the ribs beneath and plunging deep into his dark heart.

Malvinus's head lurched down under the impact. Macro twisted the sword one way, then the other, three times, before tearing it free and giving Malvinus a violent shove with his spare hand. The gang leader flopped back and fell, landing spread-eagled, his jaw slack and his eyes staring up into the clear morning sky. He blinked for a moment before he breathed one last time and went limp, eyes vacant as the life left his body.

Macro stood glaring at his enemy, chest heaving. Then he leaned over to wipe his blade on the expensive cloth of Malvinus's tunic. Sheathing his sword, he looked up at his companions and caught the amused expression on Apollonius's face.

'What's so bloody funny?'

Apollonius indicated Malvinus and the unconscious bodies of the boy and the fire tender. 'Only one man I know could ever leave a scene like this in his wake. And that's Centurion Macro. Finest officer the Roman army has ever produced.'

Macro scrutinised the spy for any trace of sarcasm, then nodded. 'Damn right. And don't ever forget it.'

CHAPTER THIRTY-SIX

As the procurator finished giving his report, Governor Paulinus folded his hands together and regarded the two men standing before him in his office. Besides Decianus, there was Prefect Cato, an officer he knew only by reputation, and an enviable reputation at that. Decianus, by contrast, was a largely unknown quantity, having only recently arrived in Britannia, and the governor's early impressions had not been favourable. Even more so given the complete breakdown in order that had gripped the streets of Londinium for several days during Paulinus's absence. There had been many deaths, and property had been looted and burned to the ground. To cap it all, someone had managed to enter the crypt beneath this very building and make off with a substantial portion of the province's treasury. It would be the governor's responsibility to report the theft and disorder to Rome, and he could imagine that the news would not go down well with the emperor and his senior advisers. Already Paulinus had in mind a scapegoat. Someone senior enough to satisfy the requirement to set an example to other provincial officials of the price paid for failure . . .

Decianus's fate would be guaranteed by the words carefully chosen by the governor to ensure that the blame fell exclusively on the procurator's shoulders. It would take no more than four months for his report to reach Rome, be read and digested, and for the warrant for Decianus's execution or exile to be sent back to Britannia. And of course, the fact that this warrant would bear Nero's seal meant that Paulinus would be able to present himself to Decianus's political allies as blameless. After all, he would be able to say with complete sincerity that he was only obeying orders.

For now, though, he would have to deal with the consequences of the recent events, and he was not a happy man. He cleared his throat.

'Gentlemen, I don't think I have ever encountered a situation like this in my long and, until now, illustrious career. You have been in the province for a matter of months, Decianus, and in that time you have managed to provoke a minor rebellion by the Trinovantes tribe, permitted the outbreak of gang warfare on the streets of Londinium and allowed some thieves to make off with two chests of silver.'

'With respect, sir, I didn't exactly allow it.'

'Silence! You were in charge during my absence. The responsibility was yours. The chests have not been recovered, so I ask you how you will make good on that matter.'

Decianus coloured and floundered a moment before he responded. 'Obviously, if we don't recover the chests, we will need to make up the shortfall by other means, sir.'

Paulinus glared at him. 'We? You're the bloody procurator. That's your job, not mine. I will hold you to your responsibilities. I don't care which poor bastards you have to lean on to repair the province's finances. Just do it.'

'Yes, Governor.'

'Very well, Decianus. Get out.'

The dismissal was curt by even the most impolite standards. Decianus opened his mouth to protest, thought better of it, closed his mouth, bowed his head and stalked away, closing the door behind him in such a manner that it was only a whisker short of being slammed.

Cato had witnessed the exchange in silence and without making any eye contact with his superior. He had long since prepared himself for the difficult questions he would be facing.

'Prefect, I suppose I'd better begin by expressing some gratitude for the part you and your comrades played in helping to suppress the disorder and eliminate the crime gangs. Although you were indeed fortunate that Decianus was quick to respond to your message once he discovered that Cinna's gang had left their usual haunts to join forces with Malvinus. I gather that without his intervention you and your Iceni allies would have been wiped out.'

'Quite possibly, sir.'

'Quite possibly?' Paulinus repeated, deadpan. 'I suppose we both have that to thank Decianus for at least.'

'Yes, sir.'

'If I understand things correctly, your veterans had a hand in provoking the violence between the gangs.'

'With respect, sir, the veterans were not mine to command. Camp Prefect Ramirus led their contingent. Very bravely, I might add. Ramirus died a hero, along with those other veterans who gave their lives for the security of the people of Londinium.'

'Very altruistic of them. But I can't help wondering why they might have been prepared to do that.'

'For Centurion Macro, sir. He had saved the lives of several of the men of the colony, and when he was attacked, they considered it their duty to stand by their comrade. As did I, and my companion, Apollonius.'

'And how do you explain the involvement of Queen Boudica and her Iceni contingent? Did you not consider it rash to endanger the wife of King Prasutagus, an important ally of Rome?'

'It was her choice, sir,' Cato replied truthfully.

Paulinus nodded thoughtfully. 'Which brings us to your part in this affair. If Ramirus led the veterans and Boudica led her warriors, what was your role? Overall commander?'

'Adviser, sir.'

'Adviser . . .' The governor raised his eyebrows doubtfully. 'I wonder if you could explain to me how you came to be in Britannia in the first place, given that you have not notified me of your arrival in the province. If I was to send a message to Rome asking if you had sought permission to be here, would I be likely to discover that your presence has not been sanctioned?'

There was no point in denying it, Cato decided. Better to tell the truth now than be caught out in a lie later on, when the consequences could not be predicted.

He cleared his throat. 'I did not think to ask permission before leaving Italia, sir. I came to Britannia to visit my old comrade, Centurion Macro, and his wife.'

'A social visit, then?'

'Yes, sir.'

'I must say, Prefect, you are unusual in the extent of the efforts you make to visit old comrades.'

'Macro is the closest thing I have to family.'

Paulinus stared at him briefly before he continued. 'Such close friendships are to be valued indeed.'

'Yes, sir.'

He unclasped his hands and sighed. 'As it happens, your presence in Britannia is something of a fortunate matter as far as my needs are concerned.'

'Sir?'

'You are no doubt aware that I am mobilising an army to

put paid to the last elements of resistance in the mountain tribes to the west of the province. Them and those Druid bastards on the island of Mona. Once they are defeated, I believe we will finally have broken the back of any organised opposition to Roman rule in Britannia.'

'I imagine so, sir.'

'That will only happen if the campaign is successful. The trouble is that I have barely enough men available for the job. All four legions are under strength, and the Second is little more than a training depot for new recruits these days. Many of the men are unfit for prolonged active service, and I'm short of good senior commanders. For example, the legate commanding the Ninth Legion, Cerialis, shows some promise, but lacks experience. The best officers from the original invasion force are either dead or discharged, and I have too many green men in their place. Which is why I need you.'

'Me?'

'You and that hard-nosed bastard Centurion Macro.'

'Macro has retired, sir.'

'That's what he might think. I hope I can persuade him to take up his sword again.' Paulinus paused briefly. 'I know about the two of you. You and Macro have a certain reputation. I know you served in the Second Legion under Vespasianus and were promoted to centurion before you were posted to other duties across the Empire. You also served as commander of an auxiliary unit on your second tour in Britannia, with Macro as your second in command. I dare say you've done sterling service in other provinces since then. That's why I need you to serve again, under me.'

Cato puffed his cheeks. 'I'm flattered by the offer. Truly. But I had no intention of remaining in Britannia for very long.'

'You misunderstand me, Prefect. It's not an offer. It's an

order. You swore an oath to serve Rome, and Rome needs you now.'

'Sir, I—'

'If you do as I ask, I will be sure to put my seal to a document saying that I summoned you from Rome to serve in the campaign. That might prove to be a very important document to have in your possession,' Paulinus added shrewdly.

Cato was cornered and could see no alternative but to agree. 'You have my sword to command, sir. But permit me a little time to say some farewells and see to my needs for the campaign.'

'Of course. A month should suffice. I expect to see you at the camp outside Viroconium a month from now. Any questions? No? Dismissed.'

Cato saluted and marched out of the governor's office, his mind troubled by the prospect of breaking the news to Claudia and Lucius when he returned to Camulodunum. Once outside headquarters, he made his way directly to the Dog and Deer, where Macro and Apollonius were waiting for him. It was a bright, warm day, and tables and benches had been set up in the street outside. Macro caught sight of him threading his way through the people who had returned to the town's streets once news of the gangs' defeat had spread across Londinium, and he called out to Parvus to bring them wine.

Parvus returned with a stoppered jar and three cups just as Cato sat down.

'That's my boy!' Macro lightly punched the lad's shoulder, and Parvus smiled in delight at the brass coin he slapped into his palm.

Cato downed half his cup before he spoke. 'Is Portia joining us?'

'No. She's busy down at the warehouse. There's a wine cargo coming in. That old fart Denubius is with her. I think she's going to make him manager of the warehouse. I'd rather that than she marries him.'

'Is that likely?'

'Fat chance. She's not going to accept handing over all her property to some husband.'

'How did it go at headquarters?' asked Apollonius.

Cato related the governor's reaction to the reports he and Decianus had provided, before breaking the news about his return to active service.

'I wonder how Claudia is going to react?' Macro arched an eyebrow.

'Quite. But if it all goes well, the campaign will be concluded before autumn, and I can return to Camulodunum.'

'What then?'

'I think we might stay for a while, at least until people in Rome have started to forget Claudia's face and it's safe to return. Might be a few years. But there are worse places to be now that the most important tribes are at peace with us. Speaking of which, Boudica and Prasutagus must have left by now.'

'This morning,' Apollonius confirmed. 'While you were at headquarters. Boudica seemed keen to say farewell in person, and to express her gratitude. I wonder what she meant by that?'

Cato shrugged and hastily raised his cup to take another sip in order to avoid being drawn on the topic. But the spy would not let the matter pass so easily.

'Is there any possible connection between that and what happened to those chests that were hidden in the cart?'

After the victory, the survivors and the wounded had celebrated at the inn, drinking themselves insensible. It was only the morning after that the disappearance of the cart had been discovered. Unable to return the chests to headquarters,

Cato had thought it necessary to swear those in the know to silence, rather than draw down the ire of the governor on them.

'In retrospect, it seems careless not to have mounted a guard on the cart,' said Apollonius.

'We can't do anything about that now,' Cato responded.

'No. I suppose not. I just hope the money was taken by those who need it most. Like, for example, the Iceni. They could use such a fortune to pay the taxes they owe. And then there's the families of Ramirus and the others who died fighting the gangs. They could do with some help.'

'I imagine they could,' Cato agreed. He caught Macro's eye, and the latter smiled knowingly.

Cato was disappointed with himself for being so transparent. It had seemed the right thing to do to reward the Iceni for their help. The tribe already had enough to contend with without the additional burden of being forced to pay taxes they could not afford. He had advised Boudica to make sure that the small hoard of silver coins was 'washed'; melted down and recast as Iceni coins so that they would not be traced back to those stolen from the provincial treasury. Those going to the dead veterans' families would be easy enough to mix in with other currency circulating through the colony without attracting attention. Cato had not revealed the fate of the treasury chests to either of his companions, in the hope of protecting them if the theft was ever traced back to him.

'We're in Boudica's debt,' said Macro. 'It would be the honourable thing to do to ensure the Iceni received some reward. Same goes for the veterans.'

Cato nodded. He topped up his cup and then those of his companions. 'A toast.'

Apollonius smiled. 'I suppose the toast should be to the honour of Rome.'

Cato thought a moment and raised his cup. 'The honour of Rome it is.'

'Aye,' Macro laughed. 'I'll drink to that. Honour and peace. We've earned it. I'm looking forward to living out my days here in Britannia with Petronella at my side.'

'About that . . .' Cato began. 'The governor needs good men to put some backbone into his army.'

'He asked for me?'

'Something like that.'

Macro sucked in a deep breath. 'I'm not looking forward to telling Petronella.'

Cato felt a puff of breeze on his cheek and glanced up to see that a band of rain clouds was approaching from the east. 'We'd better drink up. I think there's a storm coming . . .'